ETERNALLY NORTH

Tillie Cole

Copyright © 2013 Tillie Cole
All rights reserved.
Cover Design by www.damonza.com
Formatted by Polgarus Studio
Second Edition

No Part of this publication may be reproduced or transmitted in any form or by any means, electronic or mechanical, including photography, recording, or any information storage and retrieval system without the prior written consent from the publisher and author, except in the instance of quotes for reviews. No part of this book may be uploaded without the permission of the publisher and author, nor be otherwise circulated in any form of binding or cover other than that in which it is originally published.

This is a work of fiction and any resemblance to persons, living or dead, or places, actual events or locales is purely coincidental. The characters and names are products of the authors imagination and used fictitiously.

The publisher and author acknowledge the trademark status and trademark ownership of all trademarks, service marks and word marks mentioned in this book.

DEDICATION

For my Father-In-Law, Jim. Taken too soon and will be forever missed.
I hope you got your gin and tonic in Heaven!

And to all those taken by, living with, or who are survivors of cancer – you are my inspiration.
Mam and Dad, this means you!

CHAPTER 1

Out With The Old...

Let's start with an introduction.

The name's Munro, Natasha Munro – sorry I've always wanted to say that!

I'm a twenty-eight-year-old high school teacher from Newcastle-Upon-Tyne in England – well, a farm just on the outskirts of town – and I'd class myself as fun with a bubbly personality, and before you ask, no – that's not code for me being ugly, but heck, I ain't no Cindy Crawford either! But I am fab-u-lous *and* totally know how to work it!

"What *do* you look like then?" I hear you ask.

Well, where do I begin?

I have long, dark brown hair that hangs to the middle of my back, large brown eyes and light olive skin; I'm happy with my colouring. I have a small, straight nose with average-sized lips, a beauty spot under my left eye and dimples which I find excellent at getting me out of trouble!

I am not fat by any means, but I am not skinny or slender either – I like to think I'm a whole lot of va-va-voom tied up in a Coke-shaped bottle.

I'm five foot five: you know, average. My chest is… *ample* and – oh hell, who am I kidding? – my hips are in that category too, but my waist is small and pinches me in all the right places.

Like many women, my main area of trouble is my stomach – my bloody ever-so-slightly curved stomach – but I cope well enough and get a little help from my daily double-wearing of Spanx to fix this little problem – that ensures I can continue to chow down on my daily doses of French pastries and Cadbury's chocolate without too much guilt.

I bet I know what you're thinking – where the heck is this little tale going and why is her story different from any other? What happened in *her* life to make *her* stand out?

The truth is that what happened to me could happen to anyone. I'm telling you this story as sometimes truly extraordinary things can happen to ordinary people, and sometimes it's good to be reminded of that. My best friend once joked that my life would make a good book and so, here it is: my life laid out for your enjoyment.

Before we start, you need to know that this story isn't anything paranormal or so beyond the realms of reality that it's incomprehensible. There are no wizards or sparkly vampires who will appear and sweep me off my feet. There are no hobbits or elves who will request I sacrifice my life for the sake of all mankind, and I hope I'm not one of these annoyingly weak supposed-heroines who set the feminist movement back a few decades with the ridiculous choices they make.

Instead, this is the whistle-stop memoir of how a lower-middle-class girl from the north of England one day changed the way she lived her life and set off on a bumpy path that ultimately led to her very own slice of the happily-ever-after pie.

So folks, grab yourself a bowl of popcorn, a glass of wine (I would suggest you make it a large one) and when you're sitting comfortably, I'll begin.

"Well, slap my arse and call me Sally!"

The scene is set: groaning, moaning, the reverse cowboy and a rip-roaring orgasmic scream – and me, turning on the light to my supposedly devoted boyfriend going rodeo with his waif of a secretary in front of my very wide and disbelieving eyes.

What a frickin' welcome home this was turning out to be!

If someone had tried to tell me what I would find on the inside of my front door that evening, I would never have believed them. However, taking in the image that has since been ingrained in my long-term memory, left me in no doubt about the reality I was facing.

With a whip of his head in my direction, Nathan, my lovely but somewhat currently compromised boyfriend, turned a vibrant shade of scarlet and said in a flustered yet surprisingly laid-back manner.

"Hunny Bun, you're back early... erm... this is awkward... it... shit... it just...well happened...we were wet... mmm... from the rain and... well... we needed to dry off and things just kind of snowballed into... into...*this*..." he drawled on without apology, while pointing down at their conjoined bodies.

Like I hadn't already noticed that his chipolata of a penis was lodged in a vice between his secretary's legs. My eyes were practically bulging out of their sockets. Was he for real? What a total and utter wanker!

Nathan straightened, pulling his living breathing blow-up doll with him, never severing their connection, and held out a placating hand towards my furious stare.

"Sweetie, listen, I love you, and now you're here, well, I've kind of had this fantasy... so, ah, why don't you come here and, you know, join in? Triple the people, triple the fun!"

I don't know what bothered me more: the *ménage a trios* invitation or the fact that Little Miss Twig had continued slowly grinding on my soon-to-be-ex-boyfriend's dick like a Black and Decker drill bit whilst he explained to his, shall we say, less-than-impressed *current* girlfriend exactly why he was making the beast with two backs with his employee. God only knows how I mustered up the Thor-like strength to restrain myself from launching forward and fly-kicking him, then smacking the waif directly in the porn-film smile that was plastered on her overly plumped-up lips!

"Gee, *Hunny Bun,* that sounds tremendously tempting, but I think I'll pass. In fact, I'll tell you what," I said in the overly-patronising voice normally saved for only the stupidest of kids that I teach, my index finger firmly in the air to exaggerate my point. "I'll just grab my things and get out of your hair and then never see you again… as long as I live… how does that sound?"

I didn't stay to hear the response and quickly ran into the bedroom, away from the carnal sculptures currently making arse-shaped indents on my prized Italian leather L-shaped sofa.

I bee-lined straight to the sliding wardrobe and drawers and proceeded to pack my largest suitcase as fast as humanly possible.

What a prick!

With every hammock-sized bra and frilly pair of socks I pushed into my leopard print suitcase, I became more and more infuriated. The sheer audacity of him – and her! Did she not realise the impact of her little romp? *Sheesh*, mental overload: my so-called knight in shining armour, the future father to my kids, was apparently a closet Hugh Hefner.

Fighting the urge to commit cold-blooded murder, I lugged my bulging suitcase in the direction of the front room, getting myself ready for my whore of a boyfriend to begin the begging and pleading for forgiveness by planning witty and dry-humoured comebacks that would make him feel as bad as I did right then.

You would think that's what would happen next, right? That he'd grovel, tell me it was a mistake, that he loved me and that his fling meant nothing?

Not in this story, folks!

I opened the door to the front room, my anger spilling over, ready to demand, well, something – any form of apology, some explanation, a reason, just *anything!* But, there he was, my sad fucking version of Ron Jeremy still pumping into that over-processed Barbie in the budget rendition of *Debbie Does Dallas*.

Did I not even exist? As if he was still doofing the blonde, carrying on regardless after the love of his life had just caught him in the middle of vaccinating another gal with his meat injection!

Lord have mercy! *Who* and *what* have I been with for the last three years?

Like a curtain signalling the end of a performance, a red mist descended over me, and the inner queen bitch I had nurtured and relied on all these years reared her fabulous, if not slightly psychotic, head and screamed,

"You are such a dickhead, Nathan! Are you seriously going to continue boning her while I'm here, while I'm packing to leave you?"

He was. That was evident by the fact that he was still wheezing profusely and struggling to hold her legs-a-kimbo at the perfect angle in the air. Nathan had terrible asthma and any over-exertion caused him to sound like a kettle brought to the boil.

"Mmm... aww," *wheeze*, "... baby... aww... shit," *wheeze,* "... yeah... there... slap me hard, that's it! Like that..." *wheeeeeeze...*

What? Slap me? That's new!

Nathan then proceeded to flip the twig into a wheelbarrow position and resume the vigorous pummelling, avoiding any eye contact with me standing frozen in his line of sight.

"*Arghhh*, you know what, Nathan?" I bellowed over the grunts. *"You,* are a waste of time; you are selfish, arrogant and for the record –" I swiftly turned to Miss Humps-A-Lot, "– *not* that good in the sack, so knock off the fake orgasms, Blondie. His dick's way too small to deserve those kinds of noises!" With a cough and splutter, Shade Platinum Blonde 01 kindly turned down the pipes.

In hindsight, it was probably not the most productive thing to have done, but I had a sudden urge to turn to my massively unfaithful boyfriend and ask, "Nathan, out of curiosity, why did you never use the Kama Sutra moves on me?"

He looked me dead in the eye and replied with a cold smile. "That's easy, *Hunny Bun*. Elephants don't manoeuvre too well."

Well, on that note...

After taking the dignified high road of flipping the middle finger at the protagonists of the blue movie currently being enacted in my, no, my *former* living room, I made my way out into the cold, dark street, dragging my suitcase with me. I crammed it into my little banger of a car and decided on a walk. I needed to clear my head, bloody hell, not just clear it, I think only a good old lobotomy or an extensive course of ECT would be the only thing that could erase the last thirty minutes from my frazzled brain.

I set off wobbling down the road in my work-appropriate moderately high heels and laughed at the fact that the contents of my life were currently all stuffed into a rusty Nissan Micra.

How could this be happening to me? It was all going so well and to plan: move to the city – granted it's only Newcastle-Upon-Tyne and ten minutes from home, but it was what I'd always wanted. I planned to get a good job, make good money and enjoy my well-structured, traditional, normal life. There was not a part of the plan that involved my less-than-monogamous boyfriend power-driving a stick insect!

Could this day get any worse???

It had all begun with being late for work: another jumper off the Tyne Bridge had caused a huge tailback. Then I walked into school and *boom – parental attack!* I received a bollocking from a student's mother for supposedly introducing her child to the 'Dark Arts'. Yep, the Dark Arts. After setting a book report on a Young Adult thriller novel (that was written specifically for use in schools may I add), the horror-filled face of Mrs. Reilly blindsided me as I made my way into my classroom.

Apparently fictional vampires and wizards taint the sanctity of blood, encourage magic and give children impure thoughts that could result in evil behaviour. Naughty Ms. Munro, swaying the youth of today to the dark side with child-friendly and demographically-appropriate English literature. Just call me the modern day Darth-friggin'-Vader of the English private school system!

Then the day had concluded in spectacular fashion with Nathan having his unfaithful fun on my much-loved sofa; the one saving grace was that we had at least paid for the Safeguard coating and the love-fluids currently being spilled on the chocolate-brown upholstery could be easily wiped away.

Every cloud…

I bowed my head and let the sorrow wash over me. I had never been one to wallow in self-pity, but given the day's events and finding out that my ex was a closet exhibitionist who couldn't stop nailing his tramp for two minutes to kindly explain what the fuck was happening to our relationship – *I mean that's unheard of, surely?* – I was going to allow myself a short reprieve and have a pity party for one!

So with a sombre gait, I meandered down Northumberland Street and the many dark and dingy roads of central Newcastle, trying to come to terms with the fact that my life had just been flipped on its head.

After ten minutes of aimless wandering, I tilted my head and smiled in confusion at where I had ended up. The cinema. My mother would bring me here every Saturday growing up to see the current 'picture show', as the oldies called it.

I walked to the grandly decorated foyer and looked at the walls plastered with posters of current films and all their stars. I moved from poster to poster and studied the actors and imagined their lives. I bet they didn't have a care in the world. They had it all – fame, fortune and the job of their dreams.

Lucky bastards.

What did I want to be? What were *my* dreams? It was so long ago since I'd thought about that sort of thing, I couldn't actually remember – how sad is that?

I walked back outside and tipped my head to the sky. Then, like a crazy person, spread my arms and began to sob, begging the gods for a sign of what to do next, where to take my life.

I waited in silence, the only sound coming from my heavy breathing. Nothing. No shooting star or flash of divine intervention, just the sound of a bottle being smashed in the rowdy pub across the street.

With a huff of a laugh at my desperate cry for a mystic solution, I took one last look at the theatre and flinched as a light bulb on one of the poster frames popped, almost in my face. Even slightly less illuminated, I could see that the man on the poster was perfect – muscles, tattoos, brooding expression and pure gorgeousness. I bet right at that moment he was living in a million-dollar mansion somewhere, making love to some Amazonian goddess, not a care in the world.

Some people have all the luck.

As I headed back to my car, I tried to figure out what to do next. I passed my favourite bookstore and smiled at the window display – Jane Austen month, my idol. I took in the famous titles spread on luxurious red velvet, the most popular perched high on pedestals: *Persuasion*, *Emma*, *Mansfield Park* and of course *Pride and Prejudice*. The books that keep most women warm in bed *but* ruin our lives when we realise that real Mr Darcys do not come and save us from a life of loneliness after swimming through a lake.

Just as I was about to turn away, my breath caught in my throat as my wandering gaze fell on a small piece of paper showing a quote by the lady herself, tucked next to *Sense and Sensibility*.

"Why not seize the pleasure at once, how often is happiness destroyed by preparation, foolish preparations?" Jane Austen

Was this my sign? Was this the sign that I had asked for? Was Ms. Austen sending me a message from the grave that the anecdote to my current fucked up situation was to seize the day? Or was I going completely nuts? I knew it was likely to be the latter, but who isn't just a tad off-kilter? So hell, I went with it!

I grabbed my handbag, which I'd dropped to the ground during my impromptu séance, and tottered off down the street. A short way down, I turned a corner and walked straight into a homeless man sheltering in the alcove in between a row of bars.

He steadied my wobbling frame and smiled at me with a toothless grin. "Alreet, pet? Ya look bloody miserable, like. Life's never *that* bad."

I stared at the man for what seemed like an eternity and proceeded to… laugh my flippin' arse off!

Here was a man with no home, no job and no real prospects attempting to cheer *me* up. Oh, the irony!

"You're right!" I shrieked, causing several magpies to scatter around me.

I stood there in the rain, overlooking the Tyne Bridge and the twinkling blue lights of Greggs The Baker down the road.

I took a calming breath, inhaled the delicate Newcastle aroma of cheese and onion pasties and Lambert & Butler cigarettes, and thought of the many legends that this town had created – Sting, Jimmy Nail, Ant and Dec – and said to out loud,

"Man up, Natasha; you are a true Geordie: strong, focused and as hard as nails! If wor lass Cheryl Cole can get through this kind of shit, so can you!"

"*Atta girl!*" my new hobo life coach shouted. "Don't suppose you could spot me a fiver for a pack of ciggies?" he shrugged.

Laughing, I pulled out my purse. "Here's a twenty, splash out on me!"

I set off walking again, knowing there was only one place to go from here –to my best friend John. He would sort me 'reet out!

"Natasha!" shrieked John, as he opened the pink-and-purple door with superb dramatic flair, wearing his trademark white drainpipe jeans, yellow muscle T-top and thick guy-liner rimming his big blue eyes.

Before I continue, let me briefly fill you in on John Weallans. Erm… John. How to describe John…?

I know!

Think pink, glitter, unicorns and fabulous! That's him in a nutshell, and he is my soul's significant other, minus the sex and any form of physical attraction. He's the Ying to my Yang, the Ben to my Jerry and the Ziggy Stardust to my David Bowie.

John and I became best friends in High School after we met in a *'Beat-the-Bullies'* group in Grade Seven. I know what you're thinking: surely these two amazing kids were in the popular crowd? But alas, John was as bent as a butcher's meat hook, and I was as fat as a pig. Not the most sought-after attributes when picking your mates in the harsh corridors of Newcastle Tyne High in 1995.

One day, after I had been sacrificially rounded up and captured by the Grade Ten boys and symbolically roasted on a manmade spit (this really only consisted of a set of rugby posts, extra-strength electrical tape, a hockey stick and two boys rotating the device), it was 'felt' by the headmaster that I should seek comfort in a group of fellow bullied victims, and by 'felt' I mean 'forced to go', because obviously *this group* would prevent further bullying!

John was in the group after he decided to appoint himself as the head, and by 'head' I mean the *only*, cheerleader for the boys' rugby team. One look at John in a triangle-cupped bikini top, strap-on fairy wings and matching pink tutu ignited the long-lost aggression needed in the players. However, the aggression did not take place on the pitch as preferred by the coach, but on John's face and groin.

We had been best friends ever since, aptly naming our little pairing the 'Oink Fairies'.

I ran into John's arms. "The shit has hit the fan!" I said, shaking my head.

"Oh, my Gods of glitter!" His hands began to flap, and he jumped up and down on his welcome mat, which read *'Please Enter if you are Pretty and Witty and Gay'*. "You're a lesbian. I've always suspected, what with your love of khaki and your K.D. Lang obsession. It's okay, Wilbur," *Pig-related nickname.* "I'll guide you through this transition, and let me just say on behalf of the LBGT community, welcome to the land of unicorns and rainbows," he said with a graceful bow.

"Tinkerbell," *Fairy-related nickname.* "I am not a lesbian. Firstly, I like khaki because I feel soldier-strong and like GI Jane when I'm wearing it; secondly, K.D. Lang is an exceptional singer who unfortunately has a somewhat questionable style in fashion but gives me no tingles in the downstairs department; and thirdly, I enjoy pork *way* too much to switch to an all-fish diet!"

"Mmm, I like pork too," he said dreamily while leaning against his doorframe.

"We know, chick, we know," I soothed, patting his hand and walking into the warmth of his three-bedroomed Victorian semi-detached in Jesmond Dene.

Five minutes later, inside *'Casa Di Tink'*, away from the prying eyes of the suburban cul-de-sac, bags dropped in the hallway, it was safe to let the drama unfold.

Tink, eyes bright with curiosity, demanded, "Okay, spill it, what's up?" while removing the ingredients for my favourite drink, a strawberry daiquiri, from his kitchen, which was modelled on the Emerald City from the Wizard of Oz: no joke. It's amazing how much green crap you can purchase on eBay.

With a fortifying breath I told my tale, all of the gory parts included.

Five minutes later…

"Well, butter my butt and call me a biscuit!" Tink sang with a flick of his over-spiked jet-black hair, whacking the ice cube bag in earnest, mouth gaping in shock.

"What do I do? Where do I go?" I sobbed, throwing my head down to the IKEA green laminate table. *Ouch, that'll leave a bruise!*

"You'll stay here, you silly cow. We'll be roomies once more, like we were before that dick came along and took my playmate away," he said sternly, clearly insulted that I hadn't trusted him to help with my accommodation dilemma.

He continued. "It's no secret that I thought that Nathan was bad news, I just hope you use this as an excuse to actually throw some caution to the wind and start living your life, not purely existing, which you've been doing for most of your days with that slimy-skinned squid. You lost your sparkle months ago, my little Peppa Pig."

I stared at my long-time best friend. Was he right? Should I throw caution to the wind and change my ways? Had I lost my sparkle, my *je ne sais quoi*?

I thought back to the movie theatre filled with successful, happy people, and the homeless man who despite it all, found pleasure in a packet of cigarettes. Then I thought back to the Austen display and *that* quote – the quote that was practically talking to me, begging me to change. It couldn't have all just been a coincidence, could it?

Tink pottered around the kitchen, preparing to blend, when I had an overwhelming surge of anger that this was my mess of a life – my one life that I needed to live to the max and make fantastic memories in. If the homeless man could be happy, so could I – granted, his may have been due to the *Jim Beam* radiating from his pores, but still, at least he found joy! I can't remember a time when I was truly happy.

That's it. No more.

I slapped my hand down on the table top and rose to my feet (imagine me doing it in slow motion with 'Chariots of Fire' playing in the background) and I punched a fist in the air. Tink looked on with wide eyes and, feeling the significance of the moment, gasped in anticipation of my forthcoming speech, laid his right hand over his heart and fell back against the emerald-flecked granite work top.

"I am Natasha Munro and I deserve to be happy. I have a dream that one day the voluptuous vixen look will grace the catwalks again and I can channel my inner Marilyn with confidence and admiration; that I will succeed in life and be remembered as the best teacher that ever existed; and that I will love a man who loves me for me *and* my obsession with fake eyelashes and tan. Oh, and who doesn't mind that I'll always be a little bit chunky.

Screw all that has happened today! My new life starts right now, no more foolish preparations – *Carpe Diem*!"

I tipped my head to the sky, arms spread wide, "I want something new, something exciting, I want to get away, I want… I want…'"

"*I want to break free, I want to break free…*" Tink interrupted with his best Freddie Mercury impression and, ever the committed showman, made a grab for the emerald-green vacuum from the cupboard, parading around the kitchen singing at the top of his lungs, "*… I want to break free from your lies, you're so self-satisfied, I don't need you…*"

Laughing, I jumped up and snatched the feather Magic Duster and became the Brian May of our budget Queen tribute band.

After the song was done – a rendition that we were sure would place us as the winners of *Britain's Got Talent* – we sat down on the red love-seat, grabbed our daiquiris and contemplated the events of the day.

With a sigh, Tink laid his head on my shoulder and said, "Wilbur, you'll be just fine. You're gorgeous, you're an amazing teacher and the best friend a gal could ask for. I love you. You have always accepted me for me, and you don't know how special that is – I'm not your average guy by any stretch of the imagination, but you never judged me. See this as an opportunity to find someone who can make you the happiest person alive, be your everything. I mean – Nathan? Sorry to say, Wil, but a beer-bellied, balding, albino-resembling furniture shop manager is not really your Prince Charming. You deserve much more. Take the sound advice given from *Rocky Horror's* Frankenfurter: 'Don't dream it, be it."

I wiped away a stray tear from Tink´s face with my thumb and hugged him hard, kissing his cheek. I looked down, shook my head and I let out one final sigh at the day's turn of events.

There were no words.

Tink patted my knee, held my two hands in his, took a deep breath and squealed, "Now let's get trashed!"

CHAPTER 2

In With The New...

Six daiquiris followed by tequila chasers resulted in me and my favourite fairy being absolutely blitzed. On the upside, I was feeling a whole lot better about the cheating situation and, having kicked Tink's arse twice at Just Dance on the Nintendo Wii, I was feeling pretty darn unstoppable.

As we crashed on the couch, putting the world to rights, it came to me in a flash, an epiphany! I froze, and Tink grabbed my hand in reaction to my sudden stillness.

I dropped his hand, shot up from the couch and turned to stand in front of him, a slow smile forming on my face. He raised an eyebrow in question as I began to pace back and forth in front of the log fire.

"Okay, we've established that things in my life need to change, yes?"

Tink nodded in confirmation, following my every move with his bright sapphire eyes.

I continued. "I propose a new plan. I need to start a new chapter, develop a new philosophy to adhere to, one that challenges me… liberates me."

Tink went to interrupt, but I held up a hand to stop him, only spilling a little bit of my drink in the process.

"I've got it! I propose a period of time where the *only* rule is to seize the day, to go with the flow or throw caution to the wind as you put it."

Tink's face was morphing into one of utter glee at my declaration.

"It can be a test, *no*, a social experiment of sorts. I will give myself a period of time, a year or something, to change my *modus operandi*, the way that I conduct my life, and assess at the end whether it has changed for the better. If it has, I stick to it, if not…" I shrugged and looked to my bestie, who was practically vibrating in excitement, waving his hand in the air waiting for me to give him permission to speak. I gave him a regal nod to proceed.

"I say yes! And so will you, it'll be like the film, the one with whasisname… Jim Carrey. You have to say yes to everything and see if your life improves. I love it!" he slurred.

I shook my finger. "I won't commit to saying 'yes' to everything, as I think that's just stupid and could effectively land me in some sticky spots, but I will commit to taking opportunities when they arise and not overthinking the rafima… marifa… ramifications and consequences of my actions. If something feels good, I'll go with it." I nodded my head once, affirming my intention.

Tink ran to the kitchen and came back with two shots of God knows what – some orange concoction – and we knocked them back, shuddering at the burn of it running down our throats. We dived back on the sofa, and I actually felt lighter, relieved... free. Tink couldn't keep the grin off his face.

He sat forward. "So what you going to do about Nathan the dick? You're probably going to see him around. Newcastle's a small place."

I thought about Nathan parading around with his new plastic-fantastic bimbo-on-the-side and I felt sick. Tink was right. Time to put my words into action.

With a deep breath, I turned to my best friend and confided, "Tink, I'm serious when I say this, regardless of the alcohol and the sudden overhaul in my attitude and life philosophy – I need to get out of here. I've actually thought about it for a while but never dared to take the plunge," I delivered with conviction – well, conviction and a bit of intoxicated slurring.

Tink rolled his head and, with a smile offered, "Well let's go, my peppered slab of salami. Ibiza, Benidorm, Magaluf – wherever you want."

"Firstly, as if! I'm thinking those places would be great for you, with your toned physique and quest for quickies, but for a fuller-figured goddess like myself, the thought alone is giving me palpitations. Can you imagine the amount of neon Lycra I would have to purchase to survive such a fortnight? *Ugh,* no thanks!" I chided, with a grim look and a shiver to the spine.

"Shut your cake-hole, Wilbur, it'll be fun. A two week vay-cay is just what the doctor ordered," he insisted with a smug grin. "Plus you need to get laid. Elephants like you need a sexual outlet now and then, even if they don't manoeuvre too well!" he said, nudging me with his elbow and giving me a sly wink.

"Gee, thanks for that! But no, I mean I need to get away – as in move away. Newcastle is a fishbowl. It's too small for me *and* Nathan the prick. It didn't work for Nemo, and it's sure not going to work for me."

"You can't run from your problems, Wil, they'll never go unless you face them head-on."

He put a tapping finger to his lips and continued. "I'm drawn to a quote by the queen of the gays herself, Lady Gaga, who in her infinite wisdom once said *"… all that ever holds someone back, I think, is fear. For a minute I had fear. Then I went into the dressing room and shot my fear in the face."* That's you too, Wil. You are fierce enough to get through this," he mused without a hint of amusement, even though he was throwing out Lady Gaga proverbs to relate to my life. But hell, she is the new Gandhi!

"I'm not running; if anything, I'm seizing the day. Life's too short. I need to make a change, we're in agreement on that. It'll be the first step in my 'experiment'. I'm thinking big, Tink. I'm thinking international. I'm thinking of a permanent move."

Silence descended on the room while we both envisioned our lives apart, no longer joined at the hip. A broken pair of Oink Fairies.

Tink shuffled to the front of his seat, rubbed his face with his hands and shifted his attention in my direction. "Well, Wil, Newcastle probably is too small for us and our larger-than-life personalities anyway. The world is ours for the taking. And of course, you know I'll be the Dory to your Nemo in your quest for happiness," he announced as he began to line up a dangerous amount of the same orange poison-shots.

"*Wait.* Are you saying what I think you're saying?" I asked with rising excitement.

"What? You thought you'd be doing this alone? Fuck that for a bag of chips! Where you go, I go. We're the Oink Fairies, we fly and roll in mud together!" he said, kissing my hand.

"I'm pretty smashed right now and will probably not remember this in the morning, but I have never been so excited in my life. I'm peeing myself with anticipation!" I giggled as I tackled and practically strangled my most favourite person in the world with a bear hug.

"Well grab those incontinence knickers, my baby girl, because our lives are about to change."

He handed me my shots and with a 'chin chin' and a '*salute*' we toasted to the ride that was going to be our new life.

15 minutes later...

"Tink, I'm going to be sick. I cannot take all this tequila!"

Let me just take this opportunity to give an explanation for those who are unfamiliar with Geordies.

We are born loud and proud to be Northern. Being a Geordie is not simply a title due to the region we were born in, it's a culture. Our blood runs thick in black and white.

The girls are brazen and unafraid of most things — well, except the Achilles' heel to any Geordie lass... a fake tan shortage! We fight like blokes and have skin like penguins. We feel no cold and will face minus temperatures with so little on and skirts so short, that you can practically see what we've had that morning for breakfast!

We are not measured by our character and content of our hearts but by the shortness of our hem-lines and the height of our hair. Oh, and we can drink anyone, and I mean *anyone,* under the table!

Like any good Geordie, the talent of binge-drinking is innate. There is something in the Northern water that makes it possible for any one of us to consume lethal amounts of liquor in the shortest amount of time possible and still manage (granted, with a few intermittent cleansing stomach-purges) to crack on through the night undeterred.

Despite that fantastic description, most of us are classy, we just like to work hard and play even harder.

Now where were we?

Stumbling around the room with a more-than-fuzzy head, I tried to focus and fight back the nausea.

"Do not DARE fail on me now, sweet-cheeks. We have some decision-making to do," shouted Tink from across the room, while trying to decide what to dance to next: Girls Aloud or some vintage Tiffany? Such a dilemma!

Inhaling deeply and pulling myself together, I gave my body a sobering shake. "Okay, okay, I'm good now. *Soooo* how we going to do this? How in the hell do we choose where to go?" I uttered, as I tottered back to my fairy and his mammoth iDock.

"Well, hell if I know, my drunken little piglet. Let's let the fates decide," he said with his palms pointed up at the mirror ball that hung from the living room ceiling like it was an effigy of a pagan disco god.

"Fates? And just how, Mystic Meg, will the fates decide? I'm sure the fates are much too busy to deal with two drunken pissheads at midnight on a Friday."

"Fine, have you got a better plan?" my fairy demanded with an acid tongue and an arch of his perfectly plucked left HD brow.

"Well yeah, just give me a minute," I said, holding up my hand for quiet. "… Ah ha!" I yelled in triumph, and a light bulb appeared over my head. "Pass the remote for the TV."

Tink did so with a curious pout.

I looked him right in the eye. "If it's fate you want, then fate it will be. I will turn on the TV, we will close our eyes and choose a channel at random. In whichever country the show is set, then that, my fairy-weathered friend, will be our new home."

I gave a sharp nod – not a good move, *ugh*, alcohol. *No more vigorous head movements!*

My enchanted bestie shimmied and clapped in agreement and switched on the 60-inch Smart LCD. We held hands and closed our eyes. With a 'tap, tap, tap' of the buttons our future was sealed.

"I'm so excited!" squealed Tink.

"Okay, on the count of three, open your eyes… One."

Deep breath.

"Two… Thr-"

"Erm… do you hear bombs?"

"Shut up and quit stalling."

Nearly there.

"Three."

"OH, HELL NO!" was the instant response from my flamboyant partner in crime.

I opened my eyes and took in the splendour of… Afghanistan???

"What the heck is this show?" I said in a panic.

Tink snatched the remote from my tight grip and brought up the title: *Ross Kemp in Afghanistan*. Well, fate had truly turned us upside-down and smacked us right on the arse!

"Wil, I love you and everything, and you know I would do anything for you, but, well... I'm just too goddamned pretty to pull off a burkha!" he proclaimed with absolute sincerity whilst throwing himself onto the vintage white shag pile rug.

I, on the other hand, at this heartfelt plea, proceeded to break into hysterics at the sheer horror on the face of my best friend.

The Tinkster lifted his head with a scowl. "What are you laughing at? I'm serious. I'll wither and die in such a climate... and the sand. Lord, the sand! I'll be shitting out castles for eternity! However, on the upside, the exfoliation would do wonders for my complexion, and... Oh. My. Gods of glitter! I'll get to wear a headscarf and embody the iconic Little Edie from *Grey Gardens* and be *'fabulous, mother-darling'*! Mmm... Afghanistan is starting to have possibilities..." he pondered as he weighed up the pros and cons, using his hands as scales.

Pulling myself together, I turned to my bloody daft pal. "Okay, one last try and this time whatever destination is on the screen, we *WILL* be going there, war zones excluded."

Taking each other's hands once again, we closed our eyes. I had to refrain from chuckling at the idiot beside me who was chanting under his breath, "Hawaii, Hawaii, Hawaii, oh, maybe Bali?"

With a calming exhale, I tapped on the buttons once more. The thud of our hearts created a staccato rhythm. When the sound came on and we opened our eyes it was to the delightful sound of a Caribbean accent.

'Feel the rhythm, feel the rhyme, get on up, it's bobsleigh time!'

Taking in the scene before us, we turned to one another and began jumping and screaming around the room.

"We are going to Jamaica!" shouted Tink in blissful happiness.

After a thirty-second hysterical celebration involving hip bumps and high fives and tit-to-tit taps, I turned to the TV to bask in the joy of our chosen new home and abruptly noticed the snow.

Wait... snow?

"Erm, since when do they have snow in Jamaica?" *Did I miss something in Geography class?*

Tink looked over my shoulder after expertly rounding off his cartwheel and said, "Well, dip me in shit and roll me in breadcrumbs. You're right, Wilbur, look at the sign – 'Winter Olympics 1988, Calgary'."

"Calgary. Canada. Gosh! Canada, Tink, we're moving to bloody Canada!" I declared with an Irish jig.

Several dances and *Cool Runnings* quotes later – 'Kiss the egg, man' being the favoured line – it all began to sink in. We were headed to the Great White North.

I glanced at Tink, who was midway through a Fosse-inspired routine using the staircase banister for a ballet barre and said, "Well, kid, it's you and me against the world, or *Girls Gone Wild* in Calgary. I'm not sure which?"

He circled towards me on a pirouette, floated across the room and grabbed my arm with a lustful look upon his face. "One word makes this all worthwhile, Wil," he said, his eyebrows jumping up and down in a dastardly villainous fashion.

"And what's that? The Rockies? Hockey? Syrup?" I laughed, goading him on.

Shaking his head, he smirked and smouldered in a raspy voice, "Even better."

I held a breath in anticipation, eager for the response.

Closing his eyes and puckering his lips he answered, "Mounties!"

Enough said.

CHAPTER 3

Oh Canada!

"Glynis, I'm gonna need my Munro Clan kilt and my steel-capped boots, the ones that can break coccyx!" screamed my father.

The next day, after seven pints of water and a restorative fry-up, I was sitting at the farmhouse-style kitchen table of my parents' house on their farm trying to gently break the Nathan-bomb to them. As you can see, it was going well.

"Dad, calm down," I pleaded. I *sooo* did not need this right now.

With a slammed fist on the breakfast bar, my father, turning a lovely shade of crimson – and was that..? Yep, smoke coming from his ears – shrilled in a battle cry-type manner.

"The scrawny English bastard!" Cue excessive rolling of R's. "I'm gonny kill the Sassenach prick. As my ancestors before me, I will paint myself blue and cut him from naval to nose. Let the fields of Bannockburn rejoice in the sacrificial slaughter of one Nathan Skellet, another casualty of the Scottish cause: ridding the world o'wee English shits! Especially those that fuck wi' *my* family!"

I threw my head in my hands.

My father — Gordon — is the best man I know. He is also the craziest man I know. He is 100% Scottish and proud of it, as well as the most hot-headed and impulsive man on the planet.

"Calm down!" I yelled.

"I will not! That beady-eyed wee fucker slighted my daughter and thus he must pay! Glynis, get my Sgian-Dubh... and make sure its sharp!"

I jumped up and headed after my father's retreating form. "Okay, okay Braveheart, sit down," I said, grabbing his arm and returning him to his seat. "For a start, there will be no battling on my behalf. We are no longer living in the Middle Ages, so 'slighting your daughter' is perhaps too dramatic a term to use towards my ex that I lived with... out of wedlock. And Dad, your Sgian-Dubh is purely decorative for your kilt and about two inches long, so, unless Nathan has joined ranks with Grumpy and Dopey in the last twenty-four hours, it's not exactly an appropriate weapon to wield if you want to be successful in the slitting from naval to nose!"

Taking a deep breath, Dad seemed to mellow out.

"Plus we ran out of your blue face paint at Halloween when we dressed up as Smurfs."

Huffing out a sigh at not getting to beat some English meat, he seemed to restrain himself. "I'm just so angry, sweetheart. I'm ragin', ye ken?"

"I know, but let's just forget it and move on. Hey, with any luck I'll get myself a Scottish boy next," I laughed.

"Aye, that'd be guid. But nae fenians, ye hear? If they support Celtic, dinnae even bother bringing him hame! You're my wee bairn girl. My miracle," he sniffed, and wiped away a single tear.

I laid my head on his shoulder. "I know, Dad."

One parent appeased, I turned to my mother to see her bottom lip beginning to tremble.

Great, here come the water works!

"Oh, my sweet girl, how could he?" she said, rushing over to me, crushing me into her ample bosom. "And on the imported Italian leather L-shape? Has he no shame?"

"Mam, I'm fine, really," I managed to mumble out of my current suffocation.

Letting go, she grabbed my cheeks and looked me in the eye to check for fibs.

"Honestly, Mam, I think it's for the best. You know I don't let things get to me. Especially after speaking to the homeless man. I'm just pissed off that he threw a whopping spanner in my life plan. I mean I'm twenty-eight and no spring chicken but, thinking about it, I never *really* loved him; he just fit the profile I was looking for in a potential partner."

My parents furrowed their brows at how I could talk so coldly about someone I had been in a relationship with for three years, but it was true – I don't think I ever really loved him. He was just… convenient.

"But how could he?" my mother continued. "After all you have been through, the insensitive little shit! Wait, did you say you spoke to a homeless man?"

I waved my hand in front of me, dismissing her worry. "It doesn't matter about the homeless man, Mam. Please stop worrying. I'm not a charity case!" I shouted in exasperation.

My mam tutted at my little outburst. "Firstly, I do not think you are a charity case, but you have had more than your fair share of bad luck in this life, and I for one cannot believe that Nathan, knowing all of that, still betrayed you in such a way," she cried into her hands.

"I know, Mam, but it's done; I'm moving on. I think it was a blessing in disguise anyway. It saved me from a messy future divorce and gave me a new perspective on life."

She sat beside me, stroking my hair and holding my hand, nodding and staring into space.

"Erm, guys, I have something else to say in regards to said, new perspective," I started again, wanting to keep the momentum of the revelations going.

"What is it, flower?" asked my mam.

"Tink and I are moving to Calgary. In five months," I said in an upbeat tone. "Ta-daa!" I added weakly, as an afterthought, incorporating my award winning jazz hands into the reveal.

"I dinnae fuckin' think so!" My dad rose to his feet and began pacing and spouting expletives again.

I looked in my mother's direction. She was looking a deathly shade of white and had definitely stopped breathing, slouched over Brunhilde, the Munro family dachshund.

My father halted in his rant abruptly and looked me in the eye, no longer upset. "Let me get this straight. Yesterday you were living your life as normal, yes?"

I nodded.

He continued. "Then you go home and find your boyfriend with another woman, break up with him, go to Tink's, get blindingly drunk and decide to move to Calgary in Canada?"

He waited for my answer in silence.

"Erm, in a nutshell, y-yes," I stammered. It did sound kind of random, hearing it said out loud.

"You need to answer a few things for me."

"Okay." All eyes were on me.

"What the hell do you think you are doing?"

I cleared my throat. "Well, I realised yesterday that I needed to get back some *joie de vivre,* and unfortunately it took my boyfriend's infidelity to show me that. Then I went for a walk and asked for a sign, and Jane Austen spoke to me from the grave telling me to seize the day and then Tink and I got drunk and I decided that a change of scenery was exactly what I needed."

My father shook his head in disbelief. "I've have never heard anything so fuckin' stupid in all my life!"

"I second that motion!" piped up my mother dryly, with her arms crossed firmly across her chest.

That's it!

"Whether you like it or not, I am doing it, so you have five months to come to terms with it. That may sound harsh, but I want to do this, and I'm old enough and stupid enough to go through with it!"

I walked to each of my parents, kissed each of them on the cheek, and made my way out of the house feeling like Xena the Warrior Princess at standing up to my somewhat over-protective elders. I was sure they would come around in time – but until then, I headed back to my favourite fairy. It was time for another drink!

To say the following months were a blur would be an understatement. Dorothy in the tornado on her road to Oz had more structure and organisation than I did. Tink, on the other hand, was as cool as a cucumber. Having years ago been left a hefty inheritance by his eccentric and fabulously wealthy artist uncle, he had no reason to work.

However, Tink being Tink felt that not working would be to deprive the world of his unrivalled social skills, so for years had held gainful employment as a waiter in our local Italian restaurant, to enhance his verbal and, most importantly, flirting communication. Tink loved nothing more than feeding his espresso addiction while chatting to anyone and everyone about anything and everything. Coincidentally, Mario, the owner of the Italian restaurant where Tink currently worked, just so happened to have a friend in Calgary who was more than happy to organise a similar job for him there.

Luckily for Tink, and due to his healthy bank balance, his visa to Canada was accepted immediately. I, on the other hand, had several things to sort out.

I handed in my resignation at work and although it was sad to leave such an amazing team behind, I was excited for the future. My boss, Maureen, had seen a job on an online educational site that she thought I would be perfect for and after a particularly horrific Skype interview and a few tense days wait, I was offered the 'Social Science' Head of Department position at 'The Calgary School of Excellence.'

So, I was in the final stages of tying up my Newcastle life. My apartment was handed to Nathan the dick who had quickly moved in his new blonde bint – not that I was bitter or anything! I had a new job in place and all the visa paperwork had come through successfully, so my fairy and I were all systems go!

My parents, as predicted, slowly came round to the idea. Of course I had to convince them on more than one occasion that black bears could not stealthily sneak in through bedroom windows on the top floor of apartment complexes. Within a couple of months they had stopped threatening to chain themselves to the airport runaway to stop the plane from taking off and all plans to call in hoax bomb scares were put on hold indefinitely — I saw this as progress.

Tink and I arrived at Calgary International airport on July first – Canada Day – after a nine hour aeroplane ride which was made particularly uncomfortable by a moaning Tink who had bitched non-stop about the fact that his bubble-gum pink chaps were chaffing his member on the cheap polyester seats. Yep, chaps. My dad – in all his wisdom, and potentially as revenge for my moving – had thought it hilarious to give Tink a full pink cowboy ensemble complete with glitter rhinestone accents to celebrate our move to Canada's Cowtown. I had, as usual, reaped the benefits of that little gift, and had the burst ear-drums to prove it. The outfit did, however, help my camp cowboy bag a post-flight date with an air steward who had been eye-fucking my bestie for the majority of the flight and had eight hours free for a scheduled layover.

Tink exchanged his digits with his date and we jumped off the plane with uncontrolled excitement and swiftly passed through customs after receiving a very cheery 'Welcome to Canada' and 'Have an awesome day', from the enthusiastic immigration official.

We grabbed our mountain of luggage and stumbled out of the airport to meet Suzy, our 'realtor' who had been a godsend during our planning and had nabbed us the super extravagant condo, a black Smart car 'For Two' for me and a very American yellow-and-black Camaro for the Tinkster (yep, you've guessed it, it's 'Bumblebee'!).

"Well, suck me dry and call me dusty!" declared Tink as we entered our new condo on Seventeenth Avenue, downtown.

It was unbelievable. A brand-spanking new penthouse with floor-to-ceiling glass and panoramic views of Calgary. Not the best financial move, but with millionaire Tink and my whopping contribution, we had decided to throw caution to the wind and splurge.

"Well, *Dusty*. It is unreal. Can you actually comprehend that this is our new home?" I said, my voice filled with awe.

"I can and I do. Now for my little extra surprise. Come now, my little Porky Pig," Tink said as he grabbed my arm and dragged me onto the roof-top patio.

"Tah-dah!" he shouted as he pointed to the monstrous hot tub set to the left of the patio.

It was huge. As in orgy-huge.

"Tink! Wow! This is amazing! It's practically a flipping swimming pool. Thank you!" I squealed as I launched myself into his arms.

"No problem, my Canadian ham sandwich. It's probably more for me than you anyway!" he winked teasingly, lowering me back to my feet.

"Ha! Probably! What a bloody big hot tub," I commented, staring in fascination at the neon UV lights flickering below the surface.

"Well, I plan on entertaining…*A LOT*, so thought I'd make plenty of room. So many Canadians and so little time!" he sighed dreamily, staring at his new toy.

"Ewww, invest in a good water filter, please. God knows what I could catch after you and your 'friends' have 'relaxed'!" I said, turning up my nose.

"Hey! Give me some credit. You know my motto, Wil," he trilled, looking and pointing at me to give him an answer.

"Yes, unfortunately I do:

'If a lad should catch my eye,
Enough to say 'howay, way aye',
Play it safe, just in case,
And sheathe it tight, from tip to base!'

"Ugh, I hate saying that!" I exclaimed with a shiver, even though I'd delivered Tink's charming ditty with the accompanying actions of bending an imaginary person over doggie-style and repeatedly slapping their arse.

"Well, none of my precious baby batter will be floating by your head as you relax with a daiquiri, okay, sausage?" assured Tink.

"Erm… yeah thanks, chuck," I replied, trying to move the conversation on.

We walked to the edge of the balcony, and looked over at the hustle and bustle of a new and exciting city.

Tink put an arm around me and asked, "Are you happy, Wil?"

I turned to my slightly vulgar but always loveable BFF and declared, "You know, I genuinely am. I'm so unbelievably excited for this new chapter in our lives, and to be doing it with you is the icing on the cake," I said, cuddling into the nook under his arm.

Sighing deeply, he kissed my forehead, and said, "Love you, Wil. Always have, always will."

Smiling, I answered back. "You too, chuck. Always have, and always will."

"Honestly, you're my soul mate. It's such a bugger that you don't have a nice big juicy dick."

Shaking my head, I retorted, "Yeah, but I'm happy with what I've got, thanks. But speaking of big dicks, aren't you expecting company of the glorified-waitress variety?"

Chuckling, he glanced at his Rolex. "Yep, in twenty minutes."

"On that note, I'm going to unpack and catch a few Zs… I'm goosey-goosed!"

After unpacking and sorting out my whopping big new bedroom, I climbed into my California King sporting 1000 thread count sheets, and had drifted off to sleep before my head had even hit the pillow.

Tink arrived back after a few hours and, being a good boy, returned alone; he may talk like a two-bit dollar whore, but he does have some morals. Well, most of the time anyway. It seemed the lights of downtown Calgary could wait – he was too excited to try out his new Jacuzzi.

Hearing him fire up the bubbles, I jumped out of bed and pulled on my favourite red polka dot one-piece, and we wasted the evening knocking back the champers provided by Suzy and singing to the Britney back-catalogue.

CHAPTER 4

No Ordinary Teacher

After a lazy summer of acclimatising to our new homeland, arriving at The Calgary School of Excellence to prepare for the impending new term was a tad daunting.

The building was enormous and, by the looks of things, had cost a fortune to build. It boasted an ice hockey rink, American football pitch and state-of-the-art gym. It just screamed 'money'.

I could tell from the outset that this was going to make or break me as a school teacher. However, if there was one thing Natasha Munro could do, it was teach.

Fast forward thirty minutes and I was sitting in the principal's – Mrs. Thomas' - office, where she went on to tell me about the school, the ethics and rules. It was strict, a lot stricter than my old school, but I had expected it. That was stressed further by her horrified expression as she watched me unwrap my rolls of army camouflage and cow-print wallpaper for my display boards which had me quickly feeding them back into my oversized bag, along with the other contraband items I'd normally use to spruce up my classroom. Come on, a mini Henry Hoover for the desk is just too cute!

She showed me the classroom and gave me time to settle in and get everything sorted for the pupils, who would be coming in tomorrow.

Just before she left, she asked, "Natasha, can I have a word with you in my office at one?"

"Sure." I answered hesitantly.

With a smile, she assured me, "No need to worry, you're not in trouble."

"Phew! That's a relief."

"Okay, I'll see you this afternoon."

At twelve fifty-five that afternoon, I knocked on the door of Mrs. Thomas' office. She shouted me through and asked me to take a seat.

I had met Mrs. Thomas during our Skype interview and subsequent web-based planning meetings. She seemed nice. She was in her late forties and was from Vancouver. She was married to a Scottish man who had moved to British Columbia in his twenties to coach rugby. I put her good sense of humour down to this, and suspected that was why she seemed to like me so much. You know, Celtic clans sticking together.

She had talked to Maureen several times about my teaching practice and how to 'best utilise my skills'. I assumed, or rather hoped, that this was the reason for this impromptu meeting.

"Natasha, I have an interesting proposition for you. I have a project that I have been working on. You seem like an approachable young woman and Maureen has told me how good you are with the kids, especially the naughty ones. Is that true?" she queried.

"Well, yes, I suppose. I haven't had many problems with discipline in the past. I feel most kids like me," I shrugged, wondering where this was going.

"Obviously, my intention is that you are going to be running the performing arts programme after school, and we have a few students who, for various reasons, have begun misbehaving in class. Nothing big, just bad attitude, being rude to teachers, getting in fights, ditching classes, that kind of thing.

"This summer, I read an article about a teacher in Australia who became a mentor to children just like ours and, through performing arts, managed to help them work through their problems. After talking to you and Maureen, I have been convinced of you being able to do this. What do you think?" She sat back in her leather swivel office chair and awaited my response.

"It sounds amazing!" I answered back excitedly. "I'd love to see if I could get through to them. Oooh, I'm already getting ideas of how to help. One question though, do I find out why they may be acting up, for example their family situations?" I asked.

Shaking her head, Mrs. Thomas explained. "That's the kicker. You go in blind. There are laws, etc., on why, but also some information can't be shared as per request of the families. They fully support the initiative, but for their own reasons ask that you don't ask questions or delve into the girls' backgrounds. With one girl in particular, a Miss Jones – this is her first year here, she has just transferred from another school in the local area in which she only lasted one year due to personal issues – discretion is imperative," she informed me, stressing the point.

"Okay, intriguing, but I respect the need for privacy. It's a prestigious school, I'm sure that means some of the students come from powerful and prestigious parents. I'm kind of on the right lines, huh?" I cheekily probed, knowing by her small smirk that I was close to the mark.

"You could say that," she hesitantly agreed.

"And a badly-behaved child would not be good for such parents' social reputation?" I continued, fishing for more details.

"You're good, Natasha, but not as on the mark as you think. Some of the secrecy is for the child's sake too, just keep that in mind," she said pointedly, staring at me over her Chanel glasses.

"Right," I said, chastised. "Well, I'm in. When do I meet my little delinquents?"

"Tomorrow. You will have four afternoons a week with them. We are going tough on these girls. Like, *Private*

Benjamin-tough. Intense and quick, to get them back into mainstream classes," she winked.

"Well in that case, I'd better get organised," I said, rising from my seat. "Thanks for this, Mrs. Thomas. I'm excited about the challenge, and I'm flattered that you think I'm good enough to take it on."

Getting out of her seat, putting a hand around my shoulders and walking me to the door, she added, "Natasha, call me Mandy. I think you and I will get on great, and if you tame these wild ones and get the superintendent off my back, then I'll be extremely grateful."

Walking back to her desk, she added, "I see a big future for you here, Ms. Munro."

With a bounce in my step, I rushed back to the classroom, grabbed the key to the dance studio, and began to prep for my biggest challenge in teaching to date.

Arriving home that night, I was greeted by the wondrous smell of homemade lasagne and a pizza Margherita brought back by Tink from the restaurant.

"Hey, Pinky, how was your day? Do you like the school?" Tink asked while plating up the yummy grub and pouring out two glasses of prosecco.

"Tink, I love it! The facilities are out of this world, and the staff are really nice. It's a dream come true. Plus, I kind of got put on a special project today," I confided.

"Really? On your first day? You casting-couching your way to the top or what?" he laughed.

"Not quite. But it is exciting."

Tink placed our dinner on the table and gestured for me to sit. Raising his glass he announced, "*Buon appetito*", and began tucking in.

"So, don't keep me in suspense, what's the project?" he asked.

"Well, it's working with the bad kids really. Well, as bad as a thirty-thousand-dollar-a-year school can produce. My principal wants me to work with a group of girls who have been acting out. I take them four times a week at first and, through performing arts, try to change their attitudes in regard to confidence and their studies. From the sounds of it, some of these kids have got it pretty stressful at home and are basically being little shits because of it. So... *Natasha Munro to the rescue!*" I announced in my best superhero voice, although it came out a bit more like Scrappy Doo's 'Puppy Power'.

I was happily eating my carb-fest, dreaming of the Oprah-style counselling sessions I was going to have with my new 'projects', when I noticed Tink's lip was wobbling.

Looking at him and wondering what the hell was up, I reluctantly asked, "What's wrong, chuck?"

"We need to go back to Newcastle. I'm going to pack," he declared as he bolted for his bedroom door.

"What???" I asked in shock.

He glanced back, lips trembling once again and threw himself on the couch. "Wil, you can't work with kids like that here. They have guns. Oh, my Gods of glitter, I can see it now. It'll be on the news, *'Teacher tied up, tortured and shot five times in the head. Her best friend had to identify the body'*. I can't see you dead, Wil. My sensitive disposition cannot handle that kind of bloodshed!"

He was hysterical by now.

"Tink, a) They don't have guns in Canada – that's America, you idiot; b) I'm working in the most expensive school in Calgary, maybe even Canada. I hardly think I'm working with the Bronx kids here, do you?" I soothed.

Looking slightly calmer, he answered, "Really? There's no danger?"

"Well, not like you are thinking. I'm not Michelle Pfeiffer in *Dangerous Minds*, you nugget. I don't think skipping a few classes qualifies as on par with drug-dealing and gang affiliation, do you?"

"But Wil, they're rich, they could get you assassin–"

"Tink! Can you hear what you're saying? Its three girls and performing arts, for Christ's sake! What they going to do? Take me down with a hitch-kick and a full box split?" I stood, exasperated.

"Wil, look at me."

I bent down, giving my hands over at his insistence.

"Two words: *Black Swan*. That girl was *fuuuuucked up*, and she was into performing arts. Just saying, sausage. Crazies are everywhere!" he nodded his head sagely and pursed his lips in warning.

"Yeah, I know, I friggin' live with one!" I exclaimed, gritting my teeth and clenching my fists to the sky. "Now, get up. My pizza's getting cold."

"Fine, but I'm getting you pepper spray and a taser first thing tomorrow. Any bitch steps out of line on you and you pierce her with 50,000 volts of electricity. Now, that's a fucking floor show I'd pay to see!"

CHAPTER 5

Thank You For The Music

The first day of term went really well. The kids in general were some of the most well-behaved I had ever come across; a harsh stare would shut them up. I'm not used to kids not being even just a little bit lippy. At times, it creeped me the hell out. They all sat glaring at you hanging on every word you said, in a manner a bit reminiscent of *The Village of the Damned*.

My accent wasn't too misunderstood apart from being asked why I called everyone 'man' and why I said 'like' after every word but we were able to communicate well enough.

I was a bit of a surprise to most of the kids though, judging by the number of puzzled looks I got when I referred to Hitler as "that feisty bloke with a dodgy moustache from Austria", but I was confident they would get used to me. Most commented that they had never had a teacher that looked like me, and a few of the braver ones had asked if my eyelashes were really mine. I said yes; well, if I pay for the individual extensions it gives me ownership, right?

All in all, I judged it to be going well.

The time soon came for my specialist performing arts sessions, where I would meet the three members of 'Destiny's Delinquents', as I had decided to call them. Looking at the files, they seemed okay. All fifteen to sixteen, all pretty, and all brimming with a bitchy attitude.

When I walked into the dance studio they were already sitting behind their desks, awaiting my arrival. As they caught sight of me, I could see faces react in curious surprise at not having the bald Shakespeare teacher they were expecting, but me, a curvy brunette dolled up to the nines. Got to love the impact of a hot-pink peplum dress on any occasion!

"Are you our new teacher?" asked one of the Motley Crew.

"I certainly am," I confirmed, "and you are?"

"I'm Sarah Black," she answered proudly.

"Ah, Sarah, yes. How are you today?"

"Okay I suppose. What's your name?"

"I'm Ms. Munro."

"Where are you from? You sound weird," she laughed, trying her best to be condescending.

"I'm English, Sarah. That okay with you?" I asked, glaring at her over the top of the paperwork I was pretending to fill in.

"Well, err, yeah. I suppose," she mumbled, hunching over the desk and looking at me warily.

Hard work? She just shat herself at my stern voice and Ice Queen cold stare!

"Okay, so who is Victoria York?" I asked, looking up at the other two girls.

A raised hand identified a thoroughly bored girl who looked like she wished that she was anywhere but there right then.

"Right, so that just leaves Boleyn Jones," I said, pointing in the final Delinquent's direction.

"Yep, that's me," she said moodily.

"Boleyn? I love that name. I've never heard it as a forename before. Are you named after Anne?"

"Yeah, I think so. I hate it," she mumbled.

"Why? You were named after one of the most famous royals in English history. The mother to arguably the best monarch England has ever seen. I got to tell you, *I* love it. If you have any of the spark that your namesake did, you and I will get along just fine. *And* I promise that I won't behead you if you do something wrong. How's that sound?" I teased, gaining a little smirk and a shrug from her.

"Right, my little girl band, jump up and go to the costume closet. You have twenty minutes to put together the best Lady Gaga outfit I've ever seen. We are going to start with a themed movement class, and if we are dancing to Gaga you got to have a costume to match."

"What?" they screamed in horrified unison.

"Off you go. Unless you want to spend your afternoon parading those outfits throughout the school...?" I threatened.

At that, they shot out of their chairs and to the closet, huffing and puffing all the way.

This was going to be a piece of cake!

Over the first term, my classes went from strength to strength, and my after-school performing arts group were gearing up to put on their production of *Les Miserables*. My Moody Triad were, well, less moody and more open to all things theatre. Even the timid Boleyn Jones was crawling out of her shell, and consequently making new friends and becoming a lovely young lady. She would be 'mainstreamed' in no time.

I had recruited Mandy Thomas to help cast the parts for the upcoming challenging musical. We were the Pop Idol panel of The Calgary School of Excellence, and I had appointed Mandy as our honorary Simon Cowell, due to her dangerously high-waisted trousers (power trousers, she called them) and the fact that when Jonathan from Grade Nine had auditioned with a rendition of One Direction's 'What Makes You Beautiful', she had stopped him midway-through and told him he was 'distinctly average' and that he 'should try a more feminine song to suit his mousey-type vocals'.

Cut. Throat. Honesty.

We were nearly done for the day, and I was slightly concerned that I had not managed to cast 'Fantine', the lead female role. The door to the studio creaked open as we were packing away our things, and Boleyn Jones came through hesitantly.

"Boleyn? Are you okay? Do you need to see me?" I questioned.

"Erm, kind of," she replied, biting her bottom lip.

"Well, what is it, honey?" I implored.

"I... I would like to sing for you," she stated in a hushed tone.

I stared at her, gobsmacked, "You want to sing? You want to audition? I didn't know you could? You never have in class before," I said with a shocked voice.

"I... I can a bit... I think. I just get scared I'm not good enough. Can I just let you hear, and if I'm bad you can just pretend I never did it?" She shuffled her feet nervously.

"Boleyn, I'm so proud that you would even audition, it takes guts. By simply doing this, it shows how far you've come in such a short time," I praised.

"Come on, Boleyn. Let's see what you've got," barked Mandy.

Boleyn put her iPhone into the speaker and stood centre stage, looking small and timid behind the microphone.

I recognised the song immediately; it was Adele's 'Someone Like You'. Mandy and I looked at each other and cringed. It was a tough song, even for the best and most seasoned of singers.

Boleyn moved to the mic and looked up, staring straight ahead – confidence transforming her face.

Wow.

Her voice was velvet. She began to sing, and from her little mouth came the voice of an angel. It was breathtaking. Move over Charlotte Church!

Mandy dropped her pencil and grabbed my arm, her mouth hitting the floor. All I could do was stare – stare and listen. Stare as the shy, introverted girl was gone, transformed into the embodiment of confidence, owning the stage and captivating us, the audience. She was outstanding. I had never heard anything so beautiful.

Beside me, I heard sniffling, and saw the janitor had stopped her cleaning of the studio to watch with tears streaming down her cheeks, mesmerised by the timid little Boleyn girl lighting up the room.

I had found my Fantine, and Boleyn had found her passion, and by the looks of it, the key to her salvation. She looked so… happy.

The song ended and silence descended on the room. Boleyn, once again head-down and trembling, asked softly, "Ms. Munro, was that okay?"

I walked up to the stage, noticing that the whole time she was watching her shuffling feet. "Boleyn Jones. Where have you been hiding that? You were perfect. Look at me."

She glanced up shyly.

"You were *perfect*," I repeated in all sincerity. She smiled and whispered her thanks.

In my best X-Factor voice, I took her hand and shouted, "Boleyn, with two yeses, you are going through to boot camp! You are my top choice for Fantine!"

Three days later, I posted the cast list, and Boleyn suddenly found she had a new family of friends. Casts are always close, and The Calgary School of Excellence performance crew immediately took her under their protective wing. It was rewarding to see.

Later that afternoon after school, a knock on my classroom door interrupted me from the marking of a million essays on the Black Death that I had to get done by the next day.

As I opened the door, I was greeted by a fifty-something-year-old woman with dark brown hair and a kind smile.

"Ms. Munro?" she enquired.

"Yes, please come in. Can I help you?"

"Yes, I'm Mrs Nor–,… erm I mean Mrs. Jones." she announced, a little flustered.

"Oh, you must be Boleyn's mother?" I asked, shaking her hand.

"Yes. I really just wanted to come and see you and meet the woman who is changing my daughter's life," she said, smiling.

"Excuse me, I don't understand. You mean me?" I questioned, shocked.

"Ms. Munro, since you came to this school and started working with her she is a completely different person. She smiles. She's happy, she sings all day, and I didn't even know she *could* sing.

"Boleyn doesn't have an easy time at home, and has to live an unusual and, let's say, *unique* life. She moved against her wishes to Calgary two years ago, and has been in two schools already, and hasn't responded to anyone as she has done to you," she announced kindly, with a face full of gratitude.

With a lump in my throat I replied, "I don't know what to say. Thank you. That's the nicest thing anyone has ever said to me," I confided.

Getting up, Pamela took my hand again and pulled me in for a hug. "I know it may be your job, but it's her life and it's got a whole lot better since you came along," she flattered, patting my hand.

With that, she turned and walked out of the studio. I waited two minutes, and then began shimmying around my classroom with 'Spice Up Your Life' playing in my head. I grabbed my bag, and decided to ditch the rest of the marking; this called for a hot tub celebration!

As I headed to the door, I punched a *Breakfast Club*-style arm up in the air, and with a loud shout of, *"She shoots, she scores!"* ran to my Smart car, eager to tell all to the other Oink Fairy.

CHAPTER 6

The Birth of The Tudor Reign

Les Miserables was shaping up to be the best production I had ever put on, and I couldn't have been happier, but the stupidly long hours and huge pressure made me look forward to the October break like I'd never looked forward to a holiday before.

With only getting a week off school, I had decided not to go home for a visit – it took me four bloomin' days to beat the jet-lag anyhow – so I planned to have a nice chill-out week in Calgary, all kicked off with a night on the razz with Tink.

I arrived home at five o'clock after finishing some paperwork, and I was excited as hell for a good night of drinking. Tink was at the restaurant and wouldn't finish until ten that night, and I was to meet him there, prepped and ready to go.

In true Geordie style, the beauty regime had started the previous night with a soak in the bath for about an hour, using a good exfoliating brush to get my skin as smooth as Bruce Willis' head. I'd then applied fake tan, a Natasha Munro-trademark three times, to make sure I was totally tan-tastic, although the outside observer may say that I resembled a recently creosoted fence. Yes, my sheets were completely ruined, but vanity costs, people!

So, the perfect night-out colour achieved and a large glass of pinot grigio in hand, I concentrated on meticulously curling both my hair and my 18-inch clip-in hair extensions; applying lots of helpings of bronzer; gluing two layers of fabulous strip lashes firmly in place (anymore and your eyelids will struggle to function, believe me); sticking on nails like talons; adding a thick coat of scarlet red lipstick; and finally, whacking on the shortest dress I owned and the highest sky-scraper heels you can imagine! I was good to go.

Looking at the clock and feeling a little bit tipsy from the wine and obligatory few cheeky sips of Sambuca I had consumed, I realised that it was only just eight in the evening and that I was two hours early. After twiddling my thumbs and searching for something to do, I decided I'd go to the restaurant early and hang out in the back with the staff. I quickly called a cab, and fifteen minutes later arrived at a very busy Ristorante Girasoli.

In the months that we had been in Calgary, I had been to the restaurant more times than I could count. I always used the staff entrance, as they all hung out there when things were quiet or when the wait staff were on their scheduled breaks. There was always someone to talk to and always music playing, with each staff member rotating their iPhone playlists – although the back room was always a lot quieter on Tink's playlist night – *funny, hmm?*

The best thing was that you could have a laugh and talk without the patrons seeing you. Tink had truly landed on his feet working there, and he knew it too. The Italian contingent of Calgary were some of the nicest people we had met since we had moved. I had become a bit of a permanent fixture on weekend nights, always showing up to neck a grappa or two just before closing, and grabbing Tink for a night on the tiles.

I swung open the back door and saw all the staff huddled together. Now, I was a lil' tipsy from my getting-ready wine and so didn't register that this was a bit odd. I heard Carly Rae Jepsen's 'Call Me Maybe' coming through the speaker and let the music take hold of me. I began bopping in time to the beat and made my way towards the mob of servers.

As the chorus kicked in I threw in some comedy phone shapes and headed in Tink's direction, who was looking at me in a mixture of both amusement and horror. In hindsight, I should have realised something was up as he would usually have imitated my actions as I made my way towards him. However, tonight Tink was making cutting gestures with his hand over his throat. *Mmm, strange.* But in my alcohol-addled brain, I thought it was a new move, and I successfully, with superb fluidity and grace, incorporated the action into my already-outstanding routine.

When I made it to the group, I screamed, "slut drop!" at the top of my voice and began dropping to the floor in a squat position, over and over, in-sync with Carly letting her boy know that before he came into her life she missed him *'so, so bad'*.

When I looked up, I saw several sets of wide eyes focused on me, and Tink's head facing down on the tile counter, mumbling something about "Why tonight, Lord?" and groaning like he was in pain.

I put my hands on my hips and a massively confused frown on my face. "What? Why is everyone acting so weir-,"

"Ms. Munro? Ms. Munro! Mom, it's Ms. Munro!"

It was that moment that every teacher dreads while a little bit intoxicated, dancing like a stripper working for tips and frankly making an absolute tit out of themselves, the call that has you running for the hills.

Shit, a student.

I plastered a fake smile on my face and turned around, flashing the pearly whites at a table of about six people all staring at me. They were in a very dark corner with only a red table-candle illuminating the area, meaning I couldn't initially make out individual faces. I cast a quick glance at Tink who was looking a bit pale and clammy.

What the heck is going on? Why are people eating in the back room? And what is up with Tink, he couldn't have known one of my students is here?

At the table, someone second-to-right was waving their arms around like a jacked-up air traffic controller, and was frantically gesturing for me to come over. Ah, recognition hit like a smack to the face. It was Boleyn Jones.

Fuck.

Sucking in a breath, I began to make my way over to the table. Bloody hell, it was like walking the Green Mile. I searched for any holes along the way to throw myself into but tonight, it seemed, was not my night. Only smooth and polished floors led me to my doom.

"Ms. Munro! Oh my God, I can't believe it's you, you look so different," squealed Boleyn excitedly.

Looking down at myself I nodded, taking in my micro-mini LBD that tied in a cleavage-enhancing structured-cup halter and flared out with a net tutu skirt that just about covered my more-than-ample arse. I realised I looked absolutely nothing like a teacher, but like a bad extra on the set of *Moulin Rouge*.

This is just awesome.

"Hey," I said weakly, feeling like an utter knob. "Hope you're all having a nice meal."

I briefly surveyed the dimly-lit table, noting that there seemed to be near-equal numbers of men and women, all around my age or older.

In the corner farthest away from me sat an enormous hulk of a man sporting a grey woolly beanie hat, with his head resting on the heavily-tattooed arm covering his face from view. It all seemed very mafia-like.

"Yeah, we are. We are out celebrating my part in *Les Mis*. It was the first night all the family could get together in weeks," Boleyn bubbled.

Getting up from the table, Mrs. Jones held out her hands and greeted me. "Hello, Ms. Munro, nice to see you again. Sorry if Boleyn got a bit over-excited then. We didn't mean to interrupt your night."

"No problem, it's nice to see her so lively. I just wasn't expecting to see anyone back here. Sorry if you witnessed my little performance just now. It's kind of a tradition I have with the staff, it's not really meant for public viewing," I squirmed, looking down at my hands while I beamed a lovely shade of crimson.

A few laughs came from the table, and Boleyn chimed in. "I thought it was funny, Miss!"

Having not dared make too much eye contact with the rest of the patrons through utter mortification, I decided it was probably best to make my excuses as soon as possible. "Well, I'll leave you to it; I don't want to keep you from your evening. *Buon appetito.*"

I quickly turned to scurry off, and heard muffled voices behind me. I could hear Boleyn throwing an uncharacteristic strop and a gruff male voice spit something out sharply in response, but ultimately making grunts of defeat.

What is all that about? Ignore it and run. Stop embarrassing yourself.

"Oh, Ms. Munro!" shouted Mrs. Jones.

Arghhh! I turned my head slightly towards her call.

"Could we introduce you to the rest of the family?"

Noooo!!! I must have sinned badly in a past life. I just want to go and hide under a rock!

In a fake cheery tone I answered. "Sure, I'd love to."

Tink and what seemed like every Italian immigrant in Canada were all watching me with their mouths wide open.

What the fuck is going on? Is my train wreck of embarrassment really that bad? Shit, is my skirt tucked into my knickers?

Mrs. Jones (or Pamela, as she urged me to call her) came over, took my arm, and escorted me back to the table while I discreetly checked the back of my skirt, making sure I didn't have a whopping wedgie. You'll be pleased to learn that it was all good.

The introductions started with Boleyn's side of the table.

I put my hand out and said to my student. "Hi, I don't think that we've met? I'm Ms. Munro."

Boleyn began laughing whole-heartedly and shook my hand right back. "Hi! I'm Boleyn,"

"Like Anne?" I teased.

"Yeah, but don't behead me," she joked.

"Well, only if you're a good singer and can rock out to Adele like no-one's business!"

Blushing, but obviously flattered, she answered, "I think I can do that."

I winked and looked at the next person, a beautiful blonde with blue eyes who looked about my age.

"Ms. Munro, this is Samantha; she is married to my eldest son, Henry," Pamela explained, pointing to Samantha and a casually dressed man next to her.

I nodded, smiled and shook both their hands. "Hi, nice to meet you Samantha, and you too, Henry."

They both smiled back, reciprocating the pleasantries. Henry had longish dirty-blonde hair that ran just enough to tuck behind his ears. He looked like a surfer – a very good-looking surfer – maybe in his mid-thirties. Together they looked like Barbie and Ken, all good-looking and obviously madly in love. It was lovely to see.

"Next is Tate, a friend of the family," continued Pamela.

Tate was very cute, with an extremely happy disposition. I liked him instantly. He had the preppy look down to a T, with a crisp white shirt, dark denim jeans and a red dickey bow tie. He had dark hair styled in a comb-over and was cute as a button. I would bet any money that he batted for Tink's team.

"And this is?" I asked, turning to the massive bloke on the end with the beanie hat hiding most of his face. He peeked up reluctantly, and I went to introduce myself, and then stopped.

Well, shave my head and call me baldy!

"Holy shit!" I gasped and covered my hands with my mouth as if I could stuff my inappropriate cursing back in. "I'm sorry. But–"

"*Yes*, Ms. Munro. Please let me introduce my youngest son, Tudor," Pamela announced, chuckling to herself.

"Hi," he looked up briefly sporting a disgusted scowl, clearly not at all happy about my presence.

"You're Tudor North!" I blurted out.

"Am I?" he said, patting himself and feigning shock. "Shit, that's why I've been getting gawked at all night. I couldn't figure out why before you kindly reminded me of who I am. Thanks for that, you *really* must be a good teacher, so witty and quick!" he quipped dryly, turning up the right side of his mouth in a snotty smirk.

"Tudor!" admonished all of his family in unison.

I however, just stood there in shock. Partly because of who I had just been introduced to, but mainly because he had just been such an arse. If there's a sure-fire way to stop the awe of meeting a celeb, it was for them to be a complete and utter twat.

Looking rather sheepish at being shouted at by his family, he held up his hands in surrender and muttered an insincere "I'm sorry," under his breath.

That quickly snapped me out of my trance. "Apology accepted, *Mr. North,* and I'm happy that it was one that sounded so heartfelt and sincere," I retorted with venom. "I admit, I was a bit wowed there for a moment. You are Tudor *bloody* North! I've never met anyone famous before, *and* kind of don't want to ever again now. I heard that fame could do things to a man's ego," I pointed right at his face. "Exhibit A. Tudor North: arrogant and rude – alert the media." I shouted, flinging my hands in the air. I had always been one for the dramatics!

Perhaps I shouldn't speak to him like this in front of Boleyn, you know, professionalism and all – but hey, I am bloomin' pissed off!

"Yep, that's me, Tudor North: arrogant as hell, rude to anyone outside of my family, and public property to the whole fuckin' world," he remarked slyly.

This was spiralling out of control and my annoyance was at an all-time high. If we were back in Newcastle, I'd have bottled the bastard!

"Tudor! Stop it. Don't speak to Ms. Munro like that!" cried Boleyn, getting visibly upset.

Seeing that, I began to laugh, pretending his jibes had no effect on me. "Boleyn, don't get upset, I'm sure your brother is just annoyed that your meal has been interrupted. No harm done," I said soothingly.

She seemed somewhat appeased, but her eyes were wide and embarrassed.

Okay, okay, I can hear what you're asking. Who the hell is Tudor North? Well, Tudor North is a thirty-one-year-old bonafide superstar actor, as in Hollywood actor, the real McCoy. No, I'm not shitting you.

He is six foot three, ridiculously muscular in build – and by ridiculously, I mean like a four-storey brick shithouse. He has stunningly beautiful green eyes; sometimes shaven, sometimes fair, cropped hair and sports a full body of tattoos, all of which are tribal and cover most of the left side of his body. *And* he is fitter in person than he is in real life, I can now testify to that fact.

He has been on the scene for about four years, but he had recently been catapulted to the A-list with his lead role in *The Blade Reaper*, a story about a ruthless criminal-hunting vigilante, which made a record-breaking amount of money on its first weekend.

After meeting the brooding actor, I could see why he was cast as the dark superhero. And, as pissed as I was with him at that moment, I couldn't deny that he was all muscle and pure gorgeousness. Bad attitude though. What a bloody shame.

Tudor pushed his hand over the table and grabbed Boleyn's in his. He began apologising and rubbing his thumb over her knuckles to calm her down, a surprisingly gentle gesture considering the verbal rinsing I'd just received.

Slanting his eyes up towards me, he sighed. "Ms. Munro, I apologise. It's no excuse for my behaviour, but it's difficult to go unnoticed these days, and I can get slightly uncomfortable with it."

I simply nodded my head, not knowing the proper etiquette for this situation. Turning to the rest of the group, their faces all embarrassed and awkward at my expense, I decided I had made a reasonable enough idiot of myself for one night and made my excuses to go.

"Well, I'll leave you to enjoy the rest of the night. I'll move on your adoring fans too, so you don't have to feel them 'gawking' at you for the remainder of your meal," I told Tudor, using my fingers to accentuate the air quotes.

"Thanks," he whispered quietly, still clutching his sister's hand. I would have thought he was kind of sweet really, if I hadn't just been the target of his anger.

I swiftly walked back to the gaggle of waiters and laughed at their ludicrously shocked faces. Tink ran to the front and grabbed my arm, pulling me into the kitchen, out of view and out of ear shot. The Roman army followed.

"Fucking hell, Wil, you just met Tudor North! What was he like? I almost shit a disco ball tonight when he came in and asked if we could arrange a private table for him and his family. Arghhhh! Tudor *'sex on legs'* North! What I wouldn't give to sink my ball in his hole," he shrieked.

"Calm down, Tink. And you lot," I pointed to the rest of the staff, "are creeping him the hell out, so back off."

They all scurried away at the insistence of Nonna Girasoli and her trusted pasta roller, leaving me and the Tinkster alone.

"Wil, who was that girl?" he quizzed when we were no longer subject to eavesdroppers.

"That was my student, Boleyn, one of 'Destiny's Delinquents'. Think I now know why she's so secretive. Turns out her brother's Tudor bloody North, who'd have guessed that?" I mused.

"What about him? I saw him talking to you. What'd he say?"

I crossed my arms defensively. "Just introduced himself and then ripped the piss at my star-struck reaction. Came off as a moody knob really, which is a shame as I think he is the most beautiful thing I have ever seen," I admitted, expressing my disappointment.

"Apart from me of course?" asked Tink, in all seriousness.

"Yes, apart from you," I sighed.

"Well, he couldn't take his eyes off you, Wil. It was so strange. He kept staring at you before you had even realised who he was. He laughed when you came in dancing and continued watching everything you did until you went over, and then he just seemed pissed off," Tink exclaimed.

"No wonder! Have you seen the clip of me? I'm dressed up like a tart. Rule one of teaching: students and their family should not see you dressed for clubbing. Oh my God! I pulled out the slut drop too! Do you think I'll get fired over this?" I asked, suddenly panicked. "Plus, I think he hates me. Was that not obvious?"

Tink snorted in indignation. "The slut drop is your signature move, ham slice, and he doesn't hate you. He was drawn to you without a doubt. Then again it could have been your titties. They look unreal tonight," he remarked as he pushed my breasts up with his hands.

"Forget it. I want to," I gestured with a wave of my hand. "I definitely need a night out now after this. Jägerbombs ahoy! I'm up for getting completely sloshed," I hooted.

"Right well, I need to finish my shift. Sit by the counter in the back and I'll get you a daiquiri while you wait."

He stopped suddenly, as he was walking away. "Do you want me to spit in his garlic bread in revenge?"

He wasn't joking.

I laughed and shook my head. "No, but thanks for the support, chuck."

Tink just winked in response.

I took myself to the staff bar and jumped up on a stool. I felt eyes on me and when I looked back, Tudor North was glaring menacingly my way. Our eyes met and he gave a brisk nod, his mouth clenched into a rigid tight line.

What a weirdo. What did I ever do to him? Recognise him? He shouldn't be bloody famous then, if he doesn't want the friggin' attention!

CHAPTER 7

Celebrity Close Encounter

Fifteen minutes later, and I was contentedly sipping on the remains of my large daiquiri when a deep cough interrupted my thoughts.

Tudor North stood behind me with folded arms and a dangerously sexy lopsided smirk. Now he had moved away from the cover of the table I could see him in his full glory, and glo-ri-ous he was.

Wearing a fitted black T-shirt, ripped dark jeans and an oversized beanie hat tucked in at the back, he towered above me, and for once in my life I actually felt dainty next to his remarkably wide tall and sculpted body.

"You work here as well as school or something?" he asked in a low, gruff voice.

"No. Just waiting for my friend to finish work, he gets off at ten. But hello to you too. Aren't you the epitome of manners? So... *friendly* and approachable!" I jibed, feigning nonchalance.

Why is he over here?

"He?" he inquired, looking down at the floor and then back up at me, ignoring my bitchy remark.

"Yeah, Tin—, er, John."

He wouldn't get the 'Tink' reference and I couldn't be arsed explaining it to someone I frankly was beginning to detest. Although my body, currently covered in goose bumps, didn't exactly agree with my mind's assessment. His good looks were making me queasier than the super-strong daiquiri I had just necked.

"Is he your boyfriend or something?" he asked in a very abrupt and direct manner.

"*Not* that it concerns you but, *hell no!* Take a look; do you think that's my boyfriend?"

I pointed over to Tink, who was in the kitchen picking up pizzas above his head and strutting out to the main restaurant, doing his best Tyra Banks walk and screaming, "Work it, girl!"

"Ahh, guess not. He's gay, then?"

"Yep. He's as camp as Christmas and *oh*, he's a cage fighter too," I replied dryly.

He swerved to study Tink's slender frame. "What—? *Ahh,*" he nodded his head with a knowing grin. "Touché, Ms. Munro. Payback for my display of sarcasm earlier?" he commented, with the ghost of a smile.

Is he actually trying to be nice?

"Tit for tat, Mr. North. Tit. For. Tat," I scolded, exaggerating each word with a click of my fingers.

He pierced me with those forest-green eyes for what seemed like hours. I couldn't look away. Slowly licking his lips, he looked me up and down and said, "Well, I've got the tats, so…"

Redirect, reverse, and just go back to being pissed off, not turned on!

I shuffled on the suddenly-hot seat, and pulled my libido back from sneaking up his trouser leg. "He jokes! An actor with a sense of humour, who knew? Not the fuck-nut I thought, then?" I said, finally finding my poker face.

"Not always, whatever the hell that is," he murmured, seemingly slightly amused.

Phew! That voice.

"My name's Tash by the way, I feel like an S&M madam you calling me 'Ms.' all the time."

"Tash… I like it," he leaned down, his arms trapping me against the bar. He put his mouth to my ear and whispered huskily, "But I like the idea of calling you *Ms.* as well." He met my now-stunned gaze, and stepped back as if that little conversation had never happened.

He's done that to wind me up, unnerve me but… but – man, he's so hot! Oh my God, he has dimples… write me off now or let me take up residence in those little caves of cuteness!

Shuffling uncomfortably on the spot like he was nervous, he peered down at me. "So, do you want to join our table? Boleyn keeps raving about you and quite honestly I'm intrigued to hear all about the *'famous Ms. Munro'* in person. Plus, it may shut her up for the remainder of the night if you sit with us. She's been craning her neck all over ever since you came back here. Claims I was a bad brother and an even worse human being to speak to *'the best teacher ever'* like that," he declared, putting on a teenage-girl whiny voice.

"*Ahh*, so this little conversation is not altruistic, then? You want back in your sister's good books," I shook my head in mock disappointment. "And just when I thought you might have a heart, a conscience for offending little old me," I lilted, acting upset and fluttering my eyelids.

Looking at me like he was aware of my sarcasm but playing along anyway, he replied, "I admit I may have been a bit of a 'fuck-nut' as you so eloquently put it. Sorry, I really shouldn't have spoken to you like that," he apologised, one side of his mouth curving up in a devastatingly sexy way.

Trying to ignore the fact that the temperature in the room seemed to have gone up a hundred degrees, I jumped down from my stool.

"Well, lead the way, oh dutiful brother, we can't have your little sister pissed at you, can we?" I directed with a swing of my arm, earning a shake of the head from a begrudgingly entertained Tudor North.

Seated at the table next to Tudor, I fell into easy conversation with the rest of the family.

"So where are you from, Ms. Munro? I can't place your accent," asked Henry.

"You can all call me Tash. Well except you, missy. I'm still Ms. Munro to you," I said, pointing to Boleyn. "I'm from England. A place called Newcastle-Upon-Tyne. You probably don't know it. We are pretty much as far north a city as you can get to before you hit Scotland," I informed.

"Newcastle? Right. So, what brings you to Calgary?"

"Well Ti—, err, John, my roommate and best friend, and I, decided we needed a change, you know, a chance to travel. We kind of randomly just picked somewhere to live, and Calgary it was," I explained, purposely leaving out the cheating ex, Jane Austen quote, drunken decision-making and the role *Cool Runnings* played in the story.

"Wow, just like that?" remarked Samantha. "I could never do anything so drastic. I am from Winnipeg, and Calgary is about as far as I'm willing to go. My mom would kill me if I went too far from home."

"Yeah the 'rents were a bit upset, but in the end they supported it. I just have to Skype, email and text pretty much every day," I joked.

"So, no-one special here or back home?" she enquired.

"Not any more. Ex-boyfriend in England is now involved with someone else, so I'm free and single and ready to mingle with the best Calgary has to offer," I winked.

"What do you think of the Canadians, then?" asked Henry.

"Amazing. You lot are so nice. Well, nearly all of you," I tipped my head sideways and pointed my thumb at Tudor, who winced and looked down at the table. Henry, on the other hand, seemed tickled by my dig.

"Well, *most* of us are. Tudor's the exception – all broody and tortured. Just ignore him, we do," he waggled his eyebrows whilst Tudor scowled at him moodily.

Henry continued, "What about the accent though, no trouble there?"

"Nope. I love the way you say 'oot' and 'aboot'. You sound kind of Scottish, it's funny."

Everyone chuckled.

"Well, we are all very happy you have moved here. Newcastle's loss is Calgary's gain," exclaimed Pamela, smiling alongside a very cheery Boleyn.

"Thanks," I answered bashfully.

"So, Pamela, what's up with the Tudor Royal names? I love it, but I have never come across it before,"

"I studied History at University and that was my favourite period, everything about it really. So when I had Henry I knew what I would call him. Tudor was a little more difficult. I didn't like Edward, and my friend came up with the idea of using Tudor as a forename and it just stuck. Anne Boleyn was my favourite of the wives. It probably seems silly to you being from England, eh?" she asked, seemingly embarrassed.

"Not at all! It's my favourite part of our history too, so I'm in love with the names, it's super inventive! Plus,

Tudor here didn't have to create a show name, he was already equipped with one!" I teased and nudged his arm.

He looked up and sort of smiled at me... I *think*, it was either that or wind.

Wow, the icy exterior is melting.

After telling the table about my family and the ins and outs of teaching and why I chose that vocation, I decided to turn the tables on a certain socially-challenged superstar. Let's just say that I was more than a little intrigued by the guy.

"So, acting?" I declared in Tudor's direction.

"Yeah. Acting," was the enlightening response.

Undeterred, I pushed further. "How did all that happen?"

Tudor shrugged dismissively. "I kinda fell into it, but I love what I do and seem to be doing alright."

You definitely got the vibe that he didn't like to talk about his stardom too much. A modest actor too? He was full of surprises.

"Alright? You must be doing better than that for me to know your name. I'm not into action films but even I recognised you."

He just shrugged and blushed.

Henry put his elbows on the table and tilted his head, studying me. "You mean you haven't seen one of his films? You must be the only person left on the planet who hasn't."

I shook my head. "Nope, action's not my thing." I turned to Tudor. "I only hear good things though."

He nodded once, embarrassed as his mother gushed, "Oh he is, he's so talented. His film has broken lots of records. We're all so proud."

Tudor was now beaming red. I felt I should relieve him from the torture.

"So if you have just moved here, where do you all come from?" I noticed Boleyn flinch, which seemed a bit peculiar.

"Originally Victoria, BC, then Vancouver but we like here better. This is home now," declared Pamela, hugging Boleyn close. "Tate is from LA, though."

Feeling a little awkward at the reaction to what I deemed an innocent question, I carried on quizzing Tudor.

"Do you live in La-La land then too? Are you just visiting? You can't live in Calgary and be an actor surely? Are you just taking a break from escorting Victoria's Secret models to dine on lettuce leaves and strutting their angel-winged stuff at the glitzy premieres as your token arm candy?"

I gathered I had asked the wrong question by the total silence and the heads bowed down to the table.

Whoops! Foot in mouth once again. I just couldn't figure out why.

After a few moments, Tudor fixed his gaze on me. "No, I live near the family, just under the radar from the fame gig. No-one really knows I'm here. I wanted to live somewhere where people didn't really care about celebrity. No annoying photographers, you know?"

"Yeah. I can't imagine how you cope with being followed around all the time. I'd hate it. I bet by the size of you, you hardly go unnoticed very often." Tudor seemed slightly deflated by what I'd said and just nodded. I was honestly digging my own grave. I couldn't say anything right.

"It's bad when they write untrue things about you, but it comes with the job, I guess. In Calgary though, I can go pretty unnoticed, and these lot have an alias so people don't click on," he explained.

"Ah. *Jones.* I wondered what that was about."

"It's just easier, especially for Boleyn at school, you know?" professed Pamela. She shifted on her seat nervously, "I don't mean to sound out of line when I say this, but can I ask that you keep all of this to yourself? Boleyn finds it difficult dealing with Tudor's fame at school. And we have a confidentiality agreement with the principal about anonymity," she informed me, clearly embarrassed.

"It's a given. I promise," I assured them all.

There was a bit of awkward tension around the table, and so the best option seemed to navigate the conversation to Tate.

"So Tate, what's your deal?" I smiled at him, eager to find out more about the incredibly reserved cutie. He was almost a mute.

"I'm Tudor's assistant. Where he goes, I go. It's my blessing and my curse," he playfully nudged Tudor, earning a wink.

"He's a godsend. I am not organised at all, and Tate takes care of everything. I wouldn't function without him," Tudor responded, jabbing Tate on the arm.

Tate blushed. I couldn't imagine being that shy.

It was at that precise moment that everyone's favourite fairy flew in. "Here you are! I wondered where you'd disappeared to. You ready to go *par-tay*, pork chops?"

I could see the confusion on the faces of the North clan at the 'pork chops' comment, but thankfully they let it slide.

Getting up and standing next to Tink, I started the introductions. "John this is-"

"John? *Psht,* it's Tink and you know it. What's come over you?" he hissed glaring at me as though I had lost my mind.

Through gritted teeth I started again. "Fine! Tink this is Pamela, Boleyn, Samantha, Henry, Tate and Tudor. Everybody this is Tink, my best friend, roommate and fellow Geordie," I gestured in his direction.

Henry began laughing, and Samantha hit his shoulder to shut him up.

I raised a questioning eyebrow. "What?"

Henry pointed along the table. "Tash, Tink, Tate and Tudor. All T's – thank God you don't all hang out, it'd be a total nightmare remembering all your names."

I giggled. "Good job your hulk of a brother can't stand me then, eh?" I lightly flicked Tudor on his arm, but he instantly grabbed my hand and stared at me, squeezing my hand gently in his.

"I don't hate you," he mumbled, all seductively.

I couldn't look away, and felt frisky little shivers creeping up my arm from where his hand touched mine and that familiar warm sensation heading south.

Henry cleared his throat and broke the tension, "Tink? That's a strange name. Where's that from?" he asked with a curious side-look at me and his brother.

"Well, it's a funny story. Wil and I–"

"Wil?" interrupted Tudor, looking mightily confused and breaking our weird little exchange.

"Yeah, Wilbur," replied Tink, naturally assuming people would make the connection with me and the famous literary pig.

"You mean, Tash?" he clarified.

"Well, yeah but she's been Wil to me since we were twelve. You know, she was named after the pig –"

"Well, I think we'll leave it there, hey, Tink? Are you ready to go?" I interrupted, practically shouting while nipping his back and Chinese-burning his arm.

"Ow, Wil!"

I glared at him with daggers in my eyes, daring him to continue his delightful storytelling.

With a defeated huff, he spat out in a prissy tone. "Fine, yes."

I noticed Tudor silently laughing, and I rolled my eyes at him in reference to Tink. I also noticed Tate. He was staring at the self-named 'Friggin' fantastic fairy' and was practically salivating.

Tudor, having seen me studying Tate, covertly glimpsed his way too and raised an eyebrow knowingly. Tink, on the other hand, was oblivious to Tate's attention. He was too busy trying to embarrass me to notice anything else going on around him. I decided it was time to make an exit.

"Thank you for inviting me to meet you all properly, and for not holding my earlier performance against me. It was really nice to meet you. Tudor, good luck with the acting. Not that you need it but– *ah*, you know what I mean," I flustered. "Boleyn, have a nice break, and I'll see you next week. Samantha, Henry, Tate, Pamela, I hope you have a good night."

With that, Tink and I headed towards the door, arms linked and giggling when I heard. "Nice to meet you too… *Wil.*"

I whipped my head around, stopping dead in my tracks.

Tudor had twisted in his seat, an amused expression on his face, obviously tickled at my swine-themed nickname.

Tink started laughing his head off at his dig, and I proceeded to stick my tongue out at Tudor, earning a loud bellowing laugh from the Blade Reaper himself as I dragged a giddy fairy through the exit.

One-nil to him.

Tudor *Bloody* North!

CHAPTER 8

Smack-Bam Into Fate

The morning after...

I had been lying in my bed for about an hour trying to gain some form of energy to try and move so I could calm my spinning head. However, I instead found myself staring at the ceiling and thinking about recent events.

I had to say that meeting someone who is mega-star-famous was a bit strange, but then, I guess they're just people too. Abruptly meeting a superstar in the back room of a restaurant in Calgary of all places proved that they did normal things just like everybody else.

Tink couldn't shut up about meeting Tudor and I just... well I didn't know what to think. Sure, his looks were phenomenal, and all the adjectives in the world could not describe the pure animal magnetism of the man. But I was having a hard time trying to unravel the enigma that was Tudor North.

He was so dry in humour, so sarcastic in his delivery. Admittedly he was, at times, an arse who seemed to find enjoyment in winding me up immensely – that being said, he did improve a fraction as the night went on. But was that genuine or was he bullied into that by his family? He seemed unapproachable and gruff, but the real question was, was he a private person or was he really just a wanker?

As far as meeting a celeb went, I supposed it was memorable. Not something I would want to repeat very often, but it was another life experience in the *banco di vita*, as Nonna Girasoli would say.

I smelled the addictive aroma of Italian coffee and dragged my tush out of bed. Tink was in the kitchen whipping up some pancakes, sporting his novelty naked-lady apron, complete with inflatable boobs and a hairy muff. How he had never had a *Mrs. Doubtfire* moment in that get-up was beyond me.

"Hey, my little pig's trotter. How are you today?" he asked while whisking batter at a furious rate. Tink was very skilled in using his wrist.

"Okay thanks, the hangover seems to have settled. You?"

"Just peachy thanks, chuck."

Tink was his usually bubbly self and set to pouring the batter in the pan in small round pancake shapes, gradually adding chocolate chips and slices of banana.

He looked over his shoulder. "Say, did you happen go to the toilet this morning using the bathroom in the hall?"

Confused, I answered, "No, why? I always use my en-suite." I looked up at him curiously.

Turning back to the pan and flipping a pancake he said, "Mmm, it's just that someone left the seat up after taking a piss. I just naturally assumed it must have been the other man in the house." A huge grin plastered on his face.

"Fuck off, Tink!" I grumbled, still harbouring resentment from the previous night and my mistaken gender identity.

Following our encounter with the Norths, Tink and I had toddled off to Calgary's gay scene, given it had been Tink's night to choose the bars that we would drain of their alcohol. In true Tink-and-Tash fashion we didn't fail in causing a stir. Now, I was more than a little tipsy and Tink had gone AWOL after finding a giant hairy man with a handlebar moustache that he wanted to mount, so I hit the dance floor alone to stun Canada with more of my amazing moves.

I shimmied to the stage with vigour on hearing 'Gangnam Style' come pumping through the speakers and as I was riding my pony with the utmost energy and winding my imaginary lasso, my ring got hooked on a guy's chain – yes folks, his chain – that was fixed to a collar around his neck. Unfortunately the fellow didn't take it so well when I couldn't get myself unstuck as easily as one would have hoped, and he started going ape-shit right in front of my face, losing me precious Gangnam-dancing minutes.

That, coupled with my already jangled nerves from my Tudor North experience, had me seeing red and unclipping my hair extensions ready for a bitch-on-bitch take down faster than you can say *'Don't touch the face, Don't touch the face!'* Tink (along with his new hairy friend) arrived at the last moment to save the day and save me (and the chain-wearing bastard) from any real danger, but not before my adversary had mistaken me for a drag queen and suggested my show name should be *'Candy Made-my-ass-large'* – you know, something that suited my wide-frame. Nice.

Grrr... I totally could have kicked his arse!

"Aww c'mon it was funny." Tink trilled. "As if you look like a guy. *And* you said yourself that he prodded your titties. How did he not get that those bazookas are one hundred per cent real?"

"He probably thought they were chubby man boobs, after all I do look like a *'fat little slut'*, in his charming words."

Tink switched off the hob and sat down opposite me at the breakfast bar, gracefully placing a plate of delicious breakfast treats before me. "Shut up, Wil. Are you honestly bothered by what he said?" seeming genuinely concerned that I *had* taken it to heart.

"I suppose not, but it's never nice to be seen as masculine when you're a *girl.*" I exaggerated, and stuffed a comforting piece of pancake in my mouth. *Mmm... chocolate.*

"I hear ya. People often mistake me for a camp man until I speak, and then they know I'm a whole lotta female perfection," he said whilst running his hands down his sides, jumping up and swaying his hips.

"Keep making man-centred jokes at me and you will be all woman; I'll friggin' castrate you!" I warned.

"Okay I'll stop, just quit with the constant threats to my manhood. It's my best asset," he said with a grin.

"And where your brain is, or so it seems," I mumbled.

"*Anyway,* I have a surprise for you that'll turn that pout back to a snout," he informed me excitedly.

"Really? What?" I answered dubiously. Tink's surprises often left me wanting or injured or both.

"Nope, I'm not telling you yet. Go and get dressed in something sporty and meet me back here."

"Tink-"

"Wil, in the words of Nike, *just do it!*" he ordered.

"Fine!" I relented, storming to my bedroom.

I am so mature.

"Oh, Wil?" my secretive fairy shouted as I disappeared from sight.

Bending my head back around the door, I answered. "Yeah?"

"Make sure you have a shave. You're already getting a five o'clock shadow and it's only eight-thirty!"

I slammed my door and screamed.

I dressed for warmth. Most people know that Canada gets very cold in the winter but, in reality, it feels like you're at the North friggin' Pole and your next door neighbours are a penguin and a polar bear. We were only at the end of October and temperatures were already hovering at a delightful minus twenty degrees Celsius, and a light covering of snow and ice was adding a sparkly glow to everything.

I dressed in my pink puffa jacket, pink Nordic headband with snowflake motifs that left my long brown hair hanging loose down my back, exhibiting its natural wave. I had on three pairs of black thermal leggings and two pairs of socks, with leg-warmers to match. My gloves and scarf were bright white to really highlight the stunning beetroot red my face would go after two minutes in the harsh wind chill.

Yep, I was going to look *very* fetching.

I walked out of my bedroom and *bam!* I was suddenly front row in Tink's live version of Olivia Newton John's 'Let's Get Physical' video. He too was dressed for the weather and was sporting a multi-coloured neon ski suit – an outfit so bright that Joseph and his brothers would be jealous. He had teamed it with neon green mittens and a faux-fur deer-hunter hat.

Tink spotted me walking into the room whilst he was stretching out his glutes on the cow-print footrest.

"Ah-ha! You're here. Let's go shall we, my rasher of streaky bacon?"

"Where are we going, Tink?" I asked whilst reaching for my trainers, or *'sneakers'*, as the locals say. *When in Rome* and all that.

"No, Wil!" exclaimed Tink with a growl.

"What?" I quickly dropped my shoes.

"You won't need them, pork scratching," said Tink, pointing at my footwear choice. "At least not yet."

"What are we doing? And why won't I need shoes in this weather?" I asked, dreading the answer.

He dashed away and came running back seconds later with two of the most beautiful pairs of white leather, pink-wheeled roller skates I had ever seen. Not blades, but real quad boots like they use in *Starlight Express*.

Tearing up, I ran over to a smiling Tink and grabbed them from his hands, stroking the skates like Gollum with the shiny, all-powerful ring. *My precious*.

When I had composed myself, I grabbed my super-thoughtful bestie and hugged him tightly.

"They are gorgeous, just like my old beauties that that bastard bully, Stephen James, threw in a cesspool when we were fifteen."

"I know, I saw them on eBay and just had to get them for us. You never did get over losing your pair."

"Losing them? They were ripped from me and with it a piece of my tender heart, and flung into the stinking smelly depths of Spooks Woods' shit tip," I sniffed, remembering the overwhelming hurt on that fateful autumn day.

"So? You ready to try them out?" he teased.

"OMG! Yes!"

"So, where are we going to put the speed of these babies to the test?"

"I was thinking a few laps of Stanley Park and then post-skate lattes at Starbucks?" he suggested.

"You're on like Donkey Kong, my fabulous fairy!" and we raced out of the door.

CHAPTER 9

Skater-Gate Scandal

Roller skating in the park was beautiful and breath-taking. The wind whipped through my hair, the snow-capped Rocky Mountains dominated the view, and my senses were heightened. A real 'I'm alive' moment.

In our excitement over our new kinky, kitsch boots, Tink and I were flying through the park at unnatural speeds. The only other people around that early on a cold Saturday morning were hard-core joggers and a few dog-walkers. We couldn't tell if they were annoyed at the two of us or admired the sight of our obvious glee as we glided and soared, overjoyed at being reunited with our favourite teenage pastime. If we'd have had a bottle of cider in our right hands it would've been perfect.

Tink and I breezed around the path surrounding Elbow River hand in hand, pulling each other forward and swapping sides. My diva of a partner got a little bored of the mundane 'flat' routine and began to experiment with some *Dancing on Ice* moves he had recently seen on ITV One. He began humming the tune to Torville and Dean's gold medal-winning Bolero and started spinning me around whilst picking up a dangerously high velocity.

I was giggling at his antics and never even thought to look at the ground as we raced down the hill or considered what could be coming our way around the sharp bend. As I expertly pushed out of a spin, my foot slipped, and kept slipping. Tink grabbed me around the waist and we kind of shuffled awkwardly against one another, shrieking and screaming in a soprano pitch… and that was just the fairy!

Unsurprisingly, with our pink plastic wheels we couldn't gain any grip, any traction; we were going down and down and *boom!* We were taken out by an unseen force and we hit the ground hard, my wrecking ball of destruction now situated heavily on top of me, pinning me to the floor and crushing my chest. I couldn't really take much else in as a dull throbbing in my head was making me lose focus.

"What the fuck?" exploded the deep voice of my human tackling-machine. I then heard a similar ruckus to my left.

"Oh my God. I'm so sorry! Wait, Tink? Is that you?" exclaimed a gentle voice next to me.

"Well, well, well. Nice to see you again, mister, but if you were that keen to get on top of me you should have at least asked me out to dinner first, you cheeky scoundrel," Tink replied.

The other voice laughed shyly. "If you're being serious, then that I can do."

"Oh, really? Then it's definitely a date, mister," Tink confirmed, with excitement in his voice.

Too disorientated to make sense of what the hell was happening, I decided to just give in to the sleep that was looming, and it all began to go temptingly dark. I could hear bits of talking around me, most prominently Tink giggling and using his 'fuck me' voice.

OMG. I've died and gone to Fruit-Fly hell!

A string of seriously pissed-off grunts and curses brought me back to my own situation with a bang, as the human dumbbell lifted itself off my oxygen-deprived body.

"Shit. In future watch where you're go—,Tash? Tash, is that you? *Shit!*" said my personal bulldozer, as I felt rough fingers fumble across my face.

"Tink, isn't it?" the bulldozer asked someone beside me.

"Yeah," Tink answered excitedly.

"It's Tash, I think she's hurt."

I felt body heat appear near my left ear, and smelled the familiar scent of 'Fantasy' perfume by Britney Spears.

Tink.

"Wilbur? Wil, babe, are you okay? Talk to me!"

I could hear Tink begin to flap. Oh no, this was no time for a fairy meltdown.

"Calm down, sweetie, she'll be fine. Check her head, buddy," I heard the gentle voice from before instruct.

I felt the surprisingly cautious hands again from the bulldozer, this time on my head, and light breath falling on my face. I could smell him. *Mmm*... delicious.

I began to come around, eyesight re-focusing, shapes becoming sharper, sounds becoming clearer until–*"Oww!"*

Someone had just pushed something painful at the back of my head. My eyes began to water profusely.

"Tash? Can you see me? Can you hear me? Does it hurt? Fuck, there's a huge bump... aww man, it's bleeding," the unbelievable-smelling person said. I tried to sit up to see who it was. I felt a hand grasp mine and a second hand push my chest back to stop any movement.

"Wil, it's Tink. Talk to me, please."

"Tin–", *Pathetic cough*, "Tink? Wha-what's going on?" I struggled to speak.

"We had a little accident. We crashed into some... joggers," he said, sounding sheepish.

"My head. It hurts." I whined.

"Hold still, Tash," the deep voice said. "Just wait until you come around a bit more."

"Who—, who are you?" I could only hear his gruff voice. He was too close to make out a face.

I heard a small laugh and felt warm breath against my cheek. "You'll find out in a few minutes, just stay awake, okay?" he urged.

"Mmm," I felt something being put under my head, something warm and soft like a pillow. It smelt like my bulldozer. Wait, *my* bulldozer? It was woodsy, musky, and just... lovely, it reminded me of home somehow.

Fingers kept stroking my hand – Tink. I could feel it was him, but another finger was running repeatedly down my cheek and brushing away my hair, it was lulling me to relax.

"What were you doing on skates in this weather?" the voice asked harshly.

I went to answer but Tink jumped in, "I bought them for a surprise. We were only trying them out." I realised the question had been directed at him in the first place so I settled back into the pillow.

"Fucking hell, look at what's happened! What were you doing when we crashed into you? Do either of you have any common sense? Any at all? Jesus-"

"We were dancing! *Sor-ry, Dad*. Is that a crime? Anyway for your information, it was a simple two-step swing that we had already completed several times before!"

He huffed and, knowing Tink, he would have dramatically looked away and crossed his arms.

I chuckled to myself at Tink defending the roller skate dancing. What was he like? Feeling a little better, I broke the strained silence, eyes still closed. "At least we hadn't progressed to the death-defying 'head banger'," I muttered dryly.

Hands stilled and voices came at me simultaneously.

"Tash?"

"Wil!"

I opened my eyes one lid at a time, my vision coming back to me quicker now. But I was still unconscious and dreaming. I *had* to be as I saw… I saw, well, a *vision*.

"Tud–, Tudor? Tudor North?" Was it really him? Tudor North? Moody, Tudor *bloody* North!

Giving a slow disbelieving head-shake and that devastating lopsided smirk, he replied. "We need to stop meeting like this, Tash. How are you feeling?"

"Ugh! Like crap. My head is hurting... a lot," I moaned.

My stomach started to flutter at his intense green gaze.

"Yeah, you really whacked it when we fell."

"We?" I asked in confusion.

"Yes, *we*. When you took me out... with your dancing... on skates... in winter... on black ice. Yep," he pretended to think deeply. "I think that about sums the situation up," he said, a bit snippily.

"*Great*, more Tudor attitude. Just what I need!" *Shit, did I say that out loud?*

There was a sharp intake of breath above me, and then muffled giggling sounds coming from the left.

When I looked up, I saw Tudor scowling at someone, or several people, I couldn't be sure.

Had I pulled in an audience? I couldn't move my head to see. Tudor held it in a vice-like grip whilst straddling me, pinning down my body.

Yep folks, I often repeat that visual in my head too, you know, on cold and lonely nights.

He looked back into my eyes. His were sparkling, alight with humour. "Well it seems you're feeling a little better." Not a question, a statement.

"Yeah I think a little. Please can you help me up?"

He seemed worried; he had a line between his eyebrows that showed his concern.

Bloody hell, why was that sexy too?

"Hold on to me and I'll sit you up. Slowly, eh?" he instructed.

I nodded lightly, grabbed his massive upper arms, and held on tight to the ripped pythons as he pulled me into a sitting position.

Ugh, nausea.

"You feel sick?" he grunted.

"Just a smidgen," I whispered, trying to keep composure and not vomit all over him, whilst cringing about the fact that I must resemble the putrid green Wicked Witch of the West.

"I'll sit behind you to prop you up until we can move you without you feeling queasy," he announced, signalling to Tink and… yep, I thought so, Tate, to keep me upright whilst he straightened only to lower himself behind me. At least the four of us were the only witnesses to this debacle.

He shuffled close to my back and put his legs on either side. He took my shoulders and gently brought me back flush to his chest. It was all warm and cosy, and it was taking all my effort not to cop a quick squeeze of the amazingly thick thighs keeping me wedged in position.

I wonder if they are tattooed too?

Tink was looking at me with concern, and I could see him glare at Tudor from time-to-time. *What is he thinking?* He looked suspicious for a moment until he caught my gaze watching his and quickly changed his demeanour.

"You feeling better, my battered sausage?" Tink asked, cupping my cheek and returning to his chirpy, happy-go-lucky self.

I smiled and confirmed a yes with my eyes.

"Tash? You need to get this bump on your head checked out," stated Tudor, running his hands one by one over the top of my head. It felt heavenly.

I could feel his voice vibrating through me. Being so closely pushed together also enlightened me to the fact that Mr. North was huge… *everywhere* (wink wink!). That thought was definitely distracting me from the pain.

Tink looked over my head, I presumed at Tudor, and said, "I'll be back soon, pork chops, okay?" and turned to Tate, smiling. "Tate, you want to come with?"

Tate looked thrilled, and they took off. It was silent for a while, and I relaxed further into the best bed ever: Tudor's chest.

"You're an interesting character aren't you, Ms. Munro? In the space of twenty-four hours I have seen you – what did you call it? – oh yeah, 'slut drop', wipe me and my assistant out while trying to perfect another stellar dance routine, and suffer what is probably a concussion through the most idiotic pastime I've ever come across."

I could feel a single move of his chest, a small laugh.

"Yeah well, imagine if you were around me twenty-four-seven, I'd be non-stop entertainment for you," I said, it coming out a bit more snarky than I had intended it to.

Why did I always feel like a first-class fuck-up around this guy? *Mmm, probably because you are, Tash!*

"Yeah, imagine that..." he sighed, and gripped me tighter and shifted closer.

I was watching the river flow gently south when he interrupted my thoughts, his mouth at my ear. "We are going to have to get you to the hospital, Tash. Head injuries are no joke. Tink has gone to get the car."

"Mmm, okay. Are you coming too?" I blurted out sleepily before I even realised what I had said.

Oh my God, Tash, eager much? You don't even like him! Well not a huge amount, not really...

His body stiffened around me.

No, not more rejection. I seem to repel men these days.

I tried to think of something to say. I had made him uncomfortable, and his response had made me so.

As if, Tash! What were you thinking? This is Tudor North: living sex god. He is just being kind right now. He doesn't fancy you, he doesn't even know you. Why the hell would he take his kid sister's clown of a teacher to hospital? You just keep dropping into his probably perfect life like a freakin' tornado! Fix it. Now!

"I-I mean, of course you're not. Sorry, I just blurted that out, you know, head injury making me crazy and all. I'll go home and just pray that you forget the twin disaster of last night and this morning." I excused, trying to sound breezy.

"I'd never forget about you, Tash. You make a lasting impression." His arms crossed over mine, securing me tightly, his hands grazing over my clenched fists as though he was debating whether to hold them.

"I… I want to take you but, it's, it's probably just better if Tink and Tate go. Unless? No, we would have to go in a side entrance and I…"

I held up my hand to stop him and his stammering little chat with himself. My self-esteem was tumbling and I couldn't be humiliated anymore.

"Tudor, I'm sorry. I don't know why I said anything. Tink and I will be fine, we always are. I'm sorry for ruining your jog and no doubt one of your limited days off," I said sincerely.

Where is Tink?

He sighed loudly and wrapped himself around me, impossibly close. "Tash, that's not it. You could never ruin anything. You're… It's just—"

"*Wil!* I've got the car, sausage. Let's get you checked out at the Emergency Room."

Tink and Tate were walking down the hill, Tink with car keys in hand. He dropped behind a smiley Tate and blatantly checked out his arse. Tate did look cute, mind, in his jogging pants and black hoodie, with perfectly combed-over hair and striking ice-blue eyes. Tink winked at me and gave me a 'ten-out-of-ten' hand gesture.

Uh-Oh, Tate had an admirer.

I smiled back at Tink and tried to move. I heard Tudor sigh again, and I cringed at the awkwardness of this situation. I bet he wished he hadn't bothered getting out of bed that morning, now he'd faced one of Tash and Tink's Calamity Take Outs.

"Tink, help me up please," I commanded, gesturing to him with my hand.

"It's fine, Tash, I've got you. You're safe with me," assured Tudor as he gently began to lift me up, his whopping muscles flexing under his clothes.

His breathing was harsh, like he was fighting to keep himself together. Had I upset him? Angered him? I didn't know, but I honestly thought I would collapse again. Cause of death: Tudor overdose. He might be moody, but gosh, he made moody sexy. The close proximity to this guy was affecting my nerves, and other areas of my sex-starved anatomy.

When I was up straight, he put an arm around my waist and began walking with me towards the car at a snail's pace, which my aching head and I very much appreciated. His torso was too broad for me to put my arms around, so I settled for gripping tightly to his jumper. I noticed that Tink was exceptionally quiet, and I briefly glanced around to see where he was. Not for the first time, he was frowning, squinting his eyes and looking to Tudor, then looking ahead and back to Tudor all over again. I was in too much pain to even guess why.

Tudor kept me close, and I chuckled internally at the situation. An A-list movie star was walking *me*, a normal girl from Newcastle, to my car, after I had collided with him whilst roller skating on approximately one inch of ice. You couldn't make that shit up!

Arriving at the Bumblebee Camaro, Tudor lowered me into the front seat and looked as if he was about to say something and then just… didn't. I finally noticed what he was wearing, all dark clothing: gloves, a hoodie that was pulled up over his head and another woolly beanie hat, this time in black. I was desperate to pull it back and see how he wore his hair. I was hoping for shaved – he looked better that way. It was a good disguise; he looked like a generic, albeit *ma-hoos-ive*, jogger.

Tudor turned to Tate and whispered something to him. Tate nodded, turned and smiled shyly in my direction, and lowered himself into the back seat, putting a reassuring hand on my right shoulder. He was obviously not a talker, that one, just all quiet and sweetness.

Resting back against the seat, I felt something lumpy under my back. I reached behind slowly and pulled out a black scarf. What? Where? – *ah,* the pillow I had felt earlier.

I brought it to my nose and breathed in the scent that was all him, all Tudor. I smiled. Had he slipped this in the car for me to rest on? That was… unexpected. I clutched it tightly in my hands and turned my head to take in the view of the park whilst Tink was settling into the driver's side bucket seat.

Tudor stood on the embankment next to the car and watched us slowly pull away. He looked so sad and alone. As we crawled past him, I looked his way, using the scarf to support my cheek on the door frame. He was staring at me intensely, never shifting his concerned gaze, hands tucked in his sweat-pant pockets. I took the opportunity to mouth a 'thank you', and smiled at him.

His head jerked back in surprise, like he was genuinely taken back by my gratitude. Without breaking eye contact, he gave me a little nod of his head and slowly pulled his face into that heart-melting lopsided smirk.

This man is killing me!

Tink put his hand on my knee, sighed and remarked, "At least the skates didn't end up swimming in shit this time!"

CHAPTER 10

There's No Such Thing As Impossible...

It was a mild concussion. After being checked over thoroughly and forced to wait several hours at Calgary General Hospital, I was given permission to go home with the promise that someone would look after me for the next forty-eight hours.

I was given a truck-load of pain medication to take away the majority of my discomfort, and so far it seemed to be working. My hair was matted with blood from where I had sliced my scalp in the fall, but luckily it was minor and required no stitches. I was beyond happy to go home; I was tired, felt horrendous and was thoroughly humiliated.

My ego had taken a bit of a battering after my second encounter with a certain movie star. I knew I was not a Playboy model by any stretch of the imagination, but I wasn't ugly, and Tudor's reluctance towards me was bruising. I felt a pain in my heart, a physical and sharp pain, every time I thought about his reaction when I had asked him to come to the hospital with me. Realistically, I knew that Tudor was just helping a girl out in her time of need, and I berated myself that I was so bothered by the fact that his behaviour didn't mean anything more.

I had assumed that from last night's disastrous meeting that he was a grade-A twat, one who I would probably never meet again. But today, his physical actions seemed to show him in a different light. He was gentle and caring.

Had I misjudged him? Judged a book by its cover? Did he have a warm, gooey centre under that rock-hard and stunningly tattooed outer shell? And more to the point, why was I so hurt by his rejection? He was unattainable, both physically and emotionally, and I was just making my headache worse by considering something that was so undeniably impossible.

Absolutely bloody impossible.

Ahh well, enough of that now.

Tink and Tate had waited the day away with me in the ER, and it was lovely to see my normally bolshie and commitment-phobic best friend humbled by a geek-chic lovely with the sweetest disposition I had ever encountered.

Tate was very quiet in nature and only spoke when necessary, the polar opposite of me and Tink, the Odditt and Dodditt of Gobshite Central. Easy conversation had flowed and they chatted non-stop – well, mostly Tink chatted – but they each gave fleeting flirty glances and gentle touches at any given opportunity.

When we were leaving, all discharge papers signed and aftercare instructions dictated, we waved goodbye to Tate, who jumped into a nearby taxi, much to Tink's disappointment, but Tate made sure that before he left, he and Tink exchanged phone numbers and home addresses for the impending first date that had been promised during 'skater-gate'. My loved-up fairy chatted excitedly about potential venues all the way home.

Walking through the door to our condo gave me that *'there's no place like home'* feeling *à la* Dorothy from the *Wizard of Oz*. Tink placed me on the sofa and turned on the fire, making me all warm and cosy, the room only lit from the amber glow of the coals. He brushed a kiss on my head and walked towards the bathroom, where I heard the calming sound of running water. Tink may be as daft as a brush and as ditzy as all hell, but he is as loyal as they come and fiercely protective of the people he loves. I closed my eyes and let the world drift away.

"Oh no, missy! No closing those bush baby-sized shutters. Doctor's orders," chastised Tink from the end of the sofa, with his arms crossed and a disapproving look on his face.

I opened my eyes slowly and sighed heavily. "Okay, babe. Sorry."

He smiled lovingly. "Come on, sausage, I've run you a bath. Have a lush thirty-minute soak and you'll feel loads better afterwards."

Tink led me to my bathroom, where he had lit all my strawberry-scented Yankee Candles, illuminating my cream-and-gold en-suite into a sumptuous haven. My bath tub was huge and filled to the brim with bubbling vanilla foam, enticing me to envelope my aching and battered body in its depths.

Tink moved to the iDock situated on the shelf above the vanity cabinet, and within seconds Bruno Mars was serenading me about girls being perfect just the way they are. My fairy saviour helped me undress, and guided me as I sank down into the hot and soothing water. He then pulled down the gold gilded padded toilet lid and made himself comfortable.

My bestie and I for many years have had our best discussions whilst one of us soaks in the bath and the other sits astride the loo seat. We can chat for hours. Actually, for me it's weird to have a bath without the ramblings of Tink filling the room.

As I lathered up my nourishing coconut milk shampoo to try and remove the dried blood from my hair, I glanced at the toilet fairy. He was contemplating something. I knew because he had captured his tongue between his teeth, a dead giveaway to the fact that something was bugging him. He would tell me when he was ready and in the meantime I enjoyed the peace.

The intro to 'Grenade' had just kicked in when Tink spoke. "Wil?"

"Mmm?" I murmured.

"What do you think of Tudor?"

I stared at him. "What do you mean?"

He leaned forward, resting his chin on his fist. "Like, do you like him? Do you think he's nice?"

"He's gorgeous, if that's what you're getting at."

He shook his head. "No, I mean do you like *him*? His personality."

He was completely serious – very out of character.

I thought about my answer. "I don't know. He seems too abrupt and moody at times, but then today when he let that slide he was... I don't know... kind of... sweet." I shrugged. "I don't know him, Tink, and probably never will. He has a wall build up around him so high that I've decided not to think about it as it makes my head hurt," I said, trying to sound convincing.

Tink shifted uncomfortably. "I've been watching him. In fact, I made a point to watch him all last night *and* today while he played nurse."

I sat up slightly. "Is this you telling me *you* like him – like, *like* him, like him?" I asked, feeling my stomach doing more flips than an Eastern European gymnast.

"I don't want you to use Tate to get close to him. Tate's lovely and I don't want you to hurt him. He is clearly into you," I continued, scolding.

Tink lowered his wrist from his chin and glared at me, raising his pierced eyebrow. "I like Tate too, and I am not using him to get to the obviously *straight* Tudor."

"Okay," I said crinkling my forehead in confusion.

He sat up, slapping his hands on his knees. "I think Tudor likes you," he blurted out suddenly.

I simply stared at him in response.

"Hear me out, Wil. Last night everyone at the restaurant commented on how he watched you. You didn't see it, as you had no clue he was even sitting at the back table. I thought that was strange enough. But today, well today it was... I don't know how to explain it. He was about to blow a fuse at being ploughed down by us on our fabulous new skates and his face was fuming with rage, until he looked down.

"When he realised it was you underneath his bulk, his whole attitude changed. You could see it physically in his face, like he had just been told he'd won the lottery – I actually got chills. Then when he saw you were hurt, the sheer panic in his eyes was haunting. He began freaking out, and ripped off his gloves just to touch your face, took off his scarf to put under your head. I couldn't look away and nor could Tate. When we pulled away to go to the hospital, I swear he looked broken, Wil. I-I just... I am..." Tink let out an exaggerated sigh. "I just don't know what to make of it all. I can't figure him out." He physically slumped forward, the enormity of his revelations now off his little fairy chest.

I was as still as a statue, taking in everything that he had said. I shouldn't have let myself be affected, but I couldn't help it. I remembered some of what Tink was telling me: the fingers brushing across my face, the small laughs, the protective embrace and the crestfallen expression on his rugged face as we pulled away from the curb.

What did it mean? Did it mean anything at all? No, his reluctance at going to the hospital confirmed that.

"Tink, it's nothing. If he was so worried he would have took me to the hospital himself," I argued.

My frazzled bestie frowned at my words. "He talked to me about that just before I got into the car. He said that he didn't want it to be a circus, and that it would have been with him there. Said that he can't go anywhere anymore without causing riot and that your health was the priority and an impromptu autograph signing would distract the doctors from focusing all their attention on you." Tink looked away and then back to me. "Tate told me something else too. He said that Tudor hates hospitals."

I sighed. "Well who likes them?"

Tink shook his head. "No, Wil, like he *can't* go in them without freaking out. He didn't say why, but I have a feeling there's more to it than just a general dislike. Tate made it seem that he'd react like trying to get a Geordie lass to step out of the house with non-fake-tanned naturally pale skin – an absolute no go!"

He moved to kneel at the bath by my head. "Wil, I don't know if you should have anything to do with him. Something feels off to me, he seems too locked up, too distant, and the way he looks at you scares me – it's possessive, bordering on *obsessive*. There's more to Mr. North than we could ever know, and I want you to stay away for your sake. If not yours, then for mine."

"Tink, I can guarantee you that Tudor North is *not* interested in me, and I have only known him for a grand total of, what? Eighteen hours? I am not putting myself down when I say this, but I am fully aware that I am not Miss Universe and that people like Tudor North do not look at and desire people like me. I think he was just looking out for his sister by helping her clumsy teacher who he keeps unfortunately running – or should I say *ploughing* – into. It's impossible that he would feel that way for me, just... impossible. I'm not being a Debbie Downer but *him* liking *me* will never happen. We are in two different leagues. But on the off-chance of him liking me, my new-found lifestyle would encourage me to go for it, would it not?" I joked.

Tink rubbed both of his hands over his face. "You're wrong, Wil. I know it. He likes you, and stop thinking that way about yourself. You may not see all the beautiful in you, but I do, and so do an army of others, *including* one Tudor North. I know you want to live more freely, but that guy... I don't know, something is just off about him."

"Tink, babe, let's leave it there," I said, patting his hands. "Nothing will happen and nothing *is* happening between us now. It's just been a crazy couple of days, that's all. We've had more excitement in the last forty-eight hours than I think we have ever had in our lives and we are getting carried away with it all," I soothed.

Tink sighed and flicked my nose. "You *are* wrong, missy. But I'll let it go… for now," he smiled and kissed my head. "What do you say we get you out of this bath, throw on our onesies and settle down to watch an entire series of *Grey's Anatomy*?" He pretended to fan himself at the thought of all those doctors.

I nodded once and giggled at his antics. "I'm in."

In celebration of our move to Calgary, Tink and I had made an impulsive purchase of novelty adult baby-grows – *onesies* – to brave the winter nights. Both had feet and hoods and were made of the warmest fleece material.

My onesie was, you guessed it, a pig with a snout, ears, spiral tail and trotters. Tink's was a replica of *Peter Pan's* Tinkerbell costume, complete with glitter wings and a hood which looked like a blonde chignon hairstyle when erect.

We had settled on the sofa and were ogling McDreamy, McSteamy, McArmy and McBlue-eyes (our given title for Dr. Avery), with Tink bringing me a bag of frozen peas every two hours to put on my bump to numb the pain. We were ploughing through the box set, but the clock only read seven p.m. It was officially the longest day of my life.

I got to my feet to visit the little girls' room whilst Tink was re-freezing the bag of peas. I had made it all of three slow, painful steps when there was a knock at the door. I walked to the hallway and opened the giant oak-and-steel door to find Tate – looking dapper dressed in a black blazer, dress jeans, a white shirt and his staple red dickey bow –with two bunches of colourful flowers in his hands.

"Well, this is a pleasant surprise," I exclaimed as Tink came bolting around the corner, looking as though he was going to bollock me for getting up without his assistance. When he caught sight of Tate his face broke from an annoyed scowl into a sunny, happy grin.

Tate looked up shyly. "Hey, guys," he said with a wave of the flowers, passing one ridiculously huge bunch to me and one to Tink.

"I got you these," he said, kissing us both on the cheek. He lingered a touch longer than was really necessary on Tink's.

"Honey, what you doing here?" asked my giddy pal, waving his arm to welcome him inside whilst smelling his gorgeous bouquet of pink and white roses.

Tate looked to something at his side, the large second half of the double front door blocking my view. "We just came to see if you were okay," he said to me, interrupting me gazing adoringly at my favourite flowers in the whole world – sunflowers.

How did he know? Wait–,

"We?" I squeaked. Tink shot forward to grab my arm as I began to sway, losing my already-defective balance, and took my flowers off me before I dropped them.

Tate quickly moved further inside the hallway, followed by a huge hulk of man wearing jeans, a tight white V-necked long-sleeved T-shirt, hooded black leather jacket and grey beanie hat.

Tudor.

"Tash," he announced rather formally, nodding his head and then breaking into a huge grin.

Be still my beating heart. No-one should be allowed to look that good.

"Nice threads," he commented, cockily.

What? Aww shit!

Tate turned away shyly, laughing into his hands, and Tudor stood there grinning, hands in his pockets and looking directly into my eyes.

What is it with this guy and eye-contact? Does he do that in every situation?

My mind wandered back to him straddling me in the park... *Focus, Tash!*

I looked at Tink in his get-up, and then down at my own pink ensemble. *We must look like lunatics – call for the men in white coats!*

Turning back to our guests, I simply said, "Oink?" and shrugged my shoulders.

Tate burst out laughing and Tudor smirked. I turned to go back to the sofa, suddenly not feeling so good.

"Tash, you okay?" asked Tudor, silencing any giggling from the flirty fellows as he stepped forward whilst I grabbed the wall for support.

"Erm, I just got a bit faint then. I need to sit down."

I felt Tink grasp my elbow, I appreciated the much-needed steadiness.

"Tink, can I?" Tudor asked, and before I heard a reply felt a large arm encircle my waist and guide me to the couch.

My God if I was faint before, I am heading towards a complete K.O!

I inhaled. Pure woodsy, pheromone-inducing, Tudor. *Game-over, I'm down for the count!*

I was lowered to the sofa and then flanked on either side by Tink and Tate. Tudor knelt down in front of me, put both hands on my knees, and searched my eyes, obviously checking for the fixed and dilated pupils my carers had been told to look out for. If they resembled saucers we would need to go back to the hospital immediately. On seeing his expression change to one of relief, I guessed that I wasn't dying, and so rested my head on the back cushion, closed my eyes and breathed deeply to steady the nauseating dizziness.

Tudor began moving his hands up and down my leg from knee to mid-thigh; nothing had ever felt better.

After I recovered from the dizzy spell and the room was the right way around, I opened my eyes. Tink was glaring at Tudor, who I assumed had never looked away from me through my little episode. Tate, too, was fixed on him with a startled look upon his face.

It is too much to take in.

"That's better," I sighed, refocusing Tink and Tate's attention back on me.

"Wilbur, you're overdoing it. Why did you answer the door, you silly mare?" *Great bedside manner, Tink!*

"I was going to the bathroom when I heard the knock. No biggie," I shrugged.

"No biggie? You nearly face-planted the marble floor! From now on you'll use a bed pan and that's final, or I'm ringing your dad!" he threatened, and crossed his arms over his chest.

"Whatever," I dismissed.

No-one said a word for several awkward seconds. Mention of a bed pan will tend to do that to a conversation.

"I suppose a date is out of the question now?" asked Tate breaking the silence. My fairy and I both immediately snapped out of our mutual huffs to look his way.

"A date? Tonight?" squeaked Tink.

Tate blushed – *how cute!*

"I was trying to be spontaneous. I've been running around all afternoon to set it up for us."

Tink didn't know what to say. He kept opening his mouth and closing it over and over again.

Tate bowed his head and pulled imaginary lint from his jeans.

I reached over and patted his leg for reassurance. "Of course Cinderella shall go to the ball!" I confirmed weakly. Tate looked up with a relieved, beaming smile.

Tink shook his head. "Wil, I can't go, I have to stay with you for forty-eight hours remember, doctor's orders. And the date can wait, right, Pookie?"

'Pookie' lost his smile. "Of course, that was selfish. Forgive me, Tash?"

A cough interrupted the conversation.

Tudor.

I had, for most of the conversation, been struggling to breathe at the fact that Tudor was still on his knees in front of me, rubbing my thighs. His long fingers suddenly stopped their stroking at everyone's pulled attention and I allowed myself to take a deep breath, now that his fingers weren't glancing ever-so-close to my intimate areas. I mean, come on, there is only so much titillation a girl can take before she spontaneously combusts!

"I could stay with Tash," he suggested – well, kind of directed.

Three sets of eyes bugged further in his direction. "What?" we said in unison.

"I *said*," he drawled, exaggerating the words. "I can stay with Tash and look after her. You two go on your date."

"Well, dip me in honey and throw me to the lesbians!" screeched my bestie.

Tudor looked at Tink and arched a single eyebrow.

Tink stared back, and then started shaking his head profusely. "No, she is *my* best friend, and *my* responsibility and *I* will stay and look after her," he stated quite aggressively. Well, in a camp sergeant aggressive kind of way. He grabbed my hand, kissed the back of it and harrumphed loudly. I felt that if he had just cocked his leg and pissed on me, then he would have asserted his ownership rights with more clarity.

Tudor ran a hand over his stubbly chin. "I don't mind. I'll feel better doing it anyway, so I know she is alright. I kinda feel responsible for her."

Really? Why?

"She'll be fine with me," roared Tink in full on diva-strop mode.

"I didn't mean to imply otherwise. I'm simply saying that you and… 'Pookie' could have your date and I would be here to tend to all of Tash's needs."

All my needs – I feel faint again – I have needs, I have needs!

"I said n—"

"Tink!" I groaned, dizziness returning with all of the unnecessary squabbling. "You go out, chuck. I'll be fine," I implored, squeezing his fingers.

I then turned to Tudor. "You don't owe me anything, Tudor. I'll be fine on my own. What happened today was my fault, not yours. You don't need to feel guilty, and you certainly do not need to be here to babysit from some misplaced need to make it up to me."

"No," Tink and Tudor asserted simultaneously.

I flinched and looked to Tate for back up, but he just smiled sympathetically and shook his head in agreement with the two arguing brutes next to me.

"Fine! You decide what's happening. I'm going to lie down. Tink, can you help me to my bedroom?" I asked in a pissy manner, trying to get up from the low couch.

"It's okay, Tink, I—"

"No you won't," the fairy snapped as Tudor started to pull me up by my hands. "For fuck's sake, I can do this! You need to back the hell off."

"Hey, sorry," said Tudor, putting his hands up in a gesture of surrender, causing me to stumble into Tink's waiting arms.

Tink looked appeased. "Well good, at least you can follow instructions. Come on, Wil."

Tink walked me to my room, leaving Tudor watching us go and Tate still sitting on the couch, unmoving and clearly regretting his surprise date idea.

Once inside and settled on the bed, Tink began to pace. "Do you see what I mean?" he stopped and gesticulated wildly towards the closed and thankfully soundproof bedroom door.

"Tink, he was just trying to make your date happen. Which I still think you should go on by the way."

He looked so torn, bless him.

"I *do* want to go but I won't leave you alone. I fancy Tate… a lot… but I obviously care for you more. You're my priority; I've only just met the little lovely in a bow tie."

"Well Tudor has offered to stay–"

"Oh no, Wil, we have discussed this! After all you went through with Nathan, how bad of a friend would I be to green-light you getting all hot and steamy with Mr. Fort Knox out there? I can see how you look at him, your sex-deprived Fu-Fu is gagging for him, don't bother denying it. He'll break your heart if you let him, Wil."

I sank into the pillows. "He would simply be watching out for me until you get back. I don't think getting me glasses of water and bags of frozen peas constitutes 'getting hot and steamy', do you?" I laughed, but was slightly taken back by his words.

Was it blatantly obvious that I liked him? I didn't think I'd even made that decision yet myself.

Tink began pacing once more, glancing my way every now and again. His defences were crumbling.

"Tink, go be wined and dined by your new boy. He looked absolutely devastated when you refused before, and quite frankly I think you're a fool if you don't take him up on his offer," I tried to persuade him.

Tink sat on the edge of the bed and stared at me. "I think he planned to stay with you all along."

I gave him my *'as if'* face. "Tink, he came to check if I was okay, not to bully you into a date, which you want to go on, with his assistant, who just so happens to fancy the pants off you, in a grand plan to get me alone and have his nefarious way with me," I wiggled my fingers in a witch-like manner and cackled to emphasise the point.

Tink cracked a cheeky smile and went silent for a few seconds, indecision written in his expression, tongue between his lips. "Fine, you win. I'll go out and leave Mr. Dark-and-Brooding here with you," he submitted. "But know that I'm on to him," he added, pointing a perfectly manicured figure at my face and then my nether regions. "He wants a slice of your pastrami pie, Wilbur."

"Go get ready, my favourite fay. Oh, and switch on my TV. I think it's best if I stay in here. I keep getting dizzy on that sofa. We don't want any more embarrassing episodes in front of Mr. Hollywood out there."

He looked worried again so I pushed. "Go on, for frigg's sake, I'll be fine!"

With that Tink sighed, shook his head in exasperation, and blew a kiss as he opened the bedroom door, off to tell our guests the change in plan.

A night with Tudor alone, this should be interesting!

CHAPTER 11

... The Word Itself Say's 'I'm Possible!' Audrey Hepburn

I opened my blurry eyes, waking up to someone gently caressing my arm. "What the–?" I croaked.

"Tash, it's me, you fell asleep. I need you to take these tablets and put this on your head."

Tudor held out the bag of frozen peas wrapped in a towel and a bottle of pills. I tried to sit up, and felt a sickening throb in the back of my skull.

"Steady, Tash. Here let me." He moved towards the bed, and I noticed he had shed his jacket and beanie hat.

He crawled onto the bed and lifted my head gently, manoeuvring the cold bag into place, his black tribal tattoos all on display, winding seductively around the sleeve of his arms down to his wrist and creeping out of the V-neck of his T-shirt.

"You have a shaved head," I involuntarily blurted out.

Way to be cool, Tash.

Tudor glanced down at me and gave me the lopsided smirk. "Err... yeah. I normally do," he smiled, obviously bewildered by my Tourette-like assessment of his follicles.

I blushed and beamed red. "I just kept wondering what it looked like under the hat that's all – I wanted it to be shaved."

He smiled shyly. "Well, I'm glad to be of service."

Tudor handed me the pills and a glass of cold refreshing water, then watched me closely to make sure I swallowed them. He guided me back to my pillows and set the glass on my bedside cabinet.

I shuffled to make myself comfortable, pulling down my piggy hood with ears and run my fingers through my nearly dry hair.

Tudor sat back and positioned himself on the bed beside me. "What you watching?" he asked, flicking his chin in the direction of the TV.

I looked up to see an infomercial advertising some industrial-strength carpet cleaner. "Nothing, I was asleep." I glanced covertly at the Greek god sprawled out on the left side of my bed. "Are you staying in here now?" I couldn't help thinking that having him there looked, well... well... fucking incredible, truth be told.

Tudor grabbed the remote off my lap and began flicking through the channels. "I have been given orders to stay with you and keep you awake. I thought it would be easier to just lay here with you than keep running back and forth from the living room," he replied, settling on a music channel and lightly placing the remote back on my lap.

"Orders?" I asked, trying to focus on Nicki Minaj jumping around in a pink bikini singing about Starships.

"Yep, from Herr Tink," he winked and smiled.

Mortified, I shifted my gaze his way. "Oh no, I'm sorry. What did he tell you to do?"

"Hang on." Tudor slid off the bed and went into the front room. He came back with a pink, laminated sheet of A4 paper. "He left me this."

I cringed.

Clearing his throat to disguise his laughter, he handed me the sheet, which I saw was entitled:

'Mission: Keep Tash Alive'

"When did he do this?" I asked, shaking my head lightly.

"Before he left. He had it printed out already and stuck to the fridge, but he laminated it about an hour ago in case I ruined it with my clumsy sausage hands and forgot what to do, thus causing me to fail in my task. Who has a laminator in their bedroom anyway?"

I grimaced. "He can be a tad dramatic. And the boy does love his stationery; he'll find any excuse to laminate. You should see the take-away menu drawer… he has shares in Staples!" I tried to explain, but hey, it's Tink, and he marches to the beat of his own drum.

"It's no problem. I've noticed he is very protective of you, so I'm not surprised."

He pulled the sheet aside and climbed back onto his side of the bed. *His side?* At that point, I suddenly remembered the scarf that he had left with me was tucked under my pillow, which I realised may make me look like a slightly crazy obsessed fan, rather than the detached and independent woman that I clearly was.

Had he seen it? I surreptitiously ran my gaze over where I had been lying – *phew, out of sight*.

"Yeah, he is. He just doesn't like me being hurt," I explained, shifting my body to the side to make it easier to talk.

Tudor mirrored my position so we were facing each other about two feet apart. "Have you been hurt badly before?" he inquired.

"In what sense? I'm clumsy as all hell and have had a few bouts of illness, if that's what you're asking?"

He nodded and began to rub his lips together. He looked up guiltily. "What about with men?"

Well that's a bit personal.

"Erm… well, my ex-boyfriend was a huge arsehole who cheated on me in a spectacular fashion. I had been with him for a few years and no-one serious before that. I figured if he could do that to me then he wasn't worth it."

I looked down to the pillow, avoiding his eyes. "That's the reason why Tink is protective of me; he was my rock during that fallout. My God, he moved continents for me," I let out a single laugh.

Tudor nodded silently. "He seems to like Tate," he said, moving the conversation to slightly safer territory.

"Yeah. A lot I think. I've never seen him react to anyone like this before. I'm happy for them. Who knows? It could be love at first sight. Like Romeo and, well, *Romeo!*" I teased.

Tudor grinned at my joke. "I think Tate is smitten too; he doesn't really talk much about what's going on in his head but I can tell. He's a total introvert. I think Tink will be good for him, he might be able to bring him out of his shell. I'm glad. He copes with a lot working for me and never gets to meet anyone on a long term basis. Luckily, I'm here for a few months before pre-production starts on my next film. It may be the perfect time for him to meet Mr. Right."

"Yeah I'm glad too, but then they have only just met. Can something that profound really happen in twenty-four hours? Enough for that person to impact your life to such an extent?" I mused sceptically, expecting him to agree with me.

The muscled-demigod turned and fixed his hooded dark green eyes directly on mine and pierced me with a look. "I believe so."

Holy mackerel, Batman! What do I do with that titbit of information?!

Tudor suddenly changed the subject again, breaking the moment. His muscular back tensed. "Tink doesn't like me much does he?" he asked quietly, avoiding my eyes.

How do I answer that? 'No, he thinks you could potentially screw me over, shatter my soul and never let me in that Helms Deep fortress you call a heart.'

"He doesn't know you, that's all. I don't either really, and you don't know really know me. I only met you last night, for goodness sake!"

Tudor flinched at my words and rubbed my calf that was resting on top of my quilt. "I would like to know you. I don't understand it but I feel like I already kind of do. It's... weird."

Well that is a surprise.

He laid back once more and I patted his huge arm. "You have to understand a few things with Tink. He has very little family and the bit he does have are deeply religious and believe that he is an abomination who will burn in hell for eternity for being born attracted to men. When he was fourteen he came out to his parents, I thought he was so brave and encouraged it. Anyway, they freaked on an epic scale and sent him to a summer 'retreat' in back-country Alabama for teens who were sexually 'possessed by the devil'. It was horrific for him. Obviously it didn't work and he was made to leave his home and live with his uncle until he moved out to live with me."

Tudor laid his hand on his cheek, absorbing every word. "Places like that actually exist?" I knew he was finding it difficult to wrap his head around. Most people do.

"Unfortunately they do. After that he practically grew up with me and my folks. We both had a tough time at school and really only had each other for friends. He has never even had a serious boyfriend, not once. I also wonder if it is due to his parents' continued rejection of him as why he can't commit to a lover for a long period of time, but I'm no Psychologist so I let it go. We have been everything to each other for so long that sometimes it becomes blurred to both of us just what the boundaries are. If I'm hurt, he feels pain. If he's upset, I cry alongside him, and if someone he doesn't know tries to take over his caregiver role, he gets extremely defensive,"

I prodded Tudor's chest and grinned. He nodded in understanding.

"Quite honestly, I wonder sometimes if we are too close. I admit now that I was not fully invested in my previous relationship. I always put Tink first, whether that was as simple as choosing a night out clubbing over a romantic meal with Nathan, or as serious as taking his side in any argument between the two, or even missing Nathan's grandmother's funeral to comfort Tink over a horrendous argument with his parents. Tink always won.

"I worry that we've never had fully committed relationships because we don't know how to balance the love we have for our boyfriends with the fact that we are soul mates. We're a package deal – buy one get one free! Whoever eventually takes us on will have to accept that or it's a no go."

I didn't wait for Tudor's reaction to my soul bearing, as I became distracted by my favourite song coming on MTV.

"Aww, I love this song." I commented, starting to sway slightly in time with the music.

Tudor turned his attention to the TV. "What is it? Are they British?"

"Yeah, they are. It's 'Beneath Your Beautiful' by Labrinth and Emeli Sande. Just listen, it's so perfect."

We did, nearly the whole song in silence.

"The words are gorgeous aren't they? Just imagine if someone felt that way about you? To write something so incredible, and the muse was you. To love someone that much and talk about them so passionately that it only did them justice in song, to declare it for the world to hear." I sighed dreamily, "It would be everything to me, for someone to be so proud to be with me that they want everyone and their mothers to see."

I blanched. *Why did I just say that in front of him? I hope I can just pass it off as being heavily medicated.*

Tudor was silent, his gaze flashed to the end of song playing on the screen, listening to the words. When the song had reached its end and I subtly wiped away a stray tear, he shifted his body my way and ran his fingers over my head, lips pursed in concentration.

"W-What are you doing?" I croaked.

Oh fuck, is he, is he going to *kis*—.

He reached for the bag of peas and grinned. "Just removing the bag, Tash. It's been twenty minutes," he said, pointing to rule number five on the laminated instructions propped up against the bedside lamp:

5. *'Do NOT leave peas on for longer than twenty minutes at a time. You will freeze her freakin' head off!'*

"Oh yeah, thanks." I deflated like a balloon.

What the hell was that all about, Tash? Do you want him to kiss you? I thought you didn't like him? Oh shut up, I don't know, okay?!

We slouched down again, lying to face each other as before. Tudor seemed content to just lie in silence, looking at me. *Errrr,* fuck that. I certainly wasn't! To say he was intense was an understatement. He had asked a lot of questions about me, he claimed he felt like he 'knew me', and had turned me into a quivering wreck of a girl. But I didn't have the foggiest about him! How bloody rude.

"Can I ask questions about you now?" I asked, nudging his arm tentatively and attempting to use my big brown eyes to lure him in – hey, it worked for Puss in Boots in *Shrek*!

He smiled and scooted closer. Very close in fact – boundaries were blurring.

"You can ask, I'll choose to answer or not," he responded gruffly and seriously, as he rested his left hand on my hip on top of the duvet. My heart increased in speed while he looked as calm as the sea.

Go with it, Tash, throw caution to the wind and enjoy the sexiest man on the planet actually touching you in your bed! Way Aye!

"Okay. How did you become an actor?" I started off easy.

His eyes creased in amusement, he knew my plan.

"Ah, the million-dollar question. Let's see. I used to play ice hockey in Vancouver. I was playing at a pretty good level, and after a match where I was awarded MVP, I was approached by a casting agent who was scouting out people for a movie about ice hockey–"

"*The Mighty Ducks?* Did you do the 'Flying V'?" I asked, excitedly.

He regarded me blankly. "No, not *The Mighty Ducks*!" He shook his head laughing, and moved his hand to lie on top of mine. I didn't even think he had done it consciously, and our new-found intimacy didn't seem to faze him. I, on the other hand, was freaking out inside whilst trying to maintain a calm demeanour on the outside.

"It was a small–budget, indie Canadian film about how the game became professional. I was only paid about five hundred bucks. It ended up being awarded Best Film at the Toronto and Sundance Film Festivals. Long story short, I was given a small part due to my size and discovered I was pretty good at the whole acting thing. I was approached by a talent agent from the city, and she hooked me up with an acting coach and I began to audition. Up until that point, hockey was my life, but I found something I was better at, with more longevity, and I haven't looked back since."

That was easier than I had expected. "So you went from zero to hero practically overnight? Wow, that's awesome. Surreal, but awesome."

He moved his fingers and looped them in mine. He cast his green eyes down and stared at our entwined hands. "Yeah, you could say that. I have a unique look. I'll always be given certain roles, but I'm good with that. I can act too, not many bigger, thug-looking-type guys can, so I'm getting offered a lot of good parts, not just dumb muscle roles. *The Blade Reaper* franchise will take up the majority of my time over the next few years. It's going to be a trilogy."

"So no gratuitous sex scenes or romance? Just knives, guns and violence?"

He shrugged. "The idea of being cast in a rom-com gives me hives. I'm good with action. Action, I can do. I'm not good with the flowery stuff. I'm no leading man like Mr. Darcy. People find me too abrupt, too scary, and I don't think Colin Firth would have been as big a hit if he had looked like a 'roided-up wrestler, eh?" he quipped, glancing up at me with a shy smile.

"Mmm, now *that* version of Mr. Darcy would have floated *my* boat but, hey you, don't knock a rom-com. *Pretty Woman* is my most favourite romantic movie ever. You shouldn't be averse to love, mister," I scolded.

He squeezed my hand and dropped the smile. "I'm not averse to love, not if it's with the right person."

With all my inner strength, not wanting to break the intensity of the moment, I held his gaze, and was rewarded when he inched a touch closer. "I just don't want to put it on show for the masses. I hardly even do kissing scenes, they repulse me. I fucking hate kissing a woman I don't want. I feel uncomfortable getting close to people, emotionally, acting or not." His tongue wet his bottom lip. "When I'm in love, I want it to be complete heart-and-soul level, for all of my life. I'm an all or nothing kind of guy."

I'm sweating, and I think heavy breathing. I reckon he needs to rethink the 'I'm no good at romance' crap! Time for a subject change.

"So you never lived in Hollywood?"

Tudor froze, his fingers rigid in mine. He looked down at his feet. "I did for a bit, but moved back to be near my family. It wasn't for me, and they needed me more."

That was obviously a sore point. The temperature in my room went from scorching hot to ice cold. But, never one to shy away from a challenge, I pushed further. "Do you have a girlfriend, Tudor, famous or otherwise? I'm not sure being here in my bed is a good thing if you do."

He relaxed and laced my fingers once again through his. "No, I'm not good with relationships, especially with the public side I have to deal with. It's fucking crazy."

I blew out a breath I didn't know I had been holding as his stunning eyes penetrated mine.

"What I mean to say is that I haven't been interested in anyone for a very long time… until recently."

I pulled away and sat up slowly. Oh shit, I'd obviously totally misread this whole thing. I couldn't listen to him mention some Hollywood starlet he was chasing.

I needed to remove myself from this. "Can you walk me to the bathroom?" I asked abruptly.

Tudor scratched the back of his neck, frowning and rubbed his lips together. "For sure."

Tudor stood outside while I sat on top of the padded toilet seat and breathed deeply. I recounted my earlier conversation with Tink. He was right; this guy was dangerous to me. He consumed my thoughts when he was near, I became lost in him, everything about him, and I'd only just met him. The touches he gave me were as natural as breathing and were shattering my defences; they made me nervous. I needed to keep my composure. I could fall for him. Hard. But it was so easy, effortless, and I can't help but like him. Could we be just friends? Yes, friends. Nothing more. He probably saw me as that anyway.

Tudor was leaning against the wall when I opened the door. I took in the scene: he looked like James Dean. Well, if James Dean had been hitting the weights and protein shakes for a year, and inked himself up with an ungodly amount of tats. His arms were crossed, showcasing his overly defined chest; he was staring at his feet, and when he saw me he smiled his gorgeous lopsided smile. He was pure bad-boy in a six-foot-three package.

The combination of gorgeous male and the latest dose of drugs caused me to waver on my feet. Tudor approached me and, without saying anything, scooped me up and carried me back to bed.

He placed me down gently and rolled back the duvet, sliding in beside me. "Sleep now, Tash. It's okay, I'll look after you," he kissed my forehead lightly and wrapped an arm around my shoulders, moving my upper body to spread across his chest. His massive, broad chest.

I sleepily asked, "What will you do now?"

"Don't worry about me. I'll just watch a bit of TV. Just cuddle in and rest."

"Mmm okay…" I began to drift into sleep.

I could hear Tudor flicking through the music channels as I floated away. He stopped with a jerk, and I once again heard 'Beneath Your Beautiful' play from the TV.

Tudor's breathing stilled and the remote dropped to my side. He let the song play out and shifted to wrap his body around mine even closer. His lips ran back and forth along my forehead, brushing against my skin.

He slid his hand under my pillow and pulled it back almost immediately. After a few seconds his breath hitched in and he let out a painful low groan. A wool cover draped over my shoulders. It smelt of Tudor.

Fuck, he found his scarf.

I couldn't be sure, as I was nearly unconscious and internally debating how to deal with the scarf situation, but I thought I heard him whisper sadly. "Natasha Munro, you have completely bewitched me. I would like– no, I *know* I could be everything to you. But it's impossible."

CHAPTER 12

Friend-Zone

Morning came, bringing with it the sun, bathing the room in yellow hues, and Tink, leaning on one arm in my bed and regarding me with a suspicious gaze.

I groaned and stretched, pleased that my head felt less fuzzy and that the whopping lump at the back seemed to be shrinking.

"Morning, chuck," I greeted Tink sleepily.

He raised an eyebrow and clicked his fingers about an inch from my face. "Natasha Munro, you little slut!"

"What?"

It's too early for this shit.

He sat up, placing one perfectly manicured hand on his hip. "What??? I come home to find you coiled around a mammoth chunk of Canadian beef and you say '*what*'???"

Aww, bugger. Busted.

I quickly looked around the room, but no Tudor was to be seen. I turned to Tink and opened my mouth to relay the events of the previous night, when he held up a hand, effectively silencing me.

"He's not here, Ms. Desperado. He left when I came back in the early hours of this morning, reluctantly, might I add. I practically had to boot him out, and believe me that would have been a David and Goliath-style battle."

He shook his head, looking disappointed. "I shouldn't have left, should I? When he said he was going to look after you I didn't expect him to take the job quite so seriously. I didn't expect him to weasel his way into your suddenly slack knickers," he pinged the waistband of my pants to underline his point.

"Ow! I–" A cocoa butter-lotioned hand muffled my explanation.

Oh, this bitch is going down...

"You need to shut up and listen to me, Wilbur!" Tink squealed, and finding my inner Zen, I did what he asked, and gestured for him to continue.

"I walked in to check on you, only to find you both under the duvet joined together like a freakin' jigsaw puzzle: you fast asleep and him wide awake nuzzling your hair! What the fuck happened?"

I grimaced. "Nothing. He looked after me and I fell asleep... end of," I answered truthfully, and pulled the quilt over my head.

Tink immediately pulled it back down and rolled on top of me, pinning me down spread-eagle. "End of nothing, you little hussy! I knew he'd try it on. You were concussed, for frigg's sake. You don't see nurses climbing in bed with their patients, do you, stroking their arms and kissing their heads? Well, at least not until after the watershed. Why was he wrapped round you like a pretzel? And don't lie to me," he demanded.

My heart began to pound.

What did happen? Looking back we did touch a lot but in a very chaste way, and there was all that cuddling, but nothing happened... did it? No...

"Tink, calm down. Nothing happened, we talked, watched TV, he got me my pills and I fell asleep. The next thing I know, you're glaring daggers at me and I'm being interrogated by the Flamboyant Friggin' Inquisition!"

Tink leaned back against my black faux-fur head frame, flicked his hair with his hand and pursed his lips into a severe pout. "Well, fine. If you're gonna say nothing happened then I'll have to believe you. But it sure looked like something. I entered the bedroom, and when I reached the side of the bed to try and pull you both apart, he didn't even look at me, he kept his focus solely on you and said, 'I'm not leaving, so don't even ask'.

"It took Tate to persuade him to get his fine ass out of the bedroom – I was having a bitch-fit! He said he just needed to stay this one night, he only had this one night, whatever the fuck that meant. And then he finally left... in a right mood too. He slammed the friggin' door so hard it nearly fell off its hinges!"

"Tink, why didn't you let him stay if he wanted to? There was no harm in that."

What did he mean by 'he only had one night'? One night to do what?

"I made him leave as I was back to take care of you, and 'cos I thought you had given in and boned him against my wishes. I was pissed off!"

"Well I didn't, did I? And now you've upset Tudor for no reason."

"What do you care? What's he to you?" he quizzed, eyes boring into mine.

"A new *friend,* one who kindly stayed with me to let you go on a date, and you graciously kicked him out after doing so."

Tink sighed and played with his fingers, jutting out his bottom lip. "I was protecting you. I thought he was taking advantage," he whispered.

I moved my hand down my body. "No advantage taken. Anyway, like I've said a million times, he *DOES NOT* fancy me! He even mentioned some actress or someone he was interested in, for fuck's sake."

I cringed, trying not to feel the arrow through my heart at the reminder of that revelation.

Tinks eyebrows furrowed. "He did? Tater-Tot never mentioned any actress when I asked."

Pookie? Tater-Tot. Oh, I think my best friend is about to be bitten by the love bug; he only gives out pet-names when he really likes you.

"He's private, maybe Tate doesn't know." I argued.

He sighed again, theatrically this time, and grabbed me in for a hug. "Sorry Wil, I may have slightly overreacted. Are you okay?"

"Slightly? And yes, I'm fine. I have always said nothing was going on."

"Okay, I jumped to conclusions, but you must admit it looked bad."

"Call Tate and apologise to Tudor. Yes?"

I could hear his teeth grinding. "Fine," he agreed reluctantly.

Stubborn as a mule!

After failing to stay in my mood with my meddling best friend for more than thirty seconds, my curiosity got the better of me. "So how was your date? Where'd you go, what'd you do, what'd you see?"

Tink's eyes lit up and he got all mushy. He pulled the duvet back to slide under next to me and held my hand in excitement,

"Wil, it was totes amazeballs! He took me to the Calgary Tower and he had managed to hire the whole flippin' thing. It was so romantic," he gushed, releasing my hold and putting his clasped hands under his chin.

"We had a fabulous dinner, drank fountains of champagne and then we went to the viewing deck upstairs and, and… he kissed me. Ahh, it was a dream." He fluttered his long lashes.

I was elated seeing him like that. "I'm glad, hun. So you like him?"

He laid back on the pillow, staring at the ceiling. "I really like him, more than anyone before. I know it's early doors but I think he could be a definite keeper," He seemed surprised at his own strength of feeling. "Did you ever think I'd feel this way about anyone, 'cos I certainly didn't? And so quickly too?"

I shook my head in astonishment – my slapper of a bestie tamed… oh, there's those flying pigs!

"So what did you talk about?" I grilled.

"I'm still shocked that we did talk… we talked… actually talked about personal things. Normally, it's meet a guy and 'wham bam thank you ma'am' and we go our separate ways. With Tater-Tot, it is completely different; I actually care what he has to say."

"So, what did you discuss specifically?"

"Everything – jobs, our backgrounds, family. He has a great relationship with his mam, dad and older brother, and is really close to Tudor's mam. I told him about my fucked-up home life and about you and your family practically adopting me. Lots really.

"Did he talk about Tudor?" I asked.

He shrugged. "Just that he's really private, and they move a lot for family reasons. He didn't say much else. I have a feeling he's been given a gagging order on the subject."

"Mmm, probably."

Tink shuffled his body towards me. "So, what did you two talk about during the Tudor-Tash jigsaw sesh?"

I turned away, embarrassed. "Same really – family, TV, music, his acting, nothing of great substance. Oh, he did say one thing though. He thinks you hate him."

Tink was genuinely shocked and upset. "I don't hate him, I don't *hate* anyone. Negativity gives you wrinkles. I just don't trust him with you. It is my job to see you don't get hurt again, and I think he is pain and heartache all tied up in a Tudor-shaped gift box."

"Well, go easy on him, okay? I'm not going to discuss this again. I appreciate the concern but there is nothing to be concerned about. We are drawing a line under it, *capisce*?"

He smirked. "*Capisce.*"

We shook on it. Well, slapped hands twice, blew two kisses to the side and Eskimo-kissed with our noses – our own version of a hand shake.

"So what's the plan for today?" I asked.

"Pookie's going to pop around, and I thought we could have a movie day."

"Sounds good, what we watching?"

"Well, we're starting with *Priscilla Queen of the Desert*, then *The Rocky Horror Picture Show* and maybe *Mamma Mia* to finish?" he proposed, seeking approval.

I laughed. "Bloody hell, Tink, do you sneeze glitter?" I teased.

He pouted and nodded. "I sure do, and I piss pink martinis! So are you in?"

"I'm as in as you are out!"

"Then let's get this fairy show on the road," he winked.

About midday, Tate let himself in, armed with an arsenal of camp DVDs and enough sugar-filled candy that he could have been Willy Wonka himself. I settled on the sofa and Tink and Tate sprawled out on the sheepskin rug in front of the fire.

We made light conversation, and they were talking animatedly about the view of the skyline from the rotating Calgary Tower. I let my gaze wander around the room and smiled when it landed on the vase full to the brim of sunflowers. They always made me happy.

Tate interrupted my day dream. "Do you like the sunflowers, Tash?"

I beamed. "They are my absolute favourite, I can't believe you knew to get me them. Talk about being bang on."

He coughed, hiding a grin.

"What?" I inquired, confused.

"Err, I actually picked tulips for you. Tudor was watching me from the car, and when he saw me picking the tulips, he got out – even though he hates to be noticed – marched into the store and said that the tulips didn't suit you at all. He searched the shop and stopped dead in his tracks at the sunflowers. He picked as many as he could carry and took them to the counter. When I asked why he chose them, he said that they reminded him of you. Said that they were bright and bold and that they always make people smile – funny how spot on he was, eh? Plus, the woman who owned the shop had no clue who he was – so I'd say it was a successful trip all around!"

I could feel the heat rising to my face, glowing red. How weird that he knew that I adored them. What was he, a bloody flower psychic?

'Mmm, Natasha these sunflowers are the botanical personification of you and your exuberant personality.'

"Erm yeah, he picked well I guess," I said, flustered.

Tink suddenly interjected, "Why didn't he give her them himself, then? If he went through all that risk to get them for her, why let you take all the glory?" He wasn't being bitchy, just genuinely curious.

Tate squirmed. "He thought it may have looked a bit forward and he didn't want her to get the wrong idea, you know, receiving flowers from a movie star, most people would think it meant more than a 'I'm sorry I gave you a concussion' and more of a 'My dreams are coming true, a movie star loves me!'"

My heart sank right down to my big toe. If I had harboured any remaining delusion that Tudor liked me as more than a friend, maybe even just as a *'Mmm it could maybe happen one day'* or even just a *'I bet Tash would be a cracking shag'*, then that comment alone killed it.

After a few moments of increasingly awkward silence as Tate became aware he might have just put his size nine winkle-picker in his mouth, I suggested we put on the first film.

Tink looked at me as his new fellow operated the DVD, and mouthed, "You alright?"

I smiled and nodded. Tink knew what I had been fighting against in my head. I liked Tudor… a lot.

There, I've said it!

I let out a dejected sigh. "What we starting with, Tater-Tot?" I teased, using Tink's inventive pet name.

"*Priscilla* okay?" I could tell he was worried he'd offended me.

"Yep, let's watch a cock in a frock on a rock," I quoted.

He gave a shy grin, and we settled back and watched our fill of Australian drag queens bopping to the soundtrack of Cece Peniston and lots of '*fucking*' Abba.

We had just started the second film in our movie-marathon day, *The Rocky Horror Picture Show*, when there was a knock at the door. Tink jumped up and seconds later he walked back in, followed by Tudor. My fairy drew my attention and gave me his '*I told you so*' glare.

Tudor moved from behind him to meet my eyes, and gave me his lop-sided smirk. The killer Tudor smirk.

Heart. Skips. A. Beat.

"Hey, Tash. How are you today?" he asked in an upbeat tone.

He looked good, as always. Hell, who am I kidding, he looked positively edible. He had on dark-wash jeans and a fitted long black T-shirt, showing the top of his tattoo-coated pecs and as ever, a matching black beanie hat. I quickly glanced down at myself, not remembering what I had thrown on haphazardly that morning. Standard black leggings and long denim shirt with my hair in a messy bun and the puppies pushed together, creating a fabulous cleavage. Not too shabby.

"I'm feeling loads better, thanks. Cheers for looking after me last night. Sorry I wasn't awake when you left."

He smiled back at me, flashing the delicious dimples, and shrugged. "No problem, glad I could help."

I stared at him, my head tilted to the side in contemplation. He seemed different – friendlier, and not as stiff. He was speaking to me like one of the guys, where before he had been more intense.

He headed in my direction, jumped onto the couch next to me and scooped up some of the sweet popcorn I was clutching in my hands, pushing the whole lot into his mouth.

"You hungry?" I teased.

He lightly punched my shoulder. "Always hungry for your goods, Tash." he laughed.

He punched my arm, my friggin' arm! *Well shucks, friend-zone it is.*

"Tate was just telling us that it was actually you that chose the sunflowers for Wil," Tink chirped up, as I nursed the burgeoning bruise on my upper tricep.

Tudor fidgeted and blushed under the fairy's steely gaze, rubbing his lips together, exposing his dimples. "Oh, yeah... I did."

He flicked a glance my way. "They just reminded me of you. I don't know... I-"

"I love them, thanks. A nice apology gesture from a new *friend*," I interrupted, taking into consideration what Tate had just said and exaggerating our platonic status.

He looked slightly confused but chose to ignore it. "So, what are we watching? Is that Tim Currie in latex and suspenders?" he leaned forward to get a closer look.

I laughed. "Sure is. Keep watching, big boy. You're in for a real treat!"

He fell back and shuffled closer to the popcorn bowl between us. "I have a feeling this will be educational, Tash."

I winked. "Like I keep saying, if there is one thing Natasha Munro can do, it's teach!"

And so the afternoon went on, involving lots of jokes and friendly banter and absolutely no touching or all-consuming stares from Tudor. I'm going to be honest and say that I was a tad gutted about the lack of physical contact or affection, but at least we were friends. When Tudor loosened up, he was actually really nice to be around.

The rest of the week went by in much the same way. Tate would come over to see Tink, Tudor would tag along, and we would chat and watch TV or play games.

Our favourite topic of discussion was linguistics. Tudor introduced me to Canadian slang words and ribbed me about my accent. He tried to imitate me, but, like most non-Geordies, he ended up sounding like a dodgy version of Dick Van Dyke in *Mary Poppins*.

He laughed at my pronunciation of his name, *'Chew-da'*, and informed me that beanie hats in Canada were 'Tuques' (pronounced 'Toook') and woolly hats in no way resembled beans, thus 'beanie' was a stupid name in the first place. I couldn't believe he thought 'Tuque' was any better.

He explained that Canadians say 'eh' at the end of practically every sentence, and he laughed when I told him us Geordies say 'like' at the end of ours. He explained that a 'loonie' was a dollar coin and a 'toonie' was a two dollar version, and I made him say 'out house' over and over again until we could barely breathe from laughing. I explained what the difference between a 'bonny lass' and a 'canny lass' was, and introduced him to the staple terms of 'alreet', 'Aye' and of course the obligatory 'howay, man!' Tudor vowed never to go to Newcastle without me there as his personal translator.

As the days passed by, Tudor was turning out to be a close friend, something I learned he didn't have too many of, and I was happy with our new friendship. I was still not immune to him by any means, and when he flashed the dimples or when he first walked into a room, I admit I drooled a little and had to fight to keep my composure. But he was completely stunning and my body couldn't deny that, as much as I wished it could.

CHAPTER 13

Blurred Boundaries

Time passed quickly in our new life and it was soon November. The school show was just over one week away. It was snowing non-stop and I had on more layers than a Pass the Parcel present. Work was crazy–busy, the show taking up all my free time during the week, and weekends were filled with activities with my new bud, Tudor.

Saturday morning came, and my slumber was interrupted by *Simple Minds*' 'Don't You Forget About Me' coming from my phone – the personal ringtone I had assigned to Tudor.

"Piss off, Hollywood!" I answered as politely as I could at seven-thirty in the morning on my day off.

"No can do, you lazy grouch. Get up, Tash, I'm coming for you in half an hour, and its minus-fifteen and snowing, so dress warm."

"Ugh, what are you doing to me? Where the hell are we going at this time?" I asked, rubbing sleep from my eyes.

"It's a surprise. Chop, chop," he ordered cheerily. Well, as cheery-sounding as someone can be when they have a moody, brooding, and gravelly voice.

After a hot shower, I dressed in my pink snow suit, applied my truck-load of make-up, combed through my hair, leaving it down, and made my way to the kitchen to grab a slice of toast.

As I turned the corner I stopped dead at the sight of Tate buck-naked apart from a small towel wrapped tightly around his waist; actually it looked more like a face flannel.

"Well hello, Mr. Muscle," I quipped in my best seductive voice.

Tate whipped around to my direction, obviously embarrassed and clinging to his miniscule loin cloth with all the strength that he had.

"So, did you finally give up the goods and stay the night?" I asked light-heartedly.

"Erm, yeah, is that okay?" Bless, he was so embarrassed.

"Ha! Totally, chuck. I'm surprised it hasn't happened before now. Tink is not normally so… *restrained.*"

"Wil! Stop grilling my lover," trilled my sex-happy fairy, appearing at his bedroom door. He turned to 'Pookie', "You find the whipped cream okay?"

Tate held up the can and ran back into the bedroom without looking back at me. I laughed and gestured a thumbs up to Tink, who in turn pursed his lips and used his hands to create a distance of about ten inches, winked and walked backwards into the bedroom, firmly shutting the door.

Lucky bastard!

I quickly gobbled down my breakfast and, just as I was putting my plate into the dishwasher, the doorbell went.

I opened the door and there was Tudor in a black North Face jacket, black beanie hat and dark jeans, holding up white ice-skates with leopard-print laces in one hand and coffee in the other,

"For you," he said proudly, passing me the skates.

"Arghhhh! Are you serious?" I screamed, way beyond excited.

He laughed. "Yep, I can't quite pull off animal print. Thought I would take you skating – you know, the kind that is appropriate for arctic conditions."

"Har-bloody-har! But, one slight problem. I can't ice skate," I admitted.

His face contorted in shock.

Yes, yes, it possible that I can't skate. Bloody Canadians! Not everyone lives on frozen water.

"Then that we shall remedy!" he replied in a terrible William Wallace accent. Our attention was suddenly caught by a loud ecstatic groan coming from Tink's room.

I quickly looked to Tudor and winced. "I say we go, unless you want to listen to the explicit soundtrack that accompanies Tink in the throes of passion?"

He shuddered dramatically. "Let's go."

It was at that moment Tink's bedroom door flew open. We stood gaping at the buck-naked fairy standing, without shame, in his doorway.

"Tink? What's up?" I asked, and realised that it was very evident exactly what *was* up.

"I thought I heard the door." He peered around my shoulder. "Hey, Tudor."

Tudor tipped his chin in greeting.

"Well, Tink, we are off out. I'll catch you later." I announced, trying leave as quickly as possible to escape the more-than-awkward situation.

"Okay, porkie." he sang as he turned towards his bedroom on a wave.

I pushed Tudor towards the exit. Just as we were shutting the door, Tink shouted. "Wil?"

"Yeah?"

"Just so you know, don't come a knockin', if the bedroom is a rockin, but I'll try to put a sockin', while my Tatey puts his cockin'," and with that he slammed the door.

My hand stilled on the door knob and Tudor tripped in shock, righting himself on the doorframe. I grimaced and shrugged. It was typical Tink behaviour.

"Wow!" was Tudor's only response to the peep show and inappropriate verbal diarrhoea. He looked at me and we both burst out laughing. I shut the door and locked up. Tudor handed me a Tim Horton's caramel latte, and off we went to teach me how to skate.

After the millionth time of landing on my arse, I decided to throw a tantrum and retire from the sport of skating before I broke a bone. Tudor had spent the better half of two hours helping me back up off the ice and then showing off his hockey skills by speed-skating around me, manoeuvring in a hundred different directions with ease. It was slightly pissing me off that a six-foot three mountain of a man could look so graceful, while I looked like the uncoordinated mammoth version of Bambi.

We were on a pond in the back of an old ranch that spread about one hundred acres. It was weird, in the few weeks that Tudor and I had been friends we had barely stepped out in public. I knew he was a private person, but I was actually beginning to believe he was a hermit or some kind of agoraphobe.

Watching him contently glide around the ice showed that he cherished being out in the open, but he kept himself so withdrawn and hidden. It was so sad. I couldn't help but think he had completely chosen the wrong profession for himself, if his days consisted of dodging people's recognition of him and keeping all information about himself locked up tight.

Whilst I silently contemplated Tudor's career choices, the man in question saw that I had slumped down on the verge of the rink – well, pond – again, and came gunning in my direction, spraying ice all over me when he skidded to a stop.

"You bastard!" I shrieked, brushing the ice-cold flecks from my face before they melted and left track marks in my bronzer.

Tudor sat down next to me and put on a *'who me?'* expression.

"What you doing, Tash?" he trilled out in a sing-song voice.

"Giving up! I can't bloody do this, in case it had escaped your notice. I have no co-ordination and suck on an epic scale!"

Tudor ignored my outburst and grabbed my hand. "Come on, you clumsy Geordie. I'll hold on to you, there's no giving up on my watch."

I sighed and let him pull me up. Tudor grabbed my hips from behind and pushed off, forcing us to glide along. For a moment, I couldn't breathe, and then got all giggly at the fact that we had made it an entire lap without me falling arse-over-tit.

I felt his breath at my ear. "See, I said you could do it."

We were whipping around the ice with ease and I felt a moment of pure elation. Overwhelmed, I decided to spread my arms and shout. "Jack, we're flying, we're really flying!'"

I heard Tudor chuckle behind me and say, "You're so weird, Tash."

I nodded. "I'll take that as a compliment, Mr. North."

He squeezed his hands on my hips and whispered in my ear. "You definitely should."

I shivered from top to toe. He then pushed away from me, forcing me to try on my own while he skated in front, turned backwards and instructed me from about two feet away.

"Keep straight and push through the ice, one foot at a time, okay?"

"I'm doing it! Argh! I'm actually skating! Go me!"

Tudor was beaming with pride. "Okay, now try to follow me."

He turned, and I was trailing behind, when he must have seen a branch or something blocking my path and bent down to pick it up.

Like a Fem-bot lusting after a gyrating Austin Powers, I short-circuited at the peach of an arse displayed proudly in his Diesel jeans, and lost all semblance of control. My feet slipped, my arms flailed like a windmill and I began to scream.

Tudor stood up on hearing my yelp, looked back and for the second time in our short friendship, I smacked into him, taking us both to the ice at an ungodly speed. Tudor's arms gripped me around the waist and he twisted, taking the brunt of the fall, leaving me directly on top and straddling him.

He looked up at me, my gloved palms resting on either side of his head. We said nothing for a long time.

I tried to wriggle off him and he sucked in a pained breath and stopped me with a tightening of his fingers on my hips. "Don't. Move," he said through gritted teeth.

Then I felt it, a hardening, and I blushed. Tudor's eyes squeezed shut and his chest was rising and falling in an erratic motion.

Say something, break the tension. Erm, what the heck do I do?

"My, my, Mr. North. Is that a puck in your pants or are you just pleased to see me?" I quipped in a breathless voice.

Tudor instantly opened his eyes and just stared at me. I couldn't break away from the tractor beams pulling me in.

Shit, wrong time to joke?

He sighed heavily, lifted my hips up with his hands and proceeded to shake his head and laugh.

"Come on, smart mouth. Time to call it a day."

We got up carefully, trying not to press on any forbidden body parts, and he adjusted the crotch of his jeans discreetly, but not so discreetly that I couldn't sneak a peek at the extra-large hockey stick he was trying to tuck into the waistband of his jeans.

We reached land, changed into our shoes and sat for a few silent minutes on the verge, just taking in the stunning winter wonderland in front of us. I didn't know what to say. Talk about an awkward situation.

"You did well today, Tash," he said, finally breaking me out of my embarrassed trance.

"Ha! Yeah, I reckon I could go to the next Olympics," I answered sarcastically.

He grunted in amusement once under his breath.

I grimaced. "Sorry about practically dry-humping you."

He stared at me and slowly lifted one side of his mouth in amusement. "You certainly have a way with words, Tash, eh?"

"For sure!" I replied, mimicking his Canadian accent.

He patted my leg. "Come on let's go get a coffee, I think we could use one."

He helped me up, and tied my skate laces together to put them over his shoulder along with his own to carry back to his Jeep.

We were about to head back to the car when I heard my favourite song, 'Beneath Your Beautiful', playing quietly. I began looking around for the source when Tudor unzipped his jacket pocket and pulled out his phone. It was his ring tone.

He answered the call, staring piercingly at my gaping expression, his body as stiff as a board. "Hello…Yeah…I'm out at the minute…When? I'll come immediately…No problem… I'll speak to you soon."

He shut off his phone without even saying a goodbye to the caller and dropped his head, shuffling his feet. My mouth opened and closed. I tried to say something. Anything. But nothing came out.

Why did he have that song as his ringtone? Does it remind him of me? Of that night? The night we have never addressed?

Come on, Tash, embrace it. Now's a good time to tell him how you feel. Man up! You like him, so tell him.

I edged towards Tudor and said in a hushed tone, "Tudor? Why do you have that song? I'm probably totally off the mark, but… but… do you like me? Because, I… I like you, and—"

He snapped his head up, his eyes penetrating mine with an unforgiving and icy stare. "I really like that song, don't read anything into it, okay? It means nothing. *We* are nothing. I don't like you like that. You're not my type and you're my sister's teacher for God's sake!" he barked out harshly.

I swallowed and flinched, moving my head away from the sharp edge of his cutting words.

He took a step in the same direction, refusing to move from my direct line of sight. "Understood?" he growled.

I couldn't say anything. How could I, when a hole the size of the Grand Canyon had just been punched into my heart?

"Tell me, damn it!" he snapped.

I nodded my head once in comprehension. *Don't worry Tudor, I've got it. Message received.*

"Completely understood." I whispered in mortification.

And that was that, he turned and began striding away, silencing any further conversation on the subject.

I stood for a minute on my own, controlling my breathing and rubbing my chest, soothing the pain piercing my heart. Eventually, I forced my feet to move and set off, leaving the pond and my dignity behind.

When I got to the car, Tudor was already inside with the engine running, his fists clenched around the steering wheel causing his knuckles to turn white. I climbed in the back, as far away from him as possible, and he drove off, turning the radio on loud and taking me straight home without any form of communication.

He pulled to a stop outside of my complex and kept his gaze straight ahead, grinding his teeth so hard it was audible. "I have to go back home, my agent needs to speak to me. I don't know when I'll see you again. I have a lot on at the moment," he muttered through gritted teeth.

As I started to reply, he cut in adding, "Actually maybe it's best if we don't see each other again. I'm not so sure our friendship was such a good idea after all. You have feelings for me that I don't return."

He sounded distant and cold, not the Tudor I'd come to know.

I let out an exhausted, humiliated sigh, willing myself not to cry. "Fine, Tudor, have it your way. See you around… maybe. Just do me a favour and forget what I said back at the pond. I don't know what I was thinking, it was silly of me… obviously, and probably the most embarrassing moment of my life, not that you'd care, but…"

He groaned painfully, trying to reach back towards me. "Tash… wait… I–"

I swung open the door, not even acknowledging him, and shut it with force. As soon as the door was closed, he sped away in his stupid friggin' Jeep and I heard him roar a loud, "Fuck my life!" as he pulled away from the curb where I stood like a lemon. But I ignored it, turned and stormed up the steps to the condo.

I slammed the front door and walked towards Tink's room, in desperate need of my best friend. I could hear him through the walls giggling and moaning, obviously enjoying his time with Tate. Not wanting to interrupt, I fixed myself a large amaretto and Coke from the liquor cabinet and went to my room to drown my sorrows. It may have only been early in the day, but hell, I figured it was evening somewhere in the world!

I walked straight to my iDock and turned it up to the highest volume, playing Taylor Swift's 'I Knew You Were Trouble' on repeat, and sang at the top of my lungs, venting my anger and taking large gulps of my drink at every chorus, loving the burning sensation that was numbing my shattered emotions. I could totally relate to Ms. Swift – now there is a girl who knows about man trouble!

Feeling more-than-slightly buzzed, I sprawled out on my bed and smothered my mouth with my pillow which, to my vexation, smelled like the über-muscled wanker.

Fucking great!

I finally let myself remember every stabbing word he had said, and cracked from the impact of Tudor's rejection. I let out a strangled, defeated moan and sobbed uncontrollably until sleep claimed me.

How was I so off the mark and, more importantly, how do I stop wanting him so bloody much?

CHAPTER 14

Drunk As a Skunk

Tink was beyond livid.

After hearing a certain girly teen-angst song play for most of the afternoon through my supposedly well-insulated bedroom wall, he came to the correct conclusion that I was upset.

It was about eight in the evening when he retired from his all-day nookie session with Pookie – he'd exhausted himself, Tater-Tot and pretty much the entire workings of the Kama Sutra over the last twelve hours – and decided he should pop in to say 'hi' while his thoroughly sexed lover recuperated in the comfort of his whopping waterbed.

Tink opened the bedroom door for a girly chat, but instead found me absolutely paralytic on the bed under a sea of papers. In my inebriated state I had decided to seek revenge on everybody's favourite schizophrenic movie star, and had printed off several Google images of him in various paparazzi shots and movie promotional posters, and scribbled over them in my thickest brightest red pen.

Yep, you now know that I'm a psycho drunk, and needless to say, this little episode scared Tink half to death.

"Wil! What the hell?" he shrieked as he picked up an A4 sheet of paper showcasing a half-dressed Tudor on the cover of 'Men's Health' advertising his workout regime for the release of *The Blade Reaper*, his eyes gouged out and the words *'We Are Nothing'* scrawled across his protruding chest.

I lifted my head from my current art project – drawing devil horns and blackened teeth on a head shot of Mr. North – and smiled drunkenly at Tink. "My fabulous fairy is here, *finally*, after screwing his boyfriend's brains out all day! How nice of you to take a break from your back-door pummelling to witness the head-fuck that is my life!"

Tink opened his mouth in shock and began sifting through the mass of desecrated posters, his face expressing every freaked-out thought he was feeling.

"I'm going to let that bitchy comment go, seeing as though you have clearly lost your marbles. So I'll ask again: What. The. Heck. Happened?"

I fell back, and giggled at the room spinning. "What happened? Well, where do I begin? *He who shall be nameless* took me ice-skating whilst you were bumping uglies, and once again I massively cocked up and fell on top of him. Yep, and I, Natasha Munro, gave him, Mr. Unemotional, a huge, stonking hard-on!" *Hiccup.* "… then he played that song on his phone and I couldn't speak at first, but then I asked if he fancied me and I stupidly told him that I liked him. Stupid, stupid, stupid!" I hit myself in the head repeatedly.

Tink grabbed both hands to stop me.

I looked into the worried eyes of my best friend. "But why *that* song if he doesn't want me? I didn't know what it all meant, and then he shouted at me and told me '*we were nothing*' and that he never wanted to see me again, said I'm not his type," *hiccup,* "… and, and then I came home and got this bottle—"

I reached for the now near-empty bottle of booze and put a hand on my head, "Hey! Where did all the amaretto go?"

I began looking under my bed to see where the pesky liquid had run off to.

Oops! I fell off the bed and onto the floor with a thud. "… Anyway, I came home and Mr. Amaretto and I made friends and we had a little party for two."

Tink stroked my hair and I pushed out my bottom lip in sorrow. "I tried to get away from thinking of him but he was all over the internet. If he was a normal person I could easily forget, but his first name got three million results alone, three million! So, I decided to erase him, scribble him out," *hiccup* "… now he is nothing too. Just like me."

Tink turned away, trying to quell his fury and the vein on his forehead began to protrude. "Tate!!!!" he screamed, sounding remarkably like a strangled cat. I just laughed until my stomach began to ache.

He faced me again. "Ham roll, I don't understand what happened, what song? You're talking nonsense. Did you tell Tudor you liked him?"

Tate came running into the room at that moment and saw the mess on my bedspread and carpet. He picked up the pictures one by one, his face full of horror.

Tink lifted me up on the bed, and spoke to his lover. "Get him on the fucking phone now!"

Tate put his hands out. "Tink, wait, I can't call him for you. What the hell happened? What's wrong with, Tash?"

"He screwed her over, just like I knew he would! We all saw that he liked her, and we all knew he'd do something like this. Now I'll ask again, get him on the bastard phone, *now!*" he commanded.

Tate headed back to Tink's room, looking slightly unsteady on his feet, and returned seconds later scrolling through his phone, holding out a hand in a placating manner.

"Let me speak to him first, please. I'm not allowed to give his number out, it's in my contract. This is way out of my job description."

Tink turned a bright shade of red. "You have ten seconds, Tate. I mean it. I'm so friggin' angry with him."

I flipped on my side and put my hand over my mouth to muffle the hysterical giggles cascading out of me, causing the paper to crackle under my weight. Tate was pacing the room, running his hands through his hair and glancing up at Tink, who was still as a statue beside my bed, radiating pure rage.

Tate held the phone to his ear. "Tudor, it's me. Listen, erm… I'm at Tink's. Tash is in a bit of a… situation and Tink wants to speak to you… erm… she's had a lot to drink and is not doing too good."

Tate winced listening to Tudor's response.

Tink, in his fury, stormed over to his boy-toy and snatched the phone out of his trembling hands. "You total arsehole! I warned you! I told you not to do this to her!" he yelled down the phone.

Wait! He did? When?

"What the hell have you said? She is a mess and keeps talking about a song, and saying you called her nothing. How could you?" he shrieked, his voice inching up an octave.

I could vaguely hear Tudor raising his voice in response on the other end of the phone. I couldn't take the fighting. I had an idea.

As quickly as Natasha-possible, I catapulted myself off the bed and snatched the phone out of Tink's hand, ran to the bathroom and locked myself in.

I was still laughing at my scheming when I began to look for the quiet voice saying '*Tash*' that I could hear coming from somewhere in my en-suite. I looked under the toilet seat – maybe it was a gnome? I looked behind the shower door – maybe a leprechaun searching for his lucky charms? But nope, it was nowhere. Oh! Duh, it was the phone, silly drunken me!

"Helloooooo???" I sang into the mouth piece.

"Tash?" Tudor sounded relieved.

Tink was now hammering on the door, but I wasn't going to open it. No, sir-ree! I made myself comfortable on the toilet seat. *"Mr. North*, how nice to talk to you again. How are you this fine evening? Still a cold-hearted bastard with no regard for anyone's feelings?" I inquired.

"Tash, please don't. What have you had to drink? I don't know what to say," he sounded upset.

I almost – *almost* – had sympathy for him.

"Well Mr. North, I have had a few sips of amaretto and I am still trying to figure out who drank the rest. The bottle is empty and I don't know how; it was full a few hours ago. I'm suspecting goblins, but who the hell knows, eh?"

"Tash, are you drinking, well, *drunk*, because of me? Did I do this to you because of today?" he groaned sadly.

"Of course I am, you clueless knob!" I laughed harshly, all tact gone, and feisty Geordie Tash taking over. "You have crushed me, absolutely crushed me... don't you remember, you silly man? Let me remind you then," I coughed and mimicked a deep Canadian voice, "*'I don't like you like that, don't read anything into it, it was nothing, we are nothing'*. I paraphrase, but I reckon you remember well enough!"

"Please, Tash. Stop," his voice cracked. "Can I come over? Can I come and see you?"

That stilled me, all humour gone. "Come over and I'll break your legs."

His breath hitched at the end of the line.

"You were right, Mr. North. From this day we shall no longer see each other, and I don't think I can keep on liking you like this. You know what's funny? I have been falling for you, like big-style falling for you – the laughs, the time spent together, the touches, the smiles, just… you for you, not the movie star, just *you*. Just my Tudor. I thought you were special to me, I thought I was maybe special to you, too. You sometimes act like I am, you lead me on. How funny does that sound, right? Mr. Superstar liking little old me? It was stupid of me to even think it. Mr. Unattainable, Mr. I-live-to-torture-Tash. What a fool I am, but hey, at least I know now that you *are* the emotionless twat that I first suspected, and that you think me less than shit on your shoe – just another man to disregard me and toss me aside. If you try to come over I *swear* I will go Newcastle on your arse and–"

The phone was ripped from my hands by Tink, who must have finally gotten through the lock. "Tudor, I heard everything she said. Leave her the fuck alone or I'll be forced to intervene, and don't fool yourself into thinking that a fairy can't hurt you. When it comes to Wil, I'll take on anyone or anything to protect her. You got that, butch?" and he hung up.

He knelt down in front of me, putting a hand on each knee, and asked in a soothing voice, "Are you okay, my little sausage?"

With that, the floodgates of my pain opened and I cried. I cried all night long. I must have blacked out at some point, as the next thing I knew it was morning. Tink was lying next to me, and flashes of the previous day came back to haunt me.

We are nothing…

I was numb to it, numb to Tudor, numb to being treated like crap. Tink edged closer to me and kissed my head. He knew how I felt and that no words could comfort me. No explanations needed.

It was simply time to move on. No more Tudor North.

Tudor *bloody* North!

It was Tuesday before I knew it, the day before the show's opening night. I was in my classroom getting all of the final details tied up – programmes, call sheets, props lists – when there was a gentle knock at the door. In walked Boleyn.

"Hey Boleyn, are you okay?" I asked, noticing for the first time just how similar in colouring she was to Tudor. Saying that, I had also thought the burn marks on my toast looked like him that morning – tattoos included.

Yep, I'm definitely moving on!

"Yeah, Miss, I just wanted to speak to you about tomorrow night."

"Of course, come and take a seat."

Boleyn sat down opposite me, and was all smiles.

"Are you excited, chuck?" I asked her.

"Yeah I can't wait, Miss, I'm really nervous, but excited as well. Erm, I came to see you about seating tomorrow night for my family."

"Sure, how can I help?"

"Well, as you know my brother is kind of... well known. You remember you met him a while ago?"

My heart sank. Tudor had obviously not mentioned to his family that he had been seeing me, even as a friend. Just more strings to his ever-secretive bow.

I nodded at her question. "I remember, Boleyn."

"Well, he wants to come tomorrow to see me, but doesn't want to cause a commotion by sitting in the auditorium. No-one's supposed to know we're related, right? Is there anywhere he can sit out of sight? I really want him there to see me perform." She looked so nervous, it was obvious just how much her big brother meant to her.

"Well, we do have the theatre boxes. Box six is out of sight, high enough that you can't see into it from the Dress Circle and Stalls. We can put your family there, maybe? Yes, that could work. The rest of the boxes are being left empty, but in your circumstance I'm sure we can make an exception."

She squealed and clapped her hands. "That's perfect, Miss, Tudor will be so happy. He's been trying not to come, he was so reluctant for some reason, but now he has to come, doesn't he?"

I nodded gently and smiled back at her glowing face.

Boleyn got up from the chair and practically ran for the door. "See you tomorrow, Miss!"

When she was gone, I let my head fall to the desk.

Great. Tomorrow will be just great!

CHAPTER 15

The Show Must Go On

Show night, and backstage was bedlam. There were people everywhere, make-up powder was fogging up the room and enough hairspray was being sprayed to completely eradicate the ozone layer. The audience were filling the seats and the atmosphere was electric. I loved the feel of the theatre on opening night.

I had dressed to impress, wearing a cap-sleeved, fitted black dress that went to my knees; with my hair down and curled at the ends; and subtle and classy make-up. I looked good. As the director, I would have to mingle at the post-show party, and Ms. Thomas had insisted I dressed professional to please the fee-paying parents. I'm not sure how she felt about my usual attire, but I wasn't going to dwell on that.

I was busy making all of the final checks: microphones had batteries, spotlights had new bulbs, and scripts and props were in the correct places. A tap to my shoulder stopped me in the middle of counting the plastic swords.

"Ms. Munro, my family are in the parking lot. Where should I tell them to go?" asked Boleyn, portraying the perfect embodiment of Fantine, minus the prostitution and starvation.

Ugh, time to deal with Tudor.

"I'll take them through the back entrance to the boxes. No-one will see them there. Tell them to go to the south-west door. I'll meet them now."

Boleyn grabbed her phone and relayed the message. She pulled me in for a hug – a strange move for the usually unapproachable teen. "Thank you, Ms. Munro. You're the best!"

"No problem, hun. Now go and get ready. Curtain call in fifteen minutes."

I walked to the back door, and there on the other side were the Joneses – or the Norths, as they were by law. I opened the door and moved back as they all piled in.

Boleyn's mother, Pamela was the first in and she grabbed my hand as she walked by. "Ms. Munro, thank you so much for organising this. I realise we are an awkward bunch!"

Her smile was one of guilt.

"It's no problem, really," I assured her, and I meant it. They were a lovely family. Well, all except one certain heartbreaker.

"Hello Tash, nice to see you again," said Henry and Samantha in unison, the picture of happiness, his arm tightly around her shoulder and all smiles for each other.

A few paces behind them stood Tudor. I allowed myself a quick peek at him, heart in my throat. He looked bloody fantastic.

Damn it!

He wore dark jeans, a white knitted hoody with a low neck, showing the impressive chest tattoos that went to his neck, and a grey fitted blazer that clung to every ounce of his corded muscles. For once his head was absent of a hat, and teamed with his five o'clock shadow he looked positively yummy.

Tash! You are in a mood with him, remember?

He was smiling tentatively, his eyes regarding me warily. "Hey Tash, thanks for doing all this for me."

I simply nodded, pretending not to see his outstretched hand. His face fell. *Ha! Good!*

The door behind him flew open dramatically and in poured Tate and Tink, snapping me out of my Tudor-filled haze. My fairy godmothers here to save me.

My face broke into a huge smile. "Hi, Tate." I quickly hugged him before heading for my amazing and absolute best friend.

"Tink, you big fibber! You said you had to work," I chastised him whilst I grabbed him for a hug, loving his white three-piece suit with pink tie and crystal cane.

Fab-u-lous!

He just laughed. "Gotcha, sausage! As if I would miss your show. I never have before and I am not going to start now."

He kissed my head and I sighed, calming down some. "Love you, Tink." I really did; just like the real Tinkerbell, he was always there when you needed him.

"Love you too, Wil. Now, where are our seats, Director-Bitch?" he demanded, slapping my arse with the sharp end of his cane.

We began to walk up the back stairs leading us to the highest point of the theatre, where it was quiet enough to help Tudor stay incognito.

"How is she feeling?" said Pamela, obviously referring to her daughter.

I beamed. "She's great, very excited. It's a fantastic show, and her voice will knock your bloody socks off!"

Everyone laughed. "Can't wait!" said the proud mother.

I led them to their private box and made sure they were all seated. Tink immediately reached for the complimentary binoculars and demonstrated to Pookie how to use them. I suspected he already knew, but I was discovering that Tate tolerated Tink's dramatics out of pure adoration, and I for one loved seeing the look he had in his eyes when he was around my best friend – complete happiness.

I clapped my hands to get everyone's attention and said, "I will have to go on stage after the show but I'll come and get you when it's over. There's an after-party in the grand hall if you'd like to go. I can't hide you there though, I'm afraid, so just let me know what you want to do later on."

I never once looked at Tudor, although I could feel him staring at me.

"Enjoy the show!"

I turned to leave, nodding at the thank-yous and wishes of good luck. Tudor grabbed my hand discreetly as I walked past. "Break a leg, Tash," he whispered, quickly rubbing his thumb over my knuckles.

I stopped dead and nodded once, avoiding his direction. I snatched my hand back and made a speedy exit.

"Wil," Tink shouted from behind. He had followed me out and witnessed me holding the wall for support.

"You okay, hot dog?"

I stared at the floor, unable to speak for fear of crying, the emotional lump in my throat bobbing higher like a buoy.

Tink pulled me in to his chest and cuddled me tight. He knew.

"Pookie asked me to sit with them tonight, and I swear I just want to slap the beefcake silly every time I see him, *and* I have developed some pretty inventive suggestions on how to use this cane on the sod. Just ignore that he is here and have a fabulous show, yes?"

I nodded silently and he sighed, tucking my hair behind my ear. "You still like him, don't you, porky?" he whispered, gripping me harder.

I bit my lip and nodded against his chest. "I can't help it, I've never felt this way before about anyone, but it doesn't matter does it? We are nothing, remember?" I croaked, wiping away a stray tear. "Every time I ever think of him fondly, that memory snaps me right out of it."

I kissed Tink on the cheek and pulled out of his embrace. "I'll see you later, babe. I can't think about all this right now *and* do my job."

He squeezed my hands and headed back to the private box, but not before I saw Tudor peering through the privacy curtain with a grief-stricken expression upon his face, obviously having heard everything we had said.

I stared back for what seemed like an eternity, then sharply twirled away, desperately trying not to be buried by the mountain of hurt he had made me feel for the past several days.

———

The show was a huge success and Boleyn was outstanding. The production received a well-deserved standing ovation and the cast had me in tears as they presented me with a huge bouquet of red roses on stage after the show.

As I made the thank-you speeches, Tink and Tate whistled and whooped from the private box, causing curious looks in the main audience as they tried to work out who was up there. I announced the start of the after–

party, and the audience gradually began to file out, making their way to the French Revolution-themed hall.

After making sure everything was settled backstage, I made my way up the back staircase to the Norths. I pulled back the curtain to the excited sounds of the family chattering, and Tink and Tate huddled close, whispering sweet nothings in each other's ears.

As I entered, Tink – always my biggest fan – screeched and ran over, picking me up and spinning me around. "Wil, that show was amazing, the best yet in fact. I'm so proud of you! Big G and Glyn-Glyn would have loved it too."

I laughed as he grounded me, and welcomed the congratulatory hugs from Pamela, Tater-Tot, Samantha and Henry. Tudor came towards me, and Tink seeing my body freeze in anticipation of his embrace, grabbed my hand and jerked me towards him, leaving my heartbreaker the only option to simply pat me on my shoulder awkwardly and compliment me on a good show.

At least his family weren't picking up on the tension and uncomfortable vibes.

I cleared my throat. "So, who's coming to the after party?"

Everyone said yes except Tudor, who put his hands in his pockets and shook his head. "Is there a back way into the hall so I can say 'bye to Bee?"

"Err… yeah there is. It's just a corridor though, but nobody will be there, it's not been in use for years, it'll be the safest place. I'll tell Boleyn to meet you there shall I?"

"Yes, please. Is it possible for you to show me the way?"

Tink clenched my hand. I gave a squeeze back, signalling to him that it was okay. I nodded at Tudor, keeping up a professional pretence in front of the family.

"If the rest of you follow the staircase we came down and go out that door to the left, you will come right out at the hall. I'll take Tudor the back route again."

I pointed over the ledge, showing them the way out. They all began to make their way down the stairs. Tink hovered behind never letting go of my grip. I smiled at him in gratitude. "You can go too. I'm only showing him the way there."

He shook his head. "Not a fucking chance!" he declared, glaring at Tudor menacingly. For a slight guy, he had balls of steel against Mr. Hollywood Hulk.

Tudor lowered his head. "Tink, I know I don't deserve to speak to her, or even to be near her, but please can you let her show me the way to the corridor? I just want to see my sister before I leave. It's for Bee."

"It's okay. You go on with Tate," I urged.

I looked over my shoulder to see poor Tate waiting awkwardly on the top of the stairs. Bless him, he was truly stuck in the middle of this mess. Tink rubbed his face, muttering under his breath as he walked off.

I turned to Tudor, never looking up. "This way."

I began to walk ahead and felt his hand take mine. "Tash, please. Will you look at me?"

I shook my head, keeping my focus straight forward. "No, I won't. Just let me show you the way please. I have nothing to say to you." I snatched my hand back and led him to the back steps.

"Tash, please wait. I… I'm so sorry, what I said was—"

"Tudor, enough!" I said a bit too loudly, my shoulders slumping in defeat.

I turned to face him. "I can't be friends with you and I don't want an apology. Just leave it alone. I am not strong enough when it comes to you to deal with your erratic friggin' moods. You don't get to treat me the way you did and then act like this, like my friend, like you care. You led me on for weeks, spent every waking hour you could in my company, flirted with me, made me fall for you and only then made it clear how you truly felt – I'm not your type. I get it. Enough is enough, okay? I'm your sister's teacher, nothing more and I'm *nothing to you* remember? Your words, not mine."

"But–"

"No buts! Well, none except mine, walking away from you. Now, I'll show you to the corridor and get Boleyn. I'm still working tonight and will not do this here, or anywhere, for that matter. Surely you understand professionalism? You were spot on when you said we shouldn't see each other anymore. I very much agree. It's done… just… leave me alone… *please.*"

I didn't wait for his reaction and continued to lead him to the back corridor. I assumed he had followed and was through the door to the hall in record time.

I found Boleyn with her family in amongst a whirlwind of hugs and high fives and took her to Tudor. I left them to their own little celebration, and threw myself into the mob of parents to mingle and actually do my job.

By the hundredth set of parents and extended family members, I was losing the will to live. I had been meeting and greeting for about an hour, answering the same mundane questions and giving the same automatic answers, when I managed to take five minutes to grab a complimentary glass of Cava from the back bar.

I had just taken my first sip when a gentle hand on my shoulder broke me from my thoughts. I turned to see a tall blonde-haired guy smiling at me with his hand out. "Ms. Munro, isn't it?" he asked with a wide smile.

Wow, this guy was lovely. Light brown eyes and athletically built, blonde shaggy hair and a tanned face. Very nice.

I put down my glass. "Hi, yeah I'm Ms. Munro. Sorry, do I know you?"

I couldn't place him, I would definitely have remember this fine man. He was as hot as a tray of scones fresh out of the oven!

He cast a shy smile. "No, excuse me. My name is Gage. I'm Arianna Scott's brother. I saw you at the start-of-school Introduction Evening months ago, but never plucked up the courage to speak to you. "

"Oh, okay. Arianna did very well tonight, you must be very proud," I responded, automatically repeating my stock phrase and preparing to switch on to autopilot.

"Yeah, it was all great. I hear you're responsible for that?"

"I directed it, yes, but the kids were fabulous, so I can't take all the credit. It's nice to see a brother who doesn't find sitting through a two-and-a-half-hour show a chore."

He shrugged, "Well, it's not exactly my thing, but I came here to support her, and I knew her Musical Director was hot so my intentions were not entirely honourable," he teased, looking a little cheeky.

I stepped back, surprised. "Well, I'm flattered, and," I leaned in closer, "you're not too hard on the eyes yourself!"

He blushed slightly and ran his hand through his long blonde hair. I shook his outstretched hand and, laughing, went to make my excuses when Tink came barrelling over, oblivious to Gage's presence.

"Wilbur, Wilbur! Guess wh—," he whipped his head to Gage, hand on his chest, stumbling back, "... be still my beating heart. *Who* is this Californian beauty in a pea-coat?"

I observed Gage, who was looking down at his jacket and smirking.

I elbowed Tink in his ribs. "This is one of my students' brothers, Gage."

Tink shook his outstretched hand, squeaked out a "Hi, I'm Tink," and then looked at me in shock. "Not another brother of a student? Since when did schools become more successful at hook-ups than dodgy street corners?"

I took in a calming breath, *how embarrassing!* Gage simply looked confused.

I turned to my mortifying bestie. "What did you want, Tink? I'm working right now." I knew he would get the 'bugger off' tone in my voice.

"You certainly *are* working it, aren't you, girlfriend? Anyway, I came to tell you that my Pookie is taking me away tomorrow to Vancouver, a little gay-day-getaway! Apparently the scene is booming there. I'll be gone for five days, how great is that?" He shimmied his shoulders on the spot and whooped, popping his bum.

I love Tink, theatrics included, but there really is a time and a place!

"That's great. Will I see you at home tonight or in the morning before you go?"

"Yep, probably the morning. I need to get my beauty sleep! I'm going now to pack. Great show, ham roll. I'll catch you later, alligator!" he air-kissed both sides of my face and body-rolled away.

As Tink ran off, or more like split-leapt away with perfect dance fingers on his extended arms, I faced Gage again. "Sorry about that, he's my best friend and a bit… different." *Hell different? Let's say it how it is – he's off his fucking tits!*

Gage burst out laughing, and I couldn't help but join in. It was nice to laugh after days of fluctuating between episodes of depression and spontaneous crying.

"Listen, sorry to keep you, I understand that you're busy. Erm… look, I'll get to it. I know this may sound a bit forward seeing as though we've only just officially met, but how would you feel about getting a coffee sometime? Maybe this weekend if you're free?"

Wow, I wasn't expecting that!

At that moment, Tudor's face popped into my head. I shut my eyes tightly to erase the image. *We are nothing.*

"Ms. Munro, are you okay?" Gage was holding my elbow seeming concerned at my sudden change in behaviour.

I immediately opened them again. I was starting to get a headache. "Yeah, sorry, and call me Tash or Natasha. Erm…Where was I…? Yeah, what the hell, coffee would be nice."

He released a nervous breath. He seemed nice, completely different to Tudor: easy-going, happy, cheerful, slim but athletic, not ridiculously muscly and he seemed free of any visible tattoos. Not a bad boy! Coffee with Gage may be exactly what the doctor ordered; a nice and friendly, *normal,* everyday guy.

"Can I have your number?"

"Yeah, sure."

I took his mobile, entered my digits and almost dropped it when I heard a huge crash coming from somewhere nearby, but looking around I couldn't tell where. Probably just some of the props falling off their hooks.

I held out my hand. "Until the weekend, Gage."

He shook my hand and held on for a second too long. "Until the weekend."

He turned to walk away and I picked my glass back up, readying myself for another parent mingling marathon.

"Natasha?"

"Mmm?" I swung around to Gage.

"By the way, love the accent! I have a thing for Brits. Too much watching Julie Andrews movies when I was younger!" he winked.

I laughed and gave him an enthusiastic thumbs-up. He disappeared through the crowd and I couldn't help watching him go. Maybe my luck was improving after all.

I was about to step back into the fray when movement from the left of me caught my attention. The side door at the back of the hall opened wide, an arm grabbed the top of mine and I was pulled into the dark unused corridor, the door shutting tightly behind me, blocking off the guests in the hall.

What the—???

I was pushed against the hard cement wall, and looked up to find Tudor braced in front of me, encasing me in the cage of his arms and breathing heavily against my skin.

My palms and back were flat against the wall, my face mere inches from his. He squeezed his eyes shut and opened them a second later, intense emerald-green irises boring into mine.

He lowered his right arm and I felt a ghost of a touch on my hip. I gasped at the sensation. I couldn't speak. I couldn't even think to form a sentence.

Without breaking eye contact, he trailed his fingers up the side of my dress, past my stomach which tightened in response, over my ribs and finally past the edge of my breast, both of us holding in our breath. He continued up to my throat. I tried to speak, to ask what was happening. I opened my mouth and his finger lay across my lips, silencing me in advance.

His hands reached down, taking hold of mine, our fingers clasping and he raised my arms over my head, restraining me from moving. His lips brushed over my forehead, my cheeks and then moved down to my neck.

I let out a moan, it felt too good. "Tudor, God… what… *uhh*…!" I whispered.

His lips moved back north, hot breath gliding over my skin, causing me to shiver, until his lips were feathering over mine, never once kissing but so deliciously close.

I moved forward, yearning for the connection, but he moved back and exhaled a painful moan.

"I can't keep doing this, Tash. What you said to me when we went skating, I can't stop thinking about it. You like me. *'Just me for me'*. *'Your Tudor'*. God, it's all I think about," he confessed in a soft tone.

He placed both of my hands in one of his, his free hand grabbing a fist full of my hair, tipping back my head, his forefinger stretching out to run continuously up and down my cheek in a hypnotising motion, *up and down, up and down.*

"Doing what…?" I was lost to the touch.

"I-I can't keep wanting you like this and not having you... not tasting you... not being with you."

"Mmm..." was my only response, his fingers leaving my hair and moving to caress my lips, round and round, tracing the edge of my cupid's bow.

Unable to take the teasing sensation, I licked my bottom lip, brushing my tongue past his finger.

He let out a strangled hiss. "I want you. I want you *now,* so badly I can't breathe."

"You said you didn't like me, said I wasn't your type," I reminded him huskily.

He looked right into my eyes. "I lied."

He lied!

I couldn't control myself, my emotional dam broke. "Then take me... I don't care anymore."

"Tash..."

He reached down, seizing my thigh and pulled it up to cradle over his hip.

He pushed forward, pinning me hard against the cold brick, his mouth grazing across my ear, lapping at the lobe with his tongue. "I want to take you here against the wall, make you all mine, do you want that, Tash? Tell me you want that too."

"Oh my God, yes! Now, Tudor, please..." I practically screamed.

He hoisted my leg higher, letting me feel how much he did want it. He nuzzled my hair and ground his hips into mine. "I'm going to hell... I'm not supposed to let this happen, this shouldn't happen, they warned me, but I can't stop, this isn't a good idea, *us being together* is not a good idea."

He reared his head back and met my gaze. "Tell me to stop, Tash, you need to tell me to stop…" he pleaded.

He dropped his restraint on my hands and cupped my head with his other arm. His attention fell to my lips, and he rubbed his together with a lick, causing them to shine and moisten, ready for my touch.

He broke his trance, and his heavy eyes made their way back to mine. "I can't want you this much; you're not good for me. You're not meant for me, hell, I'm a fucking nightmare for you. But I have to do this, I can't stop now…"

He closed in, lips achingly close to mine, but I pulled away at the last second swaying my head to the side. My first kiss with this man would not be like this. He shouldn't regret it.

Tudor stepped back and dropped my leg. His hands lifted, and he slammed his fists against the wall above, breathing heavily.

"Tash—" he sounded like he was in pain.

"No. Stop," I commanded, my palm thrust against his chest.

"Tash, listen—"

"No, you listen," I bit out viciously.

I couldn't look at him so instead I focused on the floor. "I can't do this with *you*… I like you Tudor, probably too damn much and obviously more than you do me, but what the hell? '*You can't want me? I'm no good for you? Tell you to stop?'* Why are you here doing this? Did you think speaking to me like that would be okay? From the moment I met you, you have toyed with me so badly and I give in every time. I like you but... but, God, I have to like myself more than this, and I can't be with someone who fights so hard against wanting *me.*"

His eyes squinted shut, his jaw muscle clenching over and over. "Tash, it's complicated. *You* make this complicated for me. You don't understand!" he shook his head losing his temper.

I swallowed hard, trying not to show my hurt. "Then help me understand! It's not complicated Tudor, or at least it shouldn't be. If you want someone and they want you back its simple. It's the simplest thing in the whole friggin' world. I've had enough of complicated. I want simple, I want normal. *You're* anything but."

He expelled a venomous laugh. "You mean like *him?*"

"What? Who?" I answered confused.

"That hippy, pansy-looking guy out there? The one who was practically drooling all over you!"

"Gage?" I questioned, my headache now thumping to an almost unbearable rate. I really wasn't feeling right.

"Oh, Gage is it?" he said sarcastically. "Did you agree to go out with him? I heard him ask you?"

What the–? Has he been watching me all this time?

I tilted my chin up in defiance. "So what if I did?"

He sucked in a sharp breath, eyes wild, hitting a clenched fist against the wall repeatedly a few feet above my head.

"You can't!" he stated evenly through gritted teeth, shaking his head as he loomed over my smaller frame.

"Too bloody right I can and *I am*. What's it to you anyway? You don't want me, remember? '*We are nothing!*' I'm not going to shag you now, against this wall, just to have you regret it because I'm not good enough for you." I prodded my finger against his chest. It didn't even make him flinch.

He let out a humourless snort. "'*What's it to me?*' she says. I won't allow it, that's what! I fucking forbid it! Tash, you can't do this to me. I can't stomach the thought of you with him!"

That hit a nerve. "Do this to you? You won't allow it? You forbid it! What the hell are you going on about Tudor? You are an absolute mind-fuck. You *can't* have me, you *don't* want me, but nor can any other man? Do you see how royally screwed-up that is? You're sounding insane!"

He moved closer, an inch from my lips. He licked and rubbed his, hypnotising with the movement of his tongue. "I can't watch you be like that with other men."

"Be like what?" I asked, in total shock at his admission.

"All flirty... wanting them... you only do that for me, you're only meant to do that for me."

I physically crumpled against the wall, my head in my hands. "Tudor, I can't take this! What do you want from me? First, you're all over me like a rash, even though it's against what you want, then you reject me and now you *forbid me* from going for coffee with a guy who doesn't bloody hide his interest towards me. Who can be seen with me in public. Who seems genuinely interested in me. Who doesn't seduce me while all the time telling me he doesn't want to be with me. Who is fucking *normal*! Have I missed anything? Please, let me know? Make me understand all this shit you're putting me through!" I cried.

He just stood there, panting harshly and not moving, for what seemed like an eternity. He dipped his forehead to mine, allowing us to touch and sending an electric current shooting through my body straight to my heart.

"You're right," he whispered, resigned.

He backed away and leaned against the opposite wall. I felt exposed and empty by the loss of his physical proximity.

"I have absolutely no say in what or *who* you do. Forget I said anything. Forget tonight, it was a mistake, a fucking huge mistake." He crossed his bulging arms over his chest and looked down at the floor.

For a moment, my heart fell; the look on his face was utterly heart-breaking. Like a child who had just been told that Santa wasn't real – completely shattered.

I went to move towards him, but he stood and shook his head and began backing up towards the emergency exit, hands out in surrender.

I clenched my fists and shrieked, hurt lacing my voice. "Tudor! What are you doing to me? Why? Tell me why you're doing this? Did you mean what you said? Was all this tonight a big mistake?"

He stood completely still and lifted his head to the side, not quite looking back. "Go on your date, Tash, enjoy yourself. Forget about me. Go get married, have kids, have a good life with a *normal guy*… God knows you wouldn't get that with me."

He walked away from me once more and this time, I was sure, completely out of my life.

My head pounded, pulsing with a dull pain and I felt weak. I went to grab my coat from my office and snuck away from the party. I couldn't face anyone else.

The next morning Tink left at the crack of dawn after creeping into my room and leaving a goodbye kiss on my head.

I woke a few hours later to go to the bathroom, and then it hit me. The feeling I hadn't felt for several months: the pain, the nausea, the helplessness, the bloody evil condition that brings me to my knees.

As I lost consciousness, I just remembered thinking, *why now? Tink… help…*

And then it all went dark.

CHAPTER 16

Knock, Knock… Are You There?

I could hear the phone ringing… again. As I lay on the floor of my bedroom, a perfect view of underneath the bed, watching a cluster of lint float by my face, *Lady Gaga's* 'Bad Romance' ringtone taunting me and my current predicament.

I was present in terms of being able to see and hear, but I could not muster an ounce of energy to move. I tried to send a message to my limbs to pick themselves up and move towards the sound of my salvation; the message failed.

If I were to hazard a guess, I reckoned I had been in that spot for roughly twelve hours or so. The sun had set and cast the room in a blanket of darkness.

I drifted in and out of sleep and had managed to manoeuvre myself into various foetal positions to ease the discomfort, but I never quite managed to hoist my unresponsive carcass off the floor. I was thirsty, feverish and basically felt worse than a sheikh with a broken dick being thrown into a harem of eager women.

I'd been so blind. I should have seen the signs. When I'm stressed or not looking after myself well, my condition kicks in. I have problems with my hormones, it's something called Cushing's Syndrome, and when they are put under pressure, they can affect my already-weak immune system. It's not unpredictable; it shouldn't catch me by surprise. It was actually like bloody clockwork, a simple formula: lack of care leads to days of hell. Accidentally forgetting to take my medication may also have hindered things for me too, and then when I'm stressed everything is knocked off-kilter and I end up in that situation – face down on my bedroom floor, and this time without my favourite fairy to fly me to safety.

The real bugger of it all was that I had medication in my bathroom cabinet, but the fact that the extreme fatigue had kicked in meant I quite literally could not move. My muscles had gone on vacation. The traitorous things had probably joined Tink in friggin' Vancouver, because it was abundantly clear they were not here with me!

I could feel the dryness of my mouth through dehydration, fever ravishing my body, and my salty sweat was running into my eyes, causing them to sting and blur. I knew I was in trouble. I could imagine my parents blaming themselves for 'allowing' me to come to Canada. So much for fending for myself!

I was fading fast, that much was obvious; I was just waiting to see an obligatory oasis with a refreshing spring to tease me in my hour of need – that's what you see when you're popping your clogs, right?

What I didn't expect to see was a full embodiment of Tudor North running towards me in slow motion, white as a ghost, muscles rippling against a tight white tee and a look of concerned panic all across his face, with the theme tune from *Baywatch* accompanying his every step.

What is it with him? I am addicted. I, Natasha Munro, am a Tudaholic. I constantly think of him, being with him, him wanting me. No matter what he does to me, I cave like a junkie to a drug. Against Tudor I have no will power, and even now, at my weakest, it's the image of him coming to my damsel-in-distress call to the theme of a nineties TV show that I envision. I am royally fucked up. A glutton for punishment. Then again, if I'm going to pass through the transcendental plane, his face and fine physique are a comforting sight with which to send me on my way.

Mentally kicking my own arse, you know, as my leg wouldn't move in reality, I groaned and shut my eyes. When I opened them again, my mirage was before me, so real that I wanted to stretch out my hand to touch it, to eradicate the teasing vision.

Like a scene in a dramatic war film, the ambient sounds muted and everything occurred at a snail's pace, a slow motion Spielberg-esque director's cut of the end of my life. In a dramatic twist, I was suddenly scooped up from my impending carpeted doom by a pair of hulking arms and placed on my soft, warm bed, my eyes trying to fight the pull of blissful sleep.

I felt wetness on my lips, water running down my sandpapered throat, soothing it like a balm. A pillar of incredible strength held my head as the liquid began to take effect and my vision began to snap back into focus. My surroundings began to stitch themselves back together.

"Tash? Speak to me. Are you okay?" the voice urged.

My still-unresponsive body was guided gently back against a propped-up pillow, and my knight in shining armour moved into the spotlight above me. I knew he was real before I even opened my eyes. I could smell him and, even in my current state, I couldn't help but want the damn man!

"Tudor? Are you really here? If you are, *why* are you here?" I whispered. After last night I thought I would never see him again.

He sat on the side of the bed next to me, the mattress dipping low due to his huge frame. I rolled my head in his direction and pulled a small, appreciative smile. Despite what we had been through lately, I was bloody glad to see him.

He leaned over my body, placing his arms on either side of my chest; he took his left hand and began softly stroking my hair. I naturally leaned into his touch. He was searching my eyes, checking me over, his brow heavily creased in worry.

"Tate called. I only got his message thirty minutes ago. Tink has been trying to call you non-stop and you haven't answered all day. He was frantic, and seeing as though you only really know me here in Calgary – at least only I know where you live – he asked if I could come by and check on you."

He moved in closer and shook his head. "I don't think he was too happy about it, but he claimed I was his only option. Bee also mentioned that you didn't turn up for school today."

Oh My God! School!

I tried to sit up but only managed a painful little flop. Tudor placed a hand on my arm. "Don't worry, Tink called your school explaining you were ill. He tried to catch you there, and made your excuses when they mentioned you didn't show. He assumed you were under the weather and told me where you kept the spare key, and here I am…"

He placed his palm over my forehead to check my temperature, my neck for swollen glands and finally the pulse on my wrist which kicked into a galloping sprint as his rough and calloused hands roamed over my too-hot skin.

"I almost had a heart attack when I came in and saw you passed out on the floor. I think I've just aged thirty years. Jesus, how long were you down there?" He leaned in and brushed his lips against my forehead, swallowing hard. "To think I was at home this whole time unaware, while you were here like that."

He bent forward, putting his hands on his head, elbows on knees. "You were in trouble and no-one was here to help. You must have been so scared."

I couldn't help it, I let out a small giggle. Tudor whipped his head back, eyes wide – obviously not the response he was expecting.

"I thought you were a mirage. I knew I was in a bad way, I kind of expected the worst after waiting so long on the floor, and when I saw you I thought I was hallucinating."

He still didn't budge. No Tudor-smirk.

"Don't feel bad, Tude, this just happens sometimes. I don't know how long I've been on the floor; I've been... a little out of it. I can say, though, that despite everything that has happened between us, I've never been so glad to see your ugly mug!" I tried to crack a smile.

He raised his head, staring straight forward, his voice tinged with sadness. "Tink said you have a condition, one that's personal. What's wrong with you, Tash? He wouldn't tell me any more than that, said it was up to you. But I'm freakin' terrified, what I've just walked into was like a fucking horror film."

He tilted his head to his right, assessing me, clearly disturbed by my little episode.

I shrugged. "I just have some hormone problems, an imbalance; a syndrome. I was really poorly when I was younger and that had already left me very weak and physically worn down, and a couple of years later, this bloody hormone condition developed too. The specialists don't think the two are related – it seems I'm just a magnet for bloody health problems! If I get too stressed or run down it can send my capricious hormones all crazy and I get real tired and achy, fever-like symptoms," I paused to bite my lip – I hated talking about this. "I have medicine, in the bathroom cabinet but I couldn't get to it."

He nodded slowly, still looking slightly shaken by my confession, and then headed straight to the en-suite.

"What am I looking for?" he shouted back at me, mid-stride.

"Just bring all the bottles off the second shelf," I instructed weakly. Tudor walked into the bathroom, and I tried to move myself into a more comfortable position.

He came back out holding five different bottles. When he lifted his head to talk to me and caught me wincing, he rushed over to help.

"What's wrong, are you in pain?" he fussed, pulling the deep frown marks back on his forehead, his hands hovering over my body not daring to touch.

"I just tried to change position – it didn't exactly go as planned," I smiled timidly, trying to breathe through my nose at the griping ache in my stomach.

Tudor dropped the bottles on the bed and began pacing. "I fucking hate this, Tash. I can't stand that you're in this much pain. Do we need to go to the hospital?"

He dropped to his knees in front of me. "I'll go with you this time, I swear. Anything for you, just ask. Shall I get the Jeep?"

I shook my head as much as I could manage. "Tudor, honestly I'm used to this. I don't need the hospital but… thank you for offering to take me."

It must have been hard for him to offer, from what Tink had said.

He turned away for a second, inhaled deeply and slowly exhaled. He turned back around seeming more together. "How can I make you feel better, feel more comfortable?"

"Could you just help move me on my side, facing the door?"

He nodded and moved to place his arms under my body and with a gentleness you would not expect from such a big guy, he slowly rolled me over, placing his hand under my cheek for support.

He walked to the other side of the bed, and I sighed inwardly to myself. This was exactly the position we were in only a few weeks ago and here he was, once again, sitting on 'his side' of the bed. So much had happened between us in such a short space of time, and I still wasn't sure where we stood. I still had feelings for him though, I just couldn't help it.

Damn muscles and tattoos!

"Okay, which of these do you need?" he asked, interrupting my inner monologue, holding the bottles in his hands and looking adorably confused whilst trying to make sense of the labels. His lips were pursed in concentration with his dimples showing proudly on his unshaven cheeks. Heart-stoppingly-gorgeous.

He glanced up, eyes narrowing at my blatant ogling.

"Erm, one from the blue cap and one from the red right now, the others are for later." I said nervously looking away.

He twisted the caps open, grabbed the glass of water from the bedside table, and lifted me up to help me take them before settling beside me on the bed and running his finger up and down my exposed arm.

I realised I was still in my Lycra tank (with no bra – bugger!) and shorts that I had worn for bed. Usually this would be my worst nightmare, but right then I couldn't even bring myself to care. Much, anyway.

"What now, Tash? What happens next?" He was so worried.

"I wait for the pills to kick in, and in a couple of days all should be fine."

"*We* will wait for the meds to work you mean," he affirmed.

I groaned. "Tudor–"

"No, Tash, I'm staying, don't push me on this. You cannot be on your own. I'm here and staying put. No arguments."

Ha, I couldn't be bothered to anyway.

When I woke a couple of hours later, it was to Tudor studying my face, incredibly serious and full of gloom, only inches from me. In my exhaustion, the intensity of this didn't fully register, and I yawned, realising it was really late. It must have been nearing midnight.

"You said earlier that you can get ill like this when you are stressed, yes?"

His question caught me off guard. "Mmm-hmm," I replied, blinking the last remnants of sleep from my eyes, trying to stop myself from falling back into a much-needed slumber.

"*Why* are you stressed? And don't lie to me" he demanded, shifting closer, holding my hand, tightly.

"Erm… gosh… it's just been crazy lately. The concussion didn't really help and … erm… just other things I guess," I couldn't look him in the eyes.

"Other things being me?" he questioned, then clenched his jaw to the point that I thought it would break.

I remained silent.

"I said don't lie, Tash. Tell me straight, try to focus for me."

"Fine. I guess worrying about our… issues has definitely not helped. Or over-working at school, but nor would getting smashed on amaretto either!" I weakly tried to joke. It wasn't working.

Tudor gasped and covered his face with both hands, letting out a frustrated deep groan; I managed to move my hands up to try to pull his away. The medication was starting to kick in, thank God, and the beginnings of muscle motion were returning. When he felt my touch he didn't resist, but let me slide his hands down, and it was then that I saw his eyes glistening with hurt.

"Tudor, please. This is not your fault. I have been dealing with this for a long time, most of my life in fact. These... episodes happen every now and again. *You* have not made me like this, *you* are not responsible."

He moaned. "But I haven't helped have I? I've made your life hell for the last couple of months, due to my own fuck-ups, my own problems, none of it your fault! And last night... Jesus, what I did to you last night, making you feel like nothing... *again!* What have I done?"

He dropped his head and his shoulders slumped. "No wonder Tink hates me, he probably saw this coming. That's why he's been so hostile, so protective." He shook his head in defeat. "He knew I was no good for you and would make you ill. He could see I'd screw it all up. No doubt he will blame me for this too. Well, I deserve to be held accountable."

"Tudor, stop. I can't listen to you berate yourself. And I need to call Tink, tell him I'm okay. I'll explain how you helped, he'll be fine."

"I texted him earlier from your phone. I said you would ring him when you had woken up."

I nodded in thanks.

"Listen, Tudor, believe me when I say this, it isn't your fault. Despite all that has happened between us, all of the drama, the... misunderstandings, I can't deny that you always turn up when I need help, and for that I am truly grateful." I managed to reach my hand out and touch his. "I really appreciate that you came to help me today. I am not, however, enjoying your self-flagellation."

He was boring holes into the floor. "Can we just forget everything I've done to fuck up and start again? Please? I promise this time I'll be different, *we'll* be different. I won't lead you on and I promise you won't be victim to my personal demons. I'll be a good friend, without all the other things getting in our way. I want you in my life. I just want to let you know that my telling you *'you were nothing'* and a *'mistake'* has haunted me. I-I don't know what I was doing, what I was thinking."

He picked up a piece of my hair and began rolling it between his fingers. "As fucked up as it sounds, last night was probably one of the most amazing nights of my life, being with you like that, touching you, having you that close. I like you, Tash. More than like, but I'm dealing with some heavy things, things you can't know about and I'm struggling with balancing doing what's right and what I want. It's selfish and wrong of me, but I have to have you in my life now that I've met you. I want you, even if it can only be as a friend, if you'll agree? You just make things… better for me. I don't know how else to explain it. If I *can* explain it." He looked at me full of hope, hope that I would forgive him, that his explanation would help us move on, even if it wasn't a full disclosure into the reason for his frequent episodes of emotional whiplash.

One thing was for sure, I knew I couldn't stop liking him, he'd wormed his way into my heart. Hell, he'd wormed in, set up shop and colonised! I didn't know if his feelings towards me made me happy or whether I was annoyed. I needed more time to process all of this. But if he was being genuine and was trying to turn over a new leaf, who was I to deny him?

Be open to every opportunity, Tash!

"Of course, Tude, no bother. I want you as a friend even if there can't be anything more. I understand what it's like to work through personal shit."

He cracked his smirk, dimples out.

"What?" I asked.

"You've called me *Tude*, twice now," he told me, his face all bashful.

"I have?" *I have??? That's bloody embarrassing.*

He shifted closer, smiling and tucking his hands under his cheek. "Mmm-hmm…I like it. I've never had a nickname before."

My heart fluttered. "Well, *'I'm glad to be of service'*…"

He grew all serious again. "Can I ask a personal question?"

"I'm not telling you how old I was when I lost my virginity, or my bra size, you pig!" I scolded.

"What? *No*, I wasn't–" he spluttered.

"Gotcha!" I laughed as loud as I could manage; it sounded like a pathetic croak.

He slow-clapped. "Good one, Sunshine."

"Sunshine?" I asked, baffled.

He shrugged. "If I get a nickname so do you."

"But Sunshine? Why Sunshine?"

He fidgeted, clearly embarrassed. "That's for me to know and you to find out," he said enigmatically, playfully tapping the end of my nose.

"*Okay!* How very cryptic of you, as always. Now, fire away with your personal question. I'm intrigued."

He continued, fidgeting with his hands. I reached out and stilled his fingers, nodding my head in encouragement.

He coughed. "Erm…Well, you said you were ill before, something before this hormone problem you have now."

"Mmm-hmm."

He adjusted his position, leaning on his elbow, running his hand back and forth on the bed sheet. "Well, I was wondering… what was wrong, you know… before? When you were young. You don't have to say if you don't want to," he asked, looking very guilty for doing so.

"I don't mind telling you. It's just I don't necessarily advertise it as it was years ago, and it's in my past. I don't even mention my current condition to anyone outside of my family. It's not who I am, I am not defined by my illness, so why tell anyone about it?"

He reached out to hold my hand, he must have thought I needed some support.

I sighed heavily. "I had Leukemia when I was a kid. It was bad, and the doctors weren't sure that I would make it. Anyway, after a lot of treatment I did make it through – full remission, no relapses. I just got stuck with this bloody hormone problem a few years later, but other than that I'm all good. My parents never really got over it, are a bit clingy, but I try to live each day with a positive attitude. The way I see it, I'm alive when many of my friends – you know, other kids I met in various hospital wards – are not.

I cherish every breath I take out of respect for them. No use living in the past, I'm all for a brighter tomorrow."

He stilled, and I realised he hadn't moved for most of the big reveal.

"Tude, you okay?"

He coughed again, hunching his defined traps – you know, those gorgeous chunks of muscle between the neck and shoulder, and on Tudor they were so big they met his freakin' earlobes!

"Shit!" he whispered, interrupting my salivation over his fine physique. He was shaking, his hand was still entwined with mine in an awkward, backwards clasp, and it was trembling. He shifted back around and was staring at me, now seeing me differently.

This is why I don't tell anyone.

"Tude, it's fine. I'm fine." I hate the pity, even if it comes from a good place.

"Fuck, Tash. I wasn't expecting that. I thought maybe measles or something equally on that scale, but not... *cancer*. And this hormone thing, what happens with that? How serious is it? Can it harm you? Is it life-threatening too?"

He was panicking; I could see it in his expression and in the tone of his voice.

I began stroking his arm, something my mam used to do to calm me down. "No, don't panic. My hormones are just a bit erratic. I had surgery years ago to help and it did for the most part. The medication evens the imbalance out, but sometimes if I'm stressed or get ill they can make me feel like this – my immune system is not very strong. Oh, and it means I will always be a little bit chubby," I winked.

He scowled. "You're not chubby."

"Yeah. Okay, Tude," I spluttered, starting to pull away.

He leaned down and cupped my chin, halting my movements. "I mean it, Sunshine, you're not chubby… you're… beautiful."

There goes my temperature again.

"Tudor, it's fine. I know I'm not a rhino, actually, saying that, I *was* once referred to as an elephant… but look, *you* know, being used to the Hollywood circles, that I'm a chub, and I'm okay with that. I've made my peace with it. I'd take the gift of life over a bikini-ready body any day."

He jerked up, annoyed. "Fucking hell, Tash, stop saying that! Half of those actresses are emaciated, eating-disorder thin. Most are like that through drugs or surgery or both. I'm a big guy, I can handle a bit of meat on the bones of a woman, in fact, I prefer it. Nothing wrong with curves. I'm an ass and boob man all the way. I like something to hold on to," he said completely seriously.

I shrugged nonchalantly but was really kind of buzzing about it.

"Fair enough. I for one am glad you're a chubby-chaser. It'll help me succeed with the wicked plans I have in mind for you!"

"*Tash…*" he growled, warning me to shut up, but I saw him smirk when he thought I wasn't looking. I pulled my lips tightly together and made an exaggerated zipping motion over my mouth. He seemed mollified.

He walked around the bed and reached for the glass of water off my cabinet. "Drink," he ordered, tilting my head up. "I don't want you to get dehydrated." After a few sips, he placed the glass back down and adjusted the pillow, sitting on the edge of the bed.

"So, does it ever get any worse than this?"

I nodded. "Sometimes, but if I take my medication I'm okay. The fainting, that doesn't always happen. I got too far to the brink and Tink wasn't here to pull me back. That's the only reason this all looks so bad. It's not normally so *dramatic* of an occasion," I assured.

Tudor rubbed his hands over his face and shaved head, and looked at me in deep regard. "I don't like it, Sunshine."

He crawled over me and laid down, staring straight up at the ceiling.

I shrugged. "It is what it is. As Ron Burgundy would say '*It's part of my life*!'"

He nodded, steadfastly solemn. Bloody hell, even *Anchorman* quotes were failing to raise a smile.

I shuffled closer, laying my head on his stomach. He tensed, arms levitating in the air, not sure where to put them or even if he should touch me. I didn't care, he needed a bloody big hug. He wasn't dealing with this well, he was too intense, too fenced in.

He eventually held me in his arms. "As if I need one more reason to think about you. You're pretty much in every waking thought as it is. Now I can add worrying about this to the pile."

He sighed loudly. Bloody hell, the boy loved to brood, no wonder chicks went crazy for him! All sullen and dark – pass me a wet wipe!

"Hey, Tude?"

"Yeah?" he answered in a glum-sounding voice.

"*...don't make it bad. Take a sad song and make it better. Remember to let her into your heart. Then you can start to make it better,*" I sang. "*Nah na na nan a na naaa, Nah na na nan a na naaa, hey Tude!*"

He giggled, actually girly-giggled. I loved the sound. I was bouncing lightly with the movement of his ridiculously ripped stomach.

"You're such a dork!" He squeezed me tighter.

"Why thank you, Mr. Too-Cool-for-School."

He was quiet for a few minutes before he spoke again. "It's weird, you don't know how true those lyrics are to me."

I nodded my head in silence. I had nothing to say to that and he understood I would give no response. That kind of talk led us to bad places. We were strictly friends, as we had now agreed, who, granted, on occasion got a bit touchy-feely, a tad too flirty, a bit turbulent, but it was fine. We knew where we stood.

He tapped my arm. "Come on, let's call Tink before he flies back and castrates me. You need to sleep and get better. We'll talk more when you're stronger."

"Castrate you?" I mumbled, already dozing off, too comfortable on his lovely warm torso.

"Erm… yeah, he threatened me… again. I've never been challenged so much by such a small guy. He said if I didn't come here pronto he would cut my balls off, a threat he apparently learned from you?"

I nodded in confirmation. "Yup! You don't get brought up on a farm and not learn a thing or two about how to geld a stallion."

He shuddered. "Shit, remind me never to piss you off near a pair of shears!"

"Oh, I can do it with less than shears. A small pair of tweezers would do the trick. Now close that gaping mouth and grab my phone, and let's call the big gay queen before he gets his too-tight G-string in a twist!"

CHAPTER 17

I Just Called, To Say…

Over the next two days, Tudor turned into a beefed-up version of Florence Nightingale. He gave me my tablets and kept me fed and watered. He even changed my sheets after I managed to sweat out nearly a gallon of water during the spike of my fever.

When I was feeling slightly better and I could once again manoeuvre, albeit slowly, he even helped me take a bath. He was a true gentleman and never once took advantage, much to my disappointment. I maintained my modesty by being tightly wrapped in a towel when he dropped me in the tub and once again when he helped me back out.

Tink was on the phone constantly. After speaking to him in depth the first night, he called every two hours for updates. It took a lot of persuasion on my part to stop him from flying back and cutting his vacation short. He cried and blamed himself for not being there, but Tudor and I assured him that I was doing better every hour and that he should take advantage of Vancouver while he could.

In true Tink fashion, he had emailed a PDF instruction list of how to care for me during one of my *'Shit! Wilbur's Hormones Have Gone Nuts!'* episodes, as he had so aptly named them, and insisted that Tudor send my temperature and heart rate readings to him frequently using the spreadsheet he had devised for emergency occasions.

Tudor had been a sweetheart through it all and, as promised, treated me like a close friend. He slept next to me in bed, but assured me it was only so he could keep an eye on me at all times. He would, on occasion, sneak over to my side of the bed and spoon, but, to save us from any awkwardness, I played possum. After all, we had agreed to be just friends. Plus, I liked him being wrapped around me – I was like the meat in his fajita!

He cleaned the condo while I dozed, and when I was awake never once left me alone. Underneath that moody and hard exterior was a kind and gentle man. I tried not to get too used to this new and improved Tudor, especially the familiar warm feeling of having him with me constantly. It'd hurt too much when he left.

It was obvious that he had personal problems, or at least something was happening in his life to cause him worry, and he called his mother several times a day. He had finally told Pamela where he was and why, and even admitted that we had seen each other a few times through Tink and Tate's courtship. It still frustrated me as to why he could never just say we were friends on our own accord. But I didn't question him about it. I didn't want to hear the answer.

After spending Thursday and Friday in living hell, I woke up early on Saturday morning with the bright winter sun peeking through my curtains. I stretched, and for the first time in many hours I felt good. I tested each muscle with tiny non-jerky movements and there was no pain. I gently moved to sit up, waiting for the nausea to hit and, to my delight, it never came. I rolled my shoulders and clapped my hands silently in glee. I was turning over to tell Tudor the good news when I heard soft rhythmic breathing coming from next to me. There he was, fast asleep, looking all tousled and sexy, still fully dressed, his arms tucked under the pillow, snoring lightly through slightly pouted lips – my hulking guardian angel. He had done so much for me in the last couple of days, and our turbulent relationship seemed to be improving with each passing hour, so I probably owed him a lie-in.

In celebration of my dormant hormones, I decided that I would treat myself to a shower. An entire tub of brown sugar body scrub later, I dressed and scurried into Tink's room to style my hair and apply my much-missed shovel of make-up. I looked into the mirror and grinned; my locks were once again shiny and smooth, flowing down my back with a gentle curl at the ends, and my trusty Mac make-up collection had replenished my lackluster pallor. I had put on my red-tartan wool shorts with black tights and a black, fitted long-sleeved top that accentuated my figure, and I felt bloomin' great.

I made my way to the kitchen and began to make a proper English fry-up in honour of feeling healthy and as a big food-based thank you to Mr. Hollywood – not 'The Blade Reaper' but 'The Domesticator'! I opened the kitchen blinds, letting sunshine flood into the front room, flicked the stereo onto a country radio station and set to cooking bacon and eggs to the soothing tones of Miranda Lambert and Lady Antebellum.

As I was plating up the delicious morning feast, I heard a commotion coming from my bedroom. I turned my head to hear better, when Tudor came barrelling into the kitchen shouting my name and halting on the spot, where he found me at the cooker, spatula in hand and dolled up in my novelty apron depicting Botticelli's, 'The Birth of Venus' in all her naked glory.

"Tash? What are you doing out of bed?" he yelled.

I smiled and shook my head. "Good morning to you, too! And for your information, Mr. North, I am feeling one hundred percent better," I twirled around and gave an enthusiastic grapevine step, showcasing my resurrected kinetic abilities.

He began walking towards me and with each step his lips lifted into a joyful smile, his t-shirt and jeans all rumpled from slumber, but still managing to look like a Calvin Klein model. When he reached the kitchen island, he glanced down and spotted the calorific feast. "What's all this?"

"This, my good friend, is a celebration of my cracking hormone stability and your stellar care-giving skills. I hope you're not watching your figure, Hollywood, as this may seriously add a few pounds!"

He moved back from the island, a cheeky shit-eating grin on his face, and lifted his tight white tee to his chest, displaying his ripped abs and swirling black tattoo. "I'm pretty sure I'll be okay just this once, what do you think?" he said with a cock of his head.

Holy fuck! What do I think? Sheesh! I want to scrap the fry-up and nibble down on every tasty morsel of that muscle-laden smorgasbord! That's not a six pack, that's a friggin' brewery, and this girl's game for a piss up!

I tried to focus and picked up the spatula that I had dropped at the impromptu brawn peep-show, and managed to mumble, "Erm…yeah I think you'll be okay just this once."

I was blushing furiously, my face – with other unmentionable places – on fire!

Tudor smirked and let his T-shirt drop, knowing full well what he had just done to me. I very nearly pole-vaulted the breakfast bar to stop the material from falling back into place, but I thought it might look a bit too eager and I wasn't confident that the wooden spoon in the pan of baked beans would give me enough spring action to clear the necessary height.

Tudor began chuckling at my loss of composure. I guessed I wasn't the first victim of the '*ab attack*'.

I cleared my throat, removed my apron and instructed, "Right, take your plate and have a seat. The food is getting cold."

"Yes, sir!" he mock-saluted.

I walked past and heard a quick sharp inhale. I turned around to find Tudor staring at my arse.

"Hey! I'm up here, pervert!" I scolded.

His eyes shot up to mine, his expression guilty. "Sorry, Sunshine. I-I like the shorts. *Really like the shorts,*" he murmured under his breath.

"What?" I asked, not quite sure I had heard him correctly.

He smiled. "I said this looks nice." He lifted the plate of food to his nose and sniffed. "Yum!"

We tucked into breakfast, both feeling much happier at the fact that I'd recovered. I sent a quick text to the Tinkster letting him know I was feeling better, poured out two cups of post-fry-up ristratto coffee and moved to the couch to chill with Tudor in tow. We settled in and I switched the TV on, lowering the volume so we could chat.

I took a sip of my java. "So…"

He tipped his head to the side, and smirked. "So?"

"So, I was just thinking, now that I'm better, you're free to go back home."

His face fell as he took a long sip from his cup. He placed his mug on the coffee table and rubbed his hands together, "I suppose you're right. I should get out of your hair, you're probably sick of me."

I put a hand on his shoulder. "No I didn't mean you *have* to go. I just thought that you would *want* to… I like you being here with me."

He visibly relaxed and peeked up at me shyly. "I don't mind hanging around, you know, just to make sure you're alright today."

I felt the butterflies in my stomach again. I think they had just taken acid.

I nodded and smiled. "I'd like that."

He picked up his coffee and settled back onto the couch. We sat in comfortable silence, each catching glimpses of the other staring at the other, causing us to burst out laughing.

He patted the arm of the couch. "Okay, I'm going to get a shower. I won't be long. We'll have a movie duvet day after that if you want?"

I scrunched my face up.

"What?" he asked frowning.

"I've been cooped up in here for days. Do you fancy a walk somewhere instead?"

He rubbed his lips together. "Yeah okay. Give me ten minutes. I know just the place."

Tudor made his way to the shower. I tried very hard not to visualise him naked and wet in my bathroom, using my loofah in those hard-to-clean areas.

To distract my mucky mind, I picked up all the dirty cups and plates instead and began loading the dishwasher. I cleaned the countertops until they were sparkling, and by the time I was done, Tudor was walking out of my bedroom, stretching his arms over his head, looking like the living, breathing Canadian version of King Leonidas from *300* – completely unaware of me, frozen in place and drooling.

This is Sparta!

I quickly shook my head clear of my wanton thoughts and began putting away the cleaning supplies. As Tudor walked by the TV area, my phone started ringing from its place on the coffee table.

"Tude, would you answer my phone please? It's probably Tink calling for another update."

"Sure, no problem," he saluted, and answered the phone on the third ring.

I quickly washed my hands to remove the scent of antiseptic and I heard Tudor's voice turn ice cold, "Yes she's here. I'll just put her on."

I turned towards him, his face was rigid with anger, jaw clenching, holding out my phone.

I swallowed apprehensively and held out my hand. "What?"

He thrust the phone towards me, exhaling harshly. "It's Gage."

I nervously stared him straight in his eyes. He had me trapped in his gaze.

"T-Thanks," I whispered.

I brought the phone to my ear, Tudor never looked away. "Hello?" I answered weakly.

"Hey, Natasha, it's Gage, from the show the other night. Arianna's brother."

"Oh, yeah. Hi, Gage."

Tudor folded his arms over his chest, breathing loudly, failing to conceal his dislike of the whole situation. I couldn't take my eyes away from his magnetic stare.

"Hey, is it a bad time?" *Yes, it couldn't be worse!* "No, no, it's fine. How are you?"

"I'm great, thanks. Even better now that I'm speaking to you."

"Aww, thanks, that's sweet of you to say." Tudor made a face like a bulldog chewing a wasp at that.

"It's true. I'm calling to see if you still wanted to go for coffee? I was thinking tomorrow if you haven't got any plans, say in the afternoon sometime? I have errands to run in the morning but could call you when I'm done?"

Tash, you need to go. Gage is nice, good dating material. Tudor is a friend, he has made that crystal clear. It's only coffee, you need to do this to move on. Take a chance.

I nodded, causing Tudor to tilt his head in question. "That sounds great, tomorrow afternoon. Call me in the morning to confirm the place and time and I'll meet you there."

I could actually hear Gage smile through the line. "Awesome. It's funny, when a guy answered your cell I was worried you had got yourself a boyfriend since Wednesday, that I was too late."

I stiffened. "No… he's not my boyfriend, he's just… a friend. I'm completely single."

Tudor stumbled back, lowered his arms and clenched his fists repeatedly at his sides. I wondered for a split second if he was going to punch a hole in the wall. It certainly looked that way.

"Phew, that's a relief! I'll call you tomorrow, for sure. I'm really looking forward to it, Natasha. Have a nice afternoon."

I finally looked away from Tudor, who was as still as a photograph. "Me too. I'll see you then, Gage. Have a nice day."

I hung up and gripped the counter top. You could cut the atmosphere with a knife, so I waited about thirty seconds and turned around. Tudor was still standing in the same place, eyes focused on the floor.

I plastered on a fake smile. "So, I'm all cleaned up here. Shall we go for that walk?" I asked in an overly cheery voice.

He took a shuddering breath and darted his eyes anywhere but at me. "Erm, I-I just remembered that I have to go. I need to be somewhere else after all."

Hell no, not again!

"Tude, you promised. You said no more awkwardness. Please don't do this again." I complained as I moved around the kitchen island towards him.

He squeezed his eyes shut once and then focused his gaze back on me. "You're right, I did. But I-I can't go with you today, Tash. I need to go. Please, I need time on my own. It'll all be fine, don't worry." He sounded broken, his voice was just above a whisper and I swear his eyes were misting over.

"Tudor, you told me to go out with him only the other night, remember?" I pleaded, trying to make him understand. He told me to friggin do this!

He smiled, and nodded. "I did and you should."

He straightened and composed himself, looking normal once again and not in any way affected. "Honestly, Sunshine, go, have a good time, you deserve it. I do need to go, but I'll call you later, okay?"

He walked over and gave me a weak, one-armed hug. I knew he was lying; sure, he was an actor and his profession was to pretend, but I could read this man like a book!

He shifted away from me to walk out of the door, reaching for his car keys and mobile phone on the bookcase.

I went after him in a last-ditch attempt to salvage the situation, tugging on his arm, twisting him around. "Tudor, please, let's just go out as planned, we can do this, we can be friends without all the weirdness... Just try, for me, please."

He stilled and ran a finger down my cheek, eyes tinged with sadness, simply shaking his head: no.

My head fell onto his chest, and I relented and let go of his arm. He leaned forward and kissed my head softly; I could see he didn't want to leave but he was forcing himself to go.

He walked quickly to the door and simply bowed his head once as a goodbye. I opened it unwillingly, and he left without even glancing back. I watched him disappear around the corner to the elevator and then shut the door.

I slowly released the handle and placed my head against the cold hard wood. I guessed he was really trying, giving us the space to be friends without the drama, but should it be like this? Should it be this difficult?

I eventually peeled myself away from the frame and began to shuffle back into the living room, resigning myself to a chill-out day after all and trying to remember if I had stocked up on enough Ben and Jerry's ice-cream.

I had only just reached the couch when there was a hard continuous knock at the door.

Who the hell could that be now?

I reluctantly pulled on the handle, feeling exhausted at Tudor's sudden departure drama, and stepped back in shock when over the threshold was the man himself. There he stood, like Adonis himself; eyes shining, body tense, strong determined jaw, and hands braced on the door frame, tension pulsing from his strained muscles.

"Tudor, what the—?" I began to ask.

He was fast. He leapt forward, startling me.

"Fuck it!" he growled as he cupped my face in his strong hands, pulled me to his chest and smashed his lips down onto mine.

CHAPTER 18

Bloody Hell! What Took You So Long!

Tudor's massive frame pushed me back into the condo, devouring my lips. I heard the front door slam shut and I was pressed hard against the hallway wall. He moved his hand from my cheeks and roughly into my hair, moaning as his tongue sought entrance into my mouth. I was stunned...

He tasted delicious; all mint and sweet and *mmm*... I knew it would be like this.

Wait!

I moved my head to the side, breaking the kiss and breathing hard. He didn't stop. He began feathering kisses across my burning cheeks, creating a path to my neck, licking and nipping at my jaw line.

"Tudor, wait—" I whispered breathlessly.

He didn't.

His hands began to roam freely, his lips still fixed to my skin. His palms traced a line from my hair, skirting over my face, down to my shoulders, where they pushed the material of my shirt to the side, exposing my collar bone and the top curves of my breasts.

"You taste so good, Sunshine… I knew you would… but, God…"

His hands resumed their journey down to my chest, skimming teasingly down my side, stopping when they reached my hips. He growled aggressively and jerked them forward to rest against his pelvis before his hands drifted backwards, grasping my backside, his wet kisses burning a trail across my exposed throat.

I squirmed underneath his strong hold and heard a high pitched moan – loud, passion-filled and more than a bit X-rated. On realising it had come from me, I came to my senses, braced my hands on his chest and pushed him back.

We are going too fast. Sheesh, calm down Tash, you are NOT the Geordie version of Linda Lovelace!

"Tudor, wait… *wait!*" My body cried out in protest.

He stilled, his head resting in between the crook of my neck and shoulder, the unexpected pause causing him to exhale a low, frustrated grunt. My hands gripped his arms to steady my off-set balance, and we remained that way for several seconds, trying to catch our breath.

He lifted his head and pressed his forehead against mine, hands once again firmly on my face and his lips pressing light butterfly caresses against my swollen mouth.

My hands, in the meantime, of their own accord, were drawing circles on his enormous biceps. "Tudor, what's happening?" I murmured against his busy mouth.

He lingered on a kiss and reared back an inch so he could peer into my eyes. "I want you, Sunshine… God… please… don't ask me stop now…" he closed his eyes tightly.

"I thought you wanted to be just friends?" I managed to say, gliding my hands up to run over his closely-shaved hair, causing him to roll his eyes and expel a guttural groan.

He opened his eyes and shook his head. "No, Tash, we have never been *just friends. Can* never be *just friends.* I know you feel the same way. I've wanted you for so long, fought it with everything I had… I had to protect you… but, I can't fight it anymore, can't be without you for one more day. Please, just make me yours. I *need* you, Tash, so much."

He crushed his lips down possessively on mine, and I melted against his mouth, letting our tongues find each other. He stopped and breathed harshly through his nose, his hands gliding down my back. "Say yes. Let me have you."

I couldn't fight it anymore either. I'd wanted this man, this… *situation* for too long. Forget the Carpe Diem attitude, I just wanted him, all of him, in any way possible. I couldn't speak, so I simply nodded, giving him the permission he so desperately sought.

With that, he didn't waste any time. His hands dropped to my behind, hitching me up off the floor to sit astride his hips. He carried me straight to the bedroom, his hands slipping under the legs of my shorts, my teeth nibbling his ear and jaw, causing him to growl.

This feeling was all very new and impossibly sexy. I had never had anyone tell me they needed me, wanted me, and I had certainly *never* had anyone carry me to my bedroom before. At that moment, I was friggin' Debra Winger in *An Officer and a Gentleman – love lift me up where I belong!*

Tudor lowered me on to the bed, pulled me to the centre and crawled on top of me, diving back into a kiss, gripping chunks of my hair in his fists. Without stopping for breath, he began moving south, his tongue and gaze running down my exposed throat, over my concealed chest and stomach, causing me to jerk and tremble. He lifted himself off the bed, running his palms along my outer thighs and calves until he was standing, staring down at my laid-out body.

Without slipping from my gaze, he began to lick his lips seductively. His breathing was laboured and rough, his nostrils flared and shivers visibly racked his body. He quickly shucked off his boots, and I watched, captivated, as his hands grasped the hem of his shirt and brought it up and over his head. He was totally silent, and it was the sexist thing I'd seen in my life.

For an unknown reason, I could feel the urge to shout 'Whoomp, there it is!' bubbling up inside me, but thankfully I assessed that it may have killed the mood somewhat if I did.

I was officially now in the most erotically-charged moment of my life. It's funny, I used to think those steamy sex scenes in my mother's *Mills and Boon* novels she hid under the stairs were full of shit, but phrases such as *'throbbing member'*, *'ramming home hard'* and *'thick pulsating length,'* kind of sprang to my mind when faced with this fine specimen of a man. Hell, screw it, this could be a one-shot kind of deal, so I resolved to throw caution to the wind and go with the wanton wench vibe that this situation called for!

I re-focused and saw that the T-shirt was now off. Tudor's bronzed, bulging chest and sculpted stomach were almost fully covered in dark tattoos that wrapped around the full length of his left arm, climbing up onto his huge corded traps and his thick, muscular neck.

Jesus, he was perfect.

I shook my head once to gather my composure, biting my lip and clenching the bed sheets in my fists. He pulled a knowing Tudor-smirk, and I whimpered loudly, *needing* him to hurry.

He reached for his belt and began undoing the buckle slowly, eventually letting the leather strap fall to the floor with a thud. His fingers dusted over the top button of his jeans, snapping it open and dragging down the zip, causing the waistline to drop low on his hips, showcasing the defined V-line of his lower torso and exposing the thin patch of hair leading south of the waistband of his jeans.

"Tash, you need stop looking at me that way or I'm gonna lose it. I'm barely holding it together as it is," he announced through gritted teeth.

I pinched myself on the arm to make sure I wasn't dreaming. As I was twisting the skin on my upper arm, I peeked up to see Tudor frozen in place with a confused look on his face. I rubbed at the red mark, trying to soothe the sting.

"Ms. Munro, are you into the kinky stuff?"

"What? *No!* I was just making sure all of this was real."

He smiled tenderly. "And what's the verdict?"

"Yep, we're definitely here. Now, carry on, man-slave, and strip!"

He raised his hands high to rub over his face and head, causing his biceps to flex with the movement. "Are you ever serious? I'm pulling out all my best moves here."

I nodded enthusiastically. "I'm as serious as a heart attack, now lose the damn pants, and seize and ravish this fair and innocent maiden!"

"*Tash...*" he warned, stilling my breath and smart-ass remarks as he lowered his hands to the waistband of his jeans.

I gasped loudly and practically swallowed my tongue. *No underwear—hello, Mr. Commando!*

I couldn't look away, but I couldn't shake the feeling of being completely inexperienced and way out of my depth at what I was facing.

At *all* I was facing.

He raised an eyebrow and huffed in amusement. "What, no sassy retorts now, Ms. Munro?" as his extra-long battering ram practically hit the floor to complement his jibe.

I swallowed audibly and shook my head.

Holy mother of sphincters! I need a vodka. That or a bucket load of Vaseline! Yikes!

Tudor lifted his deliciously large legs one at a time, losing his jeans completely, and looking all perfect, excited and *very* naked. His inkings continued to his lower hip, his freakishly bulky thighs, the defined calf on his left-hand side, and were mirrored on his back – my God, his entire left side, front and back, was covered in the most knicker-tingling tattoo I had ever seen.

Ding! Put a fork in me, I'm done. Is it possible to orgasm without any touching?!

"Now you," he commanded, tipping his chin, no longer playing games.

In a moment of sheer panic, I lost all confidence. What the hell did someone who looked like him and who was as... *equipped* as him, want with me – a dumpy little Geordie? He was the definition of hot male ruggedness and I was anything but – all lumps, bumps and imperfections.

He read my expression. "What's wrong?" he questioned, worry etched on his brow.

I lifted my hands to my face to cover and hide, and pulled my knees up to my stomach, making myself small. I rubbed my eyes, trying to not be freaked out by this highly daunting situation.

I was in the process of having sex with a movie star! That doesn't happen to girls like me, surely? I was *so* out of my depth – *throw me a frickin' life ring!*

The bed dipped and large hands began creeping up the mattress on either side of my tension-ridden body. I could feel him above me, his body hovering just above mine, completely in control.

"Let me in," he demanded.

He reached down to my clamped-shut knees and pulled them apart, gently lowering himself down, his very naked body flush against my clothed one, and he forced my cupped hands gently aside exposing my terrified expression.

"Baby, *no…*" he murmured, leaning in, kissing the end of my nose and then drifting down to my mouth, brushing back my hair with his hand.

He lowered his eyes and whispered, "You are beautiful. *Believe* me, Sunshine. You're absolutely fucking incredible! I want you more than anything."

I let out a huge sigh and stared back, wanting to believe him, needing to, trying to break down years of insecurities in a matter of minutes.

He kissed the flushed apples of my cheeks and murmured. "I've never wanted anyone, no, *anything* more than you in my entire life. You have to believe me."

I smiled and blushed, hearing the sincerity in his words. I took his face in my grasp and delved into a searing kiss, causing him to chuckle against my lips.

"There she is, my kinky little minx."

I giggled back and realised at that moment that I could do this forever. How could I kiss anyone else ever again? How could I *be* with anyone ever again? You don't try filet mignon and then live the rest of your life eating Spam. My movie-star moment was going to ruin me for all others.

Tudor pulled back and clutched my hands in his. He brought each one to his lips and sat back, forcing me up on my knees. He took my hands and laid them on his broad chest, encouraging me to explore.

I broke our mutual gaze and watched carefully as my hands traced the pattern of his intricate black tattoo over his pecs and down his arms. I smiled as his skin jumped and bumped with the tickle of my fingertips as they smoothed over his tense tendons and veins.

Tudor stood still, studying me and worked on controlling his breathing. I brought my forefinger back to his chest and followed the swirls down and down, round and round, kissing his skin in the wake of my touch. I reached his hip, the muscled V-line, my new favourite part of him, and he groaned, throwing back his head in raw pleasure.

I looked up, withdrawing my hand, feeling empowered at the effect my simple touch had on this man. "Wow," I whispered, studying my finger, "I didn't realise this was such a powerful tool."

In a heartbeat his lips were back on mine, his hands on my shirt, ripping off every button. "I need to see you. All of you, naked... *now.*"

I broke from the kiss when he popped the last button, and bit my lip with nerves.

He smiled and pulled at my chin to release it, licking along the seam of my mouth with his tongue, slid my shirt off and tossed it to the floor. His eyes tore away from mine and cast down. With an impatient sigh, he pulled on my bra straps and reached behind and snapped the back with one hand, the material dropping off my body, leaving me fully exposed to his hungry gaze.

"*Shit...* Tash, you're killing me!" he groaned as if in pain.

I giggled. "I know, I know. I have a cracking set of knockers! 34FF, baby — au naturale!"

A strong arm pushed me back on the bed, and he wasted no time in pressing his hands and lips across my ample bust, my nipples tightening in response. "Can you feel how much I want you, Tash... tell me you want me too... *Say it!*" he growled.

"Yes! Yes! I want you, I want you..."

Come on, Tash! You can do better than that. Erotica it up. He's a cowboy, you're the shy stable girl. No – he's a pirate, you're a wench! Mmm... I like that... Shiver me timbers!

I was in heaven, his lips were soft and the noises of satisfaction coming from my movie star were the biggest turn-on ever. Everything was perfect, better than any fantasy I could concoct in my head. At that moment I felt… beautiful.

His right hand ghosted south, while his mouth devoured up top. He was headed for my stomach, which caused me to panic and cover it with my hands. My stomach was my least favourite area, slightly rounded and marked through years of weight problems and intrusive surgeries.

Sensing my reluctance, Tudor lifted his head, halting his exploration. He pushed back a strand of my hair, tucking it behind my ear. "You're beautiful. *Every* part of you."

"No, not there I'm not, my stomach is horrible, it's not flat, it's marked from too many treatments, it's– it's—,"

"*Therefore* my favourite part of you. It shows me your strength, determination and courage." He kissed my hands, which were covering my most hated space, his green eyes never leaving my gaze.

I released a shaky breath, and he gently removed one arm at a time, leaning down to dust kisses around my belly button and lower, adoring every mark, scar and imperfection. "Every one of these marks that you hate, I will treasure, always, as they show me how hard you fought to stay alive, that you survived against the odds and it brought you here to me. To be with me."

His hands dipped further, undoing my tartan shorts, pulling them down an inch at a time. Tudor's eyebrows danced as he lowered my clan-coloured pants, *"Auck aye the noo!"* he teased.

When he reached my feet, he removed the last piece of clothing and he whispered, "Amazing. You're fucking perfect."

I blushed and held out my arms for him to come back, I didn't like the loss. He didn't waste any time and was on top of me in an instant.

We were all hands and lips for several minutes, until he rose over me and whispered, "I can't wait, Sunshine… I need you… *now*. "

I was nervous, he was just so much more than I had ever had before, and I didn't just mean in size. I tensed as he slowly moved forward, and gritted my teeth at the initial feeling of fullness.

My invading pirate stopped and fixed his gaze on me, panting furiously. "Are you okay?"

I nodded despite the discomfort. "Just, just, keep going, I'm… it's… look, there's a lot of you to take, I'm trying to… adjust."

He blushed, leaned in and kissed me, using the distraction to his advantage, groaning loudly and ploughing forwards. A light sweat had broken on our skin and we paused, just staring into each other's eyes – enjoying the ecstasy of finally being together.

He brushed the tip of my nose with his, "Tash… you are… *fuck*… everything."

My hands ran across his back, feeling his defined muscles pulse with every movement, my hands landing on his firm backside, demanding more.

His hips became erratic and his hands reached for mine, dragging them over my head. He locked our fingers, holding hands tightly and he began to lose control.

"Tash, I need... I need... I-I don't want to hurt you, but... can I–?" he bit my shoulder, sucking the skin, unable to control the pleasure.

I nodded fast, trying to give him permission to release just as my back unexpectedly arched high and fireworks exploded behind my eyes. I could hear Tudor groaning loudly, his pace increasing further at my volcano-esque eruption.

His hands squeezed mine as he bellowed out my name – the most wonderful sound ever. He stilled, muscles straining, eyes closed and mouth gaping, before slumping exhaustedly over me, fighting to regain his strength.

As they say in Hollywood, that's a wrap! And the Oscar goes to Tudor North and Tash Munro for an outstanding debut performance in a sex scene!

CHAPTER 19

Getting To Know You…

I stared at the ceiling, tracing circles around Tudor's back with both of my hands, hypnotised by his soothing breath warming my neck, feeling safe as his arms wrapped tightly around me, holding me impossibly close.

My God! That was amazing! He actually wants me, he calls me beautiful, he makes me feel beautiful and he likes me for me, flaws and all and he doesn't need a map to my G-spot – hallelujah!

It was definitely a dream. I subtly pinched myself again. "Ow!"

Tudor exhaled loudly and lifted up his body to move directly above me, looking disapprovingly at the second red mark that was forming. "Tash! Stop hurting yourself or you will force me to restrain your hands." He smirked with bright eyes. "On second thoughts, we might be on to something there. Bruise away…"

I stuck out my tongue at him in response and he pecked my nose and stared into my eyes.

"Hey," he whispered lovingly as his finger ghosted along my cheek.

"Hey."

He closed his eyes and bit his lip, using his strong arms to lift his upper body. "Mmm, I don't wanna move." he complained.

"Then don't. I'm good with staying like this for a while yet."

He brushed my lips with his. They were so soft. "Did I hurt you? It felt too good and I lost it. I kind of ground you into the mattress towards the end."

Mmm… didn't you just. I still have the springs wedged in my spine to prove it.

I laughed and replied in a breathy, light voice, "Why no, but you *have* stolen my virtue, you thieving rotten scoundrel!"

Tudor risked a sly side-glance. "What are you on about, my crazy girl?"

"Oh just a little dirty role play I was imagining in my head during our impromptu tryst." I teased.

He narrowed his eyes sceptically. "Was I at least a dark and brooding highwayman and you the rich and prim maiden?"

"Nope, you were an unscrupulous pirate and I was the virginal wench with untapped whorish tendencies."

"Mmm… I think it'd be a best seller. Very… *saucy,*" he teased, leaning over to kiss me, differently this time, not rushed or hard, but slow and soft; one hand curled over my head, the other running gently up and down my side.

I let out a whimper, moving my hips, and he lifted from my greedy mouth and let out a single laugh.

"Again?"

I pursed my lips and nodded yes. "This wench has quite the carnal appetite, and she needs your swashbuckling... *long sword* to feed it!"

He laughed louder this time. "Well, you need to give me a few minutes to recover before you kill me!"

He pecked me on the mouth one last time and pulled away, causing me to wince. His face suddenly fell ashen. "Shit!" His eyes were incredibly wide and he shook his head profusely.

"What? What's wrong?" I questioned, slightly panicked.

His green eyes shifted to me, looking guilty. "Tash I'm sorry. We didn't use anything. *I* didn't use anything. I forgot protection, shit. I'm sorry, Sunshine. I've never forgotten before... I just got caught up in the moment and..."

I sucked in a panicked breath. "Me neither. Bugger, bugger, bugger!"

I buried my head into the pillow, muffling a curse-laden shout; he rubbed a hand over his face in worry.

After several tense seconds I lifted up, letting the duvet fall and I tugged on his arm, taking a calming breath. "Look, that shouldn't have happened, we dropped the ball.

I'm on birth control, so don't panic about that... no eggs have been fertilised in the old womb-cubator—"

I paused mid-sentence, biting my lip. It wasn't pregnancy I was concerned about. He is an actor, a very *famous* actor, one who could have – and no doubt *had* had – bimbos spreading their spindly legs for him on tap.

I glanced up to see him grinning at me. "What's so funny?" I asked, confused.

"I'm clean, Tash. No worries there. You have such an expressive face. I'd love to play you at poker!"

Strip poker. Hello!

"Oh. Well, good. Me too, I mean on the STD thing anyway. I'm as clean as a whistle... that's been polished... with bleach."

"Message received, Tash. I get it, you're clean."

I sighed in disapproval, pursing my lips. "Honestly, you pirates! You just dock your vessels where you fancy and let loose your seamen willy-nilly!"

He dived at me and rolled me on top of him, nuzzling my neck, hiding his laughter. He pulled his head back, slowly losing the humour, and met my eyes, demanding my full attention. "I haven't been with anyone in a long, *long* time, and haven't wanted to be, until you. I want you to know that."

I gave him my best *'whatever'* expression.

He put his finger on my highly arched brow, forcing it back down. "I'm serious." he pushed, forcefully.

"Why? Look at you. Hot, built and famous, you must have vadge on demand!"

He let out a loud snort. "Tash! Do you ever think before you say these things?"

I shrugged unapologetically. "It's true! You must have been knee-deep in fanny in LA. You're as hot as a menopausal woman at a *Dream Boys* concert *and* you're famous: Pure. Pussy. Magnet." I exaggerated each word with a slap on his taut arse.

He gawked at me, mouth open, before bursting out laughing. I joined in. He took my hand, kissing the tip of every individual finger before laying it over his heart. "LA is nuts, you're right. But I haven't lived there in a few years. I got sick of sleeping around with leeches, people hungry for fame. It's sickening and gets old *quick*. Since then there's been no-one special. I told you, I find it difficult to be with a girl emotionally."

"But sex is emotional." I argued.

He grew very serious. "It doesn't have to be. Sex can just be that, sex. No emotional attachment at all."

I frowned, trying to work out if we had just had non-emotional sex. He tipped my chin with his finger, forcing me to look at him. "With you it's everything, Sunshine. A rainbow of emotions." he teased playfully with his hand over his heart.

Wow! I'm like his personal Care Bear.

I pulled back and wrapped the duvet around me, viewing him critically. "You left what, three years ago?"

He nodded.

I crossed my arms. "So you're telling me you haven't been with anyone since then?" I sat back, waiting for the answer.

He grimaced shyly. "Is it not too early in our relationship for the sexual history talk?"

Relationship?

"Well, considering you just took me unwrapped, bareback, skin to skin, un-rubbered, un-sheathed—,"

He put his hand over my mouth and winced. "I get it, Sunshine."

"You sure? No more adjectives needed?"

He firmly shook his head.

"Then I'm gonna say it's exactly the *right* time to have this discussion."

He took hold of my wrists, pulling me forward, slamming me to his chest.

"You, young lady, have a mouth like a sailor, do you know that?"

I winked and clicked my tongue. *"Aye Aye, Captain!* What can I say? It's the foul-mouthed Scottish in me. Now stop changing the subject and spill, well, spill words this time. Have you really been living like a medieval monk for three years?"

He groaned rubbing his head across my lower throat. "No. I had… acquaintances that would occasionally… oblige."

"Non-emotional fuck buddies?"

"For want of a better term, yes." he said, almost regretfully.

I began tracing the tattoos on his chest. "So, when was the last time you were with one of them?"

Please don't say recently. Please don't say recently. Please don't say recently.

He grasped my face, forcing me to meet his gaze breaking my inner chant. "I haven't been with anyone in about ten months, I promise. I no longer have any contact with *them*, they are in the past, a past I'm trying very hard to move on from."

I grinned happily and smacked a kiss to his juicy full lips. "Good answer!"

He shook his head disapprovingly, waving his index finger a touch shy of my nose. "No, no, Ms. Munro, it's your turn now."

"*Pah*, that's easy. I haven't been with anyone since February, my ex, and he put me off men for quite some time, the fucking letch."

His eyes went wide. "Ah, so you've only been with women since?" he teased.

I huffed. "Yep, I've been having plenty of naked pillow fights and girly slumber parties that just for no apparent reason spiral into hours of vaginal experimentation and clitoral orgasms a-plenty! Is that what you want to hear?"

Tudor moaned loudly and lifted me against his ridiculously full crotch. "Fuck, I just got hard again!"

"Men!!!" I slapped his chest, his rock hard chest. "In all honesty Tudor, my *'acquaintances who oblige'* – as you so eloquently put it – consist of my limber-fingered right hand and my bunny-themed battery-operated friend."

He encased me in a hug and sighed. "Don't worry, I'm not into sharing, so no lesbian porno fantasies here, thank you. I only want you feasting on me. But your other methods of pleasure get an open invitation."

My heart stopped. "Hang fire and go back a bit. What do you mean share?" I blurted out in a higher pitch than was normal.

He pulled back from our embrace, confusion on his face. "What do you mean, what do I mean?"

I looked down, playing with my hands. "Well, you said you don't like to share."

He nodded in confirmation. "Yeah, *and...*?"

"Well, you can only share something that's yours," I prompted.

Bloody hell, he wasn't making this easy on me!

He smirked, and nodded slowly. "You're right."

"About what? Which part?" I squeaked.

"That you can only share what's yours."

I am so confused!

He reached down and grabbed my knees, hoisting me up to straddle him, sitting upright against my naked body, chest to chest. His hands in my hair, his gaze an inch from mine. "It may sound crazy, Natasha Munro, but I *want* to be all yours. I *want* you to be with me. Only me."

I tipped my head so we were nose to nose. "You want us to be together, like, *together* together?"

He whispered with a nervous smile. "Mmm-hmm... I want all of you, completely, *exclusively.*"

My heart did a victory somersault — fucking hell... *finally!*

I wrapped my arms around his shoulders. "*Mmm???* Well... *Okay!*" I announced, feeling stupidly ecstatic.

He beamed a Hollywood smile and kissed my collar bone. "I am yours too, you know. Completely and absolutely exclusively," he said, causing me to plant a huge wet smacker of a kiss on his inviting mouth.

With that, we picked up where we left off, cementing our new-found relationship, exploring each other's bodies until we were so exhausted we fell back to the pillows and dozed off into a comfortable sleep, happily intertwined.

I'm in a freaking relationship with Tudor North!!!

CHAPTER 20

The Little Things

I woke up to the heavenly feel of kisses down my spine.

It was a new and unexpected feeling of being treasured, and not being covered with a quilt during sex because my partner found looking at me offensive. For three years, I classed it as a special treat if Nathan actually fully removed his trousers before flip-flopping on top of me like a seal for his personal best of two minutes – *Ar-Ar!*

With Tudor, it was all different… it was nice, loving, attentive, everything I could want.

"Mmm… I could get used to this." I closed my eyes and enjoyed the loving caresses ghosting along my skin.

"How are you feeling, gorgeous?"

I smiled at the endearment. I rolled over, pulling him to lie down beside me. I took his hand.

"How am I feeling? Wow. Where do I start? Well, I can't actually believe that you're here with me, like this… finally! I can't believe that you, Tudor North, want *me,*

Natasha Munro from Newcastle-Upon-Tyne. And what I absolutely cannot believe… is how big you are in the downstairs department!" I nudged him with my arm, chuckling.

He moved in for a kiss, and my heart fluttered faster than a hummingbird's wings.

"How are *you* feeling?" I asked in return.

He lifted a strand of my hair to tease between his fingers. "How am I feeling? Well, where do *I* start? I can't believe *you're* here with me… *finally!* I can't believe that you want me, Tudor North from Victoria, British Columbia, *especially* after how I've acted towards you over the last couple of months. I really don't deserve a second, no, third chance. But mostly I can't believe that I'm gonna have to deal with one of Tink's freakin' lectures when we tell him we're together!" He tickled my ribs making me giggle.

Together. One word that evokes so much joy and happiness.

He raised himself above me, laying his hand over my heart, (which was dangerously close to my left breast*)* all playfulness on pause. "I'm gonna make you happy, Tash, I promise. No more fuck-ups."

I nodded, placing my hand above his heart too (dangerously close to his pec). "I'm going to make you happy too, Tude. *I* promise."

He grinned and meshed our mouths together, sealing the vow with a kiss.

I patted his arms. "So, now that we've stopped playing with each other's tits, I need a shower. I'm a little bit of a mess."

He pulled his lop-sided smirk. "Can I join you?"

"I have a better idea," I announced as he peppered me with kisses all over my face.

"I'm all ears."

He's all muscles!

"Tink invested in a hot tub when we moved in, it's on the deck. We could take advantage of that if you'd like?"

He nodded enthusiastically. "Only if the taking advantage would be me of you."

I guffawed. "You only have to look at me to get me to do your bidding, Mr. North, *and* you know it. That, or flash a piece of that panty-wetting tattoo."

He shook his head at my vulgarity, but then acknowledged my confession with a smirk. "Duly noted."

"Okay, let me up. I'll shower quickly and meet you out there. I think there's some prosecco in the fridge."

I moved swiftly out of the bed, purposely sashaying my apple-round arse to the bathroom. I knew I'd been successful in my seductive parade when I heard Tudor let out a low moan.

Take that Jessica Fucking Rabbit!

I loved that I had that effect on him, he made me love myself in a way I could never have done before.

Just as I was heading through the en-suite door, Tudor called out, "Tash!"

I popped my head around the door. "Yeah, hun?"

He lifted up his upper body, braced upon his elbows, his abs protruding from his stomach. "Don't bother putting on a swim suit. I want you ready and naked, no barriers between us. Yes?"

I nodded in submission and shut the door, bracing myself on the sink and looking at my wanton reflection pulling a smug smile.

Well Tash, better get chugging on gallons of cranberry juice and accept that you'll be walking like John Wayne for next few days!

Once I had showered, I headed out to the deck. Slow music was serenading through the speakers, and Tudor was in the Jacuzzi, head back and lapping up the heat.

I slid in next to him, causing him to stir and hiss through teeth. "I approve of the attire."

Or lack thereof!

He handed me a glass of bubbly, and we clinked our glasses with an obligatory 'cheers'.

He didn't meet my eyes. "*Tudor!*"

He jerked at my shriek and spilt his drink in the water. He looked completely on edge. "What?"

I shook my head in anger. "You didn't meet my eyes! Bloody hell, it must be the only time since I've met you that you haven't bored holes into these peepers!"

He started laughing. "I love looking into your big chocolate eyes, but why are you getting all worked up about it now?"

I let out a frustrated '*Argh!*' "Because, if you don't make eye contact when you toast then you get seven years bad sex," I nodded with wide eyes and pursed lips, conveying the seriousness of the situation.

Tudor lunged for the bottle of prosecco, filling our glasses to the rim. "Quick, quick, Sunshine, look deep into my eyes… not around them but right at them. You ready…? *Cheers.*"

I giggled, clinking my glass against his. "Cheers."

I moved to sit opposite him and placed down my glass, still euphoric at our newly-expressed relationship status and how relaxed he seemed to be in my presence.

Tudor set down his drink, standing slightly so I could catch a glimpse of the left, tattoo-laden cheek of his arse. He sat back down, and his arms dropped under the bubbling water, where I felt fingers grip my feet and move upwards as he grasped my ankles, making me yelp, pulling me forward through the water until I was situated on his lap. "There, that's better." He seemed very pleased with himself.

My eyes pulled tightly into a squint, trying to expel the water. "You could have just asked me to come over to you. You didn't have to dunk me." I scolded.

He intertwined his fingers around my back and answered, "Now where's the fun in that? Now come here,

I've missed your lips. And I want to cash in on our seven years of good sex."

I leaned in close, nipping his mouth before allowing him to engulf me. After several heated minutes, I pulled back and stroked his shaved head. "Tudor?"

He smiled in suspicion. "Yes?"

"Since we met, I've had these feelings for you, and now, well, I feel a lot more. Having you here, with me, is just…" I stared off towards the sky unable to finish that sentence.

He smiled and kissed the back of my hand. "Me too, gorgeous."

I didn't look his way, causing him to pull a frown. He put his finger on my chin, forcing me to meet his gaze. "What is it?"

"Well, we have slept together a couple of times now—"

"And will do so again, *soon,*" he interrupted.

I play-punched his arm. "… *and* agreed to be exclusive. But I feel I don't know anything about you really. How bad is that? I'm acting like a right slut!" I pressed my head down on his shoulder, and banged it repeatedly, groaning, "My father would kill me!" like a mantra.

I heard chuckling beneath me. "I for one am glad you are slutty with me, only me, and you're mighty good at it too. But I disagree on you not knowing me. I am more myself with you than I am with my own family. You make me happy, something I haven't been in such a long time. You make everything better. You make me a better man. Does that sound a bit cheesy?"

I shook my head and hugged him hard as I batted my lashes, acting coy.

He grinned at my playful antics. "And as for not knowing the details, here's your chance."

I raised my head so quickly that I almost got whiplash. "Really?"

"Really," he affirmed.

"Okay. Mmm… let's start easy. Favourite colour?"

"Blue. Yours?"

"Pink. Favourite movie?"

"*Spartacus*. Yours?"

"*The Breakfast Club*. Favourite food?"

"Pizza. Yours?"

"Same, or fish and chips, or a Sunday roast, or pancakes – bugger it, I have a long list!"

He laughed at me and announced that it was his turn. "Biggest turn-on in a man?"

"Monogamy, muscles, shaved heads and tattoos." He smiled and punched a celebratory fist in the air.

I ignored it, "You?"

"Mmm, let me think. I suppose a five o'clock shadow and a defined chest?"

I tweaked one of his nipples.

"Hey!" he mock cried.

"In a woman, you twat!"

"*Oh*, okay, I get it! A good sense of humour, curves, brown hair, brown eyes and… 100% trust,"

He regarded me intensely. "How many sexual partners have you had?"

"Four, including you. You, Mr. North?" I asked, my heart picking up speed as I awaited his response.

He winced. "More."

"Not good enough. I want numbers!"

No you don't, Tash, why have you asked this question?

He lowered his head. "I'm ashamed to say I don't know. I'm thirty-one. I've had two semi-serious relationships, if you can call them that and… considerably more one-night stands. We're not talking hundreds here, but there have been more than is deemed acceptable from someone of my age, put it that way."

I huffed at the fact he wouldn't confess more than this little titbit of information. I folded my arms. "That's all you're saying?"

Considerably more one night stands? Great!

He nodded sternly, and then shook his head. "Actually, there is one thing."

I glared back moodily, arms still crossed across my chest. That worked against me, I shouldn't have pushed the girls in his face. He groaned and had to struggle to tear his lusty gaze away from the view.

He took my face in his large hands. "You're number one, you're it. *Easily* the best sex of my life, and I want you for more than just one night. I'll take you forever if you'll have me. With you everything is just… different… it's just… beyond anything I could have ever imagined," he whispered swallowing the heart-felt words that hitched in his throat.

I tried to stay in a mood but his words melted my anger, and I moved to kiss his nose. "What's with all of the tattoos?" I asked while I licked the end of the tribal swirl on his lower neck.

He moved his head further to the side to let me explore. "My good buddy back in Vancouver is an artist and I asked for something one day, I let him decide. After my arm, I kinda got addicted and we kept going. He used me as a showcase for his work. Most people don't like it, think it's too much, but I'm happy with it. Tattoo's are art to me."

I smiled. "I bloody love it! It's like you're all my favourite things put on Earth to tempt me, especially the tats, they're my weakness. But why the left-hand side?"

"It's the side of the heart, the soul. It sounds stupid, but for me it was a spiritual experience, helped me rid myself of some demons I'd been carrying; they remind me that I'm strong. The left-hand side is purely for me. The right, I've been saving for someone special, a blank canvas just for them."

I wasn't expecting that level of admission. I loved how he was always able to surprise me.

"*Okay*, next question," he moved the conversation on swiftly before I got a chance to find out about those pesky demons and that someone-special tattoo plan.

"Are you close to your family?" he asked.

"Extremely. You?"

"Very."

"Can I ask a personal question?"

He nodded.

"Obviously I've met your mother and siblings, but where's your dad?"

Tudor tensed as rigid as a board underneath me, digging his fingers into my hips.

I shifted at the feeling. "Ow!"

He dropped his hands into the safety of the water. "Shit, sorry, Tash. Look, he's not in my life."

I stroked his chest and peered up, he was now staring at the stars. "Why?" I pushed.

He dropped his gaze to me looking slightly pissed off. "Tash, he's just not. Leave it there. I can't talk about it."

I stopped stroking his arm and withdrew from his lap like a scolded dog. He caught me before I could scurry too far away and brought me back to his chest, controlling his breathing, mouth sucking droplets of water off my skin. "Sunshine, I'm sorry, forgive me. I… I just can't talk about *him*. Please just understand that that topic is a no go area for me."

I sighed and accepting his apology. Hopefully in time he would tell me more about it, open up.

"Okay, my turn," I announced. He visibly relaxed knowing I was respecting his wishes. "What's your favourite song?"

He lowered his lids shyly, before peeking over his lashes hesitantly to meet my eyes. "'Beneath Your Beautiful'."

I opened my mouth but nothing came out.

"Yours?" he asked, grinning.

I whispered, "The same. You know that."

He placed a hand on the back of my head to pull me in for a kiss.

I grinned against his mouth. "That *is* why you had it as your ringtone, isn't it?"

He nodded.

"Then why did you get so angry at the pond when we went skating? You were so cold and horrible to me. If you liked me, why didn't you just say so? We could have avoided all the shit that followed."

Tudor stared at me for what felt like an eternity, and I couldn't read his expression. Was he mad, upset, pissed off that I'd brought it up?

He rubbed his lips together. "Tash, the truth is that I didn't want you to know I liked you, *how* much I liked you. Relationships are not good for me at the moment, but I could not get you out of my head, and after this I know I never will. I've never had someone affect me like you do."

He grimaced as if in pain, dragging in shallow breaths. "I can't believe I was such an ass to you though, I wish I could just go back in time and take it all back."

I sighed and nodded in agreement. "So you did have the ringtone because you liked me?"

"Yes. Every time I played it, it made me think of you, and that night, holding you, laughing with you… caring for you. It was like nothing I had ever experience before. I couldn't get you out of my head."

He kissed just below my ear and continued. "It was that night you know, after your accident, when I realised how *much* I liked you. No-one has ever made me feel like this. I can't explain it. I just want you so much that it physically hurts."

I embraced him tightly, wrapping my arms and legs around him like a spider monkey. "You don't need to explain it. I feel the same way too."

He regarded me over shy eyes. "Really?"

I kissed his nose. "Really."

"Well come here then, I want to see how you taste."

"Tudor, you've kissed me a million times by now, you know how I taste."

His eyebrows danced villainously. "Not everywhere I don't."

He picked me up as if I weighed nothing and pushed me back against the hot tub wall, balancing my backside and holding my hips up on the ledge. He started kissing me on my mouth and continued travelling south. I sucked in a breath as he reached the bottom of my stomach.

I think I can probably leave the rest to your imagination, *but* let's just say, I found out that night that Tudor would have made a fantastic synchronised swimmer!

CHAPTER 21

Breaking The Fantasy

"Wake up, sleeping beauty."

I roused from my deep sleep to see Tudor towering over me in only his black Calvin Klein boxer briefs, holding a tray filled with scrambled eggs on toast, a huge cup of steaming-hot coffee and a clipped-to-size sunflower in a small, pink vase.

I cast a shy smile. "Morning, babes. What's all this?"

Tudor leaned down and pecked a kiss on the top of my head. "This, Sunshine, is breakfast in bed. A thoroughly deserved one too. And I like that you call me babes," he grinned and winked.

I sat up, letting the duvet fall to my waist, proudly showing off the goods, and took the flower from its vase to smell. "Where did you get this?"

He dropped down on the bed and ran a finger across my neck. "I had to pop out to get some eggs and I got you these. The rest are out there for you in a vase." He pointed over his shoulder to the living room.

I gave him a brief thank-you kiss and stretched my arms high, easing the cricks from my overused body, and glanced to the window, noticing that it was still early and the sun was still rising.

My eyes squinted at the blindingly-bright glare. "What time is it?"

He shrugged his shoulders. "About eight a.m."

My mouth dropped in disbelief. "Then why the heck are we up? We didn't even get to bed until after three this morning!"

He just pursed his lips and waggled his eyebrows at me. We had spent most of the previous night in the hot tub, lazing and talking, finding out more little details about one another and just ignoring the real world for a little while. At around one in the morning, we had grown hungry and made some pancakes and brought them back to bed. I giggled quietly as I looked over to the bedside cabinet at the half-eaten midnight snack, blushing at the memory of why it had never been finished. I ran my hand down to my stomach, still sticky from the maple syrup, and smiled at the *9 ½ weeks*-esque direction the night had taken.

Tudor, noticing my train of thought, shuffled down the bed and lapped at the residue on my belly. "Mmm… still delicious, and definitely something we will do again."

That snapped me out of my trance. "Up, now, my body cannot take any more." I tried to move his humongous shoulders off my over-sexed body and failed, badly.

He crawled back up, lying flush over me, nuzzling my neck. "Fine. I'm giving you today to recover, but tonight you're mine again."

"Tudor, you haven't been home in days, and as much as I am enjoying you being here, I'm better now and you don't have to stay twenty-four-seven. Plus, I can't have any more sex, I'm exhausted! I would like to be able to walk at school on Monday morning!"

He braced his arms and moved to look at me, a little put out. "I called in at home this morning when I was out getting food, everything is good, so if you would like, I could stay one more night. You know, just until Tink gets back?"

He looked so hopeful.

I grinned at his cute, puppy-dog face. "Oh, okay then, if you *must*!"

He moved in for a not-so-innocent kiss, and after several seconds his hands started roaming south into naughty places.

I pushed him back. "Oi! Sex fiend! *NO!*"

He sighed loudly for effect and rolled over, adjusting himself with one hand and covering his eyes with the other. "Today, Tash, that's all you're getting. Then it's on," he muttered, obviously in sexual pain. I had to smile to myself. I loved the impact I had on him.

I reached for the tray of food and tucked in. Tudor lay still for a while, huffing away his frustration, and after he had got over his not-so-little 'trouser tent' – or should it be marquee? – problem, got up and wandered into the front room. Seconds later he came back in, holding out my diamante-covered pink phone.

I took it from him and checked the screen, nothing. I checked the list of missed calls, emails and messages, nada. Tudor was standing to the side of the bed, all serious-looking, arms crossed tightly over his chest. I looked back at him in confusion.

He rubbed his hand over his stubbly chin. "You need to make a call or a text, preferably."

"I do?" I asked.

He nodded his head with attitude. "You need to cancel your *date*."

"Oh shit. Gage!" I launched upright, putting my hand on my head. He ground his teeth together at the mention of Gage's name.

Wait a bloody second!

I pushed my tray away and sat up on my knees, facing Mr. Moody-arse, not even bothered that I was stark naked. "Is that why we're up so early on a Sunday morning?" I asked, slightly annoyed but also kind of proud of myself for foiling his plan.

He read my pissed-off tone right and pouted – *yes*, pouted, like an overgrown three-year-old. He spoke without looking up. "I couldn't sleep knowing that you had agreed to be with me as my girlfriend and yet your date was still planned for today. It made me…

uncomfortable. I'm not used to feeling like this and I don't like it," he mumbled and began kicking the carpet.

I tried to be angry, but the six-foot-three hulk of brawn looked too cute, and I kind of liked that he felt so jealous. I held out my hand. "Come here."

He moved as quickly as a snake, tackled me onto the bed and into my awaiting arms.

I kissed his head patronisingly. "Poor Tudor, do you have a case of the green-eyed monster?"

He narrowed his eyes. "Would you like it if I was meeting another woman today for coffee after we had just made love?"

Made love. Not had sex, but made love.

I locked still, he pulled a smug grin – he knew he'd got me.

"Pass me the phone." I held out my hand and he dropped it into my awaiting palm.

He huffed in victory. I flicked through the numbers and pressed the call button on Gage's name. Tudor wrapped his arms around my waist, laying his head on my sticky stomach.

Gage answered on the third ring. "Natasha! I was just thinking about you. I was wondering when you would be awake for me to call."

He sounded happy. I knew Tudor could hear both sides of the conversation by the tensing of his arms around my middle.

I cleared my throat. "Hi Gage, I hope you're okay?"

"I'm great knowing I'm seeing you today."

I winced, and Tudor growled, like actually growled. I looked down in surprise and shook my head in disbelief at his strange reaction.

"Erm, yeah about that…"

"*Oh*… I see, this is a letdown call, isn't it? You're not coming for coffee?" he sounded absolutely deflated.

I felt so bad, if things hadn't… escalated last night with Tudor, I'd have most definitely gone today. "Well, it's just, last night I saw an… old… *friend,* and well, we have decided to try to see if we can be more than just platonic. I don't think coffee today with you would be appropriate now, given this new development." I winced once more. Tudor relaxed and feathered kisses along my skin.

Gage sighed. "Okay, damn…" He let out a single disappointed laugh. "I should have made the coffee date for earlier in the week, shouldn't I? Or spoke to you back in September."

"I'm sorry, Gage. If it's any consolation, I was looking forward to it."

I let out a sudden whoosh of breath as Tudor gripped me tightly, knocking the wind right out of me.

"Me too, Natasha, I've been excited all week, but I guess life doesn't always give you what you want, eh?"

"I'm so sorry."

"Me too. I guess I'll just see you around."

"'Bye, Gage."

"'Bye, Natasha."

I was about to hang up when Gage spoke again, "Natasha?" he shouted so I would hear him.

"Yeah?"

"If it doesn't work out with your old friend, give me a call. My offer's an open invitation for you."

I was touched by the sentiment but the warm feeling was interrupted when Tudor growled again.

Seriously, who growls?

"I'll keep that in mind. 'Bye for now." I rushed out.

I pressed 'end' on the call and sat in silence, upset that Gage was feeling so low.

Tudor jumped up suddenly and grasped my face in his hands, swooping in for a frantic kiss. "Do you think we will last?" he blurted out anxiously, his lips still connected to mine.

What the hell?

I reared back and peered into his worried eyes. "I-I don't know Tudor, we've only just got together. Why?" I rubbed my hand over my face. "What do you think?" I asked, my nerves now starting to unravel at his random line of questioning.

He slumped opposite me and grabbed my hands in both of his. "I don't know, Tash. But what I do know is that I'll fight for you, no matter what happens. Do you understand? We may have only just got together, but I have never felt this way about anyone. I just can't wait to be with you, can't wait to be more to you that what I am now, to have figured us out. To have you forever."

I pulled my hands from his hold and placed them both on his face, pulling him in close, tying to find answers in his skittish eyes. "Hey, where is all of this coming from? I've never seen you like this before. You're worrying me."

His sudden panic over our very new relationship status was slightly unnerving to say the least. I would not have expected such a strong reaction from him over a call from a potential date, not at this early stage. If I'm honest, it was all a bit overwhelming.

Tudor's face was strained in tension, his eyes squeezing closed and his skin was growing moist under my palms, his hands low on my hips, grasping me close.

"Tudor, babes, calm down, everything's okay. We will work it out as we go along… don't worry yourself over nothing, it'll be easy." I shrugged my shoulders, trying to reassure him that it all would work out.

He huffed out a dry laugh. "Easy! Being with me is not going to be easy, Tash. I'm always travelling; my fans, or *'Tudor-Chicks'* as they call themselves can be crazy; the media always makes shit up. I'm possessive and at times get angry and I have so much going on in my life, it will be anything but easy. What if I lose you? What if you decide you can't deal with all my baggage? You won't put up with it, will you? You'll eventually see I'm not worth the trouble. You'll cut me loose."

I considered what he said. Could I do this? I at least wanted to try. To me, he *was* worth it, but it was clear there were some big things going on in his life that I couldn't understand and were making him act this way. Why was he so insecure? He had it all: looks, fame and money. Why had he done a complete U-turn from a cool, sullen and strong guy to a trembling mess after a little phone call?

I stood up, putting an end to the charade. "I'm going in the shower, and then we're going out."

"What?" he asked shocked, still perched on his knees in the middle of the bed, agonising over our unwritten future.

"What? I'm not going to sit here and dwell on *why* we will not work out. Worry about *what* can go wrong, *if* we will make it. Instead, I'm going to get ready and we are going on that walk we had planned before you burst through the door, fucked the brains out of me and made me your 'exclusive' girlfriend. Now come on, man, pull yourself around and be ready in fifteen minutes, and *don't* let what Gage said affect you like this. We will be just fine. Have faith, babes."

I walked into my bathroom without a backward glance, hearing a relieved sigh coming from the direction of Tudor, his out-of-left-field meltdown dissipating into a low simmer.

After I had shut and locked the door, I leaned against the hard wood and slumped to the floor, thinking about what Tudor had said. I already liked him too much, and I didn't know him that well at all. I mulled over what that little episode was all about, what it meant. On the one hand it was heartwarming at how highly he thought of me, how much he obviously liked me. But on the other hand, what had caused him to be so needy, so possessive, so scared? What were those pesky demons he had mentioned before in the hot tub? There must be many more pages to that story. By the looks of things, it was *War and Peace*-length and not a sweet little novella.

I must keep the faith.

I was sure Tudor would confide all of his problems when he was ready. It was funny: the thought of not having Tudor caused me pain in my soul even at that early point. How could I feel that way about someone after only a short amount of time? But I did and I had to be patient with him. He obviously needed me – he had made that very obvious.

Keep the faith.

I came out of my bedroom slightly over fifteen minutes later to see Tudor hooked on whatever was on the TV. I was heading to the closet to grab my coat and gloves when I heard his name being mentioned by the glamorous female presenter on screen, who was surrounded by pictures of him at various premieres on a plethora of LCD screens around her. *Heavens above!* He looked amazing in his formal wear.

I walked over to the sofa and sat down, trying to see what had him so enthralled. He was watching the entertainment news, the headline across the bottom reading, *'Where is Tudor North?'*

His tense eyes were fixed on the screen, his knuckles white from gripping the arms of the sofa.

I looked at him, confused, then focused back on the programme to hear what had got him so worked up.

'The question of the month is, 'Where on Earth is Tudor North?' The notorious, muscled bad-boy of the big screen has fallen off the celebrity grid over recent months, and questions are being asked as to where he is and why he's keeping himself so hidden?

We know that Tudor hails from around the Vancouver/Victoria area in Canada, so has the superstar gone back to his roots? Tudor was a firm fixture on the party scene in LA a few years ago, but after a drink-fuelled twelve months, seemed to take a step back from the limelight to focus on his burgeoning movie career. Well folks, he hasn't been spotted in about six months around Tinsel Town and we are anxious to know, why? Has he grown tired of the fame, or has he fallen in love and settled down? He has been linked to several starlets over the years, and we ran into his ex, and some say current, flame, Raquel Banks at the MTV Movie Awards, and this is what she had to say on the subject of Tudor North,

"... Tudor is doing great, we speak all the time. He just needed to get out of the media for a while to rest before the next installment of the 'Blade Reaper' franchise. Tudor and I have history, and let's just say that the flame is still brightly lit, it always will be. I can't tell you where he is, but when I visit him and his family in the next few days I'll tell him you were all asking about him, he'll appreciate the concern. I'll even give him a big kiss from all his fans out there who miss him too!"

'So is he taking time away to rest, and is he still very much involved with the beautiful blonde Raquel? Tudor Chicks –

listen up, we have a mission for you. It is your task to find him and let us know! The lucky fan will win a pair of tickets to the premiere of his next movie and a whole stash of goodies. So, go scout him out, dedicated Tudor Chicks. Are you ready? Set. Go….'

I took a deep breath and slowly rose out of my seat without looking at Tudor. I needed fresh air. I made a dash for the patio, and with each step felt myself suffocating in self-doubt, roles reversed from only minutes earlier.

Is he still with her? I didn't even know he was linked to anyone famous. Oh my God! She's beautiful, what is he doing here with me? Does he still speak to her? Is she the reason for his secrets? Is she why he fought our attraction so much?

I can't breathe.

I realised I was falling into an anxiety attack, my chest grew tight and I began to shake. I heard the patio door open, and Tudor moved in front of me and crouched on his knees. "Tash, breathe," he soothed.

I looked up and saw the anguish in his eyes. I managed to speak in a rushed tone. "Was all that true? Are you with that woman?"

He began pacing. "No, I'm not! She was a fucking mistake I made once a couple of years ago and she has clung to it ever since! She's never been my girl and never will be."

He took a calming breath and moved back to me, taking my hands in his. "Tash, look at me, please."

I did what he asked, staring him straight in his eyes looking for any dishonesty. I couldn't tell.

"I am not with her, have never been in a relationship with her. She was a one-night stand ages ago. She was the biggest leech of them all, selling the *much* exaggerated details of our night together to the highest bidder. Please, don't let this stop us from happening. Talk to me, say you still want this, want us."

He was edging to panic mode again too... *What a pair of crazies!*

"I-I... don't know. Is she the reason you have all the secrets?" My voice sounded strained, even to me.

He shook his head, moisture misting his eyes.

I let out a bitter laugh as I compared the two of us. "Why the hell would you want me when you've had that? Do all of your exes look like her? What have I got myself into? You must have been repulsed sleeping with me last night, seeing me beneath you, on top of you!" I threw my head into my hands.

He groaned loudly and pulled my hands away. "Are you fucking kidding me? You're beautiful and funny, smart and sexy as hell. You have me numbered and don't take my shit. You are worth a million Raquel Banks' and for the last time I. Am. Not. With. Her."

I surveyed him skeptically. It actually would have answered some questions if he was with the girl – the secrets he wouldn't talk about, the weird behaviour, why he pushed our attraction to the side-lines – it would make total sense.

I guessed he could read the doubt on my face. "Believe me, okay, I need you to trust me. These channels fuel gossip and ninety-nine per cent of the time it's untrue. This time it's one-hundred per cent untrue. I want you, Tash, but this is the life I'm in. You have to decide if I'm worth it to you, because you certainly are to me! I know since we've met we have managed to avoid the celebrity shit, but it's there and as much as I wish it wasn't, it is what it is and it's not going anywhere. But I want you to try. I need you to be able to handle all the crap that comes with being with me… please."

He laid his head in my lap, his arms tight around my back. We stayed that way for several minutes.

He *had* told me in advance that being with him wouldn't be easy. He was right, but it had been easy to forget that he was a public figure. I had met him in Calgary while he wasn't shooting a film, I'd never even seen him act and I'd let myself pretend he was normal for a while, but he wasn't, was he?

I was fully aware that our relationship was moving faster than a fat lass out of a slimming club but then, like they always say, when you know, you know, right? There was nothing in the past several months of my new crazy life that I would deem as 'normal', so surely falling for a massively famous, troubled, tattooed 'Bad Boy' could just be part of this parallel universe I had found myself in. For the first time in my life I wanted to be impulsive, I wanted to embark on this roller-coaster ride with Tudor, and I wanted to continue to seize the day.

Tash, just go the hell with it. After all, to live a life with no regrets was surely better than thinking on what could have been, *should* have been. Nobody ever gets to the end of their life and thinks, *'I wish I had lived more cautiously', 'I'm so happy I never tried something new'* or *'I'm glad I let the potential love of my life go because I was too scared to take a chance'.*

So here was the new Tash, the girl who would put her trust in her heart, not her head, and the one that deserved to be loved and gave her love freely to someone who would treasure it. Some people might think it rash and even stupid, but roles reversed, can you honestly say you wouldn't do the same? *Especially* if it meant that you got to ride Tudor North's very talented love-pole for the rest of your days? Multiple orgasms can be a very persuasive factor when deciding to give a guy a chance.

A whisper of a smile reached my lips as I remembered the 'real' side to Tudor, the man and not the celebrity, and the way he cared for me when I was ill. Didn't he deserve a chance? Didn't *we* deserve a chance?

Carpe Diem it is!

I lifted Tudor's head from my lap; his eyes were shut and his body tense, obviously bracing himself for my rejection. I put a hand on either side of his face and drew him to my level. He huffed out a breath and opened his eyes cautiously.

"You can trust me, Tudor, and I will trust you, and in time we can trust each other enough to disclose everything. Now, how about we take that walk?"

He looked at me warily for several seconds before his mouth lifted into a lop-sided smirk and he leaned in to kiss me. He touched his forehead to mine, relief pouring from his wide grin.

"Tudor?"

There was one last thing I needed to tell him, bearing my soul. "Please don't hurt me," I whispered.

He pressed a soft kiss to my lips. "I won't, I promise, I couldn't live with myself if I did."

He stood slowly, taking me with him, and led me back into the warmth of the apartment. He picked up my coat and gloves that had been discarded on the table and helped me into them. Walking to the closet, he reached for his jacket and car keys and held out his hand for me to take.

We began walking towards the door, when he stopped. "Hang on for just a second," he said, and darted to my bedroom.

A few moments later, he came back holding his scarf that he had retrieved from under my pillow. I blushed as he wrapped it around my neck, praying he didn't think I was a stalker, and he kissed me on the tip of my nose,

"You made me yours and I made you mine, we will work if we try hard enough."

I nodded in agreement, and he took my hand and led me out the door.

CHAPTER 22

The Wrath of a Fairy

We drove over an hour out of town to the beautiful Kananaskis National Park. Tudor didn't want to go somewhere busy or local as he wanted to spend all his time with me and not deal with the public. He apparently had just the spot that he wanted to take me, Forget-Me-Not Ridge.

On the journey he never let go of my hand and kissed me at every stop sign, every red light – basically every possible opportunity. He was demonstrating his unrivalled affection towards me after the cluster-fuck that was the lies sprouting from the mouth of that bitch, Raquel Banks.

Arriving at Tudor's chosen location, we climbed out of the car and strolled in silence for what seemed like hours, hand-in-hand, enjoying the peace and the togetherness after the emotional drama of the morning.

He led me to the top of a hill overlooking the Forget-Me-Not pond and I almost cried at the stunning view of the surrounding snowcapped Rocky Mountains. My appreciative gaze drifted over to Tudor; his eyes were closed, head back, breathing in deeply while clutching my hand to his chest. He was smiling. It was perfect. Tudor and me, and no-one getting in the way, not even skinny blonde actresses with a penchant for Tudor-based delusions.

When Tudor finally let me take a break from walking, we took a seat on a bench at one of the isolated vantage points. Snuggling into the crook of Tudor's arm, I drew together all my courage. I needed answers to some questions. I realised I had said yes to Tudor and a relationship very quickly, ignoring all of the times he had dismissed me and upset me. A twelve-hour, mind-blowing sex session can kind of do that to a girl. I probably let the feminist movement down somewhat with my acceptance of Tudor's affections after being treated so badly. I knew he was sorry, his actions more than made up for that, but I needed to talk, to help me figure it all out in my head.

I turned to my new boyfriend, who was already staring at me, rubbing his lips together in worry. I was startled to see him already waiting for me to speak. It was like the boy could read my mind.

"You have an expressive face, remember," he announced sadly.

Goddamnit Tash, you couldn't lie if your life depended on it. Well, here we go, time to forge ahead.

"I need to know why you fought us for so long. Why did you try to push me away? Why didn't you want to be with me?" I said in a rush before I chickened out from asking what I needed to know.

He sighed and glanced away. "I didn't think I was right for you, Tash. I still don't, you are too good for me. I thought if I pushed you away, then you could never want me like I wanted you and the attraction would be mine to deal with, and mine alone. But when I upset you at the pond, it nearly killed me. I freaked. Believe me when I say that you were never the problem, it was my issues that made me act like a fool. I can't even think back to what I said to you, how I made you feel. I knew I'd cave in the end, I wanted you too damn much. You can only fight so long before your heart ultimately defeats your best intentions."

"What issues made you act a fool, Tude?" I pushed.

He hesitated. "I-I... I can't say. It's not another woman, or that I'm embarrassed of you, I don't want you to ever think that. It's complicated, and I can't talk about it, but believe me when I say that I'll protect you from it. Damn it, I want to tell you but I just… can't," he slumped forward in defeat.

I rolled my head back in exasperation. What was his friggin' problem? Why did he have to hide so much?

He read my expression and gripped my hand. "Tash, this won't be forever. Hopefully it will be resolved soon, and I promise you'll know everything. I just can't tell you now, I can't risk it getting out into the public, and before you say it, I know you wouldn't tell anyone, but there's legal shit to deal with and… I just can't risk it. I just don't want you to give up on me." He leaned forward and put his head in his hands.

"Is this secret the reason you're in Calgary?"

He nodded in his hands.

"Is it why you live so close to your family? Why you fought our attraction?"

He nodded once more.

I breathed in the fresh mountain air. *Okay, I get it.* I was not exactly thrilled, but I had to trust him. He was somehow protecting his family. That was something I understood – family first.

"Okay, Tudor. I just want you to know that I'm here for you if, and when, you need to talk. It's early doors for us; we will just take every day as it comes."

He sat back, staring at the reflected trees on the calm surface of the pond, and whispered, "Thank you."

I could see it meant a lot for someone to say that they would accept him, would trust him; the tension immediately left his tight shoulders. He glanced at me, kissed my hand and smiled.

I patted his knee preemptively. The inquisition wasn't over that easily. I had one other question. "You've mentioned before that you lived in LA and you were a bit wild, and the TV report said you had a 'drink-fuelled year' – what the hell happened?"

He wrapped an arm around my shoulders, pulling me in close. "What happened? Fame, money, fans, you name it. The whole nine yards. I remember moving there and thinking that I would never be one of *those* actors, the ones you see falling out of bars, off their face on drugs or drink.

"I was in LA when I received some bad news from back home, the same news I can't tell you about, the same issue that won't fucking die. I went out that night and just drank. I woke up the next day in a strange bed with a girl I didn't know, and that became the pattern. I drank, I fucked, I forgot. It changed when I got a phone call from my mother telling me she'd seen me on TV, completely blitzed, and that she was worried about me and couldn't deal with anything else to cause her stress. I decided that night to leave LA and move back to Vancouver with my family, and as soon as the decision was made, the darkness I had been fighting lifted some, and I've never looked back.

"Raquel happened during that time and capitalised on the fling, she practically prostitutes herself out to other actors to increase her own profile, and I, the drunken sucker that I was, fell straight into her malicious trap. I actually have no memory of that night. I just woke up the next morning in her bed, both of us naked. It makes me sick even thinking about it.

"I'm no longer that lost guy, Tash. But I do have certain troubles following me, but I'm working on them. Some I can control, others I can't. But you will never be harmed, not if I can help it."

I leaned in and kissed him passionately, reassuring him. "Thank you for telling me that."

He shrugged. "Anything to keep you. I feel like you're always one revelation from slipping away, that one day I'll wake up and you'll be done with me, with us, that you will get sick of this life and sick of what being with me entails, and I'm not only talking about the fame, shit, at the moment that's the easy part.

"When we were just friends, the thought of not seeing you again gave me chills, but now that you're finally mine..." he turned his head away from my view.

I nudged his arm playfully and pulled him in for a hug. "You're stuck with me, babes, just deal with it! Plus, my va-jay-jay was pissed at me for my self-imposed celibacy over the past ten months and I'll tell you now, she ain't gonna be too happy if I withdraw the extremely-bankable Tudor-deposits she's received of late. I think she might actually shut down if I do, so you're good for a little while longer while my foof gets her fill."

His mouth dropped open, for a few seconds before barking out in hysterics, causing a deep rumbling echo around the ridge.

"Now, let's go. I'll race you back down the hill, emo-boy," and I took off, running to the footpath, squealing as I heard Tudor chasing behind me.

He caught me at the bottom and spun me around, making me dizzy. He was laughing so hard. When I shouted "Mercy", he placed me down in front of him and kissed me slowly, his hands braced on my head.

He broke the kiss and walked in front of me, then bent down slightly and looked back. "Hop on."

Well, he didn't have to ask me twice! I took a run, and jumped onto his back and he hoisted me up into a piggyback. I wrapped my arms around his neck and laid a loud smack of a kiss on his cheek.

I loved this playful side of Tudor. He began running, making me bounce around and nearly caused me to fall off his back. We were laughing so much that we didn't notice the group of teenage girls just in front of us, eyes glued to our little game. Tudor held on to my legs firmly and edged around the girls, heading in the direction of the Jeep. We heard some gasps and giggling, but Tudor kept his stride fast and never looked back. I did sneak a glance however, and noticed several iPhones being played with, but none pointing were in our direction, so I assumed we'd got by unrecognised.

We made it back to the car as the sun began to set over the hazy mountains, and Tudor opened the door for me to slip inside. He jumped in the driver's seat and leaned over to peck my cheek, seeming somewhat lighter than a few hours before. The engine roared to life and we pulled away from the parking lot at lightning speed.

As we were driving out of the exit I saw him smirking. "What are you so smiley about?"

He cast a smarmy look my way. "The day is almost done. I gave you the day to recover."

I felt the butterflies in my stomach and squirmed on the heated seat. Seeing this, he placed a hand on my upper thigh, teasing me further. I sighed in frustration. "Tudor?"

"Mmm-hmm?" He pretended to be unaffected.

"Drive faster!"

"Yes, Ma'am!"

The elevator ride was a blur, and I have no recollection of actually parking the jeep or opening the condo door. I do, however, remember Tudor shredding my outerwear at a ridiculously fast pace, pushing me against the wall and yanking down my jeans and underwear.

"Tudor, what—?"

"Here, now. The bedroom can wait," he demanded.

His jeans and boxers joined my discarded clothing on the floor, and I pictured in my head what we must look like: our top halves partially clothed, bottom halves naked, Tudor's bare arse on display and my thighs wrapped tightly around his waist, guiding him straight towards me.

Before I could argue, Tudor took me against the hard wall, my shoulder blades burning from the friction. He showed his strength by lifting me over and over while kissing me roughly, causing me to moan loudly.

I zoned out, lost in the crazy wall-sex, and didn't notice the front door opposite fling open. "Honey I'm hom-! *Arghhhhh!!! What the hell!!!*"

I opened my eyes and looked straight at a shell-shocked Tink.

Shit!

I frantically tapped Tudor's shoulder. "Tudor, stop, *stop!*"

He hadn't heard the squealing fairy and carried on regardless, his jerky hip movements tilting with perfect aim, making me groan and roll my eyes back in pleasure, determined to make me scream.

"My eyes, my eyes! I can't see! I'm blind, blind, I tell you, blind!" wailed Tink as he ran past us and into the living area.

Tudor heard that one and stilled, meeting my horrified eyes. "Tash? Shit! Is that Tink?"

I nodded quickly. I wriggled loose from Tudor's hold and bent to grab my jeans, throwing them on as quickly as I could, trying to ignore the persistent howling coming from the sofa. Tudor did the same, blushing profusely in embarrassment at being caught.

In the living room, I stood before the dramatic Geordie queen thrashing about on a mound of pink silk cushions.

"Oh, my Gods of glitter! My eyes are ruined by that hetero-horror scene! How will I ever remove the images? I'm going to have nightmares for months. I need therapy! Get me a doctor!" He raised his head from the throw cushion and saw me standing there, arms folded, tapping my foot. "And he's paying for it." Tink continued, pointing exaggeratedly towards Tudor.

"My delicate eyes can't handle what I've just seen. Get the eye drops; I need to wash away the straight! *Arghhh!* How can I go on…?" He sat up abruptly, looking around the room at a frantic pace, and started retching. "Quick somebody show me a picture of Channing Tatum, check I'm still gay!"

"Okay, enough!" I shouted.

Tink stood and stomped past me to the kitchen, knocking my shoulder with his as he passed. He withdrew the industrial-sized bottle of anti-bacterial spray from the cupboard and practically sprinted towards the recently abused wall, spraying frantically at the paintwork.

Tudor stealthily moved to stand next to me, pulling my back to his chest and laid his chin on my shoulder, watching the show. Tink turned, one hand on his hip, and marched toward us.

Staring me straight in the face, he stopped, raised his perfectly-waxed HD eyebrow and proceeded to spray my crotch with Dettol, until I knocked the bottle out of his hands.

"What are you doing?!!!" I screeched, trying to shake off the excess liquid from my nether regions.

His arms flailed in the air. "Me??? I'm trying to sanitise this rancid sex pit! Now get to the shower, missy. I have a bumper pack of douches waiting on you!"

He began pulling at my arm to get me out of Tudor's grip.

"Hey!" Tudor reached back out and tugged me back towards him.

Tink jerked at my other arm more vigorously. "Back off you big anabolic steroid, she needs fumigating due to the salty invasion of your Herman Von Long-schlong!"

Tudor snatched me back, putting himself in front of my chest. "Are you being serious?" He swerved back to me. "Is he being serious?"

I sighed. "Unfortunately, yes."

I walked around to Tudor's side, just in time to see Tink reach behind him for the remote control and fall back into a fencing position, challenging my new lover: remote arm out, left arm in the air. "Come on, you bulky bull, I'll take you. *En garde!*"

Tink began shuffling his feet forward and Tudor just stood lock still, absolutely dumbfounded at Tink's standard over-the-top-antics.

The fencing fairy lunged forward and began stabbing relentlessly at Tudor's hard stomach with the end of the remote, his only accomplishment being to turn the TV on and off at an alarming speed.

Tudor was watching Tink in amazement as he made '*Hi-yah!*' sounds and twisted his wrists to vary his shots and angles. I walked behind the prancing idiot, picked him up by the waist and spun with him in my arms, dumping him on the couch.

"*Wil,* you bitch!" Tink shrilled, jumping up and storming off to his room, but not before stabbing me in the thigh with the remote.

"Owww, witch! What the hell?" I seethed.

He put on a cocky smile from his doorway. "Not sorry, porky!" he yelled, and flipped me his middle finger, before slamming the door shut with gusto.

I groaned and dropped down onto the couch, joined seconds later by Tudor. "What the hell just happened?" he asked, in disbelief.

I looked straight ahead and shrugged. "Tink's pissed; he finds straight sex offensive to his delicate disposition."

"Wow," whispered Tudor.

I nodded silently. We sat there for about five minutes before either of us spoke.

"What do we do now?" Tudor asked, stroking my cheek.

I patted his thigh. "Oh, just sit tight, His Majesty will be making a second appearance soon enough. This is far from over. He likes to keep us waiting to make his finale all the more dramatic."

He moved closer and laid his head on my lap. "Well, I'm settling in for the night then."

I stroked his head, staring at the fireplace.

After an hour of waiting for His Royal Highness to come out of his grand chamber, Tinkerbell finally breezed into the living area, chin tilted high, coming to a stop directly in front of us. Tudor had fallen into a light sleep and I was still caressing his head on my lap.

"Babes, wake up, Tink is ready to read us the riot act," I whispered quietly whilst shaking his shoulder lightly.

Tink waved his hand around dismissively in response to me calling Tudor *'Babes'*. As if he could talk – Pookie and Tater-Tot, *really?*

Tudor got up slowly, all sorts of gorgeous as he wiped the sleep from his eyes with both hands. Once he had pulled himself around, he took my hand and quickly pecked a kiss to my mouth, then sat back, awaiting the expected rant. Tink watched the little display of affection, his mouth gaping in outrage.

I shuffled forward. "Before you start harping on at us, I just want to say that, in our defense, you were not due back until tomorrow, and that you just happened to come back at a bit of an awkward moment."

"Too bloody right I did! I came back early to check you were over your illness. Seems you were over that alright and jumped straight *under* him!"

He moved to sit on the edge of the coffee table only three feet away from the couch and crossed his legs and arms. "*So*, when did this little development happen, huh?" he barked, waving his hand around camply.

I looked down at our entwined hands and started to speak, but Tudor beat me to it. "Officially yesterday, but you could say it has been building for several weeks."

My bestie started waggling one finger like he would if he were on *Ricki Lake*. "Weeks? All I have seen is her upset or pining after you. You've been leading her on then fucking her off most of the time. You made her like you – a lot, I might add – and then you would drop her like a sack of last week's potatoes! Is that what you call 'building'? Fuck knows what foreplay would be to you then!" he shrieked.

Tudor tensed up, bowing his head. I had to intervene. "Tink, Tudor's apologised and I've forgiven him, he's explained what happened and you have to let it go. Please,

I want my best friend to support me in this," I reached forward and took his hand. He snatched it back, wiping it on his shirt as though it were infected. Mature as ever.

"Just because he apologised doesn't mean he won't screw you over. For God's sake, Wil, he says he's sorry and you open your Wendy-wide legs and let him shag you – hell, not shag, bloody roast you! He had you pinned between the wall and his red-hot poker like you were impaled on a frigging spit; you're only missing the butter and seasoning and you'd legitimately be barbeque! *And* you did it against my walnut-whip designer paint of all things! $500 a pot, Wil, $500 – it's fucking imported!"

I lowered my head in defeat, and Tudor leaned in to comfort me. I couldn't help it, I began to cry. As much as my over-the-top queen and I squabble, it's always just friendly banter. This was him really telling me what for. He was really angry – granted, it was mostly because of the paint, but it still felt like shit. How could I start a relationship with someone when my best friend, my soul mate, didn't approve?

I tucked my head into the comfort of Tudor's large chest and let the floodgates open. I pressed my head against his shirt, knowing that if I had to choose, at this point it would have to be Tink, but the pain it would cause me, knowing what could have been with Tudor, caused me to feel nauseous. I could fall in love with this man, hell, who was I kidding? I *was* falling in love with him, it *had* been building for weeks. It had been growing steadily every day since the morning of my concussion, and now that we were officially together, it was intensifying ten-fold. I couldn't help my feelings.

I heard Tudor draw a ragged breath, and looked up to see his sad eyes and him shaking his head, resigned. He kissed a falling tear on each side of my face and pressed his forehead to mine. "I won't come between you and Tink, Sunshine. I'll give you some time and see you again when it's all calmed down, okay? Look at me."

I met his gaze and shook my head; I didn't want him to leave.

"Hey, I'm not giving you up, but I'm not going to wreck a life-long friendship either. You made me yours, remember? I told you you're stuck with me."

I nodded silently, soaking my cheeks with salty droplets. Tudor moved in to give me a slow, deep kiss, and got up from the couch.

I watched him walk away, before he stopped and faced Tink. "I know you don't like me much, and I am the first to admit that my past behaviour with Tash has been horrendous and unforgivable and therefore I understand, but just know that I would do anything for her. I can't give her up, not now.

"It is my deepest wish that you and I, at some point, can move past this and be friends too. You're the boyfriend of my best friend, and I'm now the boyfriend of yours. I know you would like me if you just gave me a chance, and I hope you realise that I will never do anything to hurt Tash ever again, and us fighting is hurting her more than anything. So I'll go and let you work this out."

Tudor gave me a final strained, lopsided smirk and made his way to the door. I turned to Tink, whose bottom lip was shaking. I smiled at my bloody daft best friend. "*Tink.*"

His face crumpled and he started to cry hysterically, like only Tink can.

He dived to the couch and began to wail. "I'm sorry, piglet. I thought I was protecting you but I'm hurting you, aren't I?"

I gripped him tightly in a hug. "You are protecting me, but Tudor won't hurt me, you have to trust that too. I really like him, chuck, like, Elton John and David Furnish-style like him; I'm even going so far as to say that I'd pick him over your treasured Mother Monster Gaga at this point."

Tink swooned, complete with hand on head, and fell off the couch at my confession, fanning his face with the Madonna Sex Book we keep on the table for visiting guests to peruse.

After receiving some much-needed air, he staggered to his feet, casually licking Madonna's protruding nipple on an open page, and put his hand on my knee. "Wil, I didn't realise it was that serious, not so much that you'd renounce your Little Monster status to keep him! By all the glitter in Hobbycraft, I've been blind! Blinded by my prejudice towards the big, tattooed Canuck, but now I see you were born to be together!"

Over the top as always!

Tink released a blood-curdling shriek and ran to the doorway where Tudor was just leaving. "Tudor, come here, you big brute!" and he wrapped his arms around Tudor's neck, crying (or singing – the jury's still out) loudly, dangling off him like a necklace.

Tudor, looking very deer-in-the-headlights, glanced towards me, seeking some help. I started to laugh and gave him a thumbs-up that made him smile, and he awkwardly patted Tink on the back.

The dedicated Little Monster pulled back, all smiles. "We're now friends, big boy, but hurt my little tenderloin over there and we're gonna throw-down! *Capisce*?"

Tudor slapped his back and winked. "*Capisce*!"

Tink tilted his head to me, "Wilbur, get involved... group hug!" he sang.

I ran over and wrapped an arm around each of my guys. Tink kissed us both on the cheek and drew back. "Just so you know, I don't wanna see any more wall-fucking in the condo hallway, but feel free to spit-roast Wilbur's hungry beaver in the comfort of her bedroom."

We hid the laughter.

"You have my word," assured Tudor awkwardly.

Tink pursed his lips, accepting his promise. Just as we were breaking away from the hug, Tudor jumped, his face horrified. "He just nipped my ass!"

Tink held up his hand, *"Guilty!* And it certainly is a fine one. Thank the God's for squats! I may not want to see you porking my bestie in a live sex show, but feel free to walk round with that spank-bank-worthy tush-tush out on display… just don't bend over, 'cos then you're fair game!"

CHAPTER 23

Calling Sherlock Holmes...

If someone had told me at the beginning of the year that by November I would have a new boyfriend, live in another country and, oh yeah, that the new boyfriend would be a-hunk-a-hunk-o'-burning-superstar, well, I'd have told them to bugger off and back away from whatever substance they had been sniffing!

But here we were, in that exact situation. Tudor and I were officially a couple, and we had spent the last few weeks in a blissful and lust-filled state. Tink too was flying around on a very legal high and becoming more than a little in love with Tater-Tot. We had even developed our own little clique, the 'Four-Ts'.

But like all good things – L'Oreal's Shocking Volume Waterproof Mascara, Cadbury Crème Eggs after Easter and the perfect display that was Jennifer Aniston and Brad Pitt's marriage, to name but a few – it had to come to an end, and we were heading up Shit's Creek at a rapid speed without a paddle.

It was the last week of term in December, only four days of school left before the Christmas vacation, when the phone calls began and my loving boyfriend began to change.

Tink, Tate, Tudor and I were out at Ristorante Girasoli (once again hidden in the back room) enjoying dinner when my man received yet another mysterious call. Up until that point I had not really questioned who they were from, as Tudor had assured me that I could trust him. I assumed it was his "people" in LA talking business and then I quickly changed my mind. The problem was that he would not give me *any* information on the matter whenever I asked him, and my inner Miss Marple suspicions were aroused.

When the ringtone sounded, and he lost the 'nice-Tudor' personality I adored and adopted the 'bastard-Tudor' I was once victim to, I stilled and prodded Tink's leg under the table to give him a heads up. I had confided in Tink about the strange goings-on of late, and this was the first public call Tudor had gotten, the first opportunity for someone other than me to witness.

Tink winked once to let me know he was paying attention, and we listened as we ate our *carprese*.

"Hello… yeah, shit, okay… no I'll be there…when… no, I'll be alone… no, no-one, nothing special… yeah, I'll call you soon."

Tudor never once made eye contact with anyone during the conversation and when he was finished he slammed his phone down onto the table top, practically splitting the wood in two.

I stared at Tink, who had his eyes narrowed in suspicion. Tate's head was cast down and he was fiddling with his hands.

I cleared my throat. "Tude, are you okay?" I swallowed back the fear I felt brewing in my stomach.

"What?" he snapped.

I drew back at his aggressive tone. His manner was overtly hostile – whatever the problem was, it seemed to be getting worse.

"She asked if you were alright!" Tink bit back, defensive hackles rising.

Tudor rubbed his hand over his face and looked my way. "Yeah, I'm fine, just stop asking." He was cold and distant.

"Who was that?" I dared ask. I was *over* not knowing.

He whipped his head up to look at me and sternly shook his head. He stood abruptly, discarding his napkin on his barely-touched food and reached for his hooded leather coat, motioning to Tate that it was time to leave.

"I need to go. I'll call later, okay?" He leaned forward and brushed a meaningless kiss across my forehead.

"You're just going to leave? Leave us sitting here like numpties?" I spat out. Tudor was annoyed, and groaned in exasperation, eying Tink warily. "Tash, I need to go. Can you just get a ride back with Tink, please? This is not the time or the place to start with the questions again."

Well, that told me!

I threw down my own napkin and crossed my arms. "Fine, just bloody go then!" I turned to Tink. "Come on, chuck, I've suddenly lost my appetite."

I grabbed my bag from the back of my chair and stood, linking arms with my fabulous fairy, and stormed past Tudor. Tink tutted, clicked a finger in Tudor's face, blew a kiss at Tate, but kept up with my pace.

Tudor turned to us, trying to catch my sleeve with his hand. "Tash, please, I have to go but—"

I put up a hand. "But let me guess, you can't tell me why?"

He opened his mouth several times like he was trying to explain, but no words popped out.

I nodded once. "Thought so. Let's just go, Tink."

"Mmm... hmm. Let's split like a banana, Toots!"

By the time I had got to the car, I was shaking with anger, literally bouncing in the passenger seat with fury. I turned to Tink. "What the hell was all that about? I told you the phone calls seemed dodgy. Has Tate said anything lately about what's going on? Even just a hint?"

He shook his head. "No, not a peep! But I agree, how weird was that? Who d'you think called him? 'Cos whoever it was has royally pissed him off."

I shrugged. "I don't know. You know, over the last week he's been getting these phone calls at all hours, and every time I ask who it is he just tells me not to worry and to just 'trust him'."

Tink pulled out of the parking lot. "And do you? Trust him, I mean?"

We watched as Tate and Tudor got into the Jeep and sped away in the opposite direction.

"I think I do, but what can be so bad that he can't talk about it?"

Tink hunched his shoulders and silence filled the car for several blocks.

"Tink, did you hear him say 'No-one, nothing special'…you… you don't think he was referring to me, do you?"

He dismissed my comment with the wave of his hand. "Are you kidding? You've hardly been apart for the last few weeks. You've spent more time with him lately than most couples do in months. I think we can safely say that you definitely are someone special to him."

I sighed in relief.

Look, let me just put in my two cents worth so you know where I stand. I am not a needy girlfriend; I do not need to know every aspect of my boyfriend's life. I do however feel that I should at least gain some insight when something weird starts going on. At this point, I would have even been happy to just know how he was feeling in himself, but Tudor was keeping me at arm's length, pushing me back like the pose on the friggin' Heisman Trophy.

I'm an independent woman *('throw your hands up at me...')* and like having my own space. Equally, I thought Tudor should have his, but I was nearing my breaking point. I thought he would've confided something by now, but in between the ridiculous amounts of sex and the shower-storms of affection he had been throwing my way, he had been cold and distant, leaving no room for discussion and certainly not acting like the man I had come to know.

Tink put a hand on my knee and squeezed it gently. "Look, my greasy Bacon Buttie, you have two choices: you trust him like he has asked, or you decide you don't like the secrets and make your mind up from there. Sorry to be brutal, Wil, but demz the breaks!" I hit my head back against the head rest. "I know, I guess I'll have to trust him then, won't I? I don't want to give him up over something that may be nothing in the end, right?"

He nodded in agreement. "Right, and I don't blame you for keeping your claws into that hunk of prime cut beef... I'd like to carve me off a slice of that if he was eating on the same side of the table!"

I cracked a smile and Tink tapped my thigh. "There you go, I hate to see you doubting what you have, sausage."

Tudor didn't come over that night. I received a brief text message to say he was staying at home – the first time apart in weeks. I had never been to his place; I knew it was in an affluent area near Aspen but I had never visited, and he had never invited me either. I had always put that down to wanting to keep our relationship secret from Boleyn, and that I understood, but I was beginning to wonder…was I being kept on the sidelines? I tried not to read too much into it and just went straight to bed, not sleeping, and trying not to obsess over the ever-growing mountain of secrets.

The next morning, I went about my usual Sunday routine, planning to stay at home and get the last of my pupils' work marked before the Christmas break. I was halfway through a mammoth stack of essays on the causes of the Russian Revolution when I heard the doorbell. I headed to the door and opened it slowly to Tudor, who I noticed looked slightly, shall we say, stressed.

"Hey," I greeted, my brows pinched in concern at his sad demeanour and unkempt look. His clothes were heavily creased and his eyes looked tired and dull.

"Hey," he sounded morose.

I let him in and led him to the kitchen. "Coffee?"

He nodded, and I set to making it how he liked it – flavoured cream with sweetener, fact fans – and poured him a cup. For the first time in our 'official relationship there was tension.

I took a seat next to him at the breakfast bar and turned down the volume on the small kitchen flat-screen so we could talk.

He looked down at his mug and played with the handle before lifting his head to meet my assessing gaze. "Tash, about yesterday, I-I shouldn't have just left like that."

I expected more of an explanation, but none came. I took a deep breath. "Is that it? No 'I left because of this' or 'the person on the phone was…'? Nothing? All I'm getting is just 'I shouldn't have left'?"

He gritted his teeth at my response. "Yes, I shouldn't have left so abruptly, it wasn't right."

I tutted and went to pour more coffee from the pot – I was going to need it!

Tudor's phone dinged, and he began pressing buttons, replying to someone's text. When he put it back in his pocket I slammed my mug down on the breakfast bar. "And who was that?"

"No-one," he said, avoiding my eyes.

"Oh, so you're texting no-one? Really? Mr. Invisible sends you a message, and you reply back with a blank screen?"

He looked at me snarling. "Don't be sarcastic, Natasha."

Oh, I'm Natasha when I'm being reprimanded, but Sunshine when I'm in the sack and sucking on his dick! Nice to know!

"I'll be anything I bloody want! Who do you keep calling? It's making me nervous, Tude. I hate to sound so stereotypical, but is it another girl?"

He recoiled back on the chair, hurt written all over his face. "What? Do you really think that?"

Deep down, I really didn't, but what else was I supposed to think? I threw my hands in the air. "I don't know, okay?! You won't bloody let me in! You've been getting calls in the middle of the night, you never take me to your house, I don't even know *exactly* where you live, after a month of being together, and you are evading every single question I have about your mystery caller. Your mother doesn't know we are together, we never go out, and if we do, it is never out in public and you are acting so incredibly weird. What do you expect me to think?" I was getting irate.

"I expect you to trust me, especially now," he stated calmly.

"Yeah, trust. You want me to trust you but *you* won't trust *me* with what it is that's bothering you. Bit of a double standard don't you think?"

He held out his hand, his face looking torn. I hated seeing him like this, but I had to know what was going on. I stared at his outstretched hand. "Tash, please. Come here."

I reluctantly moved over to Tudor, and he pressed me to his chest, kissing my hair and pulling me up on his lap. "Don't lose faith in me, Sunshine, please. Just trust me on this. It won't be forever."

I drew back, taking hold of his face, searching his eyes for… something, anything, some kind of divine sign.

"Trust you with what?"

He glanced down, then up at me through damp lashes. "Protecting you."

"Protecting me? From what, babes? What should I be scared of?" I placed a hand on his cheek. It was cold and pale.

He shook his head, drawing my hand back down to kiss my palm. "Trust me," he whispered, and pulled me back into his embrace, running a hand over my head like he was relishing any time we had left together.

We stayed like that for a long time, until I was abruptly thrust back to a standing position as Tudor jumped from his chair and ran over to turn up the volume on the TV. When I looked to the screen, there was a full-sized shot of me and Tudor from our walk a few weeks ago at Forget-Me-Not Ridge. I was on his back and we were laughing. I smiled to myself; we looked very happy. However, my warm and fuzzy moment was interrupted when my oh-so-romantic boyfriend started screaming expletives and pacing from one side of the kitchen to the other while listening to the presenter, a ridiculously thin and bronzed anchorwoman who was enthusiastically sharing the details.

'Well done, Tudor Chicks. We have managed to find the missing Tudor North, and in Calgary, Canada, of all places! What he's doing there is a mystery. This photo was taken by Melissa Brown, who happened to be in Kananaskis National Park a couple of weeks ago. She claims that her attention was caught by the flirtations and affectionate games of this couple and she followed them back to Cowtown after realising who it was. The man is none other than 'The Blade Reaper' himself,

Mr. North, but the bigger question is: who is the girl? Sources say that she is not in the business, but it is clear that Tudor looks quite smitten with this voluptuous beauty. Could this be a real-life Canadian 'Notting Hill' storyline? We are on tenterhooks waiting for a statement from Tudor's people, but have no doubt that the news to come back is that the infamous Tudor 'Bad Boy' North is officially off the market. Pictures in this case really are worth a thousand words!'

Tudor was pacing, panicking, and just plain freaking out! "Fuck! Why now?" he bellowed.

Howay, man! I know you're private, but this reaction is a bit over-the-top!

I moved over to where Tudor was creating a worn-out patch on my pristine and much-treasured marble flooring and stopped the nauseating back-and-forth movement by holding his huge, two-hundred-and-fifty-pound frame in my arms. "Tudor, it's fine, they would find out at some point anyway. At least now we can live a somewhat open life. Is it so bad if we announce it to the world?"

He just stared at me, face blank, and pulled out his phone. He quickly dialed a number and left me standing, facing him with a questioning expression.

"Kate, have you seen the entertainment news?" Kate, his publicist. "I want you to issue a statement today about my romantic status, do you have a pen?"

There was a pause, and I couldn't help but smile to myself. OMG! Tense arguments be damned! In a few short hours the whole world would know about my relationship with Tudor. This was crazy, but maybe it would make everything better. Maybe all the problems had been stemming from him trying to keep us a secret, and once it was all in the open he would go back to being my sweet, loving Tudor and all would be okay?

Gosh! My mam was going to flip. I jumped up on the stool and sipped at my coffee, waiting anxiously to hear the way he would 'out' us, show the world we belonged to each other. I couldn't keep the huge grin off my face.

Rose Tint My World!

"Okay, I want you to squash it, deny it," he snapped into the mouth piece.

Yeahhh – Wait, what???

"Tell them that she is a family friend and we were just messing about. I was in Calgary to prepare for my next movie, but have left. Say, I don't know, that I was there for research or some shit. I met her here and only saw her a few times – in fact say she is in a relationship with someone else, my friend from University, and she was visiting him. Her name and credentials are not important, and there is no story so not to bother delving into it. Tell them that I am casually dating, or some spin like that, but there is no-one special. Shit, I don't care, fluff up the Banks story or something, she won't deny it, and she'll want the publicity! Just… get them off the scent. You got all that? Yeah, get it out immediately."

He hung up. *What. The. Fuck???*

Tudor turned to face me, his face torn with anguish. My grin had slipped into a grimace. I felt like I couldn't breathe. He held out his hands in a placating gesture. "Tash…"

"Just get out," I barely whispered, a tsunami of devastation washing over me, crushing my throat and all ability to speak.

"No, Tash, wait…" He tried to reach for me.

I slapped his hand away weakly, shaking. "I *said*, get out!" I finally stated at an audible volume, tears tumbling from my eyes.

"No! No, Sunshine, you need to listen to me. I said those things so they don't come here looking for pictures of us, for a story. Tash, please. I need you, don't send me away… not now, I need you more than ever. I can't do this without you."

I was breathing hard, labored and wheezing, like I'd just run the freakin' London Marathon. I guess a total thrashing of your heart will do that to you. "How could you?" I whispered, gripping the counter to keep myself upright.

He picked me up like a doll and placed me on the table top, caging me in his arms, forcing me to listen. "Tash, I can't have the media here now. I don't want a friggin' circus when we have just started out. Please, this changes nothing, I still want you. You have to believe me."

I let out a bitter laugh. "You're just embarrassed by me. I get it. Fuck the chunky normal girl, someone to pass the time with between movies, someone no-one would *ever* believe you would be with, and then go back to the glitz and glam and bloody Raquel Banks! The freakin' Barbie to your overdosed-on-protein-shake Ken!"

"No! I don't even believe you think that! And for the last God-damned time I am not embarrassed by you. Quite the opposite in fact; you're the best thing in my life! Give me time and I'll shout it from the rooftops that you're my girl, but not now, not yet!"

"Why? Why not now?"

"Trust me, Tash. Just not now!" His voice was gaining volume once again.

"You told Kate to insinuate you were dating Raquel Banks. What the hell? I thought you hated her? Was that a lie too?"

He pushed away from the counter, throwing the dish towel off the table across the room. *"Argh!* To get them away from here and away from *you*, to get the spotlight off *you*. Are you not listening to me? She's a fame whore, she'll play it up, give them a hook – she's cannon fodder, that's all."

"Why is it so bad to admit to being with me? I'm a big girl, I can handle it, believe me. I've taken on a practically unbeatable cancer diagnosis and won; I have fucked-up hormones but deal with it. What's a few paparazzi and psycho blonde Twiglets compared to that? I know my shortcomings, Tudor. I'm not naïve, but I am also super proud of who I am. You will be hard-pressed to find anyone better than me, especially when it comes to you. I adore you, I fucking worship the ground you walk on. I just want to be with you without the lies and secrets. I at least deserve that much. I want happiness in my life. I want the fairy-tale happily ever after… I want it with you." My voice was laced with hurt.

He stroked my cheek. "You are strong and brave, you blow my mind every day and I completely adore you too – you have no idea – but are you listening to me, Tash? It's not bad admitting being with you, I'm simply protecting you. We will get our happily ever after, but it can't be public, yet."

"*Why? What are you protecting me from?*" I groaned.

If I have to ask that question one more time…

He paused, pinching the bridge of his nose, controlling his emotions, debating what to tell me. He eventually sighed and bowed his head in defeat. "I'm gonna go, give you time to cool down. I'll see you soon okay." He tried to kiss my cheek as he moved past.

I pulled away. "See yourself out."

I could feel him staring at me, willing me to face at him, but I couldn't . I couldn't look him in the way he wanted, I thought I would break if I did.

He rubbed his hands over his pale unshaven cheeks and swiftly left, slamming the door for effect.

CHAPTER 24

The Fall of the Tudor Reign

Now what's a girl to do when she's feeling low and unloved? That's right, I hit the gym and worked out my frustrations.

Yeah, right!

I hit the cupboards, brought out as many things containing chocolate I could find and watched my much-loved DVD of *Wuthering Heights,* featuring Tom Hardy as Heathcliff, on the sofa decked in my (somewhat fitting) snug piggy onesie. I sat there for hours, wallowing in misery, and found myself screaming at Cathy to ditch Heathcliff as a friend or otherwise, that he was wrong for her, that he would ruin her with all his schizophrenic actions and broodiness, that she should just love Edgar Linton, have a nice loving life with Edgar Linton. No matter how much I screamed at the screen, Cathy didn't listen to me and my fantastic advice – even in death she chose the heavily-tattooed and muscly Tom Hardy interpretation of Heathcliff. Why do women always go for the bad boys? Can't live with them, can't live without them.

Oh My God!

I bolted upright, crushing chocolate wrappers under my ever-expanding arse as it dawned on me. *I* was Cathy and Tudor was Heathcliff, just instead of moors in Yorkshire we had condos in Calgary! Shit a brick! Kate Bush should be crooning about Mr. Tribal Tattoo and his perpetually confused curvy tit-bit!

Tink came in a few hours later and gasped at the amount of wrappers spread around my comatose and sugar-ravished body. After blowing a kiss and slapping his arse at Tom Hardy on the screen, he proclaimed, "Well, toss my greens and call me Caesar!" and started to wade through the sea of rubbish to reach me.

"What's he done?"

I groaned at the chocolate-induced sickness swirling in my bloated stomach. "He's issued a statement on this fine winter day telling the world that we are not together, that I'm a friend he met only briefly while prepping for a movie or some shit like that. How fucking splendid! And how was your day, darling?"

Tink squished next to me on the couch and looked at me wearily, "I saw the photo, Prosciutto."

That snapped me out of it. "And?"

"And I've already spoken to Tudor. He called me a couple of hours ago, worrying about you and the way you were feeling when he left. He explained that he had issued a denial statement, but that he was doing it to protect you, and that we were not due to cash in our *'You dare hurt Tash and we'll throw down'* deal just yet."

I sighed. "Did he tell you what he was protecting me from?"

He shook his head. "Tate reckons that Tudor is having a tough time at the moment, like, sandpaper-rough; like, non-moisturised-face-in-a-harsh-winter-rough; like, a-Northern-lass-on-the-walk-of-shame-rough; like–," I ignored the rest of Tink's beautiful analogies.

"Then why won't he explain things to me?"

He moved in for a cuddle. "Look, Wil, I love you, and I see how Tudor is with you. It makes me happy to see you together now. If he says he is keeping things from you for your sake, I'd be inclined to let it go. I wouldn't stand by and let him hurt you without issuing him a bitch slap if I thought he was being malicious and cruel."

I huffed and rammed a whole Cadbury's Dairy Milk bar into my mouth – *I know, talented aren't I?* "Easier said than done!" I mumbled through my full mouth.

"Well, keeping things from the ones you love is difficult, but sometimes if you think it's for the best, you go with that option." he said with conviction.

"Oh yeah? And how would you know, gobshite?"

He laid a hand over his chest, mouth open. "Erm… hello! Gay-boy present. I was so far back in the closet to my family, I was living in Narnia! I met the Snow Queen but out-bitched her, stole all of her Turkish Delight and ravaged Mr. Tumnus, ruining him for all other fawns!"

"Fine, you do get it... but didn't you feel better when you shared your secret?"

"Well, no-one believed me at first back in war-torn England, but then Aslan the lion—"

"Tink!"

He pursed his lips to stop from smirking. "Okay, okay! Did I feel better for coming out to the sperm and egg donors? Me, yes, I felt relieved; did they feel better? No. I was friggin' shipped off to a gay turn-around camp, and even though I found the pleasures of the oral and anal variety there, I don't know. I now think that sometimes keeping a secret may be better in the long run... for certain people. Let me tell you first hand, when someone you love so much rejects you after you've struggled for so long with such a heavy secret, that is no fault of your own, well – it crushes you. Tudor may be scared of your reaction to his issues; he needs to tell you in his own time and you need to let him."

I narrowed my eyes. "Since when did you become the wise one?"

He shrugged and batted his Hollywood Lash extensions. "I'm like a fit fookin' Yoda, only I'm tangerine-tan orange and have near-perfect syntax! Oh, and I don't think Tudor's secret is of the homo persuasion, FYI. My internal gay-dar didn't ping when I met him. My anaconda-sized treasured Sergeant Stiffy did, but that was simply in appreciation of his fine muscles."

He never fails!

"Good to know. I'm not sure I could handle two queens in my life." I said playfully, my heart feeling less heavy.

"Pisht! Everything's shinier with a bit of glitter!" he sang while throwing invisible fairy dust over the room.

"Yep, okay, for once I agree." I laughed then breathed a deflated sigh.

Tink threw an arm around my shoulders. "What's up, buttercup? You still look blue," he said with a frown.

"I just loathe frickin' secrets, they cock everything up! You'd better not be hiding anything from me. I can't handle anything else."

He coughed and removed his arm from our embrace. I shuffled to face him, "What? Why are you suddenly being so weird?" I asked, beginning to worry.

"If I'm being weird it'll probably just be the hormones."

"What? Hormones?"

He crouched down next to me, knees on the carpet, taking my hands in his perfectly-manicured ones. "Wil, I've been keeping a pint-sized porkie too." His face was so serious that I clutched his fingers tight.

"Oh my God, Tink, what is it? You're scaring me," I whispered, my heart beginning to race.

"Wil…" He drew in a shaky breath and tears filled his eyes. "It's a shock but…"

"But what???" I squeaked.

"… I'm… I'm… pregnant!"

I threw away his hands. *Prick!* "Tink!" I screamed in annoyance.

He put his hands on his hips. "Hey, can I help it if Tatey's super-sperm has defied science?"

I pursed my lips together as he moved to the floor-length mirror in the hall and felt his 'bump', before I burst out laughing.

He ran over to me diving next to me on the sofa. "Ah-ha, she smiles!!!" he shouted and pulled me in for a snuggle. "For what it's worth, sausage, I think you should trust him."

I sighed. "I'll try."

"That's all he wants."

I nudged him in his ribs. "Since when did you stick up for Mr. North? This is quite the turn around."

"Erm… about the time I saw those thrusting glutes in action! I've dreamt about them ever since. Have you noticed the dimples and the small mole just to the left of—"

"Shut up and come here!" I grabbed him and pulled him in for a bear hug, he pulled back, hissing, and winced. "What now?" I asked, not really wanting the answer.

"It's my titties, hun. Since I got knocked up they've been rock hard and hurting like a bitch," he shrugged and put a finger to his mouth. "Must be the beginning of my lactation."

I struggled to hold in my laughter. "You're a weird little freak, you know that? Honestly!"

He wiggled his fingers at me, cackling. "But I'm your little freak and you love me anyway," he said with all confidence.

"God knows I do!" I lilted.

"Well, you *and* my little Pookie."

"What?" I screeched and pulled him to arm's length. He smiled a huge, loving smile. *Aww!*

"He loves me, ham roll, me! The sun has finally come out! I bet my bottom dollar and it came out!"

"And?" I pushed.

"And, I told him I loved him too – he's my shy little field mouse," he confided coyly.

"Babe, I'm super chuffed for you! My mam will be so excited to meet him." I crushed him with another hug.

"Thanks, pork loin." He nudged me with his elbow, eying me up.

"What?"

"I think someone loves you too."

I rolled my eyes. "Moving swiftly on…"

"No! And stop rolling them eyes at me! I'm telling you, he loves you and your fine curves." He turned to me and sang, *"Tash and Tudor sitting in a tree, S-E-X-X-I-N-G, first comes love, then comes marriage, then come Tink and Tatey to complete the package!"*

I burst out laughing when he pounced on me. "Come on, Wil; bring it in, on the count of three: 'Team Four-T's!' You ready?"

I reluctantly threw in my arms, laying them over his. "One… two… three."

"Team Four-T's," we shouted in unison, and then let out several belly-laughs. Tink kissed my cheek and grasped my hand, laying his head on my shoulder and snorting with laughter at our chant. When we had calmed down, a peaceful silence filled the room. "Wil?"

"Mmm?"

"I think you love him too."

I froze and then, quick as a snit, jumped from the couch. "You want a drink, you slut of a fay?"

Tink tutted loudly at my avoidance of the topic. "You can't lie to me or yourself forever, piglet!"

I cranked up Fears on my iDock and motioned that I couldn't hear him over the music. I knew Tink's words were dangerously close to being the truth, and I wasn't ready to acknowledge it.

I went to school as normal on Monday and Tuesday, and again, I didn't see Tudor on the evenings. We spoke on the phone, though mostly it felt strained and contrived. He had agreed to come over on Wednesday to see me before I flew home on Thursday night for Christmas – it was something, I supposed.

For my final lesson of the term, I had the Grade Ten World Religions class, and in it was Boleyn Jones, who had quite quickly been taken out of 'Destiny's Delinquents' and placed back into mainstream classes. I was still at a loss as to why she was ever there in the first place, and Tudor wasn't cracking, so as ever, I was none the wiser.

I knew for a fact that Tudor had never informed Boleyn of our relationship, but I was slightly nervous that she may have seen the photo of us together on the internet or the TV, like the rest of the world – in fact I was convinced she had. If the snickers and whispers that followed me through the school corridors from her fellow classmates were any indication, she had definitely seen me aboard the back of the Tudor Express.

From the moment she walked in, I knew something was up. I stood at the door and welcomed in each child as normal. Boleyn was the last through the door. "How are you Boleyn, excited for Christmas break?" I asked cheerily.

She simply and muttered. "Oh yeah, ecstatic!"

O-kay!

"Well, someone's in the festive spirit! Cheer up, it may never happen!" I joked, trying to improve her stinking attitude whilst I turned to the board writing 'The Five Pillars of Islam' across the centre.

I heard a screech of a chair, and snapped around to face the class at the sound.

Boleyn was standing near her desk, face full of thunder. "May never happen? What the hell do you know? Believe it or not, you're not always right."

My head shot back to look at her. *What did she just say to me?* "Erm, Boleyn, please do not take that tone with me. Let's discuss this calmly." I said firmly.

Her eyes began to fill with water. "Why, are you struggling to understand me? What's wrong? Can't you understand my accent? 'Cos that'd be rich, coming from you!"

"Boleyn, this is your last warning. Reel it in, *now,* and tell me what the problem is!" I stared at her expression, and her bottom lip began to tremble, tears streaming down her face. She was becoming hysterical.

I moved around my desk pushing my arms out, trying to calm her down. "Boleyn, settle down. What's wrong? Come outside, come on," I offered as I ushered her out of the door and into the quiet corridor, using the calming voice that we were trained at University to use to soothe an irate child.

I craned my head back into the classroom. "The rest of you, create five questions that you have about the Islamic faith in the back of your books. I'll be back in a few minutes, and no talking!" I shrilled.

Boleyn was against the wall and was angry as hell as she used the sleeves of her shirt to mop up her wet cheeks. I turned to face her. "Right, what is going on? If you have a problem you can talk to me about it. Lashing out in class is not like you."

She laughed scarily. "Oh, I do have a problem…you!"

Ah, so she did see the photo then. Get yourself out of this one then, Tash!

I nodded, trying to be a calming presence. "And why is that?"

She moved from the wall to get right in my face. "Because you came into this school like Mary fucking Poppins and tried to make everything better, but you can't, can you? You're just like everyone else, helpless to do anything!"

I pinched in my brows, confused. "Boleyn, you can talk to me. Tell me what's wrong, I'm sure I can help."

She walked away for a few steps then turned back, furious, and shouted, "Why? 'Cos you're screwing my brother?"

I stepped back in shock. "W-What?"

"I know it's you he keeps disappearing to. I saw the photo, even if he won't admit to it!"

"Boleyn–" I stepped towards her.

"No! Get back. You know nothing about me, my family or my brother! Why don't you just go back to England for good? No-one wants you here! I don't want you here. I thought you would make things better but you have just fucked them up more!" She began walking backwards.

"How? How have I made things worse? Boleyn, I don't understand?" I tried to placate.

She scowled. "Just go away and leave us alone! I *hate* you! You've made it all come back! It's all going to happen again, and it's your fault!" And she fled out of the building.

Running back into my classroom, I quickly informed Ms. Thomas via the phone in my office, and was told that everything would be sorted without my help. She wouldn't tell me any more than that, and I was left reeling.

With that, school broke up for the holidays.

Merry bleeding Christmas!

As soon as school was done – literally on the bell – I went straight home. I opened the door aggressively, ruthlessly taking out my anger on the eight-foot contraption and there was Tudor, waiting on the couch.

Perfect!

I threw down my bag, walked straight past him to the kitchen and poured myself a large glass of wine. I took a long sip and turned towards my distant lover, who was now standing in the centre of the living room, looking incredibly awkward. "Where's Tink?" I asked curtly.

"He let me in as he was leaving to meet with Tate; he flies back to LA tonight for the holidays. He went to say 'bye."

I nodded, remembering Tink had told me that earlier that morning, while at the same time noticing that Tudor was decked in all black, a perfect reflection of my less-than-stellar mood. He cocked his head to the side, motioning for me to sit down next to him on the sofa.

I walked over and dropped down beside him. He looked at me cautiously, judging my mood. "So, how was your day?"

I laughed bitterly and took another swig of wine. "Oh, just peachy! Your sister went bat-shit crazy at me in class and basically announced to the entire school that I was shagging you, and then guess what? I wasn't allowed to have any say in her punishment or be clued-in as to why she went nuts at me for what seemed like absolutely no reason! Oh, she also told me to move back to England permanently as no-one wanted me here."

He threw his head back and groaned. "She doesn't need punishing, Tash. I've been with her the past couple of hours and she feels bad enough for everything she said, she's in a real bad way. She definitely doesn't need any further punishing."

"Really? Why, because she's your sister? Because let me tell you, if any other student went off at a teacher like that, they'd be at least suspended."

"Just leave it, Tash. Leave her alone," he said forcefully.

I slapped my hands down on my knees. "Oh this is priceless! *You* won't tell me what's up with you, your sister throws the mother of all wobblies and she's let off the hook, and you tell me to just leave it? All these secrets are making me crazy, Tudor. Any more and I'll be one flew over the cuckoo's nest!"

He stood up, glaring down at me. "You have no idea what we are all going through, so just friggin' leave it alone, Tash. God!"

He was a stranger to me at that moment.

I stood up to match his pissed-off stance. I was *so* done. "I'm going to ask you one more time to explain things to me, or at least tell me a hint, a tiny morsel of what you're going through. If not, then…" I shrugged.

He grabbed my arm. "Then what?"

I snatched it away aggressively. "Then we are done, Tudor."

I saw the horrified expression on his face; I didn't let it stop me in my tirade. "I have been so bloody stupid. People must be having a great laugh at my idiocy! Actually, scratch that – they wouldn't be, would they? Because nobody knows about us, I'm your dirty little secret! I mean, we got very serious way too quick with a freakin' raincloud of secrets hanging over us every step of the way. I've acted like a hormonally-charged teenager and let my attraction for you outweigh what this relationship should be, you know, an adult one, built on honesty and trust. But I have had enough. I knew deep down that I wouldn't be able to live with not sharing everything with you, or rather you with me, but I tried because of how much you mean to me. I want to give you one last chance to tell me what is going on, to salvage this, *us*, to put *your* faith in *me*, once and for all."

His face was as white as a sheet. He was shaking his head profusely. "You don't mean it."

I released an angry breath. "Yes I do, and enough is enough. I'm a good person, I should be in a good relationship. I want total honesty. Now, tell me what's going. Please."

He put his hands on the back of his head, squeezing his eyes shut. "I can't, Sunshine." And, just like that, my emotional cord to Tudor was severed, setting us both free.

I felt the water spill from my eyes but welcomed it; at least now I knew where I stood. I walked back to the kitchen, placed my empty glass down and then made my way to my bedroom. I brought out the few clothes he had left in my room, his scarf from under the pillow included, and walked slowly back towards him, holding out his possessions for him to take.

"Tash, don't," he begged. He pushed the scarf back at me, pleading me with his gaze to stop.

"Goodbye, Tudor. It has to be this way, I can't keep doing this."

He shook his head, not accepting the situation, reached for me and smashed his lips down to mine, gripping my hair in his fists, willing me to feel his kiss, his love.

I didn't respond. *Couldn't* respond.

He drew his head back. "Kiss me, Tash."

He tried again, clutching me tighter. I still didn't reciprocate the kiss, my lips tight and still against his probing tongue. It was the hardest thing I had ever done.

He staggered and whispered. "Are you serious? Are you really done with me?" Oh God, he sounded so broken.

I let my head fall. "I'm done with the secrets, with hiding our relationship – it makes me feel *worthless*, like *you don't trust me*. Just let me in and we can be together, properly, and actually give what we have a chance. I feel like we haven't even moved from the starting blocks. We take one step forward and two steps back. I'm like friggin' Paula Abdul without the tap shoes or cute cartoon cat. At the moment, I'm questioning whether I really know the real you at all."

He held my face in his large hands. "Sunshine, I can't tell you. But I don't want to lose you either. Don't make me choose. I need you. *Please.*"

I removed his hands one at a time, my voice cracking with distraught emotion. "You already have."

I kissed the palm on each of his hands and moved back. "Bye, Tudor," I whispered.

He swallowed and nodded resolutely, finally accepting my decision. "Goodbye, my Sunshine," he said breathlessly, choking on his words as he slowly edged towards the door but not before he swerved back. "I wish we could have had a real chance at this, it's just real fucked-up timing I guess. For a while there, I thought I had finally found my soul mate. Actually, I still do and I can't believe that I've just fucking lost her."

And then he left, clicking the door shut. I moved numbly to my bedroom and robotically packed to go home, trying not to trawl through my memory bank of Tudor – my bed, my bath, my heart. I took a scalding shower and, like a zombie, put myself to bed.

Later that night, I heard my bedroom door creak open and my best friend climbed into my bed and held me tight without saying a word. He let me cry on his shoulder until there were no more tears left to be shed.

'Earlier in the week, we received a photo showing what most believed was Tudor North with his new love, but boy, we couldn't have been more wrong. Tudor's people confirmed to us that the girl in question is just a girlfriend of a friend and that his on/off relationship with Raquel Banks is, at the moment, very much on. Raquel spoke to reporter Ted Smith today,

"I did see the photo, and I can assure you that the girl in question is just a friend, I know her quite well. We've all had a great laugh over all the confusion. I'm seeing Tudor this holiday, and can I just say that he will be very excited to unwrap his Christmas present, if you know what I mean!"

Well, there you have it folks. Keep tuned for more festive make-ups and break-ups after this break...'

Tink and I sat staring at the screen in the waiting lounge of Calgary International Airport and watched the entertainment report in silence. When it was over, Tink took my hand and stood, smiling a big smile. "Come on, sausage. Let's go home."

I swallowed my hurt, slapped on a determined grin and made my way to the plane bound for the UK.

There's no place like home...

CHAPTER 25

The Truth Will Set You Free

Being home was exactly what I needed. I got to spend time with my parents and my best friend, and that kept my mind from thinking about Tudor... well, *too* much anyway.

I had decided on our arrival at Manchester Airport that I would switch my Canadian phone off until I got back. Tudor probably wouldn't call anyway, but it helped me cope with the whole crazy situation better knowing that I was detached, at least electronically. I wanted my time at home to be stress-free, fully focused on catching up with those closest to me and moving on from the most turbulent – albeit shortest – relationship of my life.

My parents knew nothing about my relationship with Tudor, and Tink and I agreed to leave it that way. My mother suspected I was pining for a man, somehow she always knew the score, but due to their lack of interest in the world of celebrity, the danger of the 'rents learning about 'the photo' was small. I said that I had met someone but I didn't think it was going to go anywhere due to his personal issues. Her only concern was she didn't want me to have another disastrous relationship. My mother wouldn't have cared if my chosen significant other was a chimney sweep or the President of the United States – if *he* hurt her baby girl, then *he* had better get ready to feel the wrath of her rolling pin!

My father was in his usual fettle: rude, brash and hot-headed as hell, but it wouldn't have been Christmas without his affectionate swearing and hate-filled monologues against the English and their inferior celebratory festive traditions of 'Yule Tide' and 'Hogmanay'

Tink had proudly announced his relationship status to my mother, who already had him married off with kids (I was to embrace my 'Fruit-Fly' duty and be the volunteer surrogate, apparently). She beamed like a lighthouse at the thought of planning a civil partnership, and she made Tink promise to bring Tate over as soon as possible to meet the 'in-laws'. Even my dad was happy for the clearly-besotted Tinkster, going so far as to promise him that he would honour the occasion by going 'full Scottish' under his kilt at the assumed future wedding.

On Boxing Day, a contented Munro clan gathered around the TV, over-stuffed with food and drink and having a lazy family day. My dad was switching through the movie channels at a dizzying rate, dismissing each film as *'Pish'* or *'for eejits'* and eventually settled on one he could stomach: the Sky premiere of *The Blade Reaper,* starring none other than *(dun, dun, duuunnnn!)* Tudor North.

Tink and I were having a little tipple with my mam on the sofa when we recognised Tudor's familiar raspy-rough voice (minus his strong Canadian accent) through the very expensive surround-sound Dad had just got for Christmas. Tink, unable to disguise his shock, proceeded to spray his mouthful of Bucks Fizz all over my mother as she was polishing off her sizable third extra-strong Snowball of the afternoon.

I had never seen any of Tudor's movies – purposely, I might add – since I'd met him, and I definitely didn't want to start now, but watching him on screen, playing someone else so well was something to behold. I ended up sitting next to Dad, mesmerised, right through until the credits. Pamela was right, he was so talented and he completely blew me away, and my God, did he look fit…

Damn you, weak willpower!

There was an awkward moment when my father pointed at the ripped and bare-chested Tudor and proclaimed, "Fuckin' hell, wid ye look at the size o' that bugger! I bet he could pack a few punches tae yer mouth and yewid'nae even ken before ye lost yer teeth! At least he's no yon o these namby-pamby wee snotty-nosed shits that usually poison ma screen. He cid've stood be'side Wallace and took off a few Sassenach heeds! I'll tell ye noo, he'll be from guid Scottish stock! That's the kindy man ye need, Natasha, one that can scare the shite ootty folk!"

I smiled inwardly, knowing that my dad would have approved of us as a couple – every girl wants her father to like the one she loves, err… *likes*, I mean *likes,* people!

The next ten days at home continued in a blur of food, wine and laughter, going by far too fast but I loved every minute of it. Way too soon, it was time to get back to normality. Well, whatever normal was these days…

So there we were, back in Calgary. The third of January and minus twenty degrees – toasty!

Tink had parked Bumblebee (now sporting some excellent new snow tyres) at the airport, and we were settled in our heated seats ready to head home.

Tink was bouncing with excitement at seeing Tater-Tot again, who had already been back in Calgary for a week and was meeting us at the condo. I, on the other hand, was not looking forward to hearing their reunion all afternoon, but as Tink had already told me on the flight, "You have to like it or lump it, I'm still scarred after seeing you get pummeled against the wall by Tudor's mammoth thighs. A little bit of fairy sex-singing you can take, think of it as penance!" He did have a point, I guessed.

As we hit the highway, I decided that I had better switch my Canadian phone back on. I was surprised to see several missed calls and voicemails in my mailbox from Tudor, the latest listed two days ago. I took a deep breath and pressed my phone to my ear, bracing myself to hear his voice once more.

"Hey, Sunshine." Shit, he didn't sound too good. *"I've tried calling a few times but I suppose you've switched off your phone, being back in the UK. I... I just wanted to speak to you, see if you have had a good Christmas break? I... I'm sorry to call you, after everything, I probably shouldn't, but... I'm having a rough time at the minute, family stuff, and you always make me feel better. Anyway, I... I just want to tell you that I've been thinking of you and... I miss you... a lot. Okay, well... 'bye, Sunshine,"* and the message went off.

Tink looked at my torn face from the driver's side. "Tudor?" he guessed, and I nodded, not speaking while I swallowed the lump in my throat.

He was having family issues? That was the most he had ever told me about what was going on, how he was feeling. But we weren't even together and it was on a friggin' voice mail! How many times had I begged him to tell me something, anything, and he finally sheds some light on his problems to my phone's answering machine while I'm four thousand miles away. Frustrating is not the word!

I wondered what he meant by family issues? *Jesus! Ten minutes back in Calgary and I'm thinking of the hulking man already – I need professional help!*

I decided to file away dealing with the voicemail until later when I was in the safety of my own home and I could comfortably cope with the ever present Tudor-related issues.

We were heading downtown on Deerfoot Trail when Tink's in-car Bluetooth phone went off – 'Pookie'.

He pressed the accept button and Tate's gentle voice filled the car. "Hey, baby. You back yet?" Tate's dismembered voice asked.

I eyed Tink and saw by his expression that he too had noticed that his boy sounded off, not his usual cheery self.

"Hey, sugar tits. Yep, we are about twenty minutes from the condo. Where are you, everything okay? Wait, what's that noise?"

There was shouting and banging in the background, and Tate rushed out his next sentence in a hushed and panicked tone. "Look, I'm calling as I can't come around tonight, something's come up. I'll call you later, okay?"

I could hear police sirens wailing in the background, getting louder by the second, obviously heading closer to where Tate was.

Tink looked frantic, his hands shaking on the steering wheel. "Tatey, honey, what's wrong? Are you okay? I'm scared!"

So was I.

"I'm fine, baby, look I have to go–" There was loud shouting, banging and someone swearing.

"Tudor, *no!*" screamed a feminine voice, a voice that sounded absolutely petrified. I gripped the seat belt at hearing Tudor's name.

"Look I have to go…" The phone went dead.

I whipped my head to Tink. "Oh my God, what was all of that about? What if something's wrong with Tudor?" My voice was scaling a few octaves higher and my heart was pounding in my chest.

Tink bit the nails on his right hand. He must be really worried if he was putting his Shellac at risk. "I-I don't know," he said in a quiet, shaky voice.

I narrowed my eyes – the little liar! "What do you know? And don't lie. I can see you're hiding something by the way you can't keep your perfectly polished talons out of your mouth," I demanded.

Without checking his wing mirrors, he pulled over onto the hard shoulder, ignoring the horns and name-calling from the other drivers on the road. He laid his head on the steering wheel and groaned. "He made me promise not to tell!"

My breathing grew laboured. "Tell me what?" I screamed, shaking Tink's arm.

"Look, he didn't go into detail but when we were away, Tatey flew back to Calgary and something was going down with Tudor and his family."

"What was it?" I pushed, my heart now moving from a steady canter to a full-blown Seabiscuit gallop.

"I don't know but I think it's bad, my boy was so scared," he whimpered.

"Of what?"

"I don't know what of. Look, Wil, Tate takes his job very seriously and he signed a confidentiality agreement when he took the position, so I have no details. Believe me, I've tried but he won't crack, he's like the freakin' Enigma Code!"

Was this what Tudor had been keeping from me? It had to be. What else could it be? What the hell was going on? I had to go and find out once and for all. I needed it to move on.

I looked to Tink and he began preemptively shaking his head. *"Tink…"* I threatened. "Take me to the Aspen/Spring Valley area, at the end on Seventeenth Ave South West. I know that's the area he lives in, and, by the sounds if it, if we follow the sirens and flashing lights we'll figure out which is his house pretty damn quick."

Tink stared at me like I was crazy. "Wil, I don't thi–"

I cut him off. "Just do it, Tink, for fucks sake!" I screamed, and he quickly pulled back onto the highway and floored it all the way to the commotion at the exclusive and wealthy neighbourhood.

It didn't take us long to find the right place.

When we got there, emergency service vehicles were spread out along the long driveway of a house situated on its own in about four acres of land, completely segregated from other properties nearby. I could only assume was the residence of the Norths.

At the sight of police cars and ambulances, my fear kicked into overdrive and before the Camaro had even stopped, I was out of the door and running towards the scene. I could hear raised voices in the house from the driveway and I could make out crying, it was full of pain and anguish. My eyes began to fill up with tears in fear of what I would find.

I reached the end of the long graveled road and began sprinting up the brick stairs only to see Tate, head in hands, hunched over and crying against the side of the huge white-with-black-beams mansion – Tudor-period style (go figure).

He saw me running his way, eyes wide, and he rushed over to meet me. "Tash, what the hell? You can't be here right now," he cried, trying to usher me away.

I stood stock-still. "Where is he? What's happening?" I could hear Tudor's voice. I had to get to him, check he was okay.

"Tash, now is not a good time. You need to go." He tried to physically turn me around.

"No! I won't leave. Tell me what's going on," I bellowed.

Tate's face crumpled. He broke down and began to cry. He laid his head on my shoulder, unable to stop his torrent of emotions.

I kissed his head. "Shhhh, it's okay, sweetie, what happened?"

He let out a painful groan. "He got to her just in time, it was awful. He just lost it, and I called the police. I was in my study working on the other side of the house. It was… it was awful!" he sobbed and sobbed, drenching the shoulder of my coat.

I heard Tink running up from behind me and Tate looked up, unwrapped himself from my embrace and took off in the direction of his boyfriend. I watched him throw himself into Tink's shocked and worried arms. Unshackled, I set off in the direction of the front of the house. I turned the corner and my path was immediately blocked by an ambulance. I moved to the open doors, and inside was a young girl, bloodied and clearly shaken, clothes ripped and crying.

It was Boleyn.

Pamela North was hovering over her, fussing and petting her outstretched hand, clearly in emotional pieces. The paramedics worked on Boleyn's injuries and one of them was injecting something into her arm. I was frozen in place, I couldn't move or speak.

Catching sight of me, Pamela let out a large cry and stepped outside of the vehicle, shocked beyond measure. I suddenly realised coming here was a terrible mistake. This was clearly a very personal family matter and I was intruding, trying to involve myself in something I should never have done, all because of my own insecurities.

I opened my mouth to apologise and leave when she spoke, eyes glazed over and replaying some horror in her head. "He must have snuck in through her window and I didn't hear. What kind of mother doesn't hear? And Tudor, oh God, Tudor… just wouldn't stop. Please go see him, he needs you… please, do something… it's too much for him to cope with on his own."

The paramedic moved to the doorway and, giving me a polite nod, closed the doors. The sirens blared and blue lights filled my vision as the ambulance moved carefully up the driveway.

I looked around, trying to locate someone I knew to try and grasp some idea of what the hell was going on, but all I saw were officials and discarded Christmas decorations thrown on the perfectly landscaped, hilled lawn. With no other avenues to explore, I moved towards the front door.

Before I could reach it, two policemen came out of the main entrance, struggling with a bloodied and heavily beaten man in handcuffs. He had fair hair and was tall with a stocky build. He looked (at least from what I could make out) to be in his mid-to-late fifties and he was limping on his right foot. He exuded an air of malice; it was practically pulsing around him. I instinctively wrapped my arms around myself as he passed.

As the police officers struggled to drag the fighting man to the car, he caught sight of me watching and smiled, his mouth full of blood, droplets dripping crimson on his stubbly chin. I felt violated from his grin alone.

He began to laugh, making me shiver and I backed away. "Well, if it isn't Tudor's bitch!"

I gasped. He knew me? I was scared now and, in fear, I stepped back several more feet as the police seemed to lose their grip and had to wrestle to restrain him.

He met my gaze straight on, eyes narrowing. "Now, where have you been, little girl? I've been looking for you everywhere this past week but no-one was home. Pity really, you look positively delectable in person," he licked his lips, lapping on his own blood, causing my skin to crawl.

My head span and my heart pounded. I wasn't breathing. He'd been following me? He knew where I lived? Who was he? A stalker? A crazed fan? I couldn't speak through fear. The leer on his face was pure evil. He cocked his head and spat a mouthful of blood at my feet, making me retch.

He laughed at my reaction and tried to lean forwards. "The denial statement was good, by the way, but I knew it was bullshit. I was here, watching, waiting. I was going to finish what I started years ago before that bastard mistake of mine stopped me, stopped me from what I am entitled to do – she's mine to play with however I wish. *You* were going to be the icing on the cake, the guilt would've killed him. But hey, there's always next time, and there *will* be a next time. Make no mistake about that!" he threatened as he was hauled into the back of a police car, the police officer apologising as he walked past.

As the patrol car pulled away, the man was staring at me out if the window, smiling all the time until they were out of sight, leaving me standing alone in the snow.

Breathe, Tash. There must be an explanation for all this whacked-out, Stanley Kubrick madness. Don't vomit, keep it together... Pamela said Tudor needs you.

My inner monologue was broken by noises coming from inside the mansion. I commanded my feet to head towards the house as fast as I could. Henry, Tudor's brother, and Samantha, his wife, were sitting on the stairs directly in front of the large oak door.

Samantha was crying hysterically and Henry was as still as a statue, staring at nothing, as pale as a ghost. The door to the left of them was shut, but the crashing and banging noises emanating from behind it were loud and unyielding. I came to a halt, unsure of what to do next.

Henry noticed me first, shock clear on his face. "Natasha, what are you doing here?"

Samantha lifted her head and wiped the tears from her face. I flinched as something cracked against the wall on the other side of the door. Henry dragged a hand through his long, shaggy hair.

"He's in there, we can't calm him down. I think you had better leave him a while. We can explain everything later."

"He told you about us," I said softly. Not a question, but a statement.

Samantha stood beside me rubbing my arm. "He did. You made him very happy while it lasted," she delivered with a tight smile. I swallowed the lump in my throat. *He had told his family after all.*

"Tash, just go and come back later, please," Henry pushed once more.

I shook my head. I knew Tudor needed me, and I wasn't going anywhere. I was nothing if not stubborn (thank you, Scottish genes!). "I want to see him," I whispered.

Henry groaned and turned away, sitting back on the stairs. Samantha touched my shoulder lightly. "He's struggling to rein it in, Natasha, it's probably best to wait a while. Tudor had to deal with everything that happened today. Again. It's too much."

Still absolutely none the wiser as to what had actually happened, I hugged her quickly before walking towards the door, the three-inch piece of wood that stood between me and whatever was happening on the other side.

I took a few seconds to work up the nerve, swore quietly, put my shaking hand on the handle and pushed. The door creaked open slowly, noises of anguish amplifying as I stepped through.

I peeped my head cautiously around the door just as a chair hit the wall to my left. Undeterred, I slid through and carefully shut it behind me. In the centre of the room stood Tudor, my Tude, with his back to me, in a bloodied white T-shirt, ripped so badly that the scratched skin on his back was visible, gashes peppering his beautiful tattoos.

I inched closer to him as he kicked broken furniture, cushions and other debris around what I assumed was once Boleyn's pink-and-white bedroom. I noticed that the cream carpet had patches of blood in certain areas and the furniture was now mostly in pieces, photos scattered around like confetti.

He didn't know I was there.

"Tudor?" I spoke in a shaky voice, worried at his reaction to my intrusion.

He stilled, his back muscles bunching, his shoulders high and his breathing erratic. He slowly turned to face me, his upper lip swollen and smeared with blood, a black eye forming on his beautiful face and red welts carved into his cheeks. He turned white and just stood there, watching me in silence.

I held out my hand, willing him to take my offered comfort. "B-Babes, are… are you okay?" I was moving slowly towards him, hands still outstretched.

He released a painful cry and practically ran the short distance between us to wrap me tightly in his arms. I began to cry with him as I held his injured body in my arms. I couldn't even comprehend what he must have been through.

He was shaking and his head was tucked into the nook between my neck and shoulder. He was crying, crying so hard. I stroked his closely shaven head, trying to soothe him.

His legs buckled and he collapsed onto his knees, taking me with him, all the time gripping me tight. The fight in him instantly drained away. His hands slid to my waist and he wept – all I could do was hold him close.

It took ten minutes. Ten minutes to let it all out, ten minutes of holding him tightly in my arms and ten minutes to stop the crying. With a final shudder, he pulled back and lifted his head, his eyes severely bloodshot from all the released emotions and his face all battered and bruised.

I sat, staring at him, trying to control my rage towards the man in the police car who I assumed had hurt him. He tried to read my eyes, searching my face for a sign that I still wanted him, before tentatively leaning forward and kissing me. It was soft, brief and full of need, and this time, I kissed him right back.

He pulled away, his hand pressed to my cheek as he looked around the room. I followed his gaze with my own, surveying the chaos and destruction.

Tudor cleared his throat, his voice cracked and strained. "I need to get out of here."

"Of course," I whispered, and I stood and took his hand leading him out of the carnage.

When we were out in the hallway, Samantha and Henry rushed over. Henry wrapped an arm around Tudor's neck and pulled him into his chest. They were both struggling with their emotions and clung onto each other for support.

Henry pulled back, bracing Tudor in his arms. "Are you okay, little bro?"

Tudor nodded weakly.

Henry swallowed and whispered. "Thank you, again. You shouldn't have to keep dealing with this shit. Somehow it always falls on you."

Tudor bowed his head once in acknowledgement.

Samantha moved in and kissed his cheek and then moved to kiss mine. I smiled weakly at her, and Tudor took my hand in his, leading me to a door that led to the basement. "I need to be alone right now with Tash, I… just need some time away from all that," tilting his head in the direction of Boleyn's trashed room.

Henry tapped him on the arm and let us past, and we descended the stairs to Tudor's basement. It was unlike any basement that I had ever seen – it was practically a palace. It was bigger than most houses and it was decorated with wood and leather. A total man-cave, complete with separate kitchen and living area, but I loved it. In any other circumstances, this would have been a total turn-on, but these were not normal circumstances… These were unprecedented, these were… Well, I wasn't entirely sure. I was still completely in the dark to exactly what *had* happened and what it all meant.

Tudor led me through the dark-wood-and-chrome kitchen and sat us down on a huge black L-shaped couch, never once releasing my hand and never once uttering a single word. I rested my head on his shoulder, giving him the time he needed to talk, or not talk – I wouldn't push this time. This time it was up to him.

I honestly didn't know how long we stayed in the same spot, my head on his shoulder, his hands holding both of mine as if they were a lifeline. It was obvious that he needed time to cool down and I was happy to just be there, as a support.

The sun had begun to set when he shifted and for the first time since we moved downstairs, Tudor relaxed some and settled back against the cushions, tucking me under his arm, desperately close. I looked up at his face and his eyes were closed and tense, like he was battling with the image of something. When he finally spoke, his voice was gravelly from the strain of the day's events.

"When I was younger, things were okay at home; at that time we lived in Victoria, BC, that's where Henry and I were born and raised, and we were a typically normal family. As I grew up, I realised all was not as it seemed, not at all. I first noticed little things, like my mom would sometimes walk funny, like with a limp or a twisted ankle, and then sometimes she would have these bruises on her arms and legs, but I was too young to know what was really going on.

"I was about eight; Henry, ten, when we walked in from hockey practice to see my father pinning my mother down to the floor and beating her, punching her over and over with his fist while he was practically raping her. We didn't know what to do, we were so young – we didn't even know what sex was, for Christ's sake! Henry pushed me back to protect me and tried to pull him off her, but my dad just swatted him away like a fly. The man we idolised, our hero, was hurting our mom and we didn't know how to stop it. It was after that when we left the first time. We lived with our grandparents for a few years in Kelowna, BC, and then one day he showed up again, right out of the blue. We had no idea how he had found us but he said he'd changed, he *seemed* to have changed and my mom took him back. She wanted us to be a family, for her boys to have a dad."

He sucked in a breath, and I slipped my fingers underneath his T-shirt to run my fingers over his stomach to comfort him. I didn't want to push him. In my wildest dreams I couldn't have imagined that this was his secret.

After a couple of minutes, he lifted my chin and kissed me softly on my mouth. I smiled and cuddled back in, and he picked up where he had left off.

"At first everything was great, he was the perfect father, but then the signs appeared again: the flinching from my mother every time he moved, the bruises in places people wouldn't check and the baseball bat he started using to keep me and Henry in line. We were bigger then, both of us teenagers who trained hard at hockey. I was starting to get into weight-lifting to help with my junior varsity career and I was gaining strength by the day. Henry and I both knew how to handle ourselves, but he had my mother wrapped around his little finger, and if we stepped up to him, she would beg us to stop. He used her to control us. It went on for years and there was nothing we could do.

"I was fifteen when I found my mom crying on the bathroom floor, holding something in her hand – a pregnancy test. My father was at work. She was pregnant with Bee and that was the day we left for good. We got in the car, without any of our possessions, and moved to Vancouver and never looked back.

"Years went by and we heard nothing from him, life became normal again and the fear of him turning up went away. Bee didn't know much about Dad, we told her he had left us when she was a baby and, with two big brothers around helping Mom raise her, she didn't want for anything. She was happy, at least for a while."

He began shaking again. I sat up and took his face in my hands. "Tudor you don't need to keep going, it's okay," I reassured and I moved in to kiss his forehead.

He pulled away. "No, I want you to know, I need you to know. No more secrets, Sunshine. Never again."

I sat back and he stared off, not looking at anything in particular, eyes unfocused. "A few years back, I got my big break – you know how, I told you before – and I moved to LA to be closer to the studios. I'd been there a few months when I got a call from Henry saying that Dad had been back in touch. It just brought all these fears and feelings back, and I didn't know how to deal with this new career and the fact that... that... that *monster* was trying to weasel his way back in our lives after everything he'd put us through.

"In LA, if you're known, everything is available to you, so I turned to alcohol and tried to drink my problems away. You know the drill: I slept around and drank for nearly a year before my mom called and told me to stop being stupid and to come home. So I did. My dad had stopped calling, finally getting the message that he wasn't welcome, and things were looking better again."

He rubbed his hand across his face and his eyes once again welled up with tears. I used my thumb to rub them away and waited for him to finish the story.

"Bee was twelve when he showed up. He knocked on the front door, as brazen as all hell, like he had every right to be there. She answered and, having never seen him before, not even a picture, let him in. He claimed he was a family friend. I arrived home half an hour later, I'd forgotten a script that I was supposed to be reading for producers in downtown Vancouver, and walked in to find my father assaulting my baby sister on the living room floor. He didn't manage to rape her, but if I hadn't got there when I did…"

He let out a strangled moan and I held him tighter in my arms.

He tucked his face into my hair. "I saw red, Tash. I pulled him off her and began laying into him; I was well into bodybuilding by then and outweighed him by at least fifty pounds and could have easily beaten him to a pulp. It wasn't long before Henry came home and dragged me off him and in all the commotion, the bastard managed to get away. The police have been searching for him for over three years. God knows where he was hidden but could we hell find him. Bee took it badly and was diagnosed with an anxiety disorder; she struggled to go out of the house and would get night terrors and such high anxiety that she had to be sedated on more than one occasion. I couldn't believe it was happening. We spent over a year trying to make her better. Half the problem was that he was still out there and she just couldn't move on. The doctors advised a change of scenery. I wanted to help her, so we moved here, the last place anyone would expect and hopefully the last place he would think to come looking.

"From that moment on, I purposely fell off the radar. I kept working on my films but all social engagements and interviews were cancelled. I had the worst job in the world for coping with this type of situation, any social media post or gossip site could give away where we lived at any moment. There are thousands of pages out there solely about me and several of them only exist to track my every move. It's beyond fucked up to have fans acting as a personal GPS, especially when you have a father who is trying everything to seek you out and destroy your family. Anyway, the money from my films has helped us buy the best lawyers, private eyes and security, but my job has also made it easy for him to threaten us too.

"On movie sets, or when I've been on location – all public knowledge of course – he would send notes through the runners telling me that he would find us and finish what he started and that he blamed me for everything, for stopping him and his right to have his own daughter. *My fault!* All the police and specialists on the case warned me about involving other people and to not risk telling anyone but family about our situation, and I didn't for years.

"He was spotted a few times around Canada, but he always managed to evade the police just in time. The notes became more threatening as time went on and he made it clear that if he got the chance he would ruin my life, in any and every way that he could. He described explicitly what he would do to my girlfriend if I ever I got one, if I loved anyone as much as he '*loved*' Bee – he's a sick bastard! I knew I could never get into a relationship until he was caught. I didn't want to, I honestly thought that relationships just seemed to destroy people, rip them apart."

He pulled back and made me look into his eyes before letting out a snort of light laughter. "And then you came along and blindsided me. When you barreled into the restaurant that night I couldn't look away. I was hooked from the get-go. I fought our attraction for so long, put you through hell and never once told you why. In the end, I was weak and selfish and I couldn't *not* have you in my life. That coffee date with Gage pushed me over the edge.

"I told my mother and brother about what was happening, what I was resisting and they told me that I shouldn't – no – *couldn't* live like that: miserable and on my own forever because of him, because then he would win. So I gave in, and you completely changed my life, I finally lowered my guard to someone."

I smiled shyly at him, and he smiled softly in return, before kissing me once more. His face fell when he ended the kiss.

"About a week before you left for Christmas, my agent received an email with your picture attached. It was from him; you were coming home from school. I nearly had a heart attack when I realised he'd found us again, found out about you, and right after things had been going so well for us. I felt like we had barely been given a chance to make it work…" Tudor trailed off.

Fuck-a-duck, he was after me too? My God!

Tudor saw my face pale and hugged me tight. "The police were always ringing, telling me where he had been spotted, and I could see you were getting suspicious and I knew you were thinking the worst, but how could I explain my past without risking what we had? I needed you, but I just couldn't tell you anything.

"His picture had been circulated to local businesses and private eyes. The sightings indicated that he had made his way to Calgary, that he was here somewhere, and I decided not to tell you even then as I didn't want to scare you – I needed to protect you, protect my family. I knew though, I knew deep down that I'd lose you. Who would willingly stay in this fucked up situation?

"When you broke up with me, I felt like he'd won. He took you away, the only thing to ever make me truly happy. That paparazzi picture must have clued him in to where we were.

"The police have been looking for him for the past week, he was lying low. I thanked the Lord every day that you were in England and he couldn't get to you."

He brushed kisses onto my neck. "I was outside taking the Christmas lights down this morning when I heard Bee scream. He had gotten in through her window, which was usually always locked, but she'd opened it to let in some fresh air, and he'd seized his opportunity. When I reached the room, he was already hitting her, tearing clothes off her body while she tried to push him away. I flipped at seeing him again, attacking my sister... *again!* You turned up just after the police came and dragged me off him. If they'd let me I think I would have killed him, Tash. I fucking *hate* him!"

He sucked in a ragged breath at his admission, and I simply nodded and held him. He took my hand and played with my fingers before he grabbed them tightly in his grip.

"He mentioned you, said that he'd gone for you this morning but you weren't home."

His eyes squeezed shut, tears spilling from their corners. "Jesus, Tash, what if you had been there? What if—?"

I cut him off by putting my hands on his face. I leaned in and kissed him passionately, showing him without words what he meant to me. He didn't break away. He instantly responded and pushed me back and down onto the sofa, never leaving my lips. I could feel and taste the dried blood on his mouth but I didn't care.

He groaned and lifted his head and smiled down at me, the first genuine smile since I had found him alone in *that* room. I moaned in complaint at the interruption of our reunion kiss. "Just checking you are real," he murmured and then crashed his lips to mine once more. He stroked my head with his hand as he moved to lay soft caresses on my cheeks, my closed eyes, my neck and my nose.

This was home; this was where we were meant to be, with each other, honest and open. He pulled back his head, cupped my face, looked me deep in the eyes with a serious expression and whispered, "I love you, Sunshine. I actually can't believe how much I fucking love you."

My heart melted. I was utterly speechless at the strength and conviction of his words. I gripped him as tightly as possible to compose myself. I was shaking from the soul-shattering adoration I was feeling towards this man.

I pressed my hand to his cheek. "I love you, too, babe."

"You do?" he sighed, as though he doubted my returned affections.

"Mmm-hmm. All the way to the moon and back."

He pulled a playfully shocked expression. "That much?"

I shrugged. "No, probably more."

It was the truth.

I lifted his head closer to mine, I wanted him as near to me as possible. "Thank you for telling me everything. You don't know how much it means to me that you trust me enough to tell me all that you have been through. I will never tell another soul."

He pressed his forehead against mine once again. "Thank you for not running far away from me when I did."

"Never, you would only catch up with me anyhow. I'm not exactly what you'd call a sprinter." I whispered, jokingly.

He shifted, rolling me on top of him. He was quite content to just lie there looking at me, but after a while he pulled a frown.

"Hey, what's wrong?" I asked, worried, smoothing the creases on his face with the back of my hand

He glanced away, his face torn with sadness. "I'll never forgive myself for endangering you like that. I-I just couldn't not have you in my life. Please say you forgive me?"

I kissed his eye where a huge bruise was forming. "There is nothing to forgive. Crazy-evil Dad is going to be locked away for a long time, meaning we get to start afresh, yes?"

He pulled a timid Tudor-smirk and nodded. "If you'll have me?"

I scrunched up my face in mock contemplation. *"Ah, what the hell. I'm a sucker for muscles and tattoos!"*

He laughed out loud and tilted his head, gazing at me in unguarded affection. "God, I love you."

Now that's something I'm not going to get tired of hearing.

CHAPTER 26

No Rain, No Rainbow

Tudor cleaned himself up and calmed down considerably once his father's blood was no longer polluting his skin. When we returned upstairs, the police were there to take his statement. Tink was in the living room with Tate, who looked like he'd been put through the wringer, to say the least.

We all waited tensely in the living room whilst Tudor spent an hour with the police. As he came back into the room, I made my way to him as he took a swig of the hip flask Henry had produced.

He shrugged. "Just to settle the nerves."

"Ah, okay!" I answered in return and winked.

He took my hand in full view of everyone else, and I felt loved, publicly loved. Despite everything else that had happened that day, I adored that we could now be open with the rest of the world. Something within him had changed – calmness had settled on his usually guarded countenance and it made me so happy to see.

Henry gestured that it was time for them to head to the hospital, and I turned to my big guy. "Call me when you are done, let me know how Boleyn is doing," I said, going in to kiss him on the cheek, but he pulled back, effectively making me kiss the air. "What?" I asked confused.

"You're coming with me," he stated, as if there would be no other option.

I flashed a look at Tink who put up no resistance – he was anxious to get Tate home to our condo. I don't think Tate was really of the disposition for coping well with what had happened and had as yet been unable to untangle himself from the security of Tink's hold.

"No, Tudor, honestly it's fine. Just call me when you get back. You need to go and be with your family. I fully understand."

He nodded in agreement. "I do need to see my family, *and* my girlfriend is coming too, to support *me*."

He leaned in and whispered for my ears only, "Tash, I don't do well in hospitals, my mom was always there because of him. Henry and I received our fair share of broken bones too, and Bee... Bee had to go there, that night... I'll explain everything to you another time but I have issues with those places and I need you to be with me. You make me... I don't know... calm."

I stroked his cheek with my hand and he pulled it to his mouth and laid feather-light kisses on my palm. "Plus,

I want us there together, out in the open, for everyone and their mothers to see."

I pecked him quickly but shook my head and told him, "Babes, you're strong on your own – just look at today, how you saved your family. I shouldn't be there at the hospital, it's time for just you guys to be there for Boleyn – just family. I love how you want me to be with you, but I think tonight is much too soon for everyone else. It's a bit inappropriate."

I headed to the door. "I'll see you later, go with your brother, you'll be okay, I promise. I'll see you tonight when you get back."

He growled under his breath, dismissing my words, lunged forward and picked me up before tossing me over his shoulder in a fireman's lift, smacking my arse with his cupped hand. "For the last time, you are coming with me! Tink, take Tate home and don't expect this one back tonight."

I squealed. "Tudor put me down!"

He ignored me and began walking out of the door. I could hear Samantha giggling, a nice sound considering she had understandably spent the majority of the day in floods of tears. Tudor continued out to the car and plopped me in the back seat of a huge red Dodge Ram. Henry and Samantha climbed into the front seats and off we went to the hospital.

I sat in the large seat, frozen and stunned, mouth gaping in shock, with Tudor holding my hand as though he hadn't just gone all caveman and carried me to the car

– all we were missing was a club to the head and an obligatory grunt.

Henry looked at me through the rear view mirror and grinned. "You had better get used to being joined at his hip now, Tash. He no longer has to keep you hidden. Believe it or not, he was keeping you at arm's length before – now, he has no barriers."

I groaned dramatically and rolled my head back to rest against the seat, but, deep down inside, I broke out in a happy grin. Tudor eyed me from his side of the truck, hiding his amusement at my pleased expression, causing him to smirk.

Yes, it was lop-sided with an extra dollop of dimple. What can I say? I'm a sucker for dimples!

Boleyn was being kept in hospital overnight to assess her mental state and, although she was heavily sedated, her injuries were minor. Thankfully, it seemed Tudor got to her quickly enough that their dad didn't cause too much damage, at least not physically. Pamela was staying the night with Boleyn and only she could stay. So after a few hours of keeping her company we said our goodbyes and headed home.

I had been apprehensive about going to the hospital with Tudor, but the small smile that arrived on Pamela's lips when we walked in hand in hand made me feel less intrusive. Tudor had sat me on his lap even though there were plenty of seats around his sister's bed, and he placed absent kisses on my hands and neck for the remainder of the visit, making the ogling nurses green with envy.

Pamela pulled me in for a hug when we left and whispered, "Thank you, Natasha. He deserves to be happy, he deserves you."

I cast a startled look at her, and she winked as Tudor took my hand and led me away out of the hospital.

We arrived back at the North residence around midnight, and I was cream-crackered. It had been the longest and most emotionally draining day of my life. Tudor led me into his large bedroom, complete with the biggest sleigh bed I had ever seen, and began to undress me, grazing over my bare skin with his fingers. I was fighting to keep my eyes open and he knew it.

He huffed out a laugh and said quietly in my ear, "You are very cute when you're sleepy, Ms. Munro."

If I had been more with it, then I would've replied with a witty come back. As it was, I couldn't even be arsed to think, so just crossed my eyes and stuck out my tongue. *That'll show him cute!*

He leaned forward and took my tongue between his teeth before lifting me up and softly laying me on the bed – *hang on, how did I get naked?*

I crept under the covers as Tudor headed to his bathroom.

I snuggled into the pillows and inhaled. I took in the musky scent of Tudor from his sheets and let my eyes fall shut.

The bed dipped, and I was immediately encased in a set of huge, bare arms and pulled into an equally naked muscly chest. I felt kisses being feathered down my neck, and I arched to help Tudor take full advantage. He made his way back to my ear and whispered, "I love you, Sunshine."

I pushed myself back impossibly close causing him to moan and bite my earlobe, his breathing turning ragged.

"Tudor?"

His arm left my chest and dusted its way down to my stomach. "Mmm-hmm?"

"Do you think everything between us has gone too fast? It seems that we have got to this serious place in our relationship very quickly. Have you thought about that too?"

His hand stilled on his journey down south. "I know it seems fast, but if we feel this way about each other, why should we go slowly? Turn around, gorgeous."

I shifted onto my belly and placed my head next to his, sharing his pillow and staring straight into those emerald eyes that only hours ago were dulled by pain. I could see them sparkle when he looked at me, and no silver-tongued, flowery sentiment could express how he felt about me more than what I saw in his gaze right then.

He ran his hand through my long hair, which had fanned out around us both. "I don't want to scare you with how strongly I feel, but I need you to know anyway."

He searched every part of my face and ran his thumb over my bottom lip, his thoughts seeming somewhere else. "We weren't allowed anything of our own when we were growing up, you know, possessions, things we wanted. I never had anything that was truly mine, and anything I treasured my father would destroy to display his power over us all. All my relationships in the past have turned to shit, and quite honestly I didn't even care to be in them. I thought I would always be alone, it was safer that way.

"I have always had this fear that if I loved anything it would be taken away; even as an adult it seemed like I'd been conditioned to accept that it was just my lot in life, so I never let myself really feel for anyone or anything… until you."

I bit my lip to stop myself grinning like the Cheshire Cat. This was not the time for a celebratory Beyoncé booty-pop, but his admission had me fighting the urge to jump up and sing, *'oh-oh, oh-oh, oh-oh, oh-oh, oh-no-no'*. I made do with a little bum-shuffle on the memory foam mattress instead.

"I am well aware that most people are intimidated by me and my attitude. I know I come across abrupt, cold-hearted and moody, and I could care less – in fact, it's worked out well. Everyone would keep their distance, fewer people to get hurt. At least most people stayed clear of me. *You* however," he laughed and hitched my leg over his; "... you just spun into my life like a smart-mouthed whirling dervish and tipped me upside down.

"When I saw you enter the restaurant, decked out in that tiny dress with all that long, dark hair and those *fuck-me* red lips, I nearly fell off my seat. Here comes this stunningly beautiful girl, dancing through the door, obviously a little drunk, and not giving a shit. It was... refreshing."

I buried my head in the pillow to hide my red face; he grabbed my cheek and made me face him. "I had heard of you from my sister, who was more than obsessed with her new British teacher, and when you saw Bee that night I couldn't help but laugh out loud at the sheer horror on your face. All my family dropped their mouths at that. I guess I *had* played the part of the tortured soul at bit too much over the years, and it wasn't something they were used to me doing: laughing.

"Anyway, when you cussed me out for being rude to you, well," he rolled on top of me and kissed the tip of my nose, "... I was lost to you right then. You were tiny compared to me, but fought back like a pitbull. After that, our meetings were just a comedy of errors, but through our twisted little rendezvous I got to know you; and you, me... the *real* me."

I fluttered my eyelashes in agreement and brought him down for a kiss. He pulled back, flushed and breathless. "Quite frankly, I've never been one to care what other people say about me, and I'm pretty sure you don't either. If people want to criticise us for getting into this too quickly, I say fuck them. If we want this, what the hell are we waiting for? This works for you and me, screw everyone else. Are you in?"

He seemed a little worried for a moment before he saw it in my eyes that I couldn't agree more. "Aye. I say, fuck 'em too!" I agreed in my strongest Geordie accent.

He bellowed out a laugh and moved over me, placing his thick arms over my head and resting his forehead against mine. With a sigh he said, "I missed you, gorgeous."

I put my arms around his neck. "I missed you, too. I'm sorry my phone was off when you tried to reach me, but I saw that bloody press release at the airport and needed to just get away from it all. It kind of destroyed me."

His eyes were pained. "Sunshine, please don't apologise. You had every right; you were trying to move on. I was too, but it wasn't working out so well on my end. I won't lose you again. I want you forever if you'll have me."

He lowered his hips and moved himself between my legs, silently asking for my permission to make love to me. I nodded, and he pushed forward, his head seeking comfort in the crook of my shoulder and neck, groaning as I arched at his welcome intrusion.

He reared up clenching his jaw, breathing harshly through his nostrils. "I have to have this forever. It feels so right... *God*..." I wrapped my arms around him tighter and replied, panting, "It will be forever, babes, I promise. This is one girl that isn't going anywhere, and no-one on earth can take me from you. I made you mine, remember? Plus, I'm a stubborn cow and will kick the shit out of anyone who tries. These fake nails are not just for show: they're my bitch-fighting claws, and I sharpen them regularly!"

He tried to smile but instead bit his lip at the incredibly intense feeling of us joined together and picked up the speed of his thrusts. Comforted by my reassuring words, he reached for my hands, clasping them tightly in his and rolled us over, placing me on top, tipping us both over the edge quicker than you can say 'Holy Orgasms!'

We laid in bed, sated, my limp body sprawled over his, happy to just be together in the quietness of the night. His hand moved to my hair and he ran his fingers through it, unknotting the tatty strands. I felt like purring. In fact, I think I actually did. I was a thoroughly petted pussy. *Ahem.*

I was dozing off when I heard, "It was love at first sight for me, you know. Right from the beginning, I was crazy about you, I realise that now," he whispered, so low I almost didn't catch it.

I lifted my head to his chest and folded my arms, staring at him with my mouth open. "I-I... I don't know what to say," I said softly, unable to respond any further.

He shrugged, nervously. "You asked if I thought about why we were so serious so quickly. But everything with you was like a whirlwind and kinda bowled me over. When I saw you at the restaurant, something in me changed, and I couldn't breathe. I loved you right then;

even if I was being a stubborn dick about it, I knew deep down it was the truth."

"You didn't know me," I replied in a hushed tone, still shell-shocked by his confession.

He focused on me with sure eyes. "My soul did."

"Tudor!" I sang shyly, feeling all mushy inside.

He giggled and kissed my forehead. *"Chew-da!"* he said, mocking my accent. "I love how you say my name. I just love everything about you."

I am now a puddle on the floor.

"You, Mr. North, are a whopping big slice of Canadian Cheddar. Who knew you were so cheesy?"

He frowned and pouted. "I'm not cheesy. I'm a body builder, 'The Blade Reaper'. I can't be cheesy; I have a reputation to protect," he sulked.

I tickled his ribs, making him squirm. "Cheesy, cheesy, cheesy. But I'll allow it as it makes me love you more. Hard shell for the world, soft gooey centre for me – the girl you love. And I promise it'll be our little secret, okay? No-one will ever know you're a soppy baby bear. You got that, Yogi?"

He restrained my wrists from the guerilla tickle assault, trying to maintain his moody face, but I just ignored it and wiggled from side to side on his body in happiness and sang, *"He loves me, he wants to kiss me, he wants to hug me..."*

He shut me up by kissing me senseless and pulling me next to him, cuddling me securely in his arms.

Who'd have thought that we'd ever be here like this? At least the secrets were put to bed – literally – and now I knew the truth, it shed some light on some of Tudor's strange past behaviour.

I drew back to face him, realisation dawning. "All of this, your past, your dad, everything, is why you acted all weird when Gage said to call him if we didn't work out, isn't it?"

He swallowed cautiously and nodded his head once in confirmation. "I'd just got you, eventually, after I never thought I would. I was already stressing about losing you. When... *Gage.*"

I shook my head in disbelief at how he couldn't say his name without gritting his teeth. He glared back, clenching his jaw. "Hey, I'm still a stubborn, possessive ass, *that* won't change, and *he* likes you which means I. Don't. Like. Him."

"Tudor!"

He shrugged unapologetically. "When he told you he'd be waiting for you if we broke up, all these insecurities came back to smack me in the face, and all I could picture was the wannabe-hippy wanker taking you away from me. I have never been allowed to have anything I truly loved, Sunshine, and I loved you even then, whether you believe me or not. I freaked. Not to sound weirdly obsessive, but you're mine and I don't intend to let you go. I'm going to work on my issues, maybe talk to someone or just talk to you for now, but no more secrets, I promise. I just want to be with you more than anything in the world, and now you have me and I have you, I won't let anything break us ever again."

I placed my palm on his rough and swollen cheek. "I thought you couldn't get emotionally attached to women, Mister? You seem to be doing better at that with me – I feel like you may spout poetry at any second!"

Tudor squeezed my knee until I was squirming and giggling, but he quite quickly lost the humour. "Tash, the women I slept with before were just toys. I know that sounds harsh, but they may as well have been blow-up dolls. I felt nothing for them, and most of the time I was beyond drunk. I had to be to face being intimate with them."

"Then why…"

He sighed sadly. "It was an outlet, a way to forget everything. I was stupid. If you have never been close to anyone emotionally, and feared it would only end in misery if you did, then you crave it. Sex kind of appeased my lack of close relationships for a while. I see now that it was foolish. The women only wanted me for Tudor North the actor, not Tudor North the man afraid to fall in love."

My heart cried for him.

He stared at me in complete adoration. "With you though it's completely shattering. Making love to you, being with you… it feels like home to me. I am so happy you are mine. You're my love, the balm to my fucked up past."

I smiled against his neck and sighed in contentment. "I am yours, Tude, of that there has never been doubt. Now, let's get to sleep, today has been…" I trailed off, not knowing the words.

He squeezed me into his warm embrace, shuffling to get us in a comfortable position, "Night, gorgeous. Love you."

"Love you, too," and I drifted off to sleep in the arms of the most perfect man on the planet.

I woke in the early morning in the same position we had gone to sleep: wrapped securely in Tudor's embrace and my right arm completely dead. I moved to lie on my back to relieve my numb limb, which was wedged in a blood-stopping sandwich between Tudor's two-ton bicep and chest, when I suddenly felt woollen material on my pillow beside me. I glanced down, and lying over my left shoulder was his scarf, the scarf from 'Skater-gate' – my treasured makeshift pillow. It was back where it belonged: with me, in bed, on my pillow.

I gazed down at my hulking, tattooed bad-boy and smiled. He must have put it there during the night. I leaned forwards, kissing Tudor's slightly parted lips. Almost automatically, he lifted his shoulders off the mattress, and his hand wrapped around the nape of my neck as he drew me against him further.

Thoroughly pleased, I gently pushed him down as his eyes squinted, fighting the pull of sleep.

"Sunshine? What—?" he croaked.

"Shh… go back to sleep, babes," I cooed, running my finger gently along his face.

Tudor laid back down as instructed, pulling me over him, leaving me sprawled across his sculpted bare chest. I grazed a kiss over his heart, closed my eyes and giggled.

I was in love with a big, muscled slice of Canadian Cheddar cheese and it felt freakin' amazing!

CHAPTER 27

The Sun Will Always Rise Tomorrow

"Tink! Hurry up, man!" I bellowed as I thumped on his door for the umpteenth time. It swung open with force, and I cracked a smirk at Tink's outfit.

"Don't start!" he warned as he brushed past me, grimacing as he saw his reflection in the full-length mirror.

"I didn't say anything, did I?" I replied, holding back the spurt of laughter that was creeping its way up my throat.

'The Incident', as it was now known, was a few days behind us, and Boleyn had been released from hospital earlier that day, so we were headed for our first 'family' dinner at the Norths, as a welcome-home gesture.

The local press had gotten wind of the incident and had reported that a domestic dispute had occurred in the well-to-do area, but thanks to a well-paid publicist, an even better-paid lawyer and a seven-foot perimeter fence, the neighbours and, well, the world had no idea of Tudor's involvement.

There would be a trial, of course, and Tudor had already decided that when that day arrived he would release a statement explaining his personal involvement, alongside a substantial donation to a local women's charity. The silver lining in this whole affair was that perhaps his candid openness would help other people in similar situations by raising awareness of domestic abuse.

His "people" were still desperately working on concealing from the press his relationship to Boleyn, for her sake at school. Thankfully, due to her age, Boleyn would be hidden behind a screen when the case came to trial and would give her statements via video link. Everyone hoped that, if nothing else, we could keep her identity secret.

I was a bit worried about seeing Boleyn that night – the last time we had talked, she had told me in fairly strong terms that I was the reason her child-molesting father had returned to harm her. Not the best way to start a relationship with your boyfriend's family. But Tudor had reassured me that she didn't really mean it. We would have to see – a teenage grudge can be enduring, we've all seen *Mean Girls*. I wasn't looking forward to living with that crap, given that Tudor and I were very much back on, in a very honest, very open and very touchy-feely relationship.

So there we were, the night we officially 'met the parent' as the newbie significant others, ready to be grilled by the brood North. Tink clearly wanted to make a good impression and had dressed to impress. He was decked out in a pair of brown, shapeless corduroy trousers with a white cotton shirt and his hair combed over to the side, Tink looked positively... normal. The things you do for love, eh?

He saw me muffling my giggle in the mirror and whipped around to face me. "Toss off, porky. I'm trying to impress Tate's second mam."

He looked down at himself, slumped forward, pulled a disgusted face and sighed. "I look like an ageing closeted reject from the seventies, don't I?"

The dam broke and the laughter rushed out of me. I trotted forward to cuddle my dowdily dressed partner in crime. "It's not too bad of an outfit really, but it's not you, my fabulously fay friend – you just don't *do* Gap. Pamela wants to get to know *you,* not Norman the pot-bellied tax accountant who lives on microwavable meals for one. Go and get changed into something legendary, something that makes her believe in fairies."

He eyes widened in horror and he bolted back into his room. "You've just saved my life, Bratwurst. You know, every time someone loses their belief in fairies, one of us dies. I could have caused mass fairy-cide! I'll be back in two shakes of a lamb's tail."

Ten minutes later, Tink strutted out into the living room in black leather trousers, a black muscle tee top, Italian leather loafers and a Karl Lagerfeld leopard-print blazer with matching 1940's vintage trilby. His eyes were heavily coated in guy-liner, and he was clutching a Prada man-purse which held his essentials – God only knows what they were – but I had to admit, he looked amazing. Not a thread of polyester in sight!

He reached the couch where I had been impatiently waiting for him and, Vogued in front of me, hands framing his face, frozen in position. "Well?" he asked, pouting his lips.

I clapped my hands in applause and stood to strike a pose too, one hand on my head, the other out to the side, cutting an odd angle. "Well?" I asked in return.

He walked around me slowly, tutting and mmm-hmming, channeling his inner Anna Wintour.

I was wearing my black harem-pant jumpsuit that tied to nip in at the waist and boasted a tailored fitted shirt, with my black sequin beaded blazer over the top. My hair was loose and wavy (Tudor's favourite), and I was wearing black leather ankle boots and my new favourite 'fuck me' red lipstick.

Tink stood in front of me and smiled. "You look as hot as a cake, my love; you nearly turned me straight, but one look at those gargantuan bosoms and I'm back to loving king-sized ding-a-lings! How Tudor doesn't asphyxiate himself on those life floats mid-coitus I'll never know!"

I held his hand, ignoring his last comment, and we made our way out to Bumblebee and to our lover boys across town.

Twenty minutes – and a good sing song to Beyoncé's 'Until The End of Time' – later, we arrived at Spring Valley. This time we were able to admire the absolute palace that the Norths lived in. It was bloody huge, especially without the sea of police cars and drama.

We made our way to the front door and rapped the brass lion knocker down twice. Tudor answered, looking all delicious in a black jersey long-sleeved top with an open V-neck and black Armani Jeans. He must have just re-shaved his head that afternoon, and he sported one hell of a sexy rugged five o'clock shadow on his chiseled jaw.

He broke into a huge grin when he saw me and, after he pointed out the direction of Tate for Tink, he brought me to his chest, one arm around my waist, the other running up my spine before loosely gripping the back of my neck with his hand.

I inhaled and nearly toppled over at the scent of him. His aftershave was having a Pavlovian effect on my libido (Note to self: find out brand and drench bed sheets in it when I get home!). Tudor brushed the hair from my neck with his fingers and pressed three light kisses behind my ear, just on the spot that made me weak at the knees.

"My God, you look amazing, Sunshine! I'm half tempted to blow off dinner and drag you to my bed right now."

I giggled into his chest. "Keep talking like that and I'll definitely blow off something later," I whispered, watching his eyes widen with desire.

He pushed me outside, against the wall of the entrance way, and groaned in frustration, moving back to kiss me, his tongue spearing hot between my lips.

"Ahem!"

We were interrupted by Henry clearing his throat dramatically, hanging half out of the doorway, covering his eyes with his hands. "Tudor, when you're finished mauling our guest, Mom wants you to let her come in and *socialise*."

I jumped back in embarrassment, straightening my rumpled clothes. Tudor just smirked, absolutely no shame whatsoever at being caught. He turned to Henry and nodded. "When I'm finished saying hello to my girl I *will*."

Henry shrugged and gave a sailor's salute with his hand before he headed back inside.

I turned to my naughty macho man and shook my head in a disapproving manner. "Mr. North, that was very inappropriate, and you deserve to be punished!" I pointed at his chest, giving him my stern teaching voice.

His eyes rolled back, and he bit his bottom lip. "*Fuck*, punish me! Please! Please Miss, I've been a very naughty boy!"

I turned and walked in the direction of the front room on shaky legs, and I couldn't help but smile at Tudor's remark under his breath as I did.

"This is gonna be a long friggin' night."

As I entered the front room, everyone was seated around the monster-sized fire that dominated the space, sipping on their drinks and engrossed in deep conversation.

Pamela saw me first and jumped up to say hello. She looked lovely. Her dark, tight curly hair was styled nicely at her shoulders and she was wearing a simple green dress that went to the floor.

She smiled at me and embraced me in a hug. "How are you, Natasha? I'm so happy you came tonight. Can I take your jacket?"

I nodded my head and suddenly felt familiar hands slip my blazer off my shoulders. I glanced back to see Tudor taking it out to the coat stand in the hall.

I focused back on Pamela; she was clearly happy with her second son's act of chivalry.

"I'm great, thank you for inviting us to dinner," I tilted my head in the direction of the Tinkster, who was entertaining Samantha, Tater-Tot and Henry with one of his stories.

She swatted her hand in front of her face as if to say 'no problem', and then leaned in to confide in a hushed tone, "Thank you for not deserting him when he needed you most." She bit her lip (just like Tudor) and a distraught look passed fleetingly over her face.

I just rubbed her back in support. It would take her a long time to heal. Tudor took that opportunity to wrap his arms around me from behind and whisper in my ear, "Do you want a drink, gorgeous?"

I nodded, unable to talk due to his ever-tongue-tying presence, and he slipped away to fetch it after placing a kiss on my cheek.

Samantha had caught our little exchange and, smiling eagerly, waved me over to the other side of the room, obviously wanting to indulge in some juicy gossip about me and the Hollywood hulk.

I made my excuses to Pamela, and just as I was about to walk over to the bubbly blonde, a slight touch to my arm halted me in my tracks. I peered down to see Boleyn. She looked pale and frail, and her face was bruised and cut. I swallowed the lump in my throat to stop from bursting into tears.

I forced myself to plaster on a convincing smile and went to ask how she was, when she beat me to it. "Ms. Munro, can I show you my new room?"

She could barely meet my eyes. I could see she was wracked with guilt, and it didn't take a genius to realise it was because of our little showdown a few weeks back.

I nodded enthusiastically and gestured with my hand for her to lead the way, and we walked out the door. She headed up the stairs, glancing back frequently to make sure I was there – the poor thing was a bag of nerves.

I saw movement out of the corner of my eye in the hallway and, as I reached the final step on the first level, I glanced down to see Tudor carrying my drink back to the front room. We caught his attention, and he looked up, surprised, before his face melted into a small smile.

Boleyn shouted down, "Tudor, do you mind if I show Ms. Munro my new bedroom?"

He shook his head and smiled. "Of course not, sweetheart. I'll just be down here if you need me, okay?"

She pulled her mouth up in a shy smile, nodded and headed up the next flight of stairs.

Tudor winked at me and mouthed 'I love you' as I followed his sister, his words causing me to trip over the top step. I grabbed onto the banister for support as my knees hit the carpet, and I quickly looked down to see if anyone saw my little fumble.

Tudor stood against the wall, holding back his chuckle, and I proceeded to flip him the middle finger. He whispered loudly, "Glad I can knock you off your feet, gorgeous!"

I pretended to laugh and then let my face drop to show I wasn't amused. *Twat!*

I dusted off my knees and turned the corner to run after Boleyn, but unfortunately she had stopped to wait and had fully witnessed my fall and my little tête-à-tête with her elder brother. She was looking a bit surprised, but a faint grin showed that she had found it amusing too.

Glad to be of service!

Boleyn led me to a heavy-paneled door at the very top of the house which led to a converted loft space. As we entered the room, I gasped. It was stunning. I knew Tudor and Henry had been working for the last few days on redecorating a new room for their recovering little sister, one as far away from her old room as was possible, but what they had achieved was incredible.

I must remember to give Tudor a little extra in the boudoir for creating this!

Boleyn walked to the middle of the room and I couldn't help but notice how in only a few days she had changed so much. She was wearing baggy black leggings and a loose brown cardigan that dwarfed her tiny frame. She had pulled the sleeves down low on her arms, the cuffs covering half of her hand, which she kept bringing to her mouth. Her dark hair was unkempt and pushed back in a tight knot.

I moved further into the room, which still smelt of fresh paint, and admired the sky-blue walls and framed family photos that adorned the walls. As I moved to the rear of the room I gasped and stopped at a large glass ornament of a sunflower.

I reached out my hand to touch it, and Boleyn came and stood next to me, announcing in a small voice, "Tudor gave me that today; it's beautiful, isn't it? He said if I get upset or I can't cope that I should look at this flower and remember that I can get through anything."

Boleyn met my gaze with sadness in her eyes, her sleeve once again in her mouth. "Tudor said that you are like a sunflower to him; strong, bright and beautiful, and a reminder to everyone that the sun will always shine again, no matter what happens," she admitted, smiling shyly.

"He really said that?" I whispered, staring at the way the light reflected off the coloured petals, and she nodded.

"Yeah, just today," she replied, and she moved to sit on the sofa under the window.

At least I now know why he calls me Sunshine.

I finished nosey-ing around her new room and sat beside her. She curled up her legs on the couch and moved to face me, bottom lip trembling and water filling her sad eyes. I took her hand in support.

"Ms. Munro, I'm so sorry for shouting at you in class and for what I said."

I shook my head. "No, darling. Don't apologise—"

She gripped my hand tighter. "Please, I need to say this. I just want you to know that I wish I had never said those things. I don't want you to leave, and Tudor told me that he loves you. Please don't leave him because of me."

I squeezed her hand. "Now you listen to me, young lady, I never, ever want you to apologise again." I bent my head to meet her lowered gaze. "You can talk to me about anything and I mean, anything, okay?"

She lowered her head and wiped her nose with a tissue she took from the coffee table in front of us.

I continued, "What happened to you was despicable, Boleyn; someone your age should not have to deal with it, and for that I am so angry and upset at the universe. But I also know from experience that feeling so low and scared over something you've been through won't last forever if you don't let it.

"When I was young, I was very poorly and, in theory I shouldn't be here today talking to you, but I am. You are strong and will get through this, even if it doesn't seem like it at the moment. You will have days when it's harder than others but, on those days, you rely on your family and friends to get you through. You can even talk to me."

I took both her hands in mine and made her look up. "You're strong, Boleyn, you are going to get through this, and when you do and you come back to school, I am going to help you in any way I can. Oh, and you are *soo* gonna be singing again. Now you've shown the world your talent, they're going to want you to keep going, to keep showing off them pipes."

She giggled a little at that. "Thank you, Miss," she sniffed.

I stood, pulling her off the sofa and giving her a cuddle. "Don't thank me yet, hun. I brought Tink with me this evening, and you won't be too grateful to me after a few hours in his company!"

She giggled again, with more energy this time.

"Now come on, let's go downstairs – I'm bloody starving!"

Boleyn and I entered the room, her arm linked in mine, and everyone seemed relieved at the sight. As we began making our way through to the dining room I felt a tug on my arm.

"Everything okay with Bee?" Tudor asked, turning me around and bending his knees so he was level with my line of sight.

I pressed a kiss to his inviting lips and nodded. "Yeah, she apologised, but I told her there was no need."

I wrapped my arms around his neck. "The room is lovely, babes."

He kissed me on my cheek, my lips and my neck. "Thanks, we wanted her to be happy, you know? Well, as happy as she can be after what she's been through."

I placed a hand on his cheek in comfort. "She will be, in time."

He looked off to the distance, clearly fighting the horrific images of his sister being attacked. I pulled his face back to mine. "She showed me something else too."

He looked intrigued. "She did?"

I smiled and reached back, taking one of his hands and entwining his fingers with mine, his other hand lying flat on my back. He looked down, content at the feel of our hands playing together. I met his questioning eyes. "She showed me the glass sunflower you gave her today."

"She did?" he whispered.

I pursed my lips. "Mmm... Hmm."

"And?" he pushed.

"And, she told me what you said about it... about me."

I could see his blush rising up his body, smothering his face, and he buried his face in my neck in embarrassment. I let out a loud laugh at his reaction, my big softie getting all coy, and I stroked the back of his head.

Putting a hand under his chin, I forced him to look at me; he was rubbing his lips together with nerves. "What you said, it... it was the most beautiful thing I've ever heard," I whispered.

He lifted his lip in a lopsided smirk and shrugged, glancing up at me shyly, "You're the most beautiful thing in my life. It's all true. I... I love you, that's all."

My gaze softened, and I teased. "Soppy, Cheddary Tudor!" and wasted no time in crushing my lips against his, losing myself in his taste. Tudor groaned at my sudden attack and pushed me to the corner of the room, a large cabinet hiding us from view. He stepped back and leered at me before he opened the top few buttons of my shirt and launched his tongue at the tops of my super-pushed-up-boobs currently spilling over my black lace balcony bra.

My eyes rolled back in my head as I whispered, "Tudor, what the hell are you doing?"

He mumbled around a mouthful of flesh. "Just having a little taste to get me through the night."

"What if someone comes in? Boleyn's here for god's sake!"

"She's with my mother and we're hidden, no-one will see. Now be quiet, I can't talk with my mouth full."

Screw it. No-one will miss us for five steamy minutes!

We were wrong. Dead wrong.

We heard a surprised cough, and I pushed Tudor's puckered mouth off the top of my slightly exposed Ta-Tas to see Henry with his hand over his eyes, facing the opposite wall. "Not again! Tudor, Mom said can you stop making out with your girlfriend for once and please let her eat and actually spend time with other people?"

My hot and bothered boyfriend never looked back at his massively embarrassed big brother and instead pounced on my lips, ignoring the intrusion.

I giggled against his mouth when I heard from the next room. "Mom!!! I can't go back in there again. I think I just got knocked up from watching them! There are just some things you shouldn't see your little brother doing — heavy petting being top of the list!"

That did it; I burst out laughing and rushed to fasten my gaping top. I grabbed Tudor's hand and led him to the door. "Come on, my horny man. We need to go."

He stopped and turned, adjusting his trousers. "Erm… you go ahead, I'm just going to need a few minutes."

That made me giggle some more and, as I was walking away I heard, "This is going to be a real long friggin' night!"

Pamela brought out the first course, and my stomach rumbled in appreciation of the cantaloupe melon wrapped in Parma ham. Tudor was sitting beside me and Tink opposite.

Once everyone was settled and tucking in, Pamela began the grilling. "So, Tink, how are you finding Calgary?"

He tipped his head and smiled. "Well Pam-Pam, I'm loving it! It's colder than a witch's tit, but at least I have this gorgeous guy here to keep me warm at night, and he can make me hot in no time!"

He put an arm around his Pookie's neck and planted a wet smacker on his cheek. Tate didn't at all see the inappropriateness of his beloved boyfriend's comments and continued to smile sweetly as if the fairy had just spouted something profound and with substance.

The rest of the Norths gaped. Tink, being Tink, didn't have a clue that most people around the table weren't yet accustomed to his ways, and he carried on shoveling his starter into his mouth.

Pamela just stared at me, and I grimaced and shrugged. That was Tink – direct and unapologetic.

She continued. "So how did you two meet?" smiling at both me and the other Geordie gobshite.

Shit! I hate this story.

I went to speak, but Tink beat me to it. "Well Pam-Pam, funny story. We were twelve, it was a typical hard Northern winter, and we were both getting bullied. We met in the school's 'Beat the Bullies' group."

Tudor looked at me in shock. "You got bullied in school? Why?"

I opened my mouth to explain, but once again Tink dived in. "Because she looked like the arse-end of a truck, that's why! Can you say 'Wide-Load'?"

I dropped my fork and it clattered on the plate, making everyone freeze. I glared daggers at my soon-to-be-dead bestie. He looked back at me blankly.

"Thanks, Tink, why don't you tell them why you were there?" I challenged. His eyes narrowed. "*Because* the kids at school were homophobic," he delivered regally, a smug expression on his face.

"Oh, really? Nothing to do with you strutting your stuff in a bikini, fairy wings and a tutu, hiding in the rugby team's shower offering baby oil rub-downs with guaranteed happy endings?"

He let out a soprano shriek, making everyone flinch in their seats – well, apart from Tater-Tot, who was gazing lovingly at his boyfriend, chin supported on his hand.

"You bitch! At least I wasn't tied to a goal post and prodded with a stick!"

I laughed sarcastically. "You bloody wish you got prodded with a stick, in fact, you dreamt about it didn't you?"

He put a hand across his chest and opened his mouth in shock before snapping it shut and nodding in agreement. "True, Boo. Loves ya."

I winked and smiled lovingly. "Loves ya, too," and we carried on eating our food.

I looked up after a few silent seconds and noticed several sets of eyes frozen on us, especially Boleyn's – *whoopsy!* I just shrugged. This was normal, they had better get used to us, and what's a family dinner without a bit of friendly banter?

As the night went on, we chatted about all sorts of things. Pamela was very easy to get on with. For the mother of my boyfriend, she was pretty awesome. I think she even got used to Tink and his…*unique* personality.

Henry proved to be an excellent story-teller, and he was regaling us with a tale about the time he had taken Samantha to Mexico for her thirtieth birthday. At the mention of that, Tudor swung his chair around and gripped my arm.

"Shit, Sunshine, I don't know the date of your birthday. How did I forget to ask that?"

I shrugged and patted his leg. "It's okay, I don't know yours either – though I could probably Google it. I'm sure the Tudor Chicks have that date tattooed on their weirdly obsessive little hearts," I teased.

He leaned towards me, narrowing his eyes and dismissing my dig. "Mine's April nineteenth."

"Okay, mine's January ninth."

He shot back in his chair, nearly taking the tablecloth with him. "That's in a couple of days."

I grimaced. "Ugh, I know; I'll be twenty-nine, last year of my twenties," I said in a grumpy mood.

Tink butted in. "Mine's February fifteenth in case you wanted to put that in your calendar too. And I like diamonds, FYI."

Tudor held in a laugh. "Oh, yeah, thanks Tink, that was my next question." The fantastic fairy nodded his head, face smug, completely *not* getting that Tudor was being sarcastic.

Tudor took my hand. "What are you doing for it?"

I looked at him like he was crazy. "Erm, nothing, except probably crying myself to sleep at the loss of my youth."

Tink took a swig of his Zinfandel and whistled low. "I hear that sister, I'd be worried too with titties that size. Gravity will *not* be your friend, and you'll be tucking your droopy nipples into your socks in no time, hey Pam-Pam?" He held up a hand for a high five. Pamela paused for a moment before clapping Tink's hand in an awkward fashion and mouthing 'sorry' to me.

I took a deep, calming breath. Tudor kissed the back of my hand, pulling me from my Tink-induced mood. "We'll do something nice, Sunshine, and you'll have a good time."

I smiled. "Thanks."

We all finished at the table, and before long everyone was ready for bed. It had been one hectic week.

I found out that Henry and Samantha lived two doors down in a smaller three-bedroomed house, and Tate was going to go back to ours with Tink.

Pamela said her goodbyes and headed off to bed, taking Boleyn with her. Tudor whispered in my ear and asked me to stay with him, and I agreed, although I really didn't need much persuading. Tink's 'surprise' for Tate had arrived that morning, the box reading, 'Premium Plug Pleasure Pack'. Staying at Tudor's that night was something I deemed to be essential.

Grabbing a bottle of wine and two glasses, we headed down to the basement and curled up on the sofa, listening to Newton Faulkner on the iDock. Tudor placed me on top of him. I had come to realise that he couldn't be near me and not touch me, and most nights he wrapped me around his body like a curvy Geordie blanket – which was absolutely fine by me!

He had also shown me his newly organized room, which caused the butterflies in my stomach to go all Cirque Du Soleil. Tude, being the sweetie that he was, had cleared some of his closet and drawers and had bought me toiletries and basic clothes for the nights I would stay. I was so beyond happy with everything in my life at that moment – especially my big cuddly bear.

We were snuggling in each other's arms when he spoke. "My mother and I spoke to Boleyn's doctor today. He's recommended that she goes to a retreat in Toronto for abuse victims for a few weeks, to help her deal with everything that's happened. Mom takes her tomorrow – the sooner the better." He paused. "My agent also called this morning, and I need to go to LA a weeks' time for read-throughs and costume fittings on *The Blade Reaper II*. I knew I'd have to go soon, unfortunately."

I nodded slowly against his stomach, and my heart fell at the thought of him leaving for a prolonged period of time. I had gotten so used to him being here twenty-four seven and sleeping with him every night. I guessed this would be the start of the reality of our relationship: me being here and him being wherever it was that movie stars needed to go.

He lifted me up to his face. "Is that okay?"

I kissed him and smiled. "Of course, babes, it's your job."

He frowned. "I don't want to go without you. I'm already dreading leaving to shoot this friggin' movie. I wish I hadn't signed on to do it and just taken a year off or something to be with you."

I put my hand on his cheek. "Tudor, don't be daft. You agreed to this before you even knew I existed, it's your job. This is how our lives will be, and sooner or later we would've had to deal with it."

He pecked a chaste kiss on my head. "I'd rather it would've been later," he sulked.

I sighed. "I'll be okay with the Tinkster; he'll be pining for Tater-Tot too, but we'll come and visit you guys any chance we get." That made him somewhat brighter. I hated seeing him all sullen and down, but at the same time, it was reassuring that he was dreading being without me. But he will have a lot of… distractions, out there.

Tudor shuffled down to meet my worried eyes. "What is it, gorgeous?"

I tucked my hair behind my ear, fidgeting. "I just worry that I'm not cut out for Hollywood. It's a bit daunting for a northern girl from England to wrap my head around. But at the same time, I'd do anything to be with you."

Tudor seemed to go rigid. I grabbed his arm. "Hey, I'm not running, I swear, I'm just opening up, telling you how I feel. No secrets, remember?"

"That's not the problem."

"What is it, babe?" I asked cautiously.

He reached into his bag beside his bed and pulled out a folded piece of A4 paper and gave it to me to open. "It was released tonight."

I pulled a curious, confused face and opened the folded paper. It read:

*'**Press Release on behalf of Tudor North:** A photo was leaked to the press several weeks ago showing Tudor North with a mystery woman. There was speculation at the time that said woman was romantically linked to Mr. North. The claim was denied due to private family circumstances, but he is now able to confirm that the woman in question is his significant other. Mr. North would like to affirm that he is in a committed and serious relationship and he requests privacy and respect on this matter.'*

I dropped the paper and it floated to the floor.

"I called Kate yesterday. It will have been issued to all the major entertainment channels and public relations reps by now. I did it because I remembered a conversation that we had that stuck with me, before we were even together. You said that it would mean everything to you if someone loved you so much that they would declare it for the world to hear. Well, I thought actions would speak louder than words."

For once in my life, I had nothing to say.

Literally nothing.

Tudor fidgeted with his hands at my silence, seemingly doubting his statement release. "There will be a price to pay for this, the press will want to know all about you and they will want pictures, interviews – *oh* and a piece of your soul," he tried to joke, looking incredibly worried.

I shook my head. "I… I don't care about them, I-I just can't believe you did that."

He lowered his eyes and shuffled on the mattress. "Was it wrong? Did I fuck up?"

I shifted towards him and wrapped my arms around his waist. "Wrong? Bloody hell, I'm speechless. I thought you wanted off the radar, not to be the bloody bulls-eye target?"

He hunched his shoulders. "I want everyone to know we're together, that I belong to you and you to me. A quiet life is nothing if I don't have you."

I put my hand on the back of his head and pressed his head against mine. I whispered, "So you were never embarrassed by me?"

He moved his hands to my head, grabbing a fistful of my hair, tilting it back. "Are you kidding? How could I be? I know you have this crazy notion that you're not good enough or don't measure up, but the truth is you're out of *my* league."

I snorted at that. "Tudor I'm not perfect, not by any means."

He pressed his head back to mine, his breath fanning my skin. "No, but you're perfect for me."

It was true, we were perfect together. I just hoped we were strong enough, – no, that *I* would be strong enough – to cope with being the girlfriend of a movie star and all that it entailed. I was about to venture into unchartered territory, and I was as apprehensive as hell.

CHAPTER 28

Loose Lips

I woke up on the morning of my twenty-ninth birthday and sighed as I ran my hand over Tudor's side of the bed; it felt cold. I hated not sleeping next to him, snuggling into him and I was feeling a little apprehensive as to why he had chosen to stay away the night before my birthday. He had simply said that *"he had something to do"*.

Pamela and Boleyn were now in Toronto at the retreat, so I knew it wasn't for their benefit. I thoroughly believed that we had sorted through our secrecy issues, but something was up with him. I could just smell it.

I tried to quell my worries and jumped in the shower, dressed in the cutest grey knitted sweater mini-dress and tights, did my hair and slapped on my make-up.

Just as I was applying the last coat of mascara, my bedroom door opened and in he walked – the reason for my existence (and recent splurge at Victoria's Secret), dressed in jeans, a white muscle T-shirt, jeans and white beanie hat with Tink, who I assumed had let him into the condo.

Tink walked to where I sat, leaving Tudor to stand back at the door and sang, "Happy birthday, my pork-flavoured soul-mate!" as he handed me a large birthday bag with my name written in pink glitter glue across the front.

I opened the bag and pulled out the present – it was heavy and long. I raised a suspicious eyebrow imagining a black mambo Dildo or something worse and he rolled his eyes.

"Just open it!"

I tore off the paper and read the homemade label:

'Aged Virgin Sunflower Oil'

I bit my lip in wonder… what the hell?

I heard a snicker and looked up to my obviously tickled best friend who was laughing, holding his belly.

"I don't get it?" I stated looking first at Tink and then at Tudor who was wearing a similar expression of confusion.

Tink placed his hands on his hips sporting a seriously ticked-off look upon his heavily made-up face. "You don't get it? *You* don't get it? *I* don't get it! Everyone keeps harping on at you about sunflowers and sunshine and any other sun-related shit, and quite frankly I wanna put those comments where the *Sun. Don't. Shine!* Our condo looks like a fookin' farmers field half the time and my allergies' are at an all-time high! My eyes are red and itchy twenty-four-seven, I'm wheezing like a chubster on a treadmill, but does anyone care, *no*, because Tash is bright and warm and we need reminding of it every bloody second of every bloody day! So there you have it, my contribution to the friggin' Wilbur Sunflower Movement!"

I held in my giggle at Tinks outburst. Tudor across the room, hung his head, knowing full well it was to him whom Tink was referring.

I moved us on quickly. *"Okay...* thanks, chuck. I'll use this for our Sunday morning fry-ups!"

He nodded smugly and with that made his exit from the room. "I'll see you later, sausage when you have birthday fucked your man!" he said, slapping Tudor on the back in encouragement before he firmly closed the door leaving me with my man.

I rose from the chair and made my way across to where Tude stood. With each step my heart began to beat faster from both apprehension and the fact that I was nearly hyperventilating at how handsome he looked.

When I was mere steps from him he sprung forward and lifted me up, spinning me around. "Happy Birthday, Sunshine!" he sang.

I giggled at his playful mood and wrapped my hands around his neck, kissing his cheek. "Someone's feeling happy," I teased.

The smile on his face was blinding. "Mmm-hmm. I come bearing gifts." He released me to the floor and gestured for me to sit on the bed. I did so, just enjoying this side of Tudor's personality.

"Okay, just before we begin," he said and captured my face in his hands moving in for a not-so-innocent-kiss. He pulled back, causing me to huff in disappointment. "I missed you last night, gorgeous, too God-damned much. I can no longer sleep without you beside me."

I blushed. "Me too, babes."

He clapped his hands together. "Okay. Presents." He walked back to a bag he had placed down on the floor. "First…" He pulled out a box and I gasped when I saw the name *Tiffany & co*.

He handed me the large blue box seeming a little embarrassed. "I feel a bit of a dick now, after what Tink has just said but, here." I took it from him and opened the lid, holding my breath.

I drew back in shock. Inside, on a white silk pillow, was the most breath-taking pendant I had ever seen. The necklace cord was made of thick white gold and hanging from it was a diamond-encrusted sunflower – yellow diamond for the petals and garnet and onyx for the centre. My hands began to shake as I tried to take it out.

Tudor moved them aside and pulled it from its silk cushion. "Here, let me."

I dropped the delicate chain into his outstretched hands, and he opened the clasp and placed it around my neck. I took Tudor's face and kissed him slowly. "I love it, babes."

He brushed the tip of my nose with his lips. "Open it."

"What?"

He released a chuckle. "It's a locket, open it up."

I fiddled with the clasp, hidden behind the delicate yellow diamond leaves, and I lifted the top to reveal a photo of Tudor and me. I turned the locket to study the picture and turned to him in surprise.

He shrugged. "My mother took it at our house that night we had dinner. I didn't know she even had it until I bought this for you. She thought it would look nice inside. She wanted me to see how I was with you, how I looked at you and how everyone else can see how you've changed me. I thought it was a perfect fit."

It *was* perfect. In the picture, I was on Tudor's lap and our heads were touching, smiling contentedly, caught just after a kiss. I had always thought Tudor was ridiculously out of my league, but looking at that picture of us, at the couple in love, I thought we looked perfect – maybe he was right after all.

Tudor beamed a smile and wiped the tears from my eyes with his thumb. "Now even when we're apart, you'll always have me close." I snapped the locket shut and noticed script on the back: *'You are my sunshine'*

"Okay, and now for the main gift."

My mouth gaped in shock. "Tudor, this is enough. I don't need anything else."

He didn't reply but instead began to strip. Yep, strip, like a live showing of *Magic Mike* in my bedroom.

"Tudor, What—?" My ability to speak drew to a halt as his shirt and trousers hit the cream-coloured carpet. My gaze zeroed in. No, not where you're thinking! Okay, maybe I did peruse his lovely disco-stick somewhat, but that is not what had me sweating.

I gasped, and my wide eyes flew back to his.

He scrunched up his nose and bit his bottom lip with nerves. "Surprise! I flew to Vancouver yesterday to my artist. I just arrived back a couple of hours ago."

Low on his hip, opposite to his already body-long tribal tattoo, was a large black Maori sun, clear in the centre with thick black solar flares draping over his lower torso, set off just to his right.

"A sun?" I asked in awe.

He nodded, a shy smile ghosting on his lips.

"For me? You flew all the way to Vancouver and back in a day to do this for *me*?" I whispered.

"For you, Sunshine," he whispered back, whilst moving to stand before me and stroking my cheek with his finger.

Phew! Forget oysters, forget Viagra, and forget chocolate – okay, not chocolate, let's not get carried away – the best aphrodisiac, the best turn on in the world, is when your man brands himself with ink just for you. You may not all agree, and each to their own, but for me, *'Oh, Mamma Mia!'*

I suddenly recalled our conversation in the hot tub when Tudor had declared that he hadn't got tattoos on his right side because he had *'been saving it for someone special, a blank canvas just for them.'*

Was I that someone special? I studied Tudor's contented and happy face, and he nodded to my inner question, knowing exactly what I was thinking.

Without any warning, I pounced on him. I started at his head, placing kisses all the way down his fine body. He sucked in a breath when I got down to his stomach, perched on my knees and made a play for his 'V', that was now smothered with a sun just for me, his 'someone special' with my hot, hungry mouth.

I jumped up in record time, rid myself of my dress, faced Tudor and clothes-lined him to the bed. I began to maul him – pure, unadulterated ravishing. I had gone full nympho on his fine ass!

I licked around the ridges of hard muscle and 'my' tattoo which made him squirm and hiss. "Fuck!"

Encouraged, I sucked down harder and crept up his skin with my fingers; he burst out in laughter and curled into a protective ball. I had learned before now that a certain Mr. North couldn't take a good tickle, and I ended up laughing with him at how he begged me to stop – my tattooed muscle bad boy was now my ticklish little baby!

I crawled back over him slowly, hands on either side of his head, and he brushed a piece of my hair behind my ear. "Natasha Munro, are you trying to seduce me?"

I pressed my lips to his, stopping just long enough to say in a low, raspy voice, "Hell yeah, is it working?"

He roared and flipped me on my back. "Oh, it's working!" he rushed out.

"Yeah for me!" I clapped.

Within minutes we were joined, all politeness and tenderness gone, and passion and lust all-consuming. Tudor rolled on his back, forcing me to be on top – his favourite position, his hands full with my breasts. I controlled every move, and he surrendered willingly to my demands. His breath became uneven as he kept rhythm with our ever-increasing moans, and with one final thrust we bellowed mutual screams of release.

Exhausted, I collapsed on him, and he announced quietly, "Happy birthday, Sunshine."

I worked my hips back and forth, making him groan and grip the headboard. "And here's to many, many more." I murmured, seductively.

He replied with certainty in his eyes, "*Definitely* many, many more!" We were no longer talking about my birthday.

He reached up to take my face in his hands and ran his tongue along my bottom lip. "I love you Natasha Munro, so, so much." *Kiss.* "Thank you for saving me." *Kiss.*

I jolted back, startled. "What did you say?" I asked softly.

He nodded, assuring me of what he had declared. "You saved me, and for that I'll love you forever."

I pursed my lips and tipped my head, narrowing my eyes. "Are you saying all this because you're still inside me?"

He laughed at my incredulity but then looked out of the corner of his glittering green eyes and sneered. *"Maybe?"*

I shrieked and slapped his chest. "You pig!"

"I joke, I joke!" he protested, gripping my wrists in his hands.

His face dropped, serious again. "You really did, gorgeous. More than you will ever know."

I lowered myself to an inch from his face and kissed him passionately. He growled in pleasure, flipped me on my stomach and off we went for round two.

Happy Birthday, Tash!

We were dozing, wrapped in each other's arms, fully sated and I was so damn happy. And that's when it happened.

Thunderous hammering on my bedroom door broke us from our happy place and Tink, followed by Tate, who was covering his eyes with his hands, burst into the room, hysterical and swearing like a banshee and waving his phone in the air.

I immediately sat forward, trying to use Tudor as a shield to hide my naked state. "What? What is it?"

Tink stared down at the phone and glanced back up again. "There's been a leak to the press, it's in all the papers… everywhere. Apparently you made the evening news last night too, even in the UK," he whispered, tilting his head at Tudor.

I grasped Tudor's hand in support. "Why? Tink for God's sake, why has he made the papers? What exactly has been leaked?"

Tink winced. "Somebody has sold the story about your childhood and the abuse you suffered from your father, a very detailed story."

He looked apologetic. "It's also come to light about the recent attack on your sister and that your father is incarcerated awaiting trial for her attempted rape."

Tudor immediately jumped to his feet, wrapping the sheet around his waist and began pacing, clenching his hands over and over with frustration before walking to the wall, slamming his fists against the cement and pressing his head against it in defeat.

Tate, ever the efficient assistant, ran into the front room to make the necessary communications with Tudor's team – his PR, lawyer and agent.

My bestie, actually demonstrating some emotional intelligence for once, left to put the kettle on, leaving me alone with Tudor.

I walked towards him and took his hand in mine. He flinched and looked down, and went to pull away, frosting over again, like he always did when things got rough. This time I held on tight.

"No, don't pull away. Don't shut me out again," I begged.

He looked so torn. His go-to response in life was to carry the burden himself, to protect everyone else, but no more, not this time.

I squeezed his shaking hand in mine. "I'm here with you, Tudor. This time we will face this together. You're not alone anymore, you have me. You are not *alone*."

He stared at me for a long time, fighting his inner demons and eventually pulling me to his chest and whispering in a pained voice, "This time I have you."

This time we had each other.

After hearing the news, we immediately went to Tudor's house, where we all – Henry, Samantha, Tudor, Tink, Tate and I – gathered in the lounge to try and come up with a plan of action to deal with the fallout of the information leak on the horrific and abusive past of the Norths.

To say the atmosphere was tense was an understatement. Everybody was nervous, angry or upset, and everyone was bewildered as to who could have sold the story. A family's dirty laundry being aired to friends and neighbours was bad enough, but add into the mix that one of the key players was mega-star famous and the situation became exponentially worse.

The world now knew that Tudor, for much of his early childhood and teens, had been subject to brutal beatings, and both physical and emotional torment by his father. To be honest, the reports were so detailed in their descriptions, that even I was learning new information about my immensely private boyfriend and what he had been through: things that he hadn't even confided in me yet – and nor should he have if he wasn't ready. They were heart-breaking.

As an actor, Tudor's response must be well-calculated and thought through: one that protected his family, his career, the trial. There were so many different things at stake, not to mention the fact that the topic of all the hype was such a sensitive area. We were expecting his publicist, Kate, to arrive in Calgary from LA so she could advise Tudor on what to do next. Until then, there was nothing we could do.

Drawing on both my Scottish and English heritages to cope with the situation, I made cups of tea laced with whisky for everyone and the six of us sat around the fire, no-one saying a thing.

Henry broke the uncomfortable silence first, after shifting back and forth on his chair for near enough the last thirty minutes. "What are you planning on doing, Tudor? What do you think you will say to the press?"

Samantha moved to sit next to Henry, hands on his tense shoulders, and Tudor pulled me onto his lap and began stroking my hair. It calmed him.

He stared into the fire, watching the flames dance, lost in his personal thoughts. "I don't know. Do I ask the media for privacy and not say anything on the topic of abuse, but have it hanging over my head for the rest of my career? *Or* do I come clean and admit to what we all went through? But then that will leave me exposed, and I hate the idea of that; the world knowing all about us when we've kept it so well-hidden for so long." He laid his forehead on my shoulder, defeated. "I have no idea what to do for the best."

He gripped me tightly around the waist and groaned. I drew back and lifted his chin. "What's wrong? What's going on that head?"

He looked sheepishly to the others in the room, hesitant to talk. I looked in his eyes and urged him to explain. His head slumped forwards. "I just don't think I'm ready to talk about it to the world, it's all too raw. My family need the next few months to heal, to adjust. I was willing to talk about it all in the future with the trial, but now?"

I squeezed his hand in sympathy. He fixed his broken gaze on me. "Why, just because I act on a screen, do I have to have my entire life made public? Why should the world get to read about our problems while having their toast and coffee on a Sunday morning? Just a hot topic, gossip material to mention in passing to colleagues on scheduled breaks at work. Can you imagine it? Our past being the topic of conversation to some middle-aged couple in God knows where: *'Oh honey, have you seen this article about Tudor North, the actor? His father broke his jaw and fractured his collarbone with a chair leg when he was fifteen for spilling soda on the kitchen floor. Anyway, what time are we meeting your parents for lunch?'* That's *my* life, *our* lives that they are discussing. Why do people need to pick at every God-damned part of me just because I act? Our lives are not entertainment. *I'm* the actor. My family didn't ask to be given the lead roles in the latest fucked-up celebrity scandal."

I felt sick listening to him casually drop his past sufferings into his angry tirade. I could feel my eyes misting at the description of his injuries – a chair leg for spilling his drink? *Good God! What else must he have gone through?*

I know celebrities sign up for the invasion into their personal lives when they pursue a Hollywood career, but surely there was a line that must be drawn, especially dealing with issues like this.

I heard a heavy pain-filled sigh and turned to face Tudor. He was staring at me with regret in his eyes and pulled me closer into his embrace. "I'm sorry, gorgeous. I shouldn't have lost my cool and told you about my past in such a way."

I sniffed. "Why are you apologising to me?"

"Because I upset you with what I said."

"That's because I find it hard to hear how you were treated when you were a child. I can't stand what he did to you. What he is *still* doing to you. It's like he has this hold over you all, I just feel so helpless. I don't know how to make it better."

His eyes lost some of their tightness, and he whispered in my ear, "You're helping me, Sunshine. Just by being you." He shifted back against the chair, tucking me around his body like a comforter.

Henry coughed to catch his attention. "I'm sick of dealing with all his shit, bro. Tash is right, how long can he possibly do this to us? Maybe if we're honest and show him to be the scumbag that we know he is, then he'll have to leave us alone, he'll have no hold over us anymore. It might be, I don't know, freeing."

Samantha, obviously proud of her husband, kissed his cheek and stared at him in adoration. I had a lot of respect for Samantha; she had been supporting Henry for years and was clearly his rock. We had both fallen in love with the brothers North, and we both simply had to help them get through this. We were both strong, modern women, and I was certain that we could all do it – that we could face the situation with poise and dignity. We would make Emmeline Pankhurst proud.

Tudor was once again running his fingers through my hair and nodding gently, taking in the advice from his level-headed older brother. Henry stood and cracked his back, Samantha followed suit and they headed in our direction. He bent down, eye-level with Tudor and laid a hand on his head. "Get some sleep, and we'll figure everything out tomorrow, okay? Today has been trying for us all and I think we need to let the dust settle for a while, sleep on it."

Tudor pulled him in for a long, manly hug, and Henry winked at me as he walked out of the room, holding his wife's hand incredibly tightly – maybe he wasn't as calm as he seemed?

I looked over to Tink, who cocked his head with a tight smile and pointed to the hallway; he was going to bed too, and he took his silent boy with him. We were all staying under one roof tonight – group support to face the trials of tomorrow as a united front.

When everyone was out of the room, I snuggled into Tudor's chest in front of the fire and peppered kisses along his neck to soothe him. He nuzzled the top of my head and sighed. "What are you thinking?"

"I don't honestly know. I suppose lots of things really: us going public, what Kate will say tomorrow and, of course I'm worried about you."

He guided my head to face him. "Worried about me? Sunshine, your birthday has been ruined by my problems. Just when one nightmare ends, another begins. Why are you putting up with all of this?"

"Oh don't start!" I said a bit too aggressively and lifted myself from his embrace.

"Start what?" he asked, slightly taken aback at my attitude.

"Blaming yourself. I chose to be with you, babes, knowing everything, and still you apologise? Your father is the one to blame, not you. I love you and you don't abandon the people you love when things get tough. In fact, it's love that gets people through choppy waters unharmed. I'm not going anywhere and you need to get that through your dense noggin, butch boy!"

His lip curled in amusement at my 'dense noggin/butch boy' dig, but he still didn't look convinced.

I settled back into his lap, tracing each one of his protruding abdominal muscles through his T-shirt, trying to measure his mood. "You are not responsible for everything, every problem. I love you, I support you, and I am staying put – I'm freakin' cement!

"I've dealt with a traumatic childhood too, granted it wasn't exactly like yours, but I have some idea what it's like to lose your innocence to something out of your control and, yet still, I'm determined to make us work. I can't fight for us on my own though, Tude; you need to be in this with me. Our road to happiness was never going to be easy, but that doesn't mean that I'm not going to strap myself in and enjoy the ride – bumps, dips and all!"

He stroked my face with his finger. "I am, gorgeous, I'm totally in, but I can't help but think that all my shit is having a negative effect on you - your job, your life, everything. Are you sure I'm worth it?" he looked apprehensive.

I flicked my hair like a L'Oreal advert, stared into his eyes like I was smouldering down the lens of a camera. "You're worth it."

That at least got a wee chuckle.

He took a final swig of his bourbon tea and asked, "What do you think I should say tomorrow?"

I thought about it for a second. "I think what Henry said made sense. If you expose your father for the bastard that he is, it may liberate you in some way, make it easy for you to move on. Will it bring attention to you? Yes, of course, but you became an actor, and fame and press go with celebrity hand in hand. It's how you handle the topic that needs to be considered."

He played with the fingers on my hand. "And how would you handle it? If it was you and your family?"

I sighed in sympathy at how lost and vulnerable he seemed. I straddled his waist and wrapped my arms around his neck. "Who were your idols growing up?"

He looked at me, surprised. "Erm… James Dean, Paul Newman, Clint Eastwood – I suppose people who could handle themselves, didn't take any shit."

"And why do you think that was? Why was it those types of actors that inspired you?"

He sighed. "I guess it was because I had no control at home, I couldn't fight back against my dad, and I wanted to be like them. It's why I got so big, you know, why I body-build, and why I got the tattoos and shaved my hair. I wanted people to look at me and see someone strong, someone who could handle himself, not someone who got beat up every day for most of his early life. I suppose how I look – big and menacing – is like my armour, impenetrable. At least to most people," he said, poking me in my side, making me jump and giggle.

I loved how he was gradually revealing more about himself, opening up and trusting me. I held back the tears welling in my eyes and kissed the tip of his nose. "So imagine little… Johnny, in I don't know, Hogsville, Montana, who gets hit every day by his father and watches helplessly as his mother takes repeated beatings so his wanker of a dad doesn't go for his baby sister and him, over and over. Imagine if Johnny adores Tudor North, 'The Blade Reaper', and he woke up one morning to his hero on TV, confessing how he was abused as a child and how he was putting his energy into raising awareness of the issue and that he wanted to help other victims of abuse. It could give him hope."

Tudor was staring at me slightly dubiously, but I continued. "The press will hound you, that's a given, but is it not worth it to help even one child? To show even one person that there is more to life than the end of a fist? At least that's how I feel about it. It might be a bit naïve, but surely this is your chance to do what every celebrity says they're going to do. Give back, make a bit of the world right through the power of their art. All that crap."

He smiled at me in disbelief and pulled me into his embrace, looking at me with love. "How did I live before you? Without you?"

I shrugged teasingly. "In a constant mood, from what I can gather."

He chuckled and kissed me. "Before I got Sunshine back in my life."

He was such a mush!

I stood and held out my hand. "Come on, big boy, how about we go to bed and I'll make you forget all this for a few hours?"

His eyes lit up as he slowly lifted himself from the chair. "And how exactly will you make me forget, Ms. Munro?" he teased.

I put a hand on my hip disapprovingly. "Erm… *Scrabble* you num-nut, what did you think?"

He swept me off my feet and began to carry me to his basement. "I've got a Scrabble word for you. It's spelt S - E - X."

I put a finger to my cheek and tapped. "Hmm? You used an 'X', isn't that a triple letter score?"

He pulled my ear to his mouth. "You're gonna get a triple score," and he began to pick up speed, until he threw me on his bed and proceeded to strip.

Scrabble quickly became my new favourite game.

CHAPTER 29

*"Life is more than how many breaths you take,
but the moments that take your breath away."*
Anon

Kate, Tudor's viper publicist, was a stiletto-heeled-force to be reckoned with. She was forty, had bright red hair, was about five foot nothing and scared the absolute shit out of me! Even Tink had some verbal restraint around her – something I had never seen happen before. She was all business and got straight to the point as we gathered around the dining room table to discuss Tudor's options.

"Good news is we have found the source of the leak, the little fucker. It was a rookie cop who was paid quite handsomely by a big-time journo who he'd contacted after Boleyn was attacked. He was on the scene and identified you instantly, thought he could make a quick buck. He paid off a couple of doctors from Victoria and Kelowna to get a hold of your medical records, that's how he got the information on your injuries and accessed confidential files on your father's history – it was all there for him to piece together. Needless to say, he's being dealt with internally by the police. The bad news is that it's out now and we've got to address it, we are backed into a corner."

Tudor looked first at me and then at Henry. "I've been thinking, I feel I need to address it truthfully, all of it, full disclosure. Sunshine said something last night that I keep thinking about. She said that by me being open about it I might be able to help other people to know they're not alone and that they are not to blame. I could even work with charities – I'd love to help out. I think that if we can get something positive from all this shit then at least there's a light at the end of the tunnel. At least, I think that's the way to go. What's your professional advice?" he asked Kate.

Kate swivelled in her seat to regard me, her eyes narrowed. "You advised him to do that?"

I gulped loudly, drawing a sympathy squeal across the table from the fairy. "Y-yes. Don't shout at me!" I pleaded.

I heard a laugh next to me as Tudor shook his head. *Hey, I wasn't kidding, I was deadly serious; she's scarier than the Bogeyman!*

She raised her abnormally thin pencilled-in brow. "It's good, *and* it's what *I* thought he should do."

I began to exhale slowly now the threat to my life was averted. "You know, when Tudor told me he wanted to go public about his new little English pet, I tried everything to talk him out of it."

I looked at my squirming boyfriend's guilty expression and scowled. Kate clicked the top of her expensive pen in my face to regain my attention. "… But maybe you are good for him, at least in private. Of course, his female fans won't be happy about you, but it's good that you're average and fairly normal-looking – non-threatening, you know – but we'll cross that bridge when we come to it. For now, you've impressed me, not an easy thing to achieve," and she patted my head, patted my head like a friggin' poodle. I wanted to say something in return, but instead I kind of let out a little yip.

Kate just smirked – yep, I'm a friggin' poodle, an average, non-threatening and '*normal*' looking poodle!

Goodbye, first place at Crufts!

Kate the Viper turned to Tudor. "I'm setting up a press conference for later today, the sooner we give them a statement, the sooner we can control it. I loathe lack of control," she visibly shuddered. "Now, you need to do this alone as the press have not seen you go public yet with Little Miss Sunshine here, and we need to give them one thing at a time. Spoon feed the bastards, leave them salivating for more."

He shook his head, and folded his bulging arms across his chest. "Not happening. Tash will be sitting next to me where she belongs."

Ha, that told her! Wha—?

I grabbed Tudor's arm. "Err… Tudor, I'm not sure I can do that, and if Kate thinks I shouldn't then…"

"No," he banged his fist on the table, causing Tink to scream in response – his poor nerves had been shot ever since we had found out about the leak.

Kate clicked in Tink's face with a "Shh, pansy!" causing him to flinch back and cower in shock. I was still staring at *my* crazy muscled man, who was trying to argue his case for having me with him at the conference.

Tudor pointed at Kate. "She's sitting next to me, she's my girlfriend, *permanent* girlfriend, and *I* want her there. If I've got to address all this personal stuff, then I'm doing it with the one *I love* beside me."

He turned in my direction, eyes pleading. "I need you there, Tash, please just do it for me."

Well, what am I meant to say to that?

I lowered my head in defeat. "Fine! But I'm pissed at you for putting me on TV. I haven't even had chance to apply fake tan!" I teased.

Tink held up a finger, halting the conversation. "I have some instant dark tone Bronzante in my bag, we'll turn you from a white bap to a brown baguette in no time, my little ham roll."

I blew him a kiss and he caught it, bringing it to his cheek but then grimaced and stated, "Next time Wil, leave out the tongue. I don't like air-kiss girly frenchies."

Most of the table, now used to our antics, ignored us, but Kate sat there shaking her head, muttering something to herself about "Fucking weird Brits!"

So that was that, a press conference was going to be held later that day and I would be sitting next to my man.

My man the movie star… with the abusive past that he was about to discuss with the entire world.

That wasn't intimidating at all – Not. At. All.

Five hours later, and the press were waiting two doors down from our dressing room where we had been told to sit and wait (like Kate's good little bitch poodles).

The publicist-extraordinaire had managed to get a conference room large enough for all the press at the Saddledome stadium. I was wearing a fitted black silk vest top, stilettos and skinny high-waisted trousers, with my hair down – oh, yeah, and Tink's instant fake tan (two coats, FYI).

To say I was nervous is not exactly accurate but to save some ugly descriptions involving a high dose of toilet humour, I'll leave it at that! Tudor, at least was amused at my expense and therefore not as freaked out as I thought he would be.

He motioned for me to join him on the sofa, and I scurried over and sat down throwing my legs over his and using his presence to calm me down.

"You'll be fine, gorgeous. I'll do most of the talking. I have your back." I nodded in comprehension, obviously not convincing him.

"Tash, look at me." I met his loving gaze. "I really appreciate you doing this for me, I know it's gonna be hard but I'm truly thankful."

That soothed me some more and I smiled up at him. Tudor North, Tash Munro's personal Prozac.

In the hours leading up to the conference, Kate and the legion of lawyers she had commanded onto a conference call had briefed Tudor on what he should say, what he should and should not answer and what aspects he should discuss, particularly as the trial was still pending.

They had decided to stick to the facts – his father's abuse (no details), his life moving around and how that affected his family (excluding names and any mention of Boleyn) and also his involvement in the recent incident.

Pamela had been informed by phone, and she was happy with the road Tudor was taking, and he seemed relieved that this whole fiasco would be dealt with before he left for LA.

During the painful wait before our public debut, I was keeping myself occupied by looking around the dressing room, wondering how many stars had sat there waiting to perform. I chortled when I saw the obligatory movie-star mirror with light-bulb surround –very Hollywood. The last time I had seen one of those frames was last year outside the cinema after Nathan's sexual showpiece, where the bulb had nearly exploded in my face.

Bloody hell, I had come such a long way since then.

Wait a cherry-picking minute! Glamorous cinema posters, asking for a sign, an exploding light bulb, one hot and muscled bad boy… could it be? Was that the message all along? Mighty Zeus! It must have been. Why didn't I put it all together before now?

I suddenly sat bolt upright and shouted, "Oh My God!" My hands covered my mouth as I tried to believe what this all could mean.

Tudor jumped beside me, worry etched on his face. "What, Sunshine?"

I turned to gawk at him. Why had I never thought of it before? I asked for a sign all those months ago, and I always thought it was everyone's favourite author, Jane, from beyond the grave, but… I grasped Tudor's handsome face in my hands.

"It was you." I whispered in shock.

He looked at me like I had sprouted another head. "I'm confused."

I laughed hysterically and kissed his pouting lips. "Last year when I found Nathan with his PA, I took a walk and, in my despair, asked the universe for a sign, something to guide me, a sign that something good would happen in my life, that I would find true love.

"I saw a Jane Austen quote in a book shop window, and I thus took that as my message to live more care-free, you know, '*Carpe Diem*', and that decision ultimately led me to Calgary."

Tudor nodded at me slowly like he was witnessing me losing my mind.

"Bear with me, babes," I urged.

He motioned for me to continue.

"Just before I saw the quote, I was looking at movie posters, thinking what it must be like to live such a fantastical life." Tudor snorted loudly at that ridiculously incorrect assumption. I continued, "... anyway, a light bulb surrounding a poster popped, just like that one," I pointed to the mirror in the room. "At the time I put it down to bad electrics, but it wasn't, that must have been the message I was meant to receive, it was a sign about you."

He moved to speak and then shook his head instead. "I'm sorry, Tash, I'm still confused. Are you feeling okay? Is the stress of facing the press getting to you?"

"Tude, the poster was for *The Blade Reaper*. *You* were the actor in the picture. The sign must have been that I was meant to find *you. My true love*."

He looked up and smiled a full Hollywood happy smile, finally getting it. "So you're telling me that we were destined to be together from the beginning?"

My heart stuttered. "I guess so. Looks like we were written in the stars," I said in a hushed voice.

"I never doubted it. You're it for me. *I* knew it from the get-go."

The hosts of butterflies were back in my stomach and I moved to straddle his waist.

"So we are really doing it this time, for keeps? I'm just checking that we are both on the same page about diving in with both feet?"

Tudor's lips rose into a smug smirk, delicious dimples out on full display and he pulled me down to his mouth.

"For me it was always for keeps, and my feet have been knee deep in your love juice from our first meeting," he announced cheekily.

Ugh… Love juice?

Let it go, Tash… But love juice? What a bad choice of words! It seems I'm not the only one who says inappropriate things… Bloody love juice!

I giggled and he thrust a hand in my hair to pull me in to his awaiting lips just as Kate entered the room, spoiling the lovey-dovey moment.

On seeing us on the couch, heads bent together, my legs spread over his, she walked over and grabbed my left hand from Tudor's arm and inspected my ring finger before looking up and barking the question.

"When you said Natasha was permanent, just how permanent is she? You haven't proposed or anything stupid like that have you? Because I need to know if you have, I don't do surprises."

Tudor looked at her menacingly. "No, we are not engaged, but she is special to me and I don't intend to let her go. Marrying her wouldn't be stupid, Kate; *not* being with her would be stupid. Just leave it alone."

Kate tilted her chin. "Well okay. Not as permanent yet as I thought. At least that gives me something to work with," she muttered, not quite as under her breath as I would have liked and walked to the other side of the room waiting for our cue.

I looked to Tudor, who was biting his lip in embarrassment. "That woman is without doubt the scariest person I have ever met," I whispered, so she couldn't hear me.

He ticked his head to the side knowingly. "Yeah, but the best at what she does."

I smiled, fully believing that no-one in Hollywood could stop that freight train from barrelling through.

"Right, you two. It's time to move those saccharine-sweet hinies!" Kate interrupted again, and then peered at my backside sceptically. "Or is yours full-sugar?" she asked, and laughed hysterically to herself.

Why I ought to… cower in the corner. Jesus, grow a pair would you, Tash?!

Tudor laughed at my glowering face and seductively squeezed my 'full-sugar' arse in both hands and licked his lips, his brows dancing suggestively.

I took a calming breath and took my curvy-arse-loving man's hand. He leaned down and whispered, "If you get nervous just look at me, okay? I'll protect you. You look beautiful, by the way."

I tried to smile but grimaced instead, my nerves were beginning to take over. Tudor pulled me to his chest laying his chin on my head. "We had to do this eventually, gorgeous. We couldn't live in our private little bubble forever, not with what I do for a living."

I squeezed my arms around his back. "I know. But I loved being in that little bubble of love. It was cosy and only made for two. I like having you all to myself. I don't know how to be with you in any other way, how to share you with the world."

"You will always have me to yourself, gorgeous. The real world knows a fictional man, only you get the hundred per cent real me – fucked-up dad and all. We will figure it out as we go along. You and me forever. Yes?"

I nodded, filled to the brim with love, and pecked a quick kiss on his stubbly cheek.

I beamed from ear to ear as we walked out of the dressing room and we stood patiently in front of the closed doors that led to the massive conference room holding the eager horde of journalists and photographers.

The noise was deafening and scary, so I took his advice and looked up at my gorgeous boyfriend. He was so yummy in his black jeans; tight long white T-shirt with a deep V-neck; tattoos on display and, you guessed it, grey beanie hat, but then, he always looked gorgeous to me. Well, me *and* the world's entire female population.

My name is Natasha and I am a total Tudor Chick.

A knock on the door signalled that we were good to go, and as if someone had flicked a switch, Tudor's stance suddenly changed, and I noticed that he had taken on the persona of Tudor North – actor. He looked completely calm and confident, one hundred per cent movie-star.

Tudor glanced down at me and winked, squeezing my hand as the doors began to open. Flashing lights blinded me, my ears were deafened by the thunder of questions being fired in our direction, and I began to shake with nerves.

My eyes roved over all of the unfamiliar faces glaring at me in scrutiny. My chest grew tight, and I began to feel like I couldn't breathe, but then I saw a frantically waving hand trying to catch my attention. Standing just to the right of the hungry mob was my fabulous fairy, blowing me a kiss to show his support, wearing a red sequinned blazer that, when pulled apart, revealed a hand-made T-shirt that read, *'Tash and Tudor forever!'* in purple italic script. Next to him was Tate, who was clapping enthusiastically in his red dickey bow and tailored black suit, as Tudor and I stood proudly on show for the first time as a couple. I burst into laughter at the sight, my inability to breathe forgotten, and I nudged Tudor, pointing in the direction of the cutie twosome.

He let out an amused snort, turned to me and asked, "Ready for this, Sunshine?"

I looked up at my stunning boyfriend – my lover, my soul mate, my Tudor – and any remaining nerves stilled.

I smiled confidently and replied, "For you, babes, I'm always ready," and giggled when he waggled his brows suggestively in response.

With one final deep breath he leaned down and kissed me softly on my lips, pulled back to face the crowd and we walked forward hand-in-hand into the throng of media vultures, declaring our love to the world, for everyone and their mothers to see.

Together.

The End

ACKNOWLEDGMENTS

There are many people I have to thank for helping me achieve this dream. Firstly, a huge whopping 'ta, so much!' to my mam, dad and the rest of the clan (Yep, that includes you Sam, Marc and my awesome niece and three super-cute nephews) for housing me while I put most of this novel together.

Mam, thank you for reading every single draft, amendment and version of this book. You have supported me from the beginning and shown your unwavering commitment, even going so far to choose the actor who should someday play Tudor North on the big screen – dream big or go home!

Dad, although not your genre – as it doesn't include a warp drive, fluent Klingon or an alternate universe – thank you for supporting this venture.

To my husband, thank you for once again flipping my life (and career) on its head. If you hadn't dragged me away from Italy (reluctantly) to Canada at the very last minute, this book would probably never have happened.

Love you lots!

My biggest thanks though, *has* to go to my fabulous beta readers and editors, Rachel and Kia – *The Genius Smoggie Sisters*.

Rachel, you will never know just how much I appreciate you and all your support. Right from the drunken reveal in the Italian restaurant in London of, "This Geordie RomCom I've been writing", you have pushed me to keep going and sacrificed *way* too much of your free time to help me achieve this dream (sorry, Matt!). You have not only been an amazeballs editor, beta reader and Tink enthusiast, but also a one-in-a-million friend who, even though separated by a continent, was my shoulder to cry on (literally) through a very tough and emotionally turbulent year. I will never be more thankful for the day that I started playing the cello (even though it affected our street-cred somewhat) and met you at age nine in Junior Orchestra. If you think about it, our writing partnership started all those years ago too, in History class, with, 'La Bouche' – only this time we say words like, *vadge!* Love you lots chuck, and, remember, *'negativity gives you wrinkles.'* Mwah!

Kia, thank you for being roped in at last minute, you truly were a fairy godmother (like Tink!). You offered sound advice and guidance. You went boot-camp on my arse and helped whip this novel into shape. Plus, now you have a new-found love for transitive verbs and subordinate clauses!

Lastly, thank you to my readers. It is a very scary, yet exciting, process writing a book, then releasing it into the big wide world. It is because of you guys that I get to take the fantasies from my weird little head and put them onto the page to come to life and entertain you. I love you to the moon and back.

ETERNALLY NORTH PLAYLIST

Stuttering – Fefe Dobson

I Want To Break Free – Queen

Calgary – Fears

Call Me Maybe – Carly Rae Jepson

Collide – Leona Lewis; Avicii

Beneath Your Beautiful – Labrinth ft Emeli Sande

Love Killer – Cheryl

Easy To Break – Fears

I'm Not Your Hero – Tegan and Sara

Explosions – Ellie Goulding

Learn To Love Again – Lawson

For You – Angus & Julia Stone

Like The Sun – Ryandan

Perfect For Me – Ron Pope

Fall Down (ft Miley Cyrus) – Wil.I.Am

Dream Catch Me – Newton Faulkner

Anthems:

Tink's Anthems – Gloria Gaynor – I Am What I Am/
Lady Gaga – Boys, Boys, Boys
Tash's Anthems - Spice Girls – Spice Up Your Life/
The Rocky Horror Picture Show – Don't Dream It, Be It

Tash's Anthem for Tudor – Sinitta – So Macho
Tink's Anthem for Pookie – DJ Antoine – Ma Chérie

AUTHOR BIOGRAPHY

Tillie Cole hails from a small town in the North-East of England. She grew up on a farm with her English mother, Scottish father and older sister and a multitude of rescue animals. As soon as she could, Tillie left her rural roots for the bright lights of the big city.

After graduating from Newcastle University, Tillie followed her Professional Rugby player husband around the world for a decade, becoming a teacher in between and thoroughly enjoyed teaching High School students Social Studies for seven years.

Tillie has now settled in Calgary, Canada, where she is finally able to sit down, write (without the threat of her husband being transferred), throwing herself into fantasy worlds and the fabulous minds of her characters.

Tillie writes Romantic comedy, Contemporary Romance, Young Adult and New Adult novels and happily shares her love of alpha-male leading men (mostly with muscles and tattoos) and strong female characters with her readers.

When she is not writing, Tillie enjoys nothing more than strutting her sparkly stuff on a dance floor (preferably to Lady Gaga), watching films (preferably anything with Tom Hardy or Will Ferrell—for very different reasons!), listening to music or spending time with friends and family.

FOLLOW TILLIE AT:

https://www.facebook.com/tilliecoleauthor

https://www.facebook.com/groups/tilliecolestreetteam

https://twitter.com/tillie_cole

Or drop me an email at: authortilliecole@gmail.com

Or check out my website:
www.tilliecole.com

Printed in Great Britain
by Amazon.co.uk, Ltd.,
Marston Gate.